I0777725

By Lee Obsidian

I dedicate this novel to my father. Gone but never forgotten. I can't wait to see you again, on the other side. Rest in paradise, Dad.

Contents

The Grandmagistra's Daughter

They'll skin me alive if they catch me. Too bad they never will.

A barrage of waves traveled the surface of a lake, assaulting a young man with hair the color of forest leaves.

I mean, even if they did. How would they know? Although drenched, the young man smiled, retaliating with his own barrage of waves. *You know what. I'm not going to worry about that right now. I'm having way too much fun.*

Feminine laughter exploded into the quiet atmosphere like notes from a trumpet.

A woman just as young, wiped droplets from her mahogany eyes. "Okay, okay, you win."

"Victorious yet again," said the young man, impersonating a grandiose persona.

Laughter ensued once more, this time a duet.

Moonlight danced atop the young woman's olive complexion as she reclined to a float. "You cheat."

The young man gave a playful roll of the eyes. "Never, you just suck."

A mocking gasp escaped the young woman, and the young man wasted no time reclining to float alongside her, his spiky hair swaying in the water.

He gazed up at lantern-adorned chains caught in a tug of war with the surrounding trees. "Why haven't we come here before? This is way better than that meadow you always take me to."

"You already know why—too risky."

Specks of lake water flicked about as the young man jolted up, his handsome face wrought with irritation. "I'm sick of sneaking around all the time."

"Oh, really? Isn't that what your people are trained to do?" asked the young woman with sarcasm.

A grumpy look found the young man, but it soon crumbled behind the weight of a smirk. "This is totally different, and you know it."

"Can we just enjoy the water?"

"Okay, but think about it. It's been five months already and nothing's happened. We could get away with anything at this point."

Flipping over, the young woman rush-swam to shore.

"Babe? Where are you going?" called the young man, his face scrunched with confusion.

Splashing water was the only response he received.

What's up with her?

The young woman ascended the sandy, underwater slope, exposing her fit physique to the summer breeze. Liquid beads dripped from her silver hair, down her white bathing attire. A knit bag curled up by tree roots lured her. From it came a purple towel with a symbol emblazoned upon it. She dried herself with it.

The young man vacated the water as well and took pause. He couldn't resist admiring the anatomic view with his steel-blue eyes.

Many sensual thoughts flew like comets through his mind. "You're not going home already, are you? We have plenty of time."

"No, Obake. *You* have plenty of time. I don't think you get it. If my mom ever finds out what I'm doing, she'll…"

Obake's tongue shriveled. *Great, she hates me now.*

A dingy leather satchel waited for him; he pulled a plain towel from it and dried his black swim shorts and toned caramel skin. A pearl kimono and setta sandals clothed the young woman. Subtle looks of shame flashed from her eyes. In a contemplative manner, she sat, pushing tear drop shaped candies past her plump lips.

Obake put on his black keikogi and zori sandals then sat beside her.

"Don't worry," His heart played the drums. "One day we won't have to deal with all this."

"I hope so."

The strong trace of melancholia in her voice didn't go ignored.

"You know, next time we meet we'll be back in my neck of the woods. Want to go somewhere new or head to the usual spot?"

"The usual spot, I could use some more relaxation."

A ruffle of bushes and shuffle of sand tinged Obake's ears. He and the young woman spun around fast enough to induce whiplash.

"What do we have here?"

The forest seemed to have learned speech until an imposing man marched into the moon's field of vision. He sported a conical hat, ebony hue and jian sword. His expensive armor displayed a symbol that matched the one from the young woman's towel.

Oh shit, a Gazzo Samurai!

"If it isn't little Meilana, sneaking around in the early morning with some punk."

Obake scrambled to his feet, sand shoveling beneath them. "You know this guy?"

Meilana stood with caution, mumbling something unintelligible along the way; she couldn't peel her eyes from the new arrival.

A whistle released from the imposing samurai and the bushes began to shake. "The Grandmagistra isn't going to be happy about this."

Nine additional men wearing the same armor surrounded the couple, their hostile energy suffocating the area.

More of them? So much for never getting caught.

"I'm spending time with a friend. It's no big deal," said Meilana.

"Where I come from, friends don't cuddle together under the stars." The imposing samurai snickered. "Especially not at Illumino Lake."

The other samurai snickered, too, while Obake's focus darted between them. Most looked average except for two. One of which could be mistaken for a child. The other, a pinkish man, held extra weight that complimented his black beard and bald head, the sides of which contained stubborn spikes of hair.

Meilana whispered through fastened teeth. "You need to make a run for it."

"Are you crazy?" Obake whispered back. "I'm not leaving you."

Her tone shifted to one of confidence. "I'll be fine. They wouldn't dare lay a finger on me."

What's that all about?

"Hey now, we like secrets too. Isn't that right, fellas?" said the imposing samurai.

"Got that right boss," said a large nosed samurai as he and his companions nodded along.

Meilana ambled closer, her arms outstretched like a zookeeper trying to calm a lion. "I'm sorry. Don't tell my mom. I won't sneak out again, I promise."

The imposing samurai rolled his shoulders in an irritated fashion. "No can do. I've maintained her trust for nearly a decade. I'm not going to screw that up for you and your hormones."

Is her mom somebody important?

"Come on, Juroiza. Please!"

"I said no!" Juroiza's voice boomed with enough force to rival a demolition.

Who does he think he's talking to like that? Fire joined the blood coursing through Obake. "Hey! Do us all a favor and get the fuck out of here."

"Would you look at that? Seems we have a tough guy on our hands. What clan are you from, kid?" asked Juroiza.

"All you need to know is I'm here visiting your wife."

Juroiza laughed aloud. "You're a funny guy. I see why she likes you. Tell you what. I have a feeling you know how to fight. Why don't you show me a thing or two?"

Meilana's eyes widened with worry. The other samurai murmured with excitement.

"I'd love to," said Obake vigorously.

Meilana refused to move. "No. This isn't necessary."

Juroiza reached for the embroidered sword fastened to his back. Distress twisted Meilana's features.

Sliding past her, Obake took his stance. "I'll be fine." *Maybe I should've thought this through. How am I supposed to defend against that? Maybe I can take it from him.*

The child sized samurai came forward to receive his boss' sword.

An exhale of relief spilled from the young man. *Okay. Perfect.*

Obake rushed forward, catching everyone off guard. Vaulting through the air, he delivered a kick designed to remove his opponent's head. Both of Juroiza's arms shot up, blocking with the efficiency of steel bars. Obake's follow up elbow became snagged in Juroiza's palm. He cocked a fist, but Obake was too fast. He put a foot in Juroiza's gut like a gardener planting an apple seed. Juroiza hunched, breath shooting from his mouth. His gaze turned savage; he faked a kick then switched to a punch that sent stars prancing around Obake's vision.

Obake shook it off then rushed forward again. *I'm going to rip his head off!* He evaded a series of jabs and hooks before countering with an uppercut that Juroiza slipped. *He can't dodge me forever.*

Throwing a kick in retaliation cost Juroiza another strike to the gut. His eyes bulged while saliva sprayed between his teeth. Obake concluded his combo with a hook of his own. It connected with such force that his enemy went spiraling. Juroiza's fancy hat tumbled across the sand like a wheel on the loose.

Not so scary after all.

Meilana and the other samurai stood dumbfounded. With ferocity, each of the samurai brandished their weapons and advanced.

Juroiza thrust himself up. "No!"

Each of the nine samurai paused as if they'd combust from doing anything else.

"That was a mistake," said Juroiza, prodding the dribble of blood on his lips.

He launched a soaring knee to the head, but Obake repelled it with both hands. A leg sweep came for Obake next, when that missed Juroiza front flipped.

What is he—?

A boot rained upon Obake's head like falling hail. As his brain struggled to process the shock, he saw another boot headed his way. Seizing it, he rushed Juroiza onto his backside. As Juroiza fell, he clenched Obake's wrists then tossed him over. The sand stung Obake's back on impact.

Both combatants staggered up to face one another. A woozy spell embraced Obake, but that didn't stop him from issuing a desperate jab. Upon grabbing the jab, Juroiza jerked Obake into his knee. A heel then collided with Obake's back like an axe through wood. Obake slammed on his face so hard, it was amazing blood didn't burst from every orifice on his head. A malevolent grin spread Juroiza's lips. He then shoved his opponent's face into the sand with his foot.

No, no! He's trying to kill me. He's trying to kill me!

Obake's nose sank into the sand, preventing air. He couldn't breathe through his mouth either. Copious amounts of sand entered his mouth like an hourglass moving in reverse.

I can't go out like this. Not like this.

Almost frothing with joy, Juroiza continued grinding Obake's head into the sand. "That's right. Go to sleep little man."

Meilana hurried forward and got manhandled by two of the samurai. She lurched free and heaved an elbow at the enormous nose behind her. The samurai's head whipped back along with a dog like yelp. Her fist then deployed to clobber the mustached samurai in front of her. She ran, but didn't get far. Three additional samurai jumped in, restraining her like a vice grip.

To no avail, she squirmed and squirmed. "Get off of him!" she said, frantic terror embedded in her words.

Leave her alone, you bastards.

Juroiza's leg began lifting against his will. "What!"

Streams of sand trickled down the crevices of Obake's ears and the ridges of his cheeks as his head ascended. *I won't let him win.*

Saliva infused lumps of sand flopped from Obake's mouth, granting a much-needed breath. He growled like a cornered wolf, eyes bloodshot, face vibrating with fury.

Juroiza applied more pressure. "Get back down there!"

Obake thrust upwards with great force, sending Juroiza stumbling back.

Obake staggered to his feet, body unbalanced and fidgety, fists raised. "Time for round two."

Meilana was beyond thrilled, but Juroiza and the other samurai had the exact opposite reaction.

Retrieving his hat, Juroiza brushed it off then placed it on his head. "I have to hand it to you kid, you're one tough son of a bitch, but I think we're done here."

Juroiza also reclaimed his sword, then turned toward the forest and whistled once more. A thump went off that soon settled into a steady rhythm. Half a minute later, a gorgeous white stallion trotted along. In a paternal manner, Juroiza caressed it. The stallion nudged against him, soaking in the attention.

"Bring her to me," commanded Juroiza.

The three samurai restraining Meilana paraded her to Juroiza. She resisted with each step, but still couldn't pry herself free.

"Get off her," said Obake, shuffling at them as best he could.

"Shut up." The black bearded samurai pushed Obake back. "That's enough out of you." His voice was thick, choppy.

After forcing Meilana onto the stallion, Juroiza joined her.

The child sized samurai made his approach. "Should we accompany you to meet her mother, sir?"

"Imbecile. Never refer to the Grandmagistra that way. Show some damn respect."

The child sized samurai winced. "Yes, sir. My apologies, sir."

Juroiza sighed. "I'll ride ahead and take her back to the castle. The rest of you bring her little boyfriend. I still have questions."

Did I hear what I think I heard? No. I imagined it. There's no way she's her daughter. Right? As Obake contemplated, an epiphany washed over him like an icy wave. *What do I really know about her? Her family is…? Well, she has a sister… I think. She has a dog. No, a cat… wait. I don't know.*

His head spun with questions he wanted immediate answers to. Meilana looked back at him with unease and shame.

Her lips quivered then mouthed: "Go. Please."

Juroiza snapped the reins around his stallion and set off. In the time needed to complete a few blinks, Meilana had gone, distant thuds of stallion hooves in her wake.

Although exhausted, Obake could feel a second wind fast approaching. Each of the other samurai scowled at him, but only the one with the black beard spoke.

"We're going to have some fun with you first."

That doesn't sound good. Obake sized each of them up. *I can't fight them all.*

"What did you have in mind, Agalo?" asked the child sized samurai.

Agalo looked upon Obake, contemplating. "We're going to take you some place real fun."

Dammit. It's true. They really are going to skin me alive. After that, they'll feed me to some wild dogs. No. They'll probably make me their slave first. I have to get out of here.

Agalo gestured toward his companions. "Let's go, gentlemen."

In unison, all nine samurai whistled. A melodic stampede unleashed. Nine horses of different colors and sizes galloped into the vicinity.

The samurai mounted their steeds as Agalo circled behind Obake. "Put your hands behind your back. Won't have you doing your fancy moves on me."

Jangling chains filled Obake's ears as cold metal kissed his wrists. Before Agalo could fasten the shackles,

Obake head bunted him. The dig of teeth in his skull didn't slow him one bit. He beelined for his satchel first, then for the one available horse. After mounting it, he gave it a hard smack to the rear. Soon enough he was shifting through the trees at great speed.

He glanced back, hoping luck would've taken his side; it hadn't. All nine samurai gained on him fast. Agalo rode in tandem with the child sized samurai, affording him the luxury of unoccupied hands. He drew many arrows and let a volley hit the night sky. Some arrows streaked past Obake's head to disappear into the distance. Others ended up striking nearby trees. Unable to maneuver well became problematic for Obake. Five of the nine horsemen caught up, three in the rear with katanas at the ready. Two of the horsemen preferred weapons of a different variety, a bō staff and a hatchet. They rode up on either side, boxing Obake in.

Come on! Go faster!

Obake caught the bō staff swinging toward him, tugged it away, then threw it back. It repelled off its owner with a rowdy thud. The hatchet came swinging next. After dodging each slash, Obake felt a vibration at the rear of his horse.

Don't tell me—

He looked back to find the bō staff wielder tight roping his horse's spine. Grimy fingers soon laced around his throat. Every tree ahead blurred as the pressure intensified.

Again, the hatchet came, and again it missed. Obake pivoted his horse toward the hatchet wielder, causing the bō staff wielder to catapult into the cleaving weapon. Blood gushed from the fatal neck wound like a miniature waterfall.

Oh, shit… I've never…

The bō staff wielder's eyes rolled back as he fell, the hatchet still wedged in his neck. A sickening crunch echoed with each tumble of his body and the shadows were quick to claim him.

Unable to pry his eyes away, the hatchet wielder sustained a hard kick to the chest from Obake. As he flew from his horse, he clutched the top of the saddle, his fingers slipped thereafter. He dropped under his horse and got trampled, the snapping and cracking of his bones made Obake cringe.

What did I just do?

The horse balked then reversed back toward its crippled rider. At that moment, Obake heard another arrow whistle by. He turned a gaze to find Agalo firing again. Agalo's next arrow approached so low, Obake had to lie down. Zooming overhead, the arrow stabbed Obake's horse near the ear. It squealed then fumbled over. Obake jumped to the bō staff wielders' horse, which still ran alongside him. Upon landing, Obake peered through the canopy. An enormous wall drew ever closer; he steered his horse right at it.

I can't let them follow me any further.

Seven horsemen were still hot on Obake's trail. He reached into his satchel, which remained strapped to his torso despite the commotion. After a bit of rummaging, he retrieved two small kitchen knives. Holding both knives tight, he threw them at his targets with precision.

One knife aimed at the horsemen closest to Agalo, the samurai with the mustache. It hit him center mass, he flopped forward, dead. His body bobbed about in eerie fashion as the horse continued at full speed. Before long, the bloody corpse tumbled off, which prompted the horse to slow down. The second knife went for Agalo and his child sized partner. They saw it coming and swerved out of the way. Luck didn't shield the horseman riding behind them, so the knife plunged deep into his eye. As he fell, his foot tangled in the reins. For several feet, his body dragged across the ground. Before long, the horse noticed and halted. Five horsemen remained.

Obake pulled out a round, iron object with a button-like protrusion. Upon pushing the button, the object became hot and started to smoke. He lobbed it behind himself, right in the path of his pursuers.

Not a moment too soon, the child sized samurai steered away. The object hit the ground with a furious explosion. Nothing but smoke and debris found Obake's eyes when he looked back.

A horse then pierced through the debris, followed by a second. Of those remaining, two horses didn't make it out. The horses, along with their riders, took the full brunt of the explosion. When the smoke cleared, Obake saw them. Glued to the ground, they wailed together in agony, like ghosts singing in a quartet. Extensive damage befell the child sized samurai as well, his throat sliced open from the shrapnel. He made a repugnant gurgling noise before Agalo shoved him off the horse.

A feeling of disgust invaded Obake's headspace. *I've never killed anyone. What am I now? A monster?* He kicked the thoughts from his mind and refocused. *How do I get rid of these last two? Wait… that's it, the Nuojo Grand Chasm!*

Veering off course, Obake headed straight for a gaping chasm. Speeding up, the final two horsemen passed Obake. Agalo hopped across the chasm with ease. Along with his big bloody nose, the other horseman jumped too. Unlike Agalo, he and his horse weren't successful. Their bodies crashed back and forth against the chasm walls until meeting the jagged rocks below.

Nerves firing, Obake pet his horse. "You can do this."

His attempt to boost the animal's confidence failed. As soon as the horse saw the edge, it panicked and stopped. Obake went airborne—right into the chasm's air space. To his surprise, he cleared the chasm and found himself several feet above Agalo.

Don't shoot! Don't shoot!

The bearded samurai aimed his bow, firing a single arrow. Obake couldn't dodge it this time. It impaled his right bicep; the pain was strong, but not stronger than his will to live. He twisted, using his shoulder to slam into Agalo. They fell together, but Obake was on top, forcing Agalo to take most of the rocky ground's wallop.

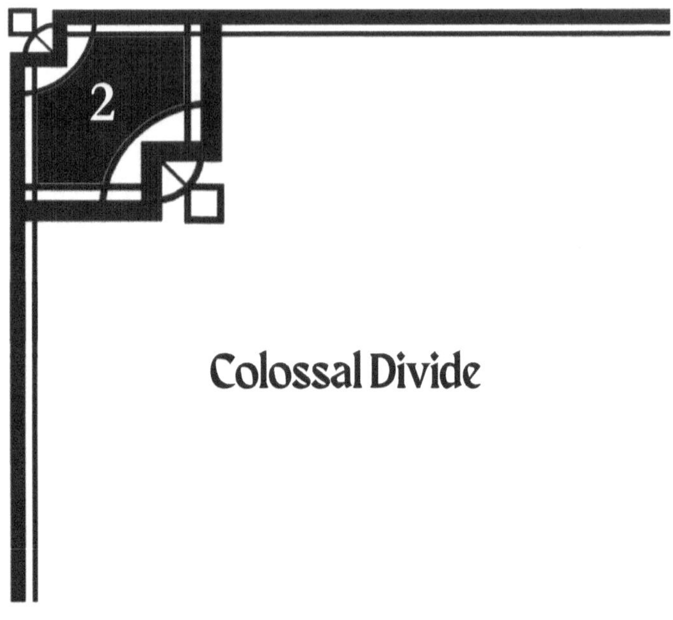

Colossal Divide

Everything was blurry and spinning, but Obake reoriented himself before long. His bicep throbbed and it showed no sign of letting up. As his vision returned, he glanced down and saw yellow teeth, black beard hair and bits of food tucked within it. A putrid stench accosted his nostrils as well. Obake was close enough to kiss his overweight pursuer. He rolled off the unconscious samurai as fast as his achy body would allow.

Disgusting! What's with this guy? It's not that hard to brush your damn teeth.

Obake wanted nothing more than to remain lying right where he was and take a long nap. He dreaded the thought of pushing his body any further. Regardless, in a fashion similar to an eighty-year-old, he climbed back to a standing position. Blood spilled over his forearm like a broken valve. Agalo's arrow pierced straight through the bicep muscle, but failed to exit. With a deep breath, Obake gripped above the arrow's tail and… panicked.

This is going to suck. I don't know if I can do this. For a second time, he inhaled. *All right, I got this. One… Two… Three!*

The arrow came free, accompanied by an awful sloshing sound. A decent amount of blood traveled the length of his arm. He took off his sash and used it as a tourniquet. Soon enough, leaking blood was no longer an immediate concern.

While gazing upon the bearded samurai, dark thoughts surged into Obake's mind. *I could stomp him out right now. Make sure he never shoots another arrow again. Or maybe I'll throw him off instead. No. I'm not a murderer.* Obake wondered if instances of this nature were what turned some warriors into cold-blooded savages. *I better go before this bastard wakes up.*

The horse Obake rode to the chasm was nowhere to be seen.

Did it fall?

Agalo's horse however, stood by with ever so quiet patience, staring at Obake with its black, orb-like eyes.

Obake approached and began petting the horse. It behaved like it didn't know what to make of the gesture. "Sorry about your friends. Believe it or not, I love animals."

Although embarrassed, he hoped the horse would reassure him somehow. Tell him he wasn't a monster. When his imagination failed to elicit a reaction from reality, he mounted the horse and searched the pouches on the saddle. All he found was a thermos filled with water and half of a sandwich. Most of the thermos' contents slid down Obake's throat, and he ate most of the leftover sandwich. The rest went straight to the horse. Again, it behaved like it didn't know how to take the kind gesture.

Up through the trees, the giant wall still loomed. A pocket watch came from Obake's kekogi. Unique patterns decorated its lid.

He flipped it open to view the ticking hands of time. *4:01 A.M. Looks like I'm not getting much sleep tonight.*

An engraving on the bottom side of the lid read: **Vai.** Obake's heart ached for the name.

I miss you, Mom.

Together, Obake and his new companion made their way and ten minutes later arrived beneath the massive sixty-foot wall. It was a beautiful sight to behold. Sandy brown stones stacked up the bottom half of the wall until they reached a partition. The upper half was a smooth surface that crawled higher, ending at a pagoda style roof. Draped in ruby colored shingles and copper accents, the roof was an architectural masterpiece. One Obake was prepared to reach.

He dismounted, then hesitated a moment before speaking. "Thanks for your help. I wouldn't have made it without you and your friends. Take care of yourself."

Obake smacked the animal on its hind and it shot off into the distance. From his satchel came two black climbing claws, each with three sharp spikes jutting from the palms. Taking a quick breath, he glanced up to brace himself for the task at hand. His ascent began when he stabbed the claws into the wall and inserted his fingertips between the stones. He also used any imperfections, unusual humps, cracks and holes, anything that enabled him to get a finger or foothold.

Despite the sting in his right arm and the physical exertion, the climb was tranquil. Whistling, serene wind brushed his ears and glistening stars grew closer. If it were possible, he would've stolen a star to keep as a memento.

Upon reaching the partition, it was time for the next step. Obake made sure his left hand had a firm grip and his feet were wedged between two blocks. Using extreme caution, he leaned back then reached into his bag. It took a mere millisecond before he found what he searched for—a wound-up black rope attached to a silver talon. The ropes slack twisted toward the ground after he unraveled it. Soon enough, the talon spun overhead like a propeller.

With a quick release, it bolted up and over the roof to latch onto its opposite side. Before trusting it, Obake gave a few tugs. Now, he dangled from a rope at thirty feet high. His ascension went fast, too fast. A spasm seized Obake's wounded arm, sending him rappelling. Gripping in desperation caused the rope to burn his fingers. Against the blocks, his feet dug in, forcing the wall to scrape up the soles of his sandals.

Before reaching the ropes end, some twenty feet above ground, he slowed to a halt. *That was too close.*

Patience on his mind, he recommenced his climb until the ruby roof greeted him.

On top of the flat, eight-foot-wide roof, he gazed to one side then the other. *Never fails to amaze me. They definitely didn't botch the name with this one. The Colossal Divide… looks like it goes on forever.* Obake found it surreal to survey the realm from on high, but it also brought him a bout of sadness. *The lengths people will go to separate themselves from each other.* Meilana circumvented his mind; he tried to push her out. He didn't want to let emotions consume him, but it was futile. They kept building until they became too strong to hold back any longer.

I'm never going to see her again, am I? There's no way I can be with her now. Why did I have to go over there tonight? His stomach performed a series of somersaults. *How could I be so stupid? The expensive things, the fancy outfits, the Gazzo Clan symbol. I mean… I knew she was from Gazzo City, but… the daughter of the Grandmagistra.*

One negative thought after the other hit his mind. *I should've figured it out. I assumed everybody from Gazzo City was rich. Why didn't I ask more questions? Stop! Come on Obake, you have to be strong. What's done is done.*

The internal agony throbbed far worse than the throbbing in his wounded arm. After a few moments of self-pity, Obake fastened the talon to the other side of the roof and rappelled with immense speed. Once halfway, he retrieved the talon and stuffed it back in his satchel. At a slow pace, he descended with his claws until he was close enough to drop the rest of the way. As his feet hit the dirt, he felt a tremendous weight lunge off his shoulders. He'd returned home.

Demon in the Walls

The stallion's hooves colliding against the dirt resonated with Meilana's auditory sensors in a muffle. In fact, in that moment, all sounds paled in comparison to the sheer volume of her worry.

She prayed, to whom… she didn't know. *Please let him escape. Don't let them kill him.*

The vulnerability percolating through her bones released warm tears from her eyes. She wept to herself, refusing to give Juroiza the satisfaction. They soon rode into a grassy clearing, putting the forest at their backs. On the horizon was a gargantuan castle.

A bout of sarcasm raided Meilana. *Back to the great Gazzo Castle, home sweet home.*

Its gothic design comprised of vibrant gray stone bricks. Gorgeous embellishments swept across it in all directions. From towers and spires waved enthusiastic silver flags. Purple draperies with the Gazzo Clan symbol hung over the ramparts, an ostentatious spectacle indeed.

Outrage strangled Meilana's sarcasm. *Why does she have to be so pretentious?* She gripped at her thighs, ruffling her kimono. *I've had enough of her shit. I won't let her do this to me anymore.* A quarter mile left of the castle lay the fossil of a Gatling gun. Rust and the elements had taken its toll on the weapon and tall grass was ingesting it. *It's returning to nature. Looks almost peaceful. Maybe I should do the same.*

While crossing the bridge leading to the castle, she glanced down at the moat. As expected, it was full to the brim with brown, murky water. She wondered what repugnant creatures might dwell there.

The stallion slowed to a halt before reaching the gatehouse. Two muscular men stood guard in front of the shiny bars. They, too, wore armor like Juroiza's.

Meilana wiped her tears away fast. Nobody seemed to notice. Upon recognizing them, the samurai saluted with nothing but the utmost respect.

"General Juroiza and the Grandheiress have returned. Open the gate!"

In an instant, the gate rose into the high archway. After passing through a short hall, they emerged in a torch lit courtyard. Countless voices erupted at once, all emanating from the city folk, busy getting ready for the approaching daylight. The courtyard was large enough to fit thousands of people at a time. Several shops lined the bottom of the ramparts; everything from food to clothing was available for purchase. Meilana took a moment to observe the elders playing chess and the children making mischief. It filled her heart with joy.

I would give anything to be free like them. They seem so happy. Loud, obnoxious trumpets reverberated from the towers. *Great, the sound of my impending confinement.*

City folk fell silent and shuffled to either side of the courtyard. Juroiza and Meilana went toward the keep at the opposite end. On the left was a stable housing a donkey who had seen better days. The stable sat between the keep's entrance and a pathway. A sign dangling from the arch above the pathway read: **Gazzo City**. Meilana could see hundreds of homes made of the same gothic design. One home harbored a plethora of potted plants on the front stoop.

I'd live in that one for sure.

Juroiza placed his stallion in a stall then stroked it on its upper neck. "I'll be back soon. Don't try to break out this time. You cost me a lot of money every time you do that, buddy."

The majestic animal looked away as if bashful. Juroiza pulled out a gleaming silver ring overflowing with keys. He unlocked and swung open the long doors of the keep. Meilana rushed in, Juroiza followed. Before he finished shutting the doors, the hustle and bustle of the courtyard reignited.

The interior of the castle was more decorative than anything outside by a long shot. A shimmering foyer that led to three branching hallways lay before them. Many glass chandeliers dazzled each hallway. Marble tiles of silver and purple accented the granite walls without effort. Two statues made of pearl surpassed the beauty of the chandeliers, floors and walls combined. One depicted a beautiful yet shrewd woman. The other depicted a man with a long flowing mustache who looked equally as shrewd.

I bet you were every bit the asshole she is. Meilana thought, stopping to gander at the two statues.

Although everything on display was beautiful, the objects left Meilana with a strong feeling of dread. Dark memories resurfaced to ignite her imagination, which conjured a grotesque demon. It observed her from the wall, syphoning what little happiness she had left.

Juroiza ushered her along. "Let's go, kid. The Grandmagistra's waiting."

Down the center most hallway they went, it led to a stairway that ascended three levels.

On the third floor, a set of double doors engraved with lavender flowers awaited them. Rather gentle, Juroiza knocked with his knuckles.

A voice doing its best impression of a calm tone called out from within. "You may enter."

Juroiza opened both doors to reveal yet another pretentious room. Inside was a balcony with a banister engrossed in thick vines. Two half oval windows sat on either side of the balcony. Each made of the finest stained-glass. They both depicted the same shrewd woman from the pearl statue, only this time, the woman was adorned with lavish battle armor. On the left, the woman sat in a stoic manner atop a noble steed. On the right, she raised a large war-hammer to the sky in triumph. Opposite the balcony rested a bed capable of fitting five full-grown adults. Next to the bed, a blonde, curly haired woman sat facing a floor mirror. She wore a purple kimono that hung loose off her smooth shoulders. Her olive skinned back aimed at the entrance while she stared at her reflection and combed her locks.

"Stay here," said Juroiza before entering and closing both doors behind him.

Unable to resist the urge, Meilana eavesdropped. Careful not to make a sound, she pressed her ear against one of the doors. Voices on the other side sounded like inaudible mumbles to her. She soon realized her effort was in vain and opted to give up. Over ten minutes later,

Juroiza returned and escorted her inside. Now, the blonde woman stared at the distant lands from her balcony.

"Here she is, Grandmagistra Izaru."

"Thank you. Please leave us."

"As you wish."

A stressful silence boiled the room. Meilana prepared to unleash, but her mother's words wrestled her anger into submission.

"Come stand with me."

The Grandmagistra's voice sounded like malevolence wrapped in a blanket of serenity. Hesitation took hold of Meilana, it felt like a trap. Despite her better judgement, she walked to the balcony. Each step was almost painful to complete. Her feet weighed a ton each. Once she arrived, the mesmerizing view stole her problems away only to return them a mere millisecond later. It occurred to her she'd never been on her mother's balcony.

"You know, one day this will all be yours," said Izaru. "There are those that would literally kill to be in your position, yet you take it for granted."

Meilana glanced at Izaru, trying to gauge her temperament. However, Izaru was difficult to read, her facial expression unwavering. Izaru turned to meet her daughter's gaze. Her eyes held a brilliant tint of yellow, her stare beyond intimidating. Their eye contact broke, Meilana's eyes burning against her mothers.

"The things I've done to secure your future bring me no comfort. But everything has been for the betterment of the Bushido Empire. I can't have you tarnishing the family reputation for some peasant boy."

Meilana went to speak, but her voice quivered. Before she could utter a word, Izaru pressed on.

"Now, you're going to tell me every detail you know about the boy you've been sneaking around with."

Shock hit Meilana like a force of nature. Her eyes attempted to leave her face and her jaw tried smacking the floor.

"First things first, what's his name and what clan does he belong to?"

The interrogation gave Meilana a bout of anxiety. Fear was trying to suffocate her to death. No way would she reveal any information, but she couldn't think fast enough to formulate a convincing lie. She hoped to disappear, go anywhere except where she was.

"I'm waiting." Izaru's tone shifted to one of open hostility.

"He's a boy from the academy mom, that's all. He's in my class."

"Interesting, if he was indeed a boy from your class, I'd know. I handpick all of your classmates myself."

Meilana spiraled through a twister of different emotions. They were high jacking her, threatening to rip her to pieces.

"Are you serious?"

"Of course, darling, it's been that way since you convinced me to let you learn with the common children." Izaru was now smug and arrogant.

"No wonder everybody in this godforsaken city treats me like I'm some sort of freak."

"They treat you like the Grandheiress that you are."

"They treat me like a porcelain doll. People are too afraid of you to risk getting close to me. I'm all alone here, always have been!"

Izaru scoffed and turned her eyes back toward the spectacular view. "Don't be so dramatic, you have everything a girl could ever want."

With resilience by her side, Meilana liberated herself from the emotional twister's clutches. "This is what *you* want! You could care less about what *I* want! You have no idea how much I hate it here. Did it ever occur to you that maybe I don't want to rule over this place?"

Meilana's sudden burst of rebellion left Izaru flabbergasted. "Enough! Give me the boy's name!"

"He's just a boy I met in the courtyard one day."

Fury shot from Izaru's eyes like a cannonball. "Tell the fucking truth! If I have to find out on my own, I will make him suffer. They're bringing him to me as we speak. You know that, right? What do you think I will do when I get my hands on him?"

The disgusting display of wrath left Meilana speechless for a moment, but words soon found their way back to her.

"You want to talk about truth? You think I don't know about you sneaking around with Juroiza behind Dad's back?"

Flabbergasted yet again, Izaru took pause and adopted an expression confirming her daughter's claims. "Mind your tongue, child. Your father's allegiance no longer resides where it should. Even a Grandmagistra has needs."

A series of urgent knocks hit the double doors.

"Juroiza, I told you to leave us."

Both of the lavender doors flew open. A look of utter shock splashed across Juroiza's face. He squeezed the words out, gasping like somebody who just sprinted a mile.

"I know… I'm sorry… but this couldn't wait." After taking a big gulp of air, he beckoned at someone next to him. "Come here, hurry."

Agalo limped inside, he kept a hand on the back of his head, but a trickle of blood carried on regardless.

Izaru looked appalled. "Agalo? What happened to you?"

Juroiza interjected like an eager child. "Tell her everything you just told me."

Agalo winced. "I'm sorry, Grandmagistra. He… he escaped. Stole my horse. We chased him, but… the others. They're all dead. He killed them! I'm so sorry I failed you."

The happiness building within Meilana was uncontainable. She smiled as big as her cheek muscles would allow and suffered a case of whiplash for it. Having witnessed Meilana's glee, Izaru yanked her close. She then scrutinized her daughter's eyes for answers, but Meilana looked away.

"Tell me who the boy is this instant!" screamed Izaru, so loud her voice cracked in protest.

Meilana's smile scattered like prey from a predator, but she didn't give in. Overcome with frustration, Izaru shoved her daughter to the floor. The last shred of respect Meilana had for her mother was out the window.

Izaru turned her attention elsewhere. "Something isn't adding up. Agalo, what can you tell me about this boy?"

"Well. He had green hair."

"Okay, that's a start. What about weapons? Did he use any against you? Did he deploy any type of deceptive tactics to escape?"

"Oh. Yeah, sort of. Um… he threw knives at us."

"What kind of knives?"

Agalo's eyes darted about. "I think they were normal kitchen knives. Couldn't see them too well in the dark though."

"Kitchen knives?"

"Yeah. Uh… he threw a bomb at us too."

Izaru stroked her chin with an investigative look about her. "Interesting, smoke bomb?"

"No. It was filled with little sharp objects."

"Shrapnel, huh? I see, I see."

Meilana grew anxious again as Juroiza offered a comment of his own. "You're not suggesting?"

"Quiet down," snapped Izaru.

Juroiza rolled his neck and shoulder in irritation. "Ah, come on. This has got to stop. You're being paranoid. I mean, what are the odds?"

"It's highly possible, and you'd be an idiot to think otherwise."

"We haven't had conflict with the ninja in decades. Why would they risk war now?"

"Those abhorrent gaikaos can't be trusted, and now my daughter's colluding with one of them."

"You don't know that." Juroiza sighed. "Plenty of samurai use knives and bombs, too. This means nothing. We can't keep traveling down this road, Grandmagistra. Please, give it up."

Izaru turned to him, fury shooting from her eyes again.

"I don't recall giving you permission to tell me what to do. You work for me. Or did you forget?"

Like a scolded pet, Juroiza backed down.

"It's normal for a girl to behave suspiciously while having a secret boyfriend. I'll give you that. Nevertheless, she's far too nervous for this to be a boy from our empire. Even for a teenager, why go through this much trouble?"

Juroiza hesitated, but ended up offering one last comment. "I understand. I just feel like we need some sort of proof, is all. We can't risk the lives of so many on a whim."

Izaru paused for a solid minute, lost in deep thought. "At dawn, go out to the scene of the incident and bring the bodies back. I'll have the doctors analyze them for any clues that may corroborate my theory. You're right, as of now I'm speculating, but my intuition has never been wrong before."

"Yes, Grandmagistra," said Juroiza, bowing so low he risked toppling over.

Izaru looked at her daughter who was starting to stand back up. "Report to your quarters and remain there until I say so."

Surprise gripped Meilana's face. "But what about the academy? My graduation ceremony is Friday night."

"There will be no more graduation ceremony. Not for you or anyone else."

Exhaustion had set in. Meilana no longer contained the energy to argue back.

Izaru turned to Juroiza. "I'll also need you to herd the cattle."

"What day and time would you prefer?"

"Friday at nightfall."

With an air of arrogance, Izaru turned back to Meilana and spoke again. "Go now, darling. Think long and hard about your defiance and what that gets you."

Seeing how vindictive her mother could be was like a punch through the gut. Meilana slouched then sulked from the room.

She took a left turn, then a right down a narrow corridor. *Yay, back to my very own personal prison cell.*

Her room opposed the décor in the rest of the castle. Each high-priced item relegated to a forsaken corner, hidden beneath a transparent veil. Two white vases towered over the rest of the items. A painting of Meilana standing with Izaru and a thin man leaned against the vases. A smaller statue of the shrewd looking man with the flowing mustache lay on the floor. Near the pile was a window decorated with a fiddle leaf fig. Despite its depressing surroundings, it was healthy and well-watered. Even the granite walls were barren. Everything had been stripped away.

Meilana drug herself over a rug covering most of the marble flooring. She plopped onto a bed she had long since outgrown. A cascade of tears raced down her cheeks, so much so she dry heaved. Darkness descended upon her once more. As she gazed around the room, she imagined the demons return. Its grotesque face peeked out of all four walls to howl with laughter.

No. Stop watching me. Go away! A wave of pressure sank her. I can't keep living this way. Anything would be better than this.

She reached under her bed, retrieved a tanto and pried the blade from its scabbard. Holding it to her wrist, she thought about dragging the cold steel up the length of her forearm.

Demon laughter grew louder, more haunting. It taunted her. "Do it!"

Meilana stalled, an epiphany was upon her. "But I have Obake now. I can run away with him."

"She'll never stop hunting you." The demon's eyes turned crazed. "You might as well kill him yourself."

"You're right. I'm no good to anyone."

Upon stabbing the blade into her flesh, she observed as the deep wound seeped blood. Seeing such a thing released her from the hazardous trance. After tossing the tanto to the floor, she cleared the sweat accumulating on her brow. The demon faces vanished and the walls returned to normal.

"Sweet Drop, may I come in?"

A familiar voice called out to her from the hall. Unsure whether she imagined it or not, she said nothing. The door to her room creaked open.

"Sweet Drop, you in there?"

The voice was real after all; Meilana dove at her tanto and threw it back under the bed.

She then sat on the edge near the headboard and covered her wrist. "Come in."

A thin, pointy nosed man waltzed over the threshold, the same man from the painting under the transparent veil. Meilana was aghast to see him.

Silver hair descended to his waistline, where it turned into two ponytails. Both tied by kiwi green ribbons. The sleeves of his shozoku dangled beside his hakama pants. He moved with fluidity, just like his outfit's many loose-fitting components.

He sat at the edge of the small bed and looked at his daughter with a joyous smile. His circular specs made him appear like a wise man that held the answers to life's many conundrums.

"I heard what happened. Are you okay?"

Meilana fixated on her fiddle leaf fig, then beyond to the starry sky. "I'm fine," she barked.

"You don't seem fine." The man continued to smile. "I know when my little girl's upset."

After a bit of squirming, she succumbed to the urge to speak her mind. "Why do you let her treat us like this? Why don't you stand up to her? Huh? Pai Liu?"

Pai Liu's smile tumbled away; his eyes converted from happy to solemn. "We've been over this Sweet Drop. Your mom is Gazzo's daughter." Pai Liu took a disgusted glance at the statue under the sheet. "I'm only Grandmaster by way of marriage. She calls the shots. Not much I can do about it."

"I still don't understand why you even married her. She's a nightmare."

Pai Liu taped a toothy grin to his olive toned face. "I married her so that I could have you."

"Yeah, right."

"No, seriously. You're the best thing that's ever happened to me."

Meilana slammed her hands on the bed in a fit of sheer frustration then re-concealed her wound. "Doesn't seem like it. You barely talk to me. Let alone spend time with me. Can't believe you still follow her stupid rules."

"Can't argue with you there. Most of her rules are very stupid."

"Then why follow them? I'm lucky if I see you once a month. I'm your fucking daughter! What? Does she think we'll plot to overthrow her if she lets us near each other?"

The glow of a proud father beamed from Pai Liu as he chuckled. "First off, language. Second, she thinks I'll make you soft."

Meilana lay back on her bed.

"I know it's not right, but try to understand. There's only so much I can do. Your mom could have me exiled or worse. At least I can help you in secret for now."

In utter disapproval, Meilana shook her head. "You could've been happy with someone else. You could've had a completely different life."

Pai Liu inhaled. "I was confused when I was your age. I craved power and wealth. Your mom fancied me and being with her gave me everything I thought I wanted. I later realized that none of it mattered. At least I got you out of the deal. I wouldn't trade that for anything."

Almost inadvertent, Meilana rolled her eyes.

Pai Liu continued. "So, what's this I hear about you having a little ninja boyfriend?"

Meilana sprang back to a seated position.

Giggles escaped Pai Liu. "Don't worry. You don't have to answer that."

"Why does she hate them so much? I mean… I know about what happened, but that was forever ago. Things are peaceful now."

"Some people are better than others at getting over things."

Meilana toiled over her father's words.

"Look, hang in there a little while longer. Once you turn eighteen, you'll be able to take control of your life. You're almost there. Don't give up now."

A more relaxed posture found Meilana.

"I guess you're right, Dad. Thanks for visiting me. I needed that."

"Yes, calling me Dad again," Pai Liu became ecstatic. "Oh, and anytime. Well, anytime I can get away with it. Your mom's a bit preoccupied at the moment."

"Do you think she'd ever," Meilana averted her gaze. "Hurt us?"

Pai Liu paused in contemplation. "Let's hope we never have to find out."

At a loss for words, Meilana gave no response.

"Well then, I'll be on my way." After kissing his daughter on the forehead, Pai Liu waltzed across the threshold, but before closing the door, he glanced back. "Should I be concerned about that?" he said, staring at the blood rising between Meilana's fingers.

"No. Um… just a scratch."

"That's some scratch. Do me a favor and have Madame Weila take a look at it, okay?"

Meilana nodded and Pai Liu gave her a wink then shut the door.

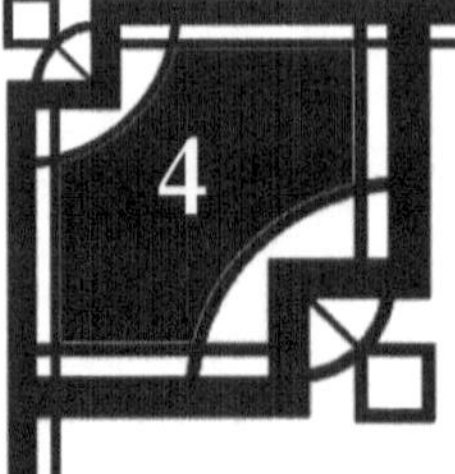

Like Grandfather Like Grandson

Shamisen notes fluttered around like a band of aimless butterflies. Obake absorbed every one of them and felt ethereal. The soothing melody was all he processed until golden light hammered against his eyelids.

He discharged a satisfying yawn while stretching each limb far and wide. "Forgot to close my blinds again."

"No, you didn't."

The ethereal feeling abandoned him. He sat up, the pain in his neck apparent once more. Even the sand scrapes on his face stung. His head pulsated so much he half expected his brain to crash through his skull. With eyelids heavier than sandbags, he had to make do with seeing through his eyelashes.

Past them, a woman with fiery red hair leaned against a wall. Large prayer beads hung from around her neck, dangling near her bulbous belly. Many lines and creases zigzagged across her face, but failed to detract from its pleasantness. While peering out the window beside her, she continued strumming her shamisen. The tune altered, deciding to bounce off the wooden walls and tatami flooring of Obake's room.

"Nana?"

The apricot skinned woman, clad in a plum kimono turned from the window with a gracious smile, her black eyes exuding kindness. "In the flesh, Froggy."

"Nana. We talked about this."

"We did. But you know your dear old grandmother's hard of hearing."

"Yeah right, Nana. What time is it anyway?"

"6:05 in the morning. Now come on. Up, up, up. I have to heal those wounds of yours. You look like you got mauled by a pigeon."

Nana propped her shamisen under the window and left the room. Obake's body ached to the point he struggled to peel himself from his bed. As he stood, his legs didn't hesitate to inform him of their disapproval.

He almost crawled to reach a half-finished fox sculpture on a lonesome desk. *This eye looks a little off.*

A knife covered in splinters laid next to the sculpture. It scraped away at the wooden fox, a left eye more befitting of the omnivorous animal started to form.

"I'm waiting," called Nana.

"No. That's okay. I'll be fine."

"Nonsense, get your butt over here. I'll add a few extra wounds myself if you don't."

Obake drug his heels to the doorway. Right next door was a bathroom half the size of his already tiny room. It had wooden walls as well, but the floors possessed straw mats instead of tatami. A wind chime hanging above the toilet gave the room an outdoorsy vibe. In the corner, a sizeable barrel filled to the brim with warm water awaited. It was just big enough to accommodate a single person, Obake limped to it.

"Hop in!" said Nana.

Obake removed his bloodstained keikogi before catching his grandmother in his periphery. Her back was to him. She hummed the same tune she performed earlier on the shamisen.

"Um… can you… get out, please?"

"I'm not looking. I used to change your diapers you know."

"Come on. I'm not a little boy anymore. I'm an adult now."

"Seventeen is hardly an adult, even eighteen for that matter. They should change the laws. I think it should be thirty, but what do I know?"

On her way out, she rolled down the cloth drape above the bathroom entrance. Obake disrobed and entered the pleasant bath. As soon as his body contacted the liquid, he felt it working to alleviate his aches and pains.

"Ready yet?" asked Nana. "I'm going to die of old age if I have to wait any longer."

"I'm ready," grumbled Obake.

She curled up the drape and waddled toward her grandson like a penguin in snow. With both hands, Obake covered his groin.

"The water feels great and all, but this will take forever. Are we still out of elixir?"

"Patience is a virtue, Froggy."

Obake rolled his eyes in annoyance. "You know I hate when you call me that."

"But it's so perfect. When you were a tiny baby, you and your green hair bounced around the house like—"

"A frog, I remember," said Obake with a sigh.

Nana chuckled as she reached into the sleeve of her kimono to fetch a wooden canister, engraved upon it, the face of a terrifying ghost. Its liquid magenta contents spilled into the bath. The bath water immolated the magenta liquid with haste. Vapor then rose from the barrel and disseminated throughout the bathroom.

"When did you get more puapo?" Suspicion crept onto Obake's face. "Wait a minute. You never actually ran out, huh?"

"Nope, I hide it from you and your grandfather. You two always use it all up. It's not easy to make you know."

"But you poured most of it in here."

"That's the trick. For minor injuries all you have to do is," She stared at Obake, inviting him to finish her sentence. "Well?"

"Take a few sips," he groaned.

"And for more serious injuries?"

"Drink half. If that's not enough, drink the whole thing."

"Exactly! Glad to see you can pay attention when you want to."

Nana tucked the empty canister back into the depths of her sleeve. "Now here's something you don't know. When you combine the Puapo Elixir with a warm bath, it accelerates your immune system. You heal twice as fast!"

Obake's entire demeanor altered. His grandmother's medicinal knowledge impressed him.

"That's some amazing shit right there."

"Amazing shit indeed."

"Why didn't you ever tell me this before?"

"You didn't need to know. You've never been injured like this."

Obake averted his eyes to the wind chime above.

"Going to tell me what happened?"

He continued scrutinizing the chime as its pipes clapped together. "That's super nice. We should put more of them up around the house."

"Thought so. You teenagers and your secrets. Don't think I didn't notice some of my knives missing either."

"I have no clue what you're talking about."

"If you say so. Whatever you're doing, I hope you're being careful."

Nana waddled to the start of the hallway then fired another gaze at Obake. He glanced back at the wind chime.

"Don't stay in there for more than thirty minutes or you'll get dizzy. Take it easy and you should be good to go by Friday, just in time for your graduation."

"My graduation is next Friday."

"I knew that," she said with embarrassment.

"Are you and Papa still coming?"

"Of course, I wouldn't miss it. Even for a sexy young man half my age."

"Come on, Nana."

Obake feigned a gag while his grandmother adopted a doe eyed smile. From another room, a gritty voice yelled out.

"Hey! Stop babying the boy, Bao-Ang. He doesn't need us there."

"Oh, hush. We're going," Bao yelled back. "Don't listen to him. I'll have your breakfast waiting for you."

She waddled out, closing the dingy drape behind her. A half hour went by like a shooting star; Obake was so relaxed he came close to exceeding the time limit.

He sprang from the bath upon noticing his imminent mistake and grabbed the robe Bao left for him.

Feeling ten times better, Obake peered at the mirror over the sink, it showed fading wounds. *Damn. This has got to be some sort of sorcery. She's a Kantasian. Yup, that's the only explanation.*

The aroma of scrambled eggs, rice noodles, steamed buns and vegetables nestled Obake's nostrils the second he entered the kitchen. It almost made him salivate; his body craved anything capable of aiding in his recuperation. Bao sat next to an elder man and they both drank from tall cups.

"About time," said the elder man.

Obake smirked and took a seat at the round table. The elder man was compact, but fearsome. Remnants of several injuries lingered on his face and only one of his eyes still functioned. The left eye harbored a painful-looking scar that slithered up his forehead and down his cheek. Similar to a gloomy day, the functional eye was foggy and gray. His hair resembled the fur of an old wolf. However, he and Obake shared the same forest green hair and caramel pigment.

The elder man regarded Obake. "Could've put some clothes on."

Having taken a sip from her cup, Bao almost spit. By pinching her lips, she prevented turning the kitchen into a splash zone.

"Yokai, stop. It's too early for that," said Bao with a rasp before taking another drink.

"You're just jealous. Not my fault you have that old, rickety ass body now. You wish you could look this good again," said Obake with a mischievous grin.

Laughter erupted like three volcanoes going off at once. This time apple juice splashed across the kitchen table. In cheerful spirit, Yokai slapped his grandson on the back multiple times.

"You're a funny guy, Green. I'm glad you're okay. You looked like shit when you stumbled in this morning."

A look of disappointment infiltrated Obake's facial features. "You saw that?"

Bao and Yokai nodded together in unison.

"Do you two ever sleep?"

"A Yokai Clan Ninja never sleeps," said Yokai. "Speaking of which, you have about ten minutes before training begins."

"What? I still have to train?" Obake looked to his grandmother. "I got mauled by a pigeon, remember?"

Bao smirked. "Nice try."

Yokai consumed what remained on his plate, then shot up. "I'll be outside. You'll owe me for every minute you're late."

Obake's eyes widened.

Yokai kissed Bao on the forehead. "Thanks for the breakfast, dear. It was tasty. I'll take care of lunch." He then made his way to the front yard.

Obake ravaged his scrambled eggs and vegetables. He then slurped down a few straggling rice noodles and shoveled another steamed bun into his mouth. Cold apple juice washed it all down.

"Chug, chug, chug," said Bao until the juice vanished. "Now hurry and put on your keikogi."

"You're not training with us today?"

"I most certainly am. I've got to finish cleaning up first."

In a rush, Obake got dressed and headed outside to a grassy field enclosed by a short bamboo fence. Yokai stood against the passing winds, his bushy mustache holding on for dear life. String trailed from his hands over to the kite of a viper some forty feet high. It swayed and slithered like a water snake on the prowl.

"Like it?" asked Yokai. "It's brand new."

For a brief moment, Obake scrutinized the kite. "I don't know. I think I like the cat one better."

"Me too," Yokai stabbed the kite spool into the grass. "Oh, and you're a minute late, Green. That'll be twenty-five pull-ups."

"Seriously?"

"Get to it."

Next to the small cottage stood a makeshift bamboo pull-up bar. It took Obake less than a minute to complete the task.

"All right, old timer. What else you got for me?"

"Here, catch."

A pipe-like object spun at Obake. It twinkled in the sunlight as he reached up to snag it from the blue sky.

"Mizuchi," he said to himself.

A naginata with a short black and gold handle sat in his palm, blade concealed by a matching scabbard. As if struck by lightning, Obake's mind found his father's face. Not long after, his mother's face drifted by, too. Both of his parent's features were so vivid, so painful. His heart rate skyrocketed until Yokai's words brought it back down.

"We'll be continuing yesterday's training. But remember. No soul energy. We'll recommence with that tomorrow." Yokai cherry-picked a few river rocks from a nearby pile. "Oh, and no shrapnel bombs either."

Obake gulped. "What do you—?"

"It's fine, but if any parents come to me saying their kid's missing a leg, you're in serious trouble."

Tingles spiraled Obake's spine as Yokai jiggled the rocks in each hand. "Now I know you worry about breaking it, but like I told you a million times, your father's old weapon was forged from galvantium. It's pretty much indestructible."

With his thumb, Obake caressed the weapon as Yokai continued.

"You were able to strike down seven last time. Let's see how well you fare today."

Obake punched one of two buttons located under the naginata's handguard. The handle extended over two feet.

"Prepare yourself!" Yokai shouted.

Obake called forth his combat stance as Yokai threw the first rock, then the second in rapid succession. With finesse, Obake rolled away from the first. It whizzed past him and crashed into a nearby boulder. He tossed away the scabbard as the second rock sailed for him. Before it smashed into his arm, he sliced upward. The projectile split in two, sending both pieces in opposite directions.

"Not bad," said Yokai as he hurled four additional rocks.

Each of which succumbed to four additional slices. Four rocks became eight against the might of Mizuchi.

Yokai had plenty more where that came from. He took six smaller rocks, placing them between his fingers. After a quick cross of the arms, he let them fly. Rocks surrounded Obake so fast that he almost lost track of them.

I don't think I can get them all.

Obake punched the second button under the naginata's handguard. The blade snaked its way from the handle by an attached chain. With a swirling motion, every projectile got sliced in one fell swoop. Pieces of rock fell like raindrops.

"I did it! How many was that, Papa?"

"Twelve. Have you been practicing?"

Obake grinned from ear to ear. "Maybe."

"Don't get too arrogant, Froggy. You're not out of the woods yet."

Bao sat on the porch. Cigarette smoke billowing from her jaws.

"Dammit, Bao-Ang. Put that thing out. It's—"

"Going to be the death of me, I know. I know."

After stabbing her cigarette in a nearby ashtray, Bao headed to the rock pile. She scooped a handful, then positioned behind her grandson.

Obake retracted Mizuchi. *Great, here comes the tag team.*

"Ready. Go!" yelled Bao.

Yokai and Bao both launched two rocks a piece. Obake jumped up, evading them all. Without hesitation the elder ninjas threw one more rock each.

They tricked me. Unable to dodge, Obake crouched in midair. *I got this.* The rocks soared over his head.

Yokai and Bao skipped their last rocks off the ground before Obake could land. One rock struck Obake's chest while the other bit into his thigh.

"Damn it!" In disappointment, Obake plopped down. However, Yokai became ecstatic. "Great job, Green."

"You were almost untouched," said Bao, dazzled.

They sat on either side of Obake before Bao spoke again.

"Now, if this had been for real, you'd be in serious trouble right about now, but superb job."

"Thanks!" said Obake with glee, handing Mizuchi over to Bao.

"We've been training you for what, a decade now? We've trained many people in our time and none have shown as much promise as you," said Yokai.

"Yeah, right. You're just saying that."

Bao gave a bright smile. "He's not lying. You really are special. Keep it up and you'll be a fine warrior someday."

A young man with a light purple faux hawk and bronze skin came walking over from a distance.

"What's up," he said, waving.

"Is it that time already?" asked Obake, retrieving his pocket watch.

Yokai glanced over his grandson's shoulder. "Yup, 7:24 a.m. on the dot. You got little more than a half an hour to get there."

Obake ascended to his feet as the young man entered the yard, bringing his skinny build and pecan-colored eyes with him. An elaborate handshake ensued between the young men.

"What's going on, Yumo? You ready for that arithmetic test or what?" asked Obake.

"Um… I think I'm going to wing it to be honest."

They both snorted then chuckled like hyenas.

"What gives, kid? You're late. How can I trust you to get my grandson to the academy on time? Twenty-five pull-ups now!" said Yokai.

Yumo looked frightened and puzzled at the same time.

Obake gave his friend a stern look. "You have to do them. He doesn't like repeating himself."

"They're just pulling your leg," said Bao, who was doing her best not to laugh.

Fits of laughter took hold of Obake and Yokai.

Yumo relaxed his tense posture. "I can never tell when you're serious or not, sir."

Yokai couldn't stop howling. "You should've seen the look on your face."

At last, Bao joined in, the laughter was too contagious. "How've you been, Yumo? How's your father doing?" she asked, in between laughs.

"Uh… he's doing fine, ma'am."

"Um, hmm. I bet he is," she said as if admiring a plate of desserts.

Yokai shot Bao a death stare as Obake hid his face behind his hands. Yumo wore a grin that screamed of discomfort.

"Have a good day at the academy, kids," said Yokai, breaking the awkwardness.

"Oh, and no ditching," said Bao.

The pair of friends avoided eye contact with her.

Obake made way for the cottage. "Uh… let me grab my bag and we'll head out." He pretended not to notice Bao's suspicious eye along the way. He returned seconds later, raring to go. "Bye. See you later."

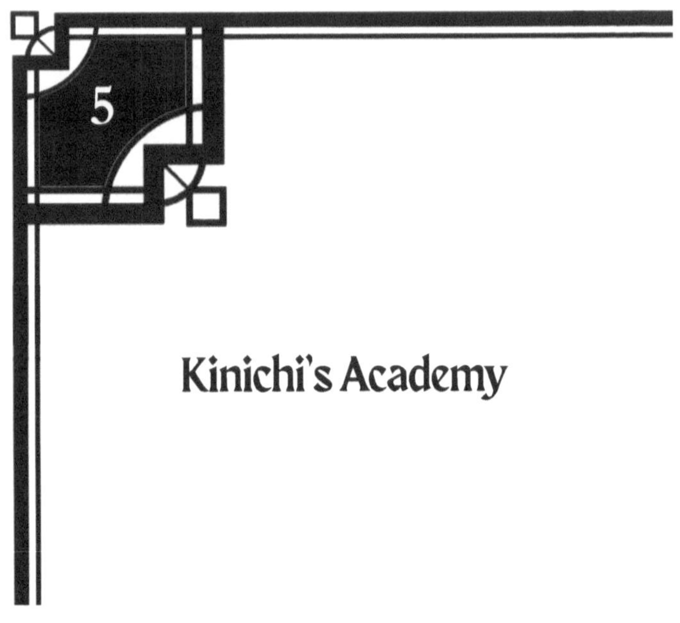

Kinichi's Academy

Yumo and Obake traversed the mountainous terrain. The bird's-eye view of the lands below was nothing short of remarkable.

Before long, the pair encountered two trails. One led down the mountain. The other led to a path where the trees did their best impersonation of a corridor. They chose the latter, where a handful of other teenagers were walking ahead.

With a hint of wonder in his eyes, Obake gazed around. *I can't stand the academy, but at least I get to enjoy the Tree Corridor on the way.*

Obake hadn't thought about Meilana all morning, but with each step her memory clawed its way back to the surface. He thought about the many times they ventured through the very same corridor together. Holding hands and giggling like small children. He remembered all the times he took her to Taulon Falls. All the times they kissed, all the times they almost—

"Why're you so quiet?" asked Yumo.

Meilana burrowed her way back into Obake's subconscious. "Sorry, I was thinking about something."

A mischievous grin dawned on Yumo's face. "Thinking about Tezza, huh?"

"Why would I?"

"Come on. You know she wants it. You don't see her giving you the googly eyes in class?"

"I try not to."

"What? She's so sexy. If you don't jump on that I will."

Obake gave a light shrug of the shoulders. "Be my guest. I'm not interested."

Yumo scrunched his face as if a foul odor entered his nose. "You must be gay."

A hearty laugh bellowed from Obake's core. "No, dumbass. I got my eye on somebody else."

"Oh. Let me guess. Is it Katshi? No, Naivu?" Yumo bit his bottom lip. "I love that nice ass she's got."

"She does have a nice ass, but nope. Not her."

Yumo flung his arms up and down. They looked like the wings of an exhausted stingray. "So, you're not going to tell me?"

"Nope, I'm keeping this one to myself."

"Are you serious right now?"

"Sorry."

"That's messed up. It's not like I'm going to tell anybody."

Obake sent Yumo a harsh side eye. "Yeah right, remember in second year when I told you I liked Morrgo? You went right up to her—"

"All right, all right, but in my defense, that was when we were kids."

"They called me Love Doctor for months."

Yumo laughed so hard all the nearby critters scurried off. "Oh, yeah, I forgot all about that. Good times."

Midway through the Tree Corridor, at the base of the trees, were five turtle statues made of brass, three in a row on one side and two in a row on the other. Each turtle possessed a shell full of spikes and a wangjin hat.

"Are they ever going to replace that one?" asked Yumo, pointing to the side that contained only two statues.

In the middle of them rested an empty pedestal.

"The Zoza Statue? Doubt it. If they wanted to replace it, they would've done it years ago."

"Kind of creeps me out. What if it came to life and walked away?"

"I bet it did. It's been hiding in your attic all these years, waiting for the best time to devour you."

"You read way too much Zhai Foong."

Obake gave a cheerful chuckle.

"Did you read the latest issue yet?" Yumo continued.

"Not yet. I'm so far behind. I'm still on the 'Life after Death' saga."

"Catch up already. I mean… that's my favorite part of the story, but that came out like a year ago."

"You know some people say it's true, right?"

"Yeah, that would be awesome, but I don't know. Dying, traveling to another realm, fighting a giant dragon, coming back to life… too good to be true."

"I don't know. A lot of people can wield their soul energy. That alone is pretty crazy, if you think about it."

"Okay. Okay. You got a point."

The friends finished traversing the mile-long Tree Corridor before they knew it. As they exited, their academy revealed itself in the valley, a pagoda style castle, watching from below. Its cerulean walls, imperial red roof tops and gold accents conveyed a near picturesque surrealism. About two hundred children waited at the foot of its gates. A winding trail lay before them and the valley.

"Want to race down the Serpentine Trail?" asked Yumo.

Obake smirked. "I'd rather not have to take you to the hospital."

"Whatever." Yumo chuckled. "So, you're still going to help me out later, right?"

"Help you with what?" Obake's face sagged with annoyance. "You're still trying to go back to the Yokai Ruins?"

"Yup, I need that money."

In disbelief, Obake shook his head. "You actually think you're going to get a Stinger?"

"I don't think so. I know so. My dad said he'll get me one for graduation."

Obake executed a playful shove. "Looks like you're screwed then. You know your goofy ass didn't get enough points."

"Whatever. You're just mad I'm about to be riding while you're walking."

"Yeah, right. I'll believe it when I see it."

"Look. I heard him talking to the neighbor. He said he's going to get it for me tonight."

Yumo became so thrilled that Obake started to believe him.

"Why do you need the money then?" asked Obake.

"I can't leave it all basic. You know I have to spice it up. I want the all-purpose tires, the custom seat and the enhanced engine. The ladies are going to be all over me when they see it."

"I got weird vibes the last time we went there. Something's off about that place."

"I'm not planning to stick around. We'll grab the money and get out of there."

"How do you even know it's still there? Bandits probably swiped it by now."

"Bandits don't loot there anymore. They already got everything worth taking a long time ago."

Obake swiveled his head and groaned in frustration. "Why did you have to drop it anyway?"

"Not like I did it on purpose."

"You know we might run into whatever made that sound last time, right?"

Yumo shuddered. "I hope not. That was too scary. But believe it or not, I thought about that."

A well-crafted dagger with a wavy blade came out of Yumo's shirt pocket.

Obake slid its scabbard open and inspected it, an expression of admiration developing. "It's gorgeous. We can't let Batta see this though."

"Of course not. He'd flip."

Obake resumed walking.

Yumo trailed behind him. "If something jumps out on us, we'll take care of it."

"How am I going to make it to Genopai someday if I'm busy cleaning up after you?"

"Don't worry. Your dreams of becoming a 'ninja for hire' will come true. You should have more faith in yourself."

"They're called bounty hunters. How many times do I have to tell you that?"

"Yeah, yeah. Are you down or what?"

Obake halted again, looking at his friend with suspicion. "Are you feeling okay? It's not like you to go charging into danger like this."

"You know what they say, money talks. Plus, I'll have you with me."

"All right, fuck it."

Yumo thrust his fist into the air. "Yes. Hey, you never know. Maybe this time you'll find what you were looking for."

"Doubt it, like you said. The place has been completely ransacked."

"I still can't believe your grandparents won't tell you what really happened."

"Me either. They're hiding something. Even Sensei Kinichi won't tell me what happened to them."

A sad vibe struck like an unexpected storm.

"They supposedly died when the so-called 'ginyai' showed up. Monsters from another realm, yeah right. Maybe they're the ones reading too much Zhai Foong."

"Think it could've been the brekkas?"

"Come on. You know I don't like that word."

"My bad. Samurai. Better?"

Another side eye slipped from Obake.

"So, could it have been them or not?" continued Yumo.

"No way, a full-blown war would've broken out."

Yumo placed a hand on his friend's shoulder. "Maybe it's hard for them to admit that it was a random disaster."

"Still, if they wanted me to believe them, then why not be more convincing? More details would help. They're so vague and act weird whenever I bring it up." Obake sucked his teeth. "What if it did happen, though? Did my parents run like cowards or fight like warriors?"

"I hate to say it, but a freak accident probably caused that fire. It's sad, but even great ninjas like your father don't always go out like heroes. I'm sorry."

All Obake could muster in response was a solemn nod. Pressing on, the friends soon reached the valley. The academy gates remained shut tight. Children crowded about, all of them from the ages of ten to seventeen. They came in every color, shape and size as well.

"I still can't believe all of you hike here every day," said Obake.

Yumo crossed his eyes and pursed his lips. 'Have to get your education somewhere.'

Laughs rumbled from Obake's belly. "Your dad doesn't talk like that."

"Yes, he does. To be fair though, my town doesn't have an academy anymore. It got shut down before we were born. Some drunkard ran it. Genopai has one, but that's like three hours away by automobile."

"Damn. I'm lucky I live up here then. Do you think it's worth it though?"

"Well, supposedly this academy turns out the most successful students. Guess we'll see how true that is in a week or so."

Obake and Yumo drifted into the thick of the crowd. The academy's three levels towered above. Everyone appeared infinitesimal by comparison. Two falcon statues made of pure gold mounted opposite corners of the uppermost roof. They gleamed bright under the blanketing sun.

A stout, disgruntled looking woman wearing a beige complexion arose behind the gates. Despite her feminine qualities, an undercurrent of masculinity peeked out. Patches of black hair spiked from her chin and upper lip. The hair on her head was patchy as well. She walked with an obvious limp, but did her best to hide it. Some children giggled at the sight of her. As the woman opened the gates, a loud gong signaled the imminent start of classes. The adolescent horde swarmed inside like a colony of ants trying to fit down a single tunnel. Obake and Yumo waited for the swarm to thin out and they weren't the only ones. Through the many bobbing heads were two stationary ones. An ivory boy with slicked back hair and hooped earrings occupied a bench. Next to him was a stocky, coconut skinned boy whose hair looked struck by lightning.

Obake nudged Yumo in the ribs. "Look."

"Ow. What's your problem?"

"Look stupid." Obake pointed at the boys with his forehead. "The assholes."

Yumo glanced over at them. They were busy providing harsh commentary on any student unfortunate enough to get caught in their gaze. Even the faculty wasn't safe from their savage opinions.

"There goes the groundskeeper again, looking terrible as ever. She could use a new wardrobe if you ask me," said the slick-haired boy, he couldn't pry his eyes from the woman who'd just opened the gates.

The stocky boy smirked and nodded. "She could use a better haircut too."

"They're pathetic," said Yumo, as one would when talking about maggot infested food.

Obake nodded. "That's an understatement. Can't they just slip off the side of the mountain already?"

As the crude duo glanced around, their sights landed on Obake and Yumo.

"Take a look, Jevoss." The slick-haired boy slapped his cohort on the arm then pointed. "If it isn't our best buddies."

"Here we go again." Yumo sighed.

"You guys still haven't found anything better to do with your time?" asked Obake with a strong trace of loathing.

The slick-haired boy swaggered over to Obake. "What could be better than ruining your day, shrub head?"

He was thin and lanky, as if he considered eating too much of a hassle.

"I'd rather look like a plant than a worm," snapped Obake.

Yumo roared with laughter.

The stocky boy left the bench too. "Bald boy here thinks something's funny, Eshra. Can you believe that?"

"What do you think we should do about it?" asked the slick-haired boy.

Stiffening his chest, Jevoss took several aggressive steps toward Yumo. "He won't be laughing much with a black eye."

Obake intervened. "Back up."

"Or what?" Eshra stiffened his chest as well. "Going to use your little defiler powers on us?"

"You're just mad because you're a feeble. I bet you wish you could use your soul energy," said Yumo.

Clenching their fists, Eshra and Jevoss both seethed with offense.

"I doubt you guys want a repeat of last time," said Obake with an air of cockiness.

Eshra grinned, detestable words on the tip of his tongue. "Luck, that's all it was. This time I'll send you home so fucked up your mom won't even recognize you. Oh, wait… you don't have one of those."

Red smeared Obake's vision like a murder scene, a tsunami made of every negative emotion colliding within him. Visions of Jevoss and Eshra's bloodied, battered bodies lying in the dirt sprang forth. Obake wanted the visions to become real as soon as possible. He thought about the samurai he killed the night before. How confused it made him feel. Killing Eshra and Jevoss would feel different, somehow, he knew it. After all, this was personal.

With glee on their ugly faces, Eshra and Jevoss beamed at each other.

Obake lunged, snarling like a ravenous tiger, but Yumo held him back.

"I'll kill both of you bitches!" He thrashed at Eshra and Jevoss. "Come here! Come here!"

While Yumo struggled to keep Obake back, Eshra and Jevoss taunted him.

"Calm down. Stop!" screamed Yumo.

Obake didn't let up. "I'll slit your throat cock suckers!"

"What's going on over there?" said the patchy-haired woman, heading their way.

Jevoss and Eshra tried departing the scene.

"You two, wait right there." The patchy-haired woman paused to examine the scene. "Everything all right over here?"

It took an immense amount of willpower, but Obake regained control of himself.

"Yeah," said Obake, through bated breath.

"Yup. Everything's fine, Miss Jiaou. All good here."

Yumo sounded much more convincing, but not convincing enough.

"If I see any more funny business, all four of you will be taken directly to the Supreme Sensei. Do I make myself clear?"

"Crystal," said Yumo as Obake nodded along.

Eshra and Jevoss fought back the urge to laugh.

Miss Jiaou scowled at them. "You two get to class—now."

She sent Jevoss and Eshra away. Only after they were a suitable distance did she grant Obake and Yumo permission to proceed as well. As they made their way through the gates, she watched them, her square jaw and thorny upper lip more apparent than ever.

I don't think I've ever been this close to her before.

"Now listen to me, boys. My mother always told me… 'never take responsibility for other people's trash.' You'd do well to remember that."

After her parting words, Miss Jiaou vanished amidst the colorful flowers of the garden that started at the gates and spread to surround the academy.

Other people's trash. What does she mean?

Obake and Yumo entered the foyer; it was empty aside from a few stragglers. Most of the other children had already found their respective classes.

"We're going to be late," said Yumo as he and Obake made a run for it.

The academy's interior was a beautiful shade of brown, so vibrant it bordered on golden. Light fixtures hung from the walls. They all matched the falcon statues on the roof. A decorative staircase divided the center of the foyer. Walls on either side of it held three doors each. All of which displayed a class name or designation. They found the classroom labeled: **Art of Arithmetic** and scraped inside before the late gong.

A petite woman stood at the front of the class with a wicker bin full of scrolls. "Aren't we cutting it a bit close?"

"Sorry Sensei Gwell," murmured Obake.

She had brown hair so long it tickled the floor. Her bifocals were hideous, but the pretty bronze face beneath them caused many of the boys to fawn over her.

"Have a seat, gentlemen," said Sensei Gwell.

The voice floating from her was so calming, it was safe to assume she found yelling unbecoming.

Her parka flapped and fluttered as she paced in front of a chalkboard littered with equations.

As Yumo found his seat in the back, Obake made his way to the front row. Eshra and Jevoss were also present, but their seats were isolated from the rest of the class.

"If you've been paying attention and have studied like I suggested, then this test should be a breeze. If not, you might be in trouble."

Obake glanced at Yumo who rubbed his closed eyelids like a stressed parent. Next to Yumo was a tanned, blonde girl. She put her hazel eyes to use by staring at Obake with extreme affection.

Sensei Gwell's voice returned. "Eyes forward."

With a snap, Obake turned to her. She regarded him with her freckled face.

"Most of you already have enough points without this test. However, for a select few, this will be the deciding factor on whether or not you pass my class. As you all know, you need this class to graduate."

Obake's mind went haywire. *Son of a bitch, I knew I should've studied.*

Sensei Gwell waltzed down the aisles and delivered the scrolls to every student. When the scroll landed on Obake's desk, it came with a bout of anxiety.

I hate arithmetic and whoever invented it.

Opening the scroll, Obake winced as if he expected equations to leap from the page and devour him. To his surprise, only a few of the equations looked difficult.

Wait a minute. This doesn't look so bad.

One after the other, he tackled each question, growing more confident all the while.

"Bring it here."

Obake looked up to see Sensei Gwell beckoning Eshra, who was standing between the blonde girl and a dark-haired girl. The blonde occupied a level beyond embarrassment. Her face shrouded behind her bright locks. Eshra approached his sensei with a fist clutched at his side.

"Give it to me."

Eshra feigned ignorance.

"I won't ask twice."

He handed a small piece of paper to the sensei, and she began reading its contents.

Hi, Obake!

Um… it's hard for me to say this, but it's our last year and you still haven't made a move. I think it's adorable that you're too shy to approach me. Actually, I think everything about you is adorable. Well, if you haven't figured it out yet, I like you and I was wondering if you felt the same way. Please write back and let me know soon.

Your not-so-secret admirer,

Tezza

Obake now occupied the same level of embarrassment as his admirer. He stared at his desk as the entire class combusted with laughter.

Even Sensei Gwell chuckled. "Okay, settle down class. Finish your tests."

Before long, the end of class gong went off. The students wasted no time making hasty retreats.

Sensei Gwell ushered them along with some semi ominous words. "Your tests will be graded tonight. You'll know your fates come tomorrow morning. Enjoy the rest of your day."

Through the shuffle of bodies, Obake made eye contact with Eshra who began making foolish expressions.

Yumo stepped in between. "Let it go. He's not worth it. He's trying to get you to ruin your graduation. Don't let him win."

"Fuck him. Why should we keep letting him get away with this? He's been a problem for years."

"Kick his ass after we graduate. For now, let's get to Sensei Pelssa's on time."

Yumo entered a room labeled: **Language Mastery.** Obake lingered, hoping to catch Eshra and Jevoss in the hall. He gave up then found them already seated inside. They chose desks right next to each other, which further enabled their obnoxious behavior. Loud talking, throwing writing utensils and burping were a few of their favorite disruption tactics.

Jevoss flipped a pencil off the edge of his desk. He then watched it bounce off the ear of a small boy sporting a bowl cut. "Ding! Ding! Ding! Three points for me."

Obake thought about attacking them right then and there, but after careful consideration, he realized it would be smarter to catch them alone.

Sensei Pelssa was present, but lacked the desire to do anything about the mayhem ensuing in his classroom. An odd fellow, he had pale skin and retained an awkward shaped physique. Each of his extremities were thin like metal rods, his torso however, resembled an upside down hot-air balloon. Reclined in his chair, he kicked both feet up on his desk. A book titled: **Never Too Late to Get a Date** in his grasp.

The near two-hour class breezed by in what felt like two minutes. Obake and his one hundred ninety-nine classmates landed in the second-floor dining hall. That many students crammed together made the dining hall claustrophobic.

Miss Jiaou stood behind a buffet table with a cooking apron draped over her torso. Obake smiled at her, grabbed a tray and swiped as much food as it would allow. Everything from watermelon to shrimp made its way into his meal. Yumo and Obake sat alone. They spent the start of their hour-long lunch people watching and trading items.

"Two more classes and we're home free," said Yumo.

"So, we don't have to go to the Yokai Ruins anymore?" replied Obake with sarcasm.

"Well… we're home free *after* that."

Forty-five minutes into lunch and Obake's food had vanished to the pits of his stomach, which still weren't satisfied. He decided to partake in a second helping. As he returned to the lunch line, the dark-haired girl form Sensei Gwell's class jumped in front of him.

"Uh…?"

"Come talk to my friend," said the dark-haired girl.

Behind her, Obake found Tezza giving a cutesy wave.

"But I was—"

"Don't be shy."

The eager girl yanked Obake by the arm and weaved him between a few tables until he was face to face with Tezza.

"Hi," she said, gazing at him with longing.

Obake looked away; it was all too much. "Uh… hey." His eyes darted all over the dining hall. To his relief, nobody paid them any attention.

"That was pretty embarrassing, huh?" continued Tezza.

"What? Uh… yeah."

"Sorry about that. Stupid Eshra is always messing things up."

Every time Obake's eyes found Tezza's, he looked elsewhere. "He sure is, can't say I'm a fan."

"So, um… did you have time to think about my note?"

"Look… you're pretty and everything, but—"

"Wait! You don't think…?" Tezza's entire demeanor changed in an instant. "I don't like you like that. I meant like… you know… a friend."

Obake froze. His adolescent brain couldn't comprehend what was happening. "You… you did?" he asked, more perplexed than ever.

"Yeah, duh."

At last, he developed the courage to look her straight in the eyes. He could see deception hiding within them.

Tezza scoffed. "Boys are such idiots." She then flipped her hair and strutted away, accompanied by her friend.

"All these years we called you Love Doctor for nothing."

Standing close by was none other than Eshra and Jevoss. They were smiling from ear to ear.

"Does it ever get any better for you, shrub head?" asked Jevoss.

The end of lunch gong sounded throughout the dining hall. As Eshra and Jevoss walked past Obake, they each slammed their shoulders into him.

At that moment, Yumo arrived. "You all right?"

Obake wasn't listening. Too busy keeping a watchful eye on his enemies as they exited the dining hall. Aware that Yumo would try to stop him, Obake faded into the crowd. Like a shark circling prey in the open sea, he hunted them. A perfect opportunity presented itself when they entered the bathroom.

Opening the bathroom door, the young ninja tiptoed inside. He expected his enemies to be at the urinals, but they weren't. Next, he checked the sinks and sure enough, there they were, washing their hands without a care.

Obake's voice filled the bathroom. "Hurry up!"

Eshra and Jevoss became startled. They whipped around to find the source of the voice.

"What do you think you're doing?" asked Eshra.

Jevoss grimaced as Eshra's worm-like body made its way over to Obake. "Sorry, shrub head. We don't give potty training lessons."

Jevoss and his stocky build found its way to Obake as well. Despite the two-on-one odds, Obake didn't flinch.

Eshra reached behind his back and brandished a small switchblade. "How bout I—"

Before Eshra could finish his threat, Obake struck him in the neck. Eshra dropped the knife and stumbled backwards, clutching his throat. Charging forward, Obake shoved Eshra into the sink. It cracked open, releasing a geyser of water. Jevoss charged, too, much like a bull. Obake sidestepped, forcing Jevoss to bust full force through the bathroom door, tumbling into the hall for everyone to see.

Hoping to escape into the crowd, Obake dashed out. He then felt himself shift toward the floor. His shoulder smacked hard against it and his neck whiplashed. He expected to see Eshra, but an ebony man with a bristly mustache peered down at him instead.

"Get up, both of you!"

With ease, the muscular man lifted Obake and Jevoss to their feet. Eshra attempted to get by undetected.

"Where do you think you're going? All three of you follow me," said the ebony man.

Soon enough, Obake found himself in a cozy little office, a comfortable armchair beneath his bottom. Sitting next to him was the ebony man, Jevoss, and Eshra. He eyed the shelves fixed to each wall, and the books packed within them.

Does he really read all those?

A nonagon desk hogged a majority of the office space. Upon it, a nameplate read: **Supreme Sensei Kinichi**.

All three students waited for an hour, the class outside the door had yet to conclude. Like an eagle, the ebony man watched them. Obake jiggled his leg, Eshra twiddled his thumbs, and Jevoss stared at the carpet.

In walked a man with light brown skin, he appeared to be the same age as Obake's grandparents. The wrinkles on his face were just as profound. Yet he had a relaxed, prestigious aura about him. Long gray hair and a long gray beard attributed to that. As he moved, his blue and white robes resembled water moving in midair.

"If it isn't Mr. Batta, what can I do for you and these fine young scholars?"

"Supreme Sensei, I caught these three fighting in the bathroom on the second level. They caused extensive damage to the sink and door. I even confiscated a switchblade."

Kinichi pulled open a drawer and out came a purple box. After shuffling through it, he released a small bar of chocolate.

He took a bite and savored the taste. "Would any of you like one? I have plenty."

Kinichi held the box out, shaking it before each of them.

Mr. Batta looked confused. "No thank you, sir. I'm on a no sugar diet."

"Are you positive? They taste exceptional."

"Yes. I'm positive."

Once again, Kinichi looked at each boy. They all shook their heads as if the gesture were some sort of trap.

"Sir, these boys—"

"Would you say detention is in order?"

"Detention is too lenient, don't you think?"

"Depends on your perspective, judging by their injuries, I'd say they've been punished enough for their transgressions."

"But, sir? What about the damages? What about the switchblade? None of them are eighteen yet."

"Yes, of course. However, we do live in a land that faces the possibility of war from forces beyond a giant wall." Kinichi pointed in the direction of Bushido Empire. "It's not uncommon for our people to arm themselves."

"They were going to use it on each other. Not the samurai. They're just kids. They have no right. As watchman it's my job to—"

"I understand your position, but each of them will be eighteen sooner rather than later. Nobody was harmed either. I say we consider ourselves lucky."

Mr. Batta was beyond flustered. "Yes… yes sir."

Kinichi peered at Eshra, who wouldn't dare meet the Supreme Sensei's gaze. "I will be confiscating your knife for the remainder of the year. Come see me on graduation day with your parents if you'd like to retrieve it." He turned back to the watchman. "Don't worry about the damages. Miss Jiaou will repair them in no time. And do me a favor, escort these gentlemen to the caretaker's office. Dr. Kauzo will see to it they get patched up nicely."

Mr. Batta looked as if he'd had the wind ripped from his sails. "Right away, sir."

"I'll be on my way then. I have a class to finish up. I'd hate to keep the students waiting any longer."

◆◆◆

Dr. Kauzo was handsome, copper toned and younger than any other faculty member. Obake found it hard to believe he wasn't in fact a student.

"Haven't seen you in here for a while. How's life?" asked the doctor.

Obake glanced around the mid-sized room. "I'm doing all right. Feels weird to be putting this place behind me soon though."

Charts displaying human anatomy and medical certifications plastered the walls. Dividing screens implemented for patient privacy stood in sequence. Not the most advanced place to practice medicine, but it sufficed.

Dr. Kauzo examined Obake for wounds. "I don't blame you. You've spent almost eight years of your life here." He paused, pointing out the faint bruising around Obake's neck. "Hmm… looks like you're developing a knack for injuries."

"That should be gone soon."

The doctor put away his magnifying glass. "Well, I don't see anything to be too concerned about. The other kids are ok too. I don't think you'll have to worry about their parents coming after you."

"Thanks, Doc."

◆◆◆

"The next time I see you better be at graduation. Or else," said Dr. Kauzo with a warm smile.

"You got it."

◆ ◆ ◆

The late gong for final period had rung, but Obake wasn't the only one lurking the halls. At the top of the first-floor stairs was a funny-looking woman in odd clothing. She spotted Obake and went at him as if he'd stolen something, her braided hair dawdling behind her like a tail.

"Young man, you missed my class," she said in a high-pitched squeal.

Her honey complexion wasn't indicative of her personality in the slightest.

"Sorry Sensei Oldro, I—"

"Where were you?"

"I was in Dr. Kauzo's office."

"You'd better not be lying. I will personally see to it you receive the harshest of punishments if you are."

"I swear."

"I've warned you and your little friend about ditching before, have I not? **Science of the Human Realm** is not to be taken lightly."

"Yes, ma'am. I never said—"

"Do you have your homework? You can't pass without it."

"Yeah, it's right here."

"Chop. Chop. I must be on my way. Believe it or not, there are students who truly care to learn."

Obake pulled the homework from his satchel. Sensei Oldro snatched it and stomped away with her head held high and mighty.

Obake mumbled under his breath. "Fucking bitch."

He then finished his trek back to Kinichi's Chamber on the third level, his last period. With the hope of avoiding attention, he opened the chamber doors slow and steady. To his dismay, everybody turned at the sound of the squeaking doors.

Why does everybody always have to stare like that? What am I? Some kind of caged animal?

The grandiosity of the chamber always garnered an eye of admiration from Obake. Its high ceiling coated with gold leaf complimented the solid oak flooring. Ocean paintings, landscapes and soaring falcons gleamed from certain segments of the surrounding walls. In between those hung weapons, ranging from swords and spears to hammers and bokkens.

"How good of you to join us," said Kinichi.

Obake sat beside Yumo in the fourth of seven rows.

Yumo leaned close for a whisper. "I thought you got expelled or something."

"I'm surprised I didn't," whispered Obake.

Against the wall, opposite the entrance, sat three platforms, one stacked on top of the other. The higher they went, the smaller they became. On each platform, stairs were fixed to either side. **July 6th, Year 772. Genesis, Final Lessons** was scrawled across a rollaway blackboard that stood in front of the platforms.

With a stick of chalk, Kinichi wrote a single bullet point: **The Forru Concordat.** "How many of you know what this is?"

He scanned from side to side until a hand erected.

"That's the peace treaty between us and the samurai, right?" said a chubby boy with glasses.

"Don't you mean the brekkas?" blurted a male voice.

The class unraveled into a giggle fest.

Kinichi ignored the outburst. "Correct, wonderful answer. It's a document that was enacted by Grandmaster Forru. He hailed from a place in the Shinobi Empire called Genopai City. No doubt most of you have heard of such a place."

Every student in the class went silent. They sat transfixed, their attention glued to the Supreme Sensei.

"As you are all well aware, we are currently not on the best of terms with our neighboring empire. However, what you may not be privy to is how things came to be this way."

A thin girl with a chin level hairdo extended her hand.

"Yes, you there."

"Haven't they always been our enemy?"

"Not quite. We've had many different experiences with the samurai."

Gasps scampered around the room.

"At first, we were united together under the Council of Ten. An organization comprising Grand Monarchs, Masters and Magistras alike. Half from the Shinobi Empire and half from Bushido. Unfortunately, a famine struck that disrupted the delicate trade operations. That ordeal ultimately led both factions into conflict."

A brown skinned boy from the back of class yelled, "That's it?"

"You'd be surprised. Sometimes that's all it takes," answered Kinichi.

All fifty teenagers wore stunned expressions.

"After years of warring, Grandmaster Forru opted for peace and single-handedly rallied most to his cause. Both empires dispatched their best Kantasian sorcerers and sorceresses. Together they built the Colossal Divide."

"What were they trading, sensei?" asked Yumo.

"Food and medicine mostly. Actually, that brings me to my next point. The original two clans that came to squabble were the Gazzo Clan and the former Yokai Clan."

Every student made it a point to stare at Obake again.

"Why tell you this now? Why haven't I taught this aspect of our genesis before you ask?"

Stole the question right out of my mouth.

"First and foremost, now that all of you are graduating soon… I believe it is imperative I arm you with the knowledge necessary to keep you safe."

Kinichi folded his arms behind his back and stood very statuesque. "You may or may not encounter samurai during your individual journeys, but I prefer you all be prepared should that happen."

Dead samurai flickered like a flame in Obake's thoughts.

"Second, those who don't know their past are doomed to repeat it."

Obake's nerves flared at the thought of dealing with the samurai again.

"Last, we can't move forward as a people if we continue to build on a foundation of lies."

The short-haired girl raised her hand again.

"Yes, what is your question?"

"My mom told me the brekk—I mean, the samurai were power hungry."

"I heard that Gazzo's wife cheated on him with a ninja," said another student.

"I heard that too," said a student in the front row. "I heard they skin people alive."

Kinichi peered at Obake. "You see, a certain someone went through great lengths to cover up the truth. Many counterintelligence measures were put forth. Those involved ensured that numerous versions of said story were released to the public."

Obake found himself flabbergasted. *Papa?*

"But rest assured scholars, I have all the details. We will study this subject more thoroughly starting tomorrow and continue until the end of the year. For now, open your books to chapter nine."

Mystery in Yokai Ruins

Happiness, joy and bliss, the Yokai Ruins were anything but. A thick haze of despair invaded every nook, cranny and crevice. Every chipped stone, every cracked statue, and every dilapidated building told a story of pain and suffering. Many of the rooftops seemed to have been torn off by a giant. Apertures penetrated the walls of several buildings, resembling the handy work of explosives experts. Burn marks streaked across every surface, melted dishware strewn about. Broken and overturned furniture lay in the dirt beside tapestries torn to shreds. The countless lives lost pervaded in spades. Did their spirits still linger, unable to move on?

"Let's get this over with. I don't want to be here all day," said Obake.

"Relax. We'll be out of here in no time."

Although compelled to gripe at Yumo, Obake refrained, instead opting to scrutinize his surroundings again. The city comprised pagoda style architecture interwoven with baroque, evidence of a once flourishing collection of diverse minds. Obake remembered the spots he rummaged through before. He remembered the places he looked for answers yet came up empty.

"There it is." Yumo ran toward the least decrepit building in the city, a tall house in a large cul-de-sac. "Come on, let's go."

On the way they passed a decorative fountain in the center of the cul-de-sac, a family of frogs presided in the swampy water of its base.

At least somebody likes it here.

Next to the tall house, a cathedral surmounted with substantial proportions and great embellishments. All of the damage upon it didn't detract from that. However, like Yumo, Obake found himself allured by the tall house.

Why does this house always feel so familiar?

A domed roof with a sharp needle mounted the tall house. Long double doors made of platinum barred entry. Expensive in appearance, yet helpless against the blazing flames of old. The doors melted and warped into each other like an abstract painting.

Yumo's head moved from side to side, examining the former doors. "Dammit. Why didn't they put windows down here?"

"You said that last time. It's obvious they wanted it to be difficult to break into. This place was probably important."

"Well, looks like we're climbing again."

"How do you even know this is the right building? You could've dropped it in any of these."

"This is the one. I'm positive."

Along with Yumo, Obake walked to the foot of the tall house, his curiosity piqued. *I shouldn't get my hopes up. It'll most likely be like last time. I need to accept that. There's nothing for me to find in there.*

Yumo analyzed the exterior, then without warning jumped onto a short brick wall. He wobbled a bit, relocated his equilibrium then hopped up to a ledge like protrusion on the wall of the house. His hand stretched as far as it could toward the windowsill above, but couldn't reach it. At last, he grabbed hold with an inelegant foot thrust. The second-floor window's shattered glass left shards jutting from the frame. Yumo slipped between them unscathed.

"You coming?" he asked.

Obake scoffed, then jumped onto the brick wall, then up to the protrusion. With his fingers gripping it, he pressed both feet against the house then launched himself through the window.

"Show off," said Yumo, rolling his eyes.

Vestiges of a hard-fought battle cluttered the room. A hole in the roof and the sight of blood stains triggered a nebulous memory. Obake could see himself floating. No, he was in the arms of another. Panicked breathing and a pulsating heartbeat thumped against his eardrums. He was moving fast, wind brushing against his cheeks then, blackness.

What was that?

"You're going to kill me."

Snapping out of his daydream, Obake found that Yumo had stopped walking. He was staring through a hole in the wall adjacent to the cathedral which also had a hole.

"Wrong place, huh?"

"Yup, you were right. It happened in the cathedral. I remember now." In embarrassment, Yumo scratched the back of his head. "I had the money until we ran from whatever made that creepy noise."

"You think it's still in there?"

"I hope not." Yumo side eyed the hole in the wall. "But if it is, we're prepared."

"Don't tell me—"

"Uh- huh. We have to jump again. Unless you want to waste time looking for another way in."

"Looks like we're jumping then."

Upon completing a series of elaborate stretches, Yumo faced the hole like it was his archenemy then sprinted full speed.

"Don't die!" screamed Obake.

Yumo hurdled through the hole and fell a few feet into the other hole in the cathedral. A sense of eeriness pervaded Obake as he stood there alone. Regardless of the horrors, he was very much attracted to the house.

"Are you alive up there?"

"Relax, I'm on my way."

Obake charged as if he aimed to tackle the hole into oblivion. Instead, he vaulted through it and felt the thrill of danger pulse within his bones as he plummeted.

"Please tell me you got the right place this time," said Obake, landing inside the cathedral.

"It is, don't worry," replied Yumo while glancing around.

Despite the hole, darkness drenched most of the room, causing the left side to vanish. However, the right side of the room was different. In the center of the wall, was a stained-glass window with a strange jewel-like emblem upon it. Dust made it difficult for light to get through, but a few stubborn rays managed. Two hallways, one to the right of the window and one to the left, led into the shadows as well.

"So, who do you think Supreme Sensei was talking about?" asked Yumo.

"I have an idea."

"Same here. I didn't want you getting all pissed off at me for saying it, though."

"It's ok. My grandparents have been hiding things for too long. They need to come clean already. I'm fed up with being in the dark."

"Like I said earlier, all that ginyai stuff is likely make-believe."

"I've been thinking that for a while now. I mean… where's the evidence? No armor, no weapons, no remains, no nothing."

Yumo stopped listening, his concern, a distant object. "Finally!"

He skipped across the room toward a small pouch on the floor. A jangle of coins reverberated as he picked it up.

"I'm shocked. Didn't think it would still be here. I was ready to laugh at you."

"Told you, dummy," said Yumo, opening the pouch.

"You're one to talk. You could barely even find the right place."

"Yeah, yeah. All that matters is I'm rich and you're not."

"Rich, huh? Let's see then." Skeptical, Obake peered into the pouch. An assortment of decorated coins peered back. "Okay, you got a bunch of carnelians, typical." He shuffled the pea-sized red ones aside. "Not bad, there's even some sapphires in here." Jealousy went off like fireworks as he shuffled away the grape sized blue ones. "Emeralds! How did you get emeralds?" Five green coins the size of sliced beets sat at the bottom of the pile.

"Told you I was—"

A nightmarish growl burst from the left side of the room, slashing the quiet to ribbons. Obake's heart tried crawling through his ribs. With no hesitation, Yumo sprinted down the hallway to the left of the stained-glass window. His pouch tumbled back to the floor in the process. After picking the pouch up, Obake caught Yumo and latched onto his wrist. Yumo screeched and almost jumped apart from his own skin.

"What is this? Déjà vu? Take this." Obake slammed the money into Yumo's chest. "We didn't come here just for you to lose it again.'

"I know. I'm sorry."

"Where's the dagger?"

"Fuck that. Let's just get out of here!"

"In case it catches us," said Obake, holding out his hand. "Here."

As Yumo handed off the dagger, the acute sound of running bounced amidst the hallway. Something fast, something heavy and something strong barreled right at them. From the darkness emerged a massive grizzly bear, but this bear was far from ordinary. It reeked of death and displayed a body full of open wounds. Behind the many wounds were dirty bones and ruptured organs.

Yellow stained fangs, proportional to large knives, poked from its rancid gums. Claws, even bigger than that, poked from its massive paws. Roaring nonstop, the undead grizzly gained on Obake and Yumo.

"Run!" screamed Obake with boundless terror.

As the grizzly's blood curdling growls closed in, the friends ran for their lives. The bear moved too fast to evade for long, despite its undead state.

"Use your Shadow Cloud and teleport us out of here!" said Yumo as he ran ahead.

Obake gripped the dagger in both hands and closed his eyes, concentrating hard. The grizzly ran right behind him now. A cloud of shadow began emanating from Obake's entire body. It came out in quick, short bursts then stopped.

"Watch out!" screamed Yumo, who had arrived at a dead end.

Obake opened his eyes, but not soon enough. He smashed into Yumo full force, sending both of them crashing through the fragile wall. They fell twenty feet to the first floor. Debris assaulted them from overhead. To their surprise, the grotesque bear didn't follow. With its soulless eyes, it stared at them from above.

Back on their feet, the friends hiked over the rubble. The bear remained in their sights until the new surroundings stole their attention. Sun had a much easier time infiltrating this area. Regardless of its many bruises, the ceiling loomed in glorious fashion. Pipe organs fixed along a balcony glistened in the spots where dust was less prominent. A stained-glass window, depicting four ethereal individuals, glistened in spots vacant of dust as well. Two of the individuals were women, two were men. Each of them held out upturned hands, accommodating the same jewel emblem from the window upstairs. Below that was a rostrum with four pedestals stationed in front of it. One had devolved into stone crumbs long ago. Another was cracked and chipped a great deal. The other two looked to be in pleasant condition.

Yumo gazed around in awe. "Wow. This place must've been beautiful back in the day." He held a finger to his left brow, keeping a slight gash on it from dripping.

"You all right?"

"I'm good. Nothing I can't handle."

Through snapped pews and leaning support beams, the boys navigated to the exit door on the side. It wouldn't open, they pounded and kicked, but it stayed in place.

"Now what?" asked a perturbed Yumo.

"There's got to be another exit around here somewhere."

Yumo pointed to the spot they had crashed through. "The bear's gone. It's gone!"

Jitters paraded around Obake's arms and fingertips as he awaited the creature's imminent re-emergence. Not knowing whether to run or fight, hide or freeze.

Yumo located the main exit and ran to it, but rubble barricaded its doors. Hoping to make a dent, he started tossing the rubble aside. No matter how much he scraped, the pile didn't diminish.

"What are you doing? Help me out."

"That's not going to work."

"Why can't you teleport us out of here?"

"I don't know. It's not working. I've never done it under this kind of pressure."

"We're dead. It's going to eat us alive."

"I don't know about you, but I'm not going out like that."

"We can't fight that thing."

"Then why did you bring this dagger, Mr. We'll Take Care of It?"

"That was before I knew we'd be up against a dead bear."

"That's our way out," said Obake, spotting another side exit hidden behind a fallen support beam.

Yumo went to kick it open, but the undead grizzly blasted in. Ripping from its hinges, the door cartwheeled away. Like a pig during slaughter, Yumo squealed and became sandwiched between the floor and the grizzly. It chomped at Yumo's horrified face, but thanks to his adrenaline-induced muscles, the bear couldn't reach. The grizzly shifted, aiming to bite into Yumo's throat instead. Obake leapt onto the grizzly's upper back, its fur coarse like wires. He unleashed the dagger from its scabbard and plunged it into the bear's skull, causing wailing and ferocious thrashing to ensue. While holding onto fur that threatened to shed, he stabbed it several times in the snout. The grizzly stood on its hind legs, elevating Obake eight feet high. It rocked from side to side, causing the patch of fur in Obake's grip to shed. He slid down to the bear's mid back before gripping a new patch of fur.

Yumo hurled pieces of debris at the undead terror. With each successful impact, it wailed louder. He then fished out a sharp piece of wood and gutted the grizzly. Putrid innards spilled onto the ground. As if nothing happened, the bear continued standing tall.

"Die already!" shouted Yumo, who was now angry more than anything.

Obake scaled the wiry fur, mounted the bear's shoulders and stabbed once more. This time he struck the temple. The bear moaned then dropped like a falling tree.

"We did it!" exclaimed Yumo.

"Hopefully it stays dead this time."

"If you hadn't… if you didn't…" Yumo put a hand on Obake's shoulder. "You'll make a great bounty hunter someday. No doubt about it."

A warmth came over the young ninja. "I'll always have your back. Don't ditch me next time, though. Okay?"

"Sorry, I was freaking out."

"Don't worry about it. I'm just glad we're not dead."

"I got your back, too, you know."

"Well, if I didn't know before, I sure do now. You messed that thing up."

"Not going to lie, I almost puked."

They escaped the cathedral through the busted door and soon arrived back in the cul-de-sac.

Yumo took one last glance at the cathedral. "That's definitely a Kantasian cathedral."

"You think so?"

"It has to be. I thought that started in Saidaku though?"

"I don't know much about it, to be honest."

"Well, they still worship the Guardians, so you know they're out of their minds. Have you ever been to a sermon?"

"Nope, seems so boring."

"You're lucky. My dad makes me go sometimes. I hate it."

"Sucks to be you."

"I think it's all a bunch of nonsense, but don't tell my dad I said that."

"Your secret's safe with me."

The grizzly's terrible image replayed at the front of Obake's mind. "Wait, does this mean my grandparents were telling the truth after all?"

"What? Oh no, I'm pretty sure that was a wraith."

"Isn't that like a ghost or something?"

"Not exactly. Let me educate your ass really quick."

Obake chortled.

"There are some Kantasians out there that like to dabble in the dark arts."

Intrigue lifted Obake's eyebrows as high as they could go.

"There aren't very many of them because once they get caught, they're exiled. I wonder how long that thing's been lurking around and why nobody ever saw it before."

"Maybe they didn't live to tell the tale."

By the time Obake and Yumo made it through the Tree Corridor, night had swallowed day.

"I better see you riding that Stinger tomorrow."

"You will. Just you wait."

"Oh, and watch out for bears."

Yumo laughed then clutched his elbow.

"You going to be okay?"

"I'll be fine. It didn't get me that bad thanks to you."

Obake smiled. "It's kind of late. Want to crash at my place? My grandparents won't care."

"Thanks, but my dad is probably pissed enough as it is. I was supposed to be home hours ago."

"You sure? We've been needing somebody with your skills to take a look at our fuel tank. It's been acting up again. That'll buy you some of my nana's famous breakfast for sure."

"Not going to lie, I'm tempted, but I'll have to pass. Maybe I can swing by tomorrow and take a look for you, it's probably an easy fix."

"You're the man. By the way, let's keep this little adventure to ourselves. You know what'll happen if anyone finds out we've been in the ruins."

"I was about to say the same thing."

The elaborate handshake that started their adventure ended it as well. Yumo wandered down the trail into the starry night while Obake approached his not-so-distant home. He could see the lights inside flickering incessantly.

Upon arrival, he went around back and opened a metal box filled with teal stones. Using a single-handed shovel, he funneled the stones into a fuel tank. After a few cranks of the attached handle and a few kicks to the tank, an engine purred, and the lights in the cottage stabilized. Jovial chatter and merry making burst from inside. Three voices were present instead of the usual two. Obake went around front to find Kinichi stumbling outside with a bottle of liquor in his hand.

"Obake! Splendid to see you. We missed you at dinner."

"Sorry. I was hanging out with Yumo."

"Mischief making per usual, I assume."

"Uh… something like that."

"Well, you have a wonderful night. I'll see you bright and early tomorrow morning."

Kinichi floundered toward the direction of the Tree Corridor.

"Are you going to be ok by yourself, Sensei?"

Kinichi paused to release a rumbling burp. "I certainly hope so."

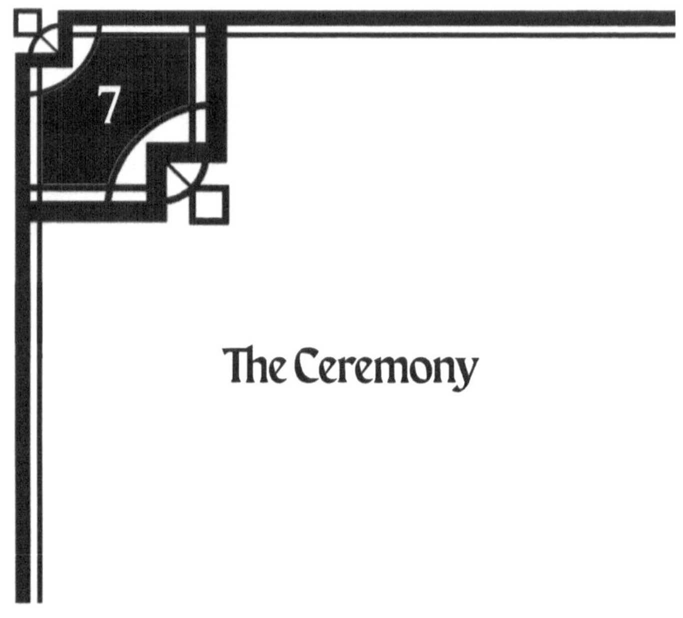

The Ceremony

"How did you sleep?" asked Bao upon Obake's arrival to the kitchen the following morning.

"Great. What about you? Still drunk?" he replied with a comedic undertone.

"No, of course not. Although, I wish I were. My back is killing me."

Obake circled behind her and initiated a delicate back massage.

"You're such a sweetheart."

"Where's Papa at?"

"He had to run out. He'll be back any minute."

Obake discovered his breakfast and began devouring the buttery pancakes, scrambled eggs and congee.

"Good. Because I need to talk to you guys," he said with a full mouth.

"Is everything okay, Froggy?"

The front door creaked open and in came Yokai with a fist full of fresh herbs. "Fantastic. I don't have to wake Sir Lazy Bum over here."

"I'm surprised you're not hung over, old man."

"Hangovers are for the weak. Besides, I can't be hung over on a special day like today, Green."

Like a curious cat, Obake tilted his head.

"Ceremony time."

"What? Today? Right now? Doesn't that take a while?"

"Don't worry. We have enough time." Yokai glanced at the clock on the wall. "It's only 6:07 a.m."

Yokai went to the sink and gave the black herbs a quick bath.

Maybe I should bring it up later.

Obake regarded three framed photos on the mantle above the fireplace. One depicted Yokai and Bao smiling from a boat in the ocean. Another depicted Obake, Bao, and Yokai playing cards together on the porch. All great memories, but it was the last photo Obake admired most. It depicted dozens of warriors standing side by side, each wearing a ghost-like green mask. The terrifying ghost from Bao's puapo canister mirrored the masks exactly.

"Well. I wanted to talk to you guys about something."

"I'm sure whatever it is can wait."

Bao interrupted with concern. "Surely we could—"

"Absolutely not, this is far too important."

"This is important, too," said Obake, determined to get answers.

"Patience, you'll get your chance. Now get dressed."

Obake pouted all the way to his room. With a begrudging attitude he put on his kekogi then met his grandparents in the front yard.

Yokai pointed to the peak of the mountain. "Rare flowers are growing at Cliffs Edge right now."

"I know. They're used to make Puapo Elixir. What about them?"

"Your task will be to retrieve one of those flowers."

"One? That's so easy."

"While Bao and I do our best to stop you."

A lump found its way in between Obake's vocal cords, he gulped it down.

"We will show you no mercy. You will be treated as an enemy. Don't go easy on us. We will not offer you the same courtesy. Now that your wounds are healed, I expect a stellar performance."

Obake glanced at his grandmother, whose demeanor was also serious.

"The last thing I want to do is bury my only grandson. Don't let us down."

Yokai fetched the naginata leaning against the cottage wall and handed it over. Mizuchi's cold steel supplied a supreme level of confidence to Obake.

"Are we using—"

"Yes. Soul energy will be required if you want to survive this. I know you've had a hard time using it under pressure, but your enemies will not care about your stage fright."

Obake didn't like when his grandfather went from witty old man to fierce warrior.

"I don't know why I have trouble with it. I just… choke."

"You'll get better. It's like I always say. Soul energy is like a muscle."

"Or like breathing," added Bao.

"Even better," said Yokai as he continued.

"You're born with muscles and you're born inherently knowing how to breathe, right?"

Obake nodded in response.

"However, you have to work out in order to build those muscles. You have to train if you want to hold your breath longer underwater. All it takes is a little practice."

"I understand, but I'm no good at it."

Bao spoke with an air of intensity. "Have some faith. This test should help you. If it doesn't, then I worry nothing will."

Obake never saw his grandparents so serious before. Not when he broke valuable decorations by accident, not when he got poor grades in the academy, not even when he failed to make curfew. They were all of a sudden behaving like people going off to war.

"This should go without saying, but never attempt to harness soul energy without a conduit. A well forged weapon, a well-crafted piece of jewelry, a sturdy set of armor. Anything like that will do."

Obake became impatient.

"Yes. We can't emphasize that enough. Soul energy is extremely demanding on the body. Conduits drastically reduce the toll it takes," said Bao.

"The better the conduit, the better the results," Obake cut in, an effort to speed up the conversation. "I know all of this already."

Yokai grimaced. "We're just making sure. Plenty of warriors have taken this lesson lightly and paid the ultimate price."

Obake rubbed a hand through his hair. "I'll be careful."

"I knew a kid growing up that used a metal spinning top," Bao cocked her head. "Crazy girl."

With a burst of speed, Yokai was off, moving faster than Obake had seen anyone move in his seventeen years of existence.

"Good luck," said Bao.

Her waddle turned into a nimble dash as she followed in her husband's wake. They both entered the Tree Corridor and disappeared without a trace.

Where did that come from? They're not playing around this time. Mizuchi slipped in his sweaty hand. *This is it. Now or never.*

As if the wind were propelling him forward like a sailboat, Obake bolted after them. He still couldn't see them or even sense their presence as he traversed the land. The Tree Corridor fast approached and… nothing. Obake entered expecting to find them hiding among the treetops, but they weren't there.

Fatigue of a long-distance sprint stung his legs. *I should've paced myself.* He looked to either side of the corridor, into the forest and still no elder ninjas in sight. *Where are they?*

A slimy, purple blob, like something found in a bog, rolled onto his path. Before he could evade the strange object, it exploded. The vibration sent him rolling through the dirt as a cloud of dust inundated him. Seeing beyond a three-foot radius became impossible. Obake's ears rang so loud he couldn't rely on them either.

Shrill screeches broke through the ringing seconds before sonic waves knocked Obake into a tree. While he crawled to a crouch, another bog bomb landed in front of him. It burned as he hurled it through the air. His head soon slammed to the ground thanks to the bomb exploding above it.

Dust cleared and Obake saw him. Yokai was hiding among the trees after all, behind a camouflaged cloth that he tossed away before dropping down. A three-fanged, claw-like weapon was strapped to each of Yokai's arms. They glinted against sun rays peeking through the leaves. Like an owl descending on a mouse, he stabbed at Obake. The young ninja barreled away just in time.

Obake swung his naginata and winced as it came mere inches from Yokai's throat. "No!"

He imagined blood spraying out, but Yokai blocked the attack with little effort. Mizuchi struck several more times, stronger and faster with each consecutive blow.

Yokai deflected them. All the while, a disappointed demeanor developed. "Not good enough!"

As the clang of metal resounded, Bao leapt from underground, a kodachi firm in her grasp. She too had been hiding by way of a camouflaged cloth. After a long inhale, she intonated a potent shriek. With the ringing gone, Obake heard every piercing octave. The volume was almost loud enough to shred his eardrums. More sonic waves came spiraling. Flipping over top of them, Yokai let the waves slam into his grandson. Obake's feet left trenches in the dirt as he skidded backwards. In that moment, he allowed himself to view his grandparents as enemies.

I won't let them beat me.

Yokai and Bao stood side-by-side. Bao took another deep breath while Yokai raised his arms overhead. A bog bomb, double the size of the last two, formed between his open palms. When her lungs reached capacity, Bao unleashed another sonic wave. Obake ran straight at it and went airborne, letting it spiral under his legs. Yokai reeled and chucked his purple bomb. Upon releasing Mizuchi's chain, Obake rotated his entire body like a typhoon. Mizuchi's blade slashed the bomb, repelling it back from where it came. It exploded between the old couple, sending them opposite directions. They crashed into the turtle statues on opposite sides of the corridor.

After retracting Mizuchi's blade, Obake ejected it once more. The chain wound itself around a distant tree branch. Obake pulled himself to it by retracting once more. Over and over, he repeated the action until the Tree Corridor was in his wake.

Instead of hooking a right and descending into the valley, he hooked a left, ascending toward the summit. Cliffs Edge awaited him in the distance. His heart filled with hope. He was eager to hear his grandparent's praises, eager to tell Yumo about his triumph.

While grabbing hold of the first rocky ridge, another sonic scream struck. The ridge crumbled to powder in Obake's hand, forcing him to hit the dirt. Another bog bomb blasted him back; he flopped around like a fish in a net.

Bao and Yokai gained on him, heaving more bog bombs and sonic screams. Persevering through the onslaught, the young ninja shoulder rammed Bao. Two additional bombs released. Obake sidestepped the first and repelled the second, Yokai suffered the impact.

The ascent to the summit left Obake feeling prideful until he heard another sonic scream. He turned to brace for it when the day light dimmed. Overhead, a black silhouette passed under the sun. His grandmother was flying! Her sonic scream allowed her to maintain a steady altitude. Yokai peered from atop her backside. Dozens of explosive bog pellets dropped from his hands. It was impossible to dodge them all. Clenching his eyes, Obake dug deep within himself, summoning strength from his very essence. As the pellets rained and explosions went off around him, he vanished in a cloud of shadow. Shock overcame Bao and Yokai as their grandson re-emerged above them.

Obake double kicked Yokai in the back, hard. "Was that good enough for you?"

The elder ninjas crashed down in pain. On the other hand, Obake landed softer than a feather. For a split second, he thought about checking on them, but teleported all the way to the summit instead.

Radiant ocean water met Obake's vision the moment he burst from the Shadow Cloud. *There it is, the Hoitunji Ocean. Never fails to impress.*

At his left, a small distance away, sat the Yokai Ruins. To the slight right, a thin strip of rock extended over the blue water. A bed of magenta flowers swayed at the very edge. Behind them stood a slab of stone with an inscription on the top: **Those who have fallen in this life will rise in the next.** Hundreds of names were listed below that. Two of which made Obake forget why he was there. **Vai, Bakemono.** He read the names again and again until he heard footsteps approaching from behind. That very instant, he ran over to the flowers, pried one from its roots and held it high.

"Yes!" he screamed.

Bao and Yokai came over the ridge, smiles of glee on their faces.

In his front yard, Obake sat cross-legged in a circle with his grandparents. They each kept their eyes shut while black herbs burned from a bowl in the circle's center. A sweet fragrance encapsulated every one of his senses. He felt relaxed beyond what he thought possible. All of his worries fled to the back of his mind; his parents, Meilana, the samurai, the undead bear, the bullies, all of it. The worries fled so far they were almost nonexistent.

"A Yokai Ninja's duty is to protect his home, his clan and his family. The Yokai Ninja takes no joy in the killing of others, but must sometimes do what is necessary to maintain peace."

His grandfather's words swam around his mind like a shark at play.

"Emotion is not your enemy. The Yokai Ninja is fueled by it. Emotions are powerful tools when controlled. Unstoppable when used wisely. A Yokai Ninja controlled by emotions is doomed to fail."

Bao's words were striking as well.

"A Yokai Ninja who values these principles can overcome any and every obstacle." Yokai and Bao now spoke in unison. "Do you swear to uphold the values and traditions of the Yokai Clan?"

"I do," said Obake, speaking with pride.

"Do you swear to strike down those who threaten peace whenever and wherever they reveal themselves?"

"I do."

"Do you swear to always protect your family and clan?"

"I do."

"Then you're hereby bestowed the mantle of Yokai Ninja. For now, your training is complete. You may rise."

Obake sat down a boy, but stood up a man. He became empowered, ready to accomplish feats deemed impossible, prepared to take on the realm.

"This is... I've wanted this since I was a little kid. I don't even know what to say right now."

"You don't have to say a word," Bao's eyes gleamed with admiration. "Just know that you deserve this."

"You did it, Green. To be honest, you had me worried there for a minute, but you surprised the shit out of me," said Yokai.

Obake soaked in the praise like beach sand under the ocean.

"The one critique I have is your lack of stealth. Always keep that in mind," Yokai tapped his head. "Deception is a precious asset."

"You're right. I guess I get over excited and forget about it."

Chuckles departed Bao and Yokai.

"Now remember, as of now, you're a Genin. But you'll have plenty of time to climb up the ranks," said Bao.

Obake smiled. "Well in that case, what're we waiting for?

"No way, slow it down." Yokai gave a weary laugh. "I'm going to need a nice break after that. My muscles aren't what they used to be."

"After what I saw, I don't blame you. I never knew you two could fight like that."

Like a pair of little girls receiving compliments, Yokai and Bao blushed.

"We needed you to see how dangerous an actual battle could be," said Bao.

Yokai gripped his grandson's shoulder. "There's no way to tell who's a Soul Wielder at first glance. It'll serve you well to always be prepared. You also never know when we might face our next threat."

"About that, I was in the Yokai Ruins yesterday."

"You what?" said Yokai, adopting a defensive disposition.

With an undertone of anger, Bao piled on. "You know that's forbidden."

"Yeah, but how else am I going to get answers?"

"Answers? Answers to what?" Yokai's defenses mounted.

"You know, like… what really happened to my parents."

The elder ninjas fell dumbstruck, unable to look at their grandson.

"Please. I'm begging you. I need this."

"I won't," said Yokai.

"Why won't you tell me? Huh? I deserve to know. You guys don't even let me see pictures of them anymore. All I have is a pocket watch, the armor you keep in your room and vague descriptions to remember them by."

Attempting to close the gap, Bao stepped forward, but Obake took several dismissive steps back.

Bao's eyes welled up. "Obake please, we—"

"We what? We will tell you when you're older? We will tell you if you graduate?"

"Calm down," grunted Yokai.

"No! I'm sick of waiting. No more excuses. Tell me what happened to them."

Yokai inhaled deep. "You already know the ginyai—"

"Always with the damn ginyai! What does that even mean? All you've ever said is that the supposed 'ginyai' killed them. That's it. What's the rest? I want to know everything!"

Unable to make eye contact with his grandson, Yokai turned his back.

"I searched for evidence of these 'ginyai', too. Know what I found? Jack shit. Did you guys make it up?"

Tears streamed down Bao's cheeks. "That's utterly ridiculous. We would never invent something like that. The Great Strife was real. It happened."

"It was the most devastating ordeal we ever experienced. I wouldn't wish what happened to our clan on my worst enemy." Yokai spoke with despair ingrained in his voice. "I understand why you're upset. I understand you feel left in the dark, but trust me. Knowledge can be a heavy burden to bear, sometimes too heavy. You're better off not knowing."

"That's not for you to decide," barked Obake.

"It is as long as you're under my roof."

"Then I won't be under your roof!"

Yokai whirled around, he couldn't mask his shock.

"You know you should consider taking a page from your pal Kinichi's book."

Bao peeked from behind her tear-drenched hands and glanced between her two family members.

"Oh, yeah, I know you had something to do with the samurai incident. Kinichi basically said so himself. He's going to start teaching the whole class about it today. Looks like I'm not the only one tired of all the lies."

"He wouldn't."

"Want to bet?" Obake stormed away toward the Tree Corridor.

"Come back, Obake!" screamed Yokai.

With reluctance, Obake turned to meet his grandfather's gaze.

"I will tell you this. They fought valiantly and died with the greatest of honor. They were the best of us and will never be forgotten."

Obake's eyes emulated his grandmother's, but his fury wouldn't let the tears fall. Without another word, he shook his head in disappointment and departed.

Tungsten Scepter

A rumbling engine found Obake inside the Tree Corridor.

No way.

Yumo sped along on a sleek motorcycle. Its iron wheels left figure eight track marks as he went. His sudden screech to a halt almost left Obake with a face full of dirt and gravel. With the engine killed, Yumo popped the kickstand and pushed up his goggles. A small band aid stuck to his left eyebrow. The gorgeous motorcycle gave Obake a temporary reprieve from his stewing anger.

"I'm sorry I ever doubted you," said Obake with adoration.

"Didn't I tell you?"

"You definitely did."

"I'll have a girlfriend by the end of the day. Watch. I can't wait to see the stupid looks on Jevoss and Eshra's faces."

"That's going to be priceless."

Obake examined the craftsmanship. "A Stinger: Model 0. Classic, I didn't even know these were still around."

"I got super lucky. My dad found it in some old junkyard."

"What? I would've never let this go if I were them."

Obake opened the Stinger's fuel tank to find it full of teal stones. "How much zoganite does it take?"

"Eight pounds, I'll be able to go a hundred and seventy-five miles before I have to fill up again."

"You're so lucky. Looks like you already made all the modifications too."

"Sure did, took me forever. That's why I'm running so late. I didn't sleep much either. This thing is addicting."

"I bet. I wouldn't even go to the academy if I had one of these."

Yumo reignited the engine, releasing teal smoke from the exhaust pipe. "Sorry I didn't have time to look at your fuel tank. I can fix it after the academy though."

"Don't worry about it. How's the eye?"

"Stings like crazy, damn bear."

"I would've brought you some puapo, but I'm not on the best of terms with my grandparents right now."

"Oh yeah, I saw them. They didn't look too happy."

"That's their problem."

"Still keeping secrets?"

"Their favorite thing. It'll never end."

"You'll have to find out the truth some other way."

"Yeah, I'll figure it out somehow."

"All right, well I'll see you down there."

Wrinkles of insult appeared on Obake's forehead.

"I'm messing with you." Yumo laughed, then brought his backpack around and fetched another pair of goggles from its depths. "Hop on."

Obake and Yumo yelled from exhilaration as they cascaded down the Serpentine Trail. The gong signifying the imminent start of classes met their ears. Revving the engine harder, Yumo careened to the front entrance where Miss Jiaou stood.

"Well, now. Aren't we luxurious today?"

The pair dismounted fast.

"Have you forgotten the rules?"

They decided it would be in their best interest to play dumb.

"No bicycles. No skateboards. No scooters. No glissaders or motorized transporters of any kind."

"Uh… we forgot," said Obake with a pathetic level of conviction.

"Well, in that case let me remind you we are on a mountain. What if you were to fall off? Wouldn't be pleasant now, would it?"

Yumo slid his goggles up. "I know, but I'm almost eighteen so I figured it would be okay."

"You figured wrong."

"Look, I was going to hide it in the garden. Can I?"

"No other options come to mind. I certainly won't send you back home on that thing. Does your father know you drove that here?"

"Uh… no," said Yumo with the same level of pathetic conviction as Obake's previous lie.

The boys walked through the garden.

Miss Jiaou was sure to follow. "Be sure to secure that thing. There are those who'd find great satisfaction in stealing it."

From Yumo's backpack came a lock and chain. "That's why I have this bad boy." He fastened the Stinger to a burly tree.

"Careful not to leak any zoganite. Don't make more work for me."

"I won't. Don't worry."

"Hurry now. You have a few minutes left."

"Hey, Miss Jiaou."

With one brow raised, the groundskeeper glared at Yumo.

"Can you keep an eye on it for me?"

"Most certainly not."

Yumo applied his best puppy dog impression. "Please?"

"Oh, all right. Now hurry along."

Obake returned his goggles to their rightful owner. Right above the forehead is where Yumo's goggles went, and his Stinger key dangled from a golden chain. Like an expensive necklace, he wore it with pride.

"Seriously?" asked Obake.

Yumo smirked. "What?"

Shaking his head, Obake entered the academy. Miss Jiaou and Yumo weren't far behind.

"It was so easy to get through the mountains today," said Yumo.

Obake set sight on Sensei Gwell's classroom. "Don't rub it in. I still have to walk."

"Where do you two think you're going?"

They turned to see Miss Jiaou pointing at a sign on an easel. It read: **Assembly in the Supreme Chamber Today**. Joy erupted from the duo.

"Yes. I hope it lasts all day," said Obake as he and Yumo raced to the third floor.

The chamber doors were thick, but they didn't stop student chatter from leaking into the hall. The chatter didn't stop two familiar voices from coming around the corner.

"Thanks. My stomach was hurting so bad. I'm surprised I didn't pass out."

"Anytime, we have to look out for each other."

"I hope I'm not a burden."

"Of course not, but your mom should be feeding you, too. This isn't right."

"Not much I can do about it. She's always too strung out to think straight."

"You should tell the Supreme Sensei."

"No way, I can't. My mom would go crazy."

"Well, you have lunch to look forward to, I guess."

Obake and Yumo each took a peek and glimpsed Eshra and Jevoss departing into the Supreme Chamber.

"Did you hear that?" asked Yumo with surprise.

"Damn. That's rough, even for Eshra."

Carrying on, the friends entered the chamber. They shuffled between almost two hundred students before the late gong blared.

"I sometimes wonder if you two delinquents will ever get your acts together."

Sensei Oldro appeared among the crowd, wearing a sharp scowl.

Obake scowled back. "What?"

"You two were very close to being late. Yet again," she continued, disdain shooting from her eyes.

"But we weren't late," said Yumo.

"Ah. Ah. No back talk. Find your seats."

She shooed the boys away like a dreadful queen would a couple of peasants. They took refuge from her wrath near the front of the chamber, sitting cross-legged on the hardwood floor.

"What's with her? I'm going to go off one of these days, I swear."

Yumo grinned. "We should put one of those little needles in her seat."

"I'm so down. Monday?"

"Let's do it. That'll shut her up for a while."

Hysterical laughter burst from the boys as other students took their seats. The rollaway blackboard proved absent, leaving the three platforms unobstructed. Faculty members found their seats on the bottom two platforms. Pretending not to notice them, Sensei Gwell ignored all the boys drooling over her. Dr. Kauzo smiled and conversed with a group of students. Without a care, Sensei Pelssa still read from his book. Even when seated, Mr. Batta towered at least a foot above everyone else. Sensei Oldro kept glancing at Obake and Yumo, the disgust on her face blatant for everyone to see. Miss Jiaou sat last and began squirming, none too happy with her seating arrangement.

Over ten minutes passed before Kinichi appeared, striding from his office located to the left. The students simmered down as he took his place atop the third and highest platform. He grasped a tungsten scepter, the top of which contained four sharp curves.

"What is that thing?" asked Obake.

Yumo couldn't take his eyes off Kinichi. "Maybe he's planning to punish Sensei Dumb Bitch for us."

Kinichi raised a silencing hand. "Quiet down now, scholars." A white and red shawl covered in angular symbols draped his body. "I have a considerable announcement to make."

What was left of the chatter died out, followed by an uneasy stretch of silence.

"It brings me great joy to disclose that today will be my last day as Supreme Sensei of this academy."

Sensei Pelssa's book flopped to the floor; he opened his mouth, but words evaded him.

Sensei Oldro bolted to her feet. "What's the meaning of this?"

Mr. Batta stood as well, his muscle-bound body slumped with sadness. "You're leaving us?"

Kinichi refused to look at him. "Not exactly my friend."

"Well then what's going on and… why're you holding that weapon?" asked Sensei Gwell.

Hysteria trumpeted through Sensei Oldro's voice. "If you're leaving, then who will assume your position?"

"Unfortunately, there will be no successor," said Kinichi.

"Are you closing the academy?" asked Dr. Kauzo with urgency.

"I would say that is the safest conclusion to draw."

"I have bills to pay!" yelled a fuming Miss Jiaou.

Dr. Kauzo continued. "How could you do this to us? What about the students?"

"I know you're all upset, but I have waited far too long. Longer than any of you could fathom."

Sensei Pelssa apprehended some of his elusive words. "Brings you great joy? To leave us high and dry? Is that it?"

"Worry not. Nobody will suffer long. I've grown fond of some of you during my tenure. It almost pains me to have to do this."

"A warning would've been nice!" roared Sensei Gwell.

"Well, yes, but… that would've ruined everything."

Kinichi raised his scepter to the ceiling; a diabolical smile curled his lips. A scarlet flash burst from the scepter, enveloping everyone. Cold dread seized Obake when he saw it. No matter how hard he tried, he couldn't draw breath. Once the flash dimmed, a strange sensation raced throughout Obake's body. He scrutinized his arms for traces of bugs. Certain he'd see some crawling beneath his skin, but there was nothing. He turned them over, expecting to see something swimming within his veins, but again… there was nothing.

What's happening to me?

The horrible sound of students vomiting by the dozens gave him the strength needed to force a breath.

Obake swallowed so much air his lungs applauded. Yumo on the other hand, sat clutching his stomach in agony. Yellow bile leaked through his gritted teeth. Obake tried to rise, but couldn't bypass whatever invisible force held him there.

Why can't I move?

Right in front, a brown-haired boy convulsed and tore away at his own clothing. He wailed in pain as his flesh altered. Clumps of hair fell from his scalp and his color drained to a snowy white. The teeth in his mouth became fangs, and boney nubs popped through his fingertips and toes. Wails of pain turned to growls of hunger.

This isn't real. I must be losing it.

Tezza came crawling through the writhing crowd. As she transformed, her tear-soaked eyes fell upon Obake. They begged for help, but the last trace of humanity escaped her.

Everyone else in the chamber transformed as well, Sensei Gwell, Mr. Batta, Dr. Kauzo, Sensei Pelssa, Miss Jiaou and Sensei Oldro. All were no more. The students were gone too, tall and short, fat and skinny, light complexion and dark, every last one of them. In their places stood gruesome creatures with blood-shot eyes, tattered clothes, protruding spines and exposed rib cages. Aimless, the creatures howled and ran into one another.

A miniature cyclone of energy shot to the center of the chamber, just below the ceiling. It sent scarlet rays circling around. Each creature fixated upon it, their crazed eyes glazing over. They became rooted in place, quaking and grunting like mindless beasts. Saliva dripped from their mouths onto the floor, mixing with the vomit at their feet.

Obake's muscles warped and his skin tingled. His breakfast tried to wiggle up his esophagus. Convulsions came for him as well, followed by overwhelming heat. He desired nothing more than to remove his clothing, but with every fiber of his being he suppressed it, all of it. His unyielding resistance even shattered whatever held him in place.

While sweat leaked from every pore, Obake checked on Yumo again, but he was gone. Frantic, he searched and searched. He soon spotted his friend stumbling into a room on the right side of the chamber. Yumo looked very different. Unlike the others, he was sprouting black feathers all over his body.

Obake motioned toward him, but the chamber teeter tottered, halting his progress. Shutting his eyes, he waited for the dizziness to subside.

"How did you?" Although no longer soothing, Kinichi's voice was unmistakable. From the top platform, he glared at Obake. A look of astonishment plastered on his visage. "You son of a bitch."

Kinichi aimed his scepter and fired a scarlet bolt of energy. Obake shielded himself behind one of the creatures. Sustaining the bolt, it dropped dead against the floor. Miss Jiaou's face was upon it. Her facial features remained intact despite the hideous modifications.

The dizzy spell over Obake faded, allowing him to start a mad dash toward Yumo's location. Several additional bolts fired from Kinichi, all of which missed their marks.

As Obake drew near Yumo, a creature standing before the doorway dove at him. He caught it by the throat, digging his nails into its slimy skin. Its mouth opened wide, letting out a vile stench and a long pink tongue. Snaking its way over, the tongue licked Obake's cheek. With a shove, he held the creature at arm's length. Relentless, it tried to taste him again. The gangly stature reminded him of someone that he soon recognized as Eshra.

Sounds of a switch pulled Obake's attention back to Kinichi. The wall behind the platforms parted down the middle and both halves slid sideways. An enormous stone obelisk marked with dozens of runes revealed itself. Although hard to see, its ancient design shone beneath a translucent, white, energy barrier. Kinichi stood in awe before it. Two more creatures broke out of their trances and approached Obake.

He slammed Eshra into one creature then tossed him into the other. "Get out of my way!"

All three tumbled across the floor. As Obake reached the platforms, two more creatures attacked. Ferocious slashing and chomping ensued. Evading their strikes, he knocked them both into a pack of their cohorts.

A scarlet vortex burgeoned from Kinichi's scepter. Dozens of creatures became caught within its pull. Golden fragments of light ruptured their chests, spraying blood around the vicinity. They let out chilling screams while the arms of death embraced them. Each golden fragment wore the face of who it belonged to.

Kinichi guided the contorting faces into the translucent barrier surrounding the obelisk. "Nothing prettier than a freshly plucked soul."

Heavy cracking blared each time one made contact. Obake considered taking Yumo and fleeing, but as the thought entered his mind, so did another.

'I will tell you this. They fought valiantly and died with the greatest of honor. They were the best of us and will never be forgotten.'

Yokai's words resonated far more than the desire to flee.

I don't know what this is, but I have to stop it.

Obake dashed toward the platforms, Kinichi launched a flurry of scarlet bolts his way. He slipped past them with a burst of agility and went to kick Kinichi's legs out from under him. It stunned Obake to see his kick phase right through his sensei's legs.

What was that?

Multiple punches discharged from Obake, but each one phased through Kinichi as if he weren't even there. Kinichi grinned before punting Obake in the gut with the bottom of his scepter. Obake tumbled down the platforms, landing face to face with a dead, beastly version of Sensei Oldro.

Kinichi continued summoning golden souls. "Wait there, I'm almost done."

All over the chamber creatures dropped into pools of their own blood and vomit. Cracks became ever present throughout the translucent barrier. They spread each time a soul struck. Soon, twenty creatures remained. Despite the carnage, they stood still, eyes devoid of consciousness.

Defying Kinichi's order, Obake stormed the platforms. This time he lunged for the scepter. Once again, his hands phased through.

"Winning isn't one of your strong suits, is it, boy?" said Kinichi, the sharp end of his scepter slicing at Obake.

Twisting out of its way, Obake sent an elbow crashing into Kinichi's nose. *Yes! I got him.*

Obake followed with a kick to the head, but his foot phased through again. Kinichi retaliated with another bolt, but Obake ducked. Whiffs of burnt hair tickled his nostrils.

Obake's punches came too fast this time. "Asshole!" They made Kinichi's head whiplash. "What did you say about winning?"

Blood trickled down Kinichi's chin as fury trickled into his expression.

Taunts from Obake continued. "Give it up. This is turning into elder abuse."

As Obake went to continue his assault, Kinichi slammed his scepter to the ground. Thousands of scarlet sparks discharged, driving the young ninja across the chamber floor. Before long, he came to a stop amidst the corpses of his former classmates.

Kinichi pulled out the last souls and sent them crashing into the translucent barrier. Unable to sustain any more damage, the barrier shattered. Shards sailed through the air then vanished into nothingness.

Scarlet energy radiated from Kinichi's scepter. The obelisk reacted and started to transform. Its entire composition went from stone to an array of pink, kaleidoscope-like patterns. With a hypnotic glare, Kinichi's eyes shone. He reached out and crept toward the now shimmering obelisk. Its surface rippled like water, swallowing his hand. Overcome with satisfaction, Kinichi placed his foot inside as well.

Obake clambered over the dead, Dr. Kauzo and Sensei Pelssa among them. "Hey, fuck face! Leaving already?"

With a deep sigh, Kinichi backed out of the obelisk. "I see it's going to take more than that to kill you, boy. You really are your father's son."

Obake gasped. "You have no right to talk about him, traitor!" Jitters set into his musculature. "Why're you doing this? These were innocent people, innocent kids!"

Kinichi offered no response. He instead amplified his scarlet energy, it flared in erratic fashion, licking the ceiling and scarring the walls. The shawl covering his torso flapped despite the lack of wind. His eyes turned green and all of his skin began melting onto the already fluid infested floor. Neither his clothing nor his shoes could stop it. Skin seeped through as if he were wearing nothing at all. Not a single stain appeared as the gore dropped in rivulets. Younger, dark gray skin appeared where the old brown had been. A pointy nose formed and long ears grew. Oversized, clawed hands supplanted the frail, wrinkled ones. Thin ashen hair turned blood red, full and spikey. The man Obake once knew was now an entity he always struggled to believe existed. Extreme guilt penetrated his emotional state.

It's true. They are real! I want to go back, forget about it all. The ninja squeezed his eyes so tight they throbbed. *Papa was right. I thought I wanted this.* When he reopened them, nothing had changed.

Again, he tried, but the gray man didn't transform back into Kinichi. His classmates and senseis didn't transform back into humans.

'I understand why you're upset. I understand you feel left in the dark. Trust me. Knowledge can be a heavy burden to bear, sometimes too heavy. You're better off not knowing.'

Yokai's words replayed in Obake's mind.

Why didn't I listen?

Jumping down, the gray man released another set of sparks. Every creature blasted away to the chamber's perimeter. Obake saw Jevoss and Sensei Gwell's dead stares rolling within the fleshy piles.

"Let's try this again," said the gray man, closing the gap between them.

As soon as his enemy was within range, Obake struck. *Why couldn't I tell? This thing was here, all this time. Right here!*

With ease, the gray man evaded, so Obake followed with an axe kick. His attack collided with a scarlet energy shield summoned by the gray man. The shield then blasted forward, mowing Obake over. He ricocheted between the shield and floor until it passed over him.

The scepter transformed into a sizzling, scarlet, energy whip. It slashed at Obake who vaulted from the floor. Wood splintered into a massive, hideous scar. Mr. Batta's beastly corpse beckoned Obake who rolled toward it. He lifted Mr. Batta's arm and another crack of the whip severed it. Now in possession of the arm, Obake rushed in for the kill. The gray man swung his scarlet whip, but Obake vanished, leaving a Shadow Cloud in his wake.

When he re-materialized, Obake bashed the arm against the gray man's face. As if it were a hammer, he brought the arm down a second time. Before the arm could connect again, it disintegrated into fleshy chunks.

The gray man knocked Obake away. "Clever, but that doesn't make for a good conduit, boy."

Summoning another scarlet shield, the gray man propelled it at his enemy. It twisted and scraped gashes into the hardwood floor. Obake had time enough to get to one foot. Bracing for collision, he extended both hands. As the shield crashed into them, his arms threatened to snap. The shield shoved him backwards as he planted his other foot. Both of his zori sandals frayed with every slide across the floor. Utilizing absolute force, he pushed the shield back from where it came. It spiraled at its creator, who dispersed it with a flick of his scepter.

This might be my last chance.

Obake flew into a drop kick, but like many of his prior attacks, it phased through. He tumbled to the floor as the gray man pointed his scepter. Expecting to dodge whatever attack was in store, Obake jumped. To his surprise, an attack had yet to start.

First, the scepter followed him through the air, only then did it fire. A scarlet bolt hit Obake dead center of the chest. With a sickening crunch, he dropped to the floor.

9

Through the Gateway

The gray man prodded Obake's body with his scepter, but it remained lifeless.

"Just when I thought you'd become an expert at dodging those."

Crouching, he checked Obake's inner wrist and neck. Both lacked a pulse. "The emperor will be pleased to see your rotting corpse." He kicked the young ninja over onto his face then took a moment to survey the aftermath. *My greatest masterpiece yet.*

Once more he ascended the platforms to stand before the obelisk. It had reverted to stone, but another radiation of scarlet energy remedied that. The pink patterns were slow to return, but did so nonetheless. With confidence, the gray man walked into them. They enveloped him like water would a diver. He soon floated within a sea of the pink kaleidoscope patterns. Their aesthetic traveled every which way unto infinity.

I forgot how beautiful it is in here. I feel so weightless.

Memories of days long past rushed his mind. He remembered swimming there with hundreds of other ginyai.

I was so nervous that day. If there weren't so many of us, I wouldn't have gone through with it.

As he had done in the past, he swam. Another stone obelisk revealed itself from a distance. As it drew closer, his determination shrank.

I've come this far. I can't back out now. Can I? Everything I've done. It'll have been for nothing.

Unable to decide, he floated there for several minutes.

Dammit. I hope he understands.

He swam close to the dormant obelisk; its design was different from the one prior, but the runes were the same. Energy burst from his scepter and a transformation ensued. However, pink patterns didn't appear this time. The image of a cave manifested instead. It swayed and wobbled like reflections on the surface of a puddle. Before another thought encumbered by hesitation could trouble him, he swam straight in. His weight returned to him and the ground steadied beneath his feet.

The cave's immense size teemed with various forms of wildlife. Off to one side were large pots filled to the brim with black liquid. Blind, tailless squirrels drank from them with vigor. Beside that were tables adorned with tools, vials, candles and half eaten food; a welcome feast for blue lizards with long necks.

On the opposite side, large insects with square teeth crawled around strange contraptions. Each of which stood broken amongst the stalagmites. Four eyed bats with overbearing wings hung between the stalactites. They screeched, warning others of the gray man's presence. Stalagmites and stalactites made the cave's entrance appear like a roaring mouth. Beyond that were smoky clouds, a vibrant ochre sky and a massive volcano.

Mount Drakoba, still as ominous as ever.

As the gray man exited, the sound of scurrying footsteps tapped his eardrums. Once outside he found nothing but an expansive barren wasteland. He gazed upon the dry, fruitless soil from no less than a hundred feet high. No foliage or additional wildlife could be seen, just an ocean of ochre water and a cluster of thin, serrated pillars.

Well, this hasn't changed much.

Inhaling down to his core, he let the smell of sulfur invade his nostrils.

Ahh, that's it, feels good to be home.

Traveling from the cave was an undertaking. Its location at the top of a towering cylindrical mountain made sure of that. The gray man spent a while descending its broad yet treacherous trail; he spent a while more reaching the ominous cluster of pillars.

Reluctant, he entered, his stomach rumbling with each step. Fatigue had come to visit. It took a bit of wandering about, but doubt came to visit as well.

Don't tell me I went and got myself lost.

He had long since passed skeletons of those unlucky enough to do just that. Their remains still held traces of flesh, but there wasn't much else to speak of. Someone had pillaged everything from their clothes to their valuables. The gray man suspected who would do such a thing.

"Look, guys."

Four plump individuals came from behind one of the pillars. Each of them had a different shade of yellow skin and tusks that jutted from behind their bottom lips. They sported excessive jewelry made from various bone fragments. Necklaces, earrings and bracelets embellished each of them. The plumpest of the bunch had a nose ring and several eyebrow piercings as well. Clubs fashioned from the leg bones of creatures far bigger twirled in their hands.

"What are you doing way out here? Lost?" asked the individual with facial jewelry.

A cautionary stance swept over the gray man. "I'm simply passing through, friend."

"Friend? I don't make a habit of befriending ginyai I don't know."

"Look. I don't plan to cause trouble."

The individual with facial jewelry glanced at his companions. "That's fine and all, but… we do."

His companions nodded along.

The gray man readied his scepter. "There's no need for this. The emperor unified us long ago."

"Yeah well, he's not here, is he? Besides, I don't think he'll make a fuss over one dead hagazo."

Scarlet sparks shot skyward from the gray man's scepter. "I'd tread lightly if I were you."

"How cute, little sparkles," said the shortest member of the quartet.

"You stand before the emperor's Chief Sorcerer," said the gray man.

A lazy eyed member of the quartet spoke up. "Strange. There hasn't been one of those in almost two decades."

"I'm not surprised. No one could replace Jinenji."

The group gave a brief pause before erupting in hysterical laughter.

"Jinenji? The coward who ran while everybody was busy fighting the humans? That Jinenji?" asked the slimmest of the quartet.

Jinenji said nothing, the cold pinch of embarrassment held his tongue.

"You might want to pick another identity, 'friend.' Everyone from here to Magyor was ordered to kill Jinenji should he ever show his ugly mug again," said the individual with facial jewelry.

"Gentlemen, I'm extremely tired and hungry. Can we do this some other time?"

"Listen here Mr. 'Jinenji.' It's been nice chatting with you and all, but we're starving too. Come to think of it. We haven't had your kind in a while."

As the quartet stampeded, Jinenji transformed his scepter and whip slashed them all in rapid succession. The one with the lazy eye was the first to go; the scarlet whip divided him straight down the middle. Innards spilled free, as did a vile stench. The slimmest and shortest both had their heads lopped clean from their shoulders. Blood gushed, turning into red rain that lasted for a few seconds. Terrified, the one with facial jewelry made a run for it. Jinenji was quick to take his legs. His new bloody stumps met the ground with a sickening splatter. Ear-splitting screams echoed throughout the cluster of pillars.

"Going somewhere?" asked Jinenji.

"No, please. We were—"

Jinenji's boot proved adept at skull crushing. After spitting on the mush of brain matter, he trekked on. It wasn't long until his path became clear. He put the cluster of pillars behind him while a towering building shaped like an octahedron standing atop a tetrahedron came before him. Its iron walls were flat and smooth save for the imprint of large double doors, a few designs and a massive eye insignia. Below it were dozens and dozens of other buildings. All made of the same intimidating iron work.

Omni Eye City, I never thought I'd see this place again.

Half a mile later, he arrived at last. Comfort evolved within him as he took it all in. Seeing so many ginyai was familiar, yet foreign at the same time. Through the flood of busy bodies, a small shack caught his eye.

Argett's Fish House.

The name alone made his mouth water; he could almost taste his favorite dish. A tangerine-colored woman with spots and floppy ears stood at the clerk's window. A long line resembling a colorful centipede streamed from it, the one obstacle between Jinenji and a fresh meal. His stomach couldn't wait, it demanded sustenance.

Jinenji rushed to the front of the line. "I'll have rodau chicken with potatoes, please."

"Hey. What's your problem? No cutting," said a furry woman at the front of the line. She looked like the result of a wolf crossing with a leopard.

Stupid wudaigo, mind your own business.

"It's fine. I used to come here all the time," replied Jinenji with irritation in his voice.

He locked eyes with the clerk who stood a little above three feet.

"We appreciate your patronage, sir, but that's not fair to everybody else."

"I'm also a friend. Isn't that right, Argett?"

"Friend or foe, you have to wait like everybody else," said an older woman standing near the grill.

She and the clerk shared the same species, but unlike the clerk, her attention span had little time for Jinenji. She was too busy chopping up a fish with antlers.

"Can't make an exception, not even for me?"

Jinenji's voice finally drew her attention. All it took was a single glance. Argett's cleaver dropped, clanging against the cutting board. Her shock ridden expression said it all. Jinenji's entire body went tense.

"You shouldn't be here," said Argett.

Not her, too.

Adopting a calm tone, Jinenji spoke again. "Argett relax. I just need some food and I'll be on my way."

A scream flew from the top of Argett's lungs. "It's Jinenji!"

Everyone in the vicinity stared. Some wore puzzled looks, while others beamed hatred at the sorcerer.

"But that's impossible," said a voice from somewhere in line.

"Whoa. It is him. I've seen that scepter he's got in all the history books," said a wudaigo boy.

In an instant, everyone turned hostile and surrounded Jinenji.

"Stop! The books are a lie."

"You calling our emperor a liar? You fucking deserter," shouted Argett, who had retrieved her cleaver.

"No, I'm… Listen, it's all a misunderstanding."

Rocks appeared out of thin air to pelt Jinenji in the forehead. Punches he couldn't determine the source of clocked him, followed by kicks to his back. As the mob went into full attack mode, he conjured a scarlet shield. He defended himself from every additional strike. City folk repelled one after the other.

From the back of the crowd, a growl of a voice yelled out. "That won't save you for long. You piece of shit!"

Many ginyai in sturdy black armor approached as well, their spears fit for stabbing. A revving motor bled through the ruckus.

"That's enough." A vermillion-skinned woman with black horns pulled up, an iron, two-seater vehicle as her transport. "The emperor would like a word with this one."

The mob, along with the ginyai in armor, dropped on bended knees.

Argett's body shook. "Yes, of course."

Jinenji lowered his shield. *No, not you. Anyone but you.*

"Get in," said the vermillion woman with no shortage of sass.

Overcome by thoughts of running, Jinenji didn't obey.

"What? Never seen a Surface Bolt before?" asked the vermillion woman.

Jinenji glanced at her vehicle and the dark blue smoke emitting from its exhaust, but he didn't move.

She grimaced at Jinenji's lack of urgency. "I won't tell you twice."

Dispersing his shield, the sorcerer climbed into the Surface Bolt. *Why hasn't someone decapitated you yet?*

"Try anything and you're dead," she barked before driving off.

Her vehicle went so fast, several of the city folk dove to avoid getting clobbered. In a matter of minutes, they reached the building adorned with the eye insignia. The vermillion woman pulled up to a podium and input a number code into its interface. It resembled the interface built into the vehicle's dashboard. Once the code was accepted, the set of double doors opened inward to a foyer lit by lamps harboring blue light. Their glow filled the atmosphere, giving Jinenji a sense of impending doom. As soon as they were inside, the doors returned to their former position.

Skidding to a halt, the vermillion woman yanked Jinenji from the vehicle. With the utmost of force, she shackled his hands and feet then took his scepter.

She then guided him into a dreary corridor, shoving him every time he moved too slow for her liking. "Pick up the pace."

Before long, the pair arrived at a fortified door. She knocked upon it four times in rhythmic sequence. Midway up the door, a slit appeared, followed by two beady little blue eyes. A plump, yellow man like those from the wasteland granted them access.

"Hurry it up," he said, his corpulence jiggling behind an open vest.

Jinenji entered and spotted a regal man across the room. Every hair on Jinenji's body rose like the fur of a startled house cat; an overwhelming urge to faint came next. The regal man sat in a grandiose iron throne with his bearded chin resting against his knuckles. An old, yet deep scar journeyed the top of his bald scalp. He had burgundy skin and black horns like the vermillion woman. However, his horns were far bigger. They swept up to the sky then curved back toward his muscle-bound shoulders. His regality was further accentuated by his blue battle coat and glistening silver armor.

Despite Jinenji's arrival, another hagazo retained the regal man's gaze. Unlike Jinenji, this one was tall; his six-inch platform boots amplified that trait. His expensive glasses went well with his long purple ponytail and light gray skin. A black lab coat with an eye insignia on the chest hugged his slim physique. Behind him hung a brown, wrinkled sheet, it wiggled and moaned as he paced before it.

Should've known he'd still be around.

"Your Grandeur, may I?" asked the hagazo man.

Amusement spread over the regal man's features. "I thought you'd never ask."

The brown sheet came down, revealing a green, scaly woman with shark like features. Her eyes emanated pure contempt, a stark contrast against her royal attire. Even more so against the glimmering crown attached to the fin on her head. She writhed with aggression, but to no avail. Thin wires bound her neck, wrists and ankles. Every time she moved blood leaked out. Again and again, she tried speaking, but the gag in her mouth prevented that.

The hagazo man looked at the green woman with curiosity. "Seems like she's ready to talk."

"Let's see what our friend Celeste has to say, Doctor," said the regal man.

With a swift tug, the doctor ripped the gag from Celeste's mouth.

"You motherfuckers! You'll die for this! I'll make sure—"

The doctor re-administered the gag as Celeste nipped at him and missed, prompting the doctor to slap her.

"You horrid bitch, you nearly took my fingers!"

Whipping around, the doctor awaited the regal man's consent. He gave it, nodding with anticipation. With every crank of the contraption's lever, the wires cinched tighter and tighter. An expression of sorrow appeared on Celeste's face, followed by a stream of tears. All at once blood sprayed from her neck and each of her limbs. Her body fell to the ground along with her severed hands, feet and head. Thick blood pooled as she faded from the land of the living. Before the blood could reach his pristine boots, the doctor scampered away.

A belly laugh spilled from the regal man. "What? Can't stomach your own inventions?'

"It's the germs, Your Grandeur. Deplorable, I must say."

"What a shame. I was hoping we'd get something useful out of her." The regal man's eyes trained on Jinenji. "Should we strap you in next?"

Jinenji's heart threatened to leave his body in the same manner as digested food. The vermillion woman shoved Jinenji at the throne; his shackles tripping him to his knees.

He looked up to find he was at the regal man's feet; he didn't dare look any higher. "Emperor Tazuro, please forgive me. What I did was inexcusable. I'm here now to set things right."

The emperor's three-clawed foot gripped Jinenji's head, grinding it on the cold floor. "Now why would I do a thing like that? You committed treason the minute you fled that battlefield," His voice boomed with each spoken word. "You didn't care for the fate of your comrades, the fate of your emperor."

"Your Grandeur, please, I destroyed the barrier around the Gateway. You can finally finish what you started."

"Indeed. You've served a purpose. But what further need of you is there?"

"I've studied the humans for the last seventeen years. I know their weaknesses. Their combat capabilities. I can share all the knowledge I have."

"You make a compelling argument. But I'm afraid you can't be trusted. I'll take my chances without you."

Tazuro reached behind his head, lifting a handle like protrusion from his throne. A large steel sword with a long isosceles blade emerged. An eye insignia fashioned into the hand guard surveyed the room.

"I killed the boy! Bakemono's son, he's dead. I can take you to his corpse."

"And what of Bakemono himself?"

"Dead! He died at the Gateway, right after he sent you back here."

Tazuro removed his foot, inverted his sword and let it plunge.

Before it punctured Jinenji's back, he stopped. "I suppose killing my enemy's off spring redeems you somewhat."

Jinenji's wincing face settled into a look of bewilderment.

"Planning to stand up sometime soon?" asked Tazuro.

Jinenji stammered to his feet, his shackles rattling like tambourines. "I also found your old sword, but I'll need help retrieving it."

Euphoria swept over the emperor. "There's the Jinenji I remember."

Tazuro's reaction allowed Jinenji to feel some euphoria of his own. "May I ask what the plan is? Rally the troops?"

"No. I have something else in mind."

Jinenji glanced over at the doctor who was smiling like a child with a treat.

"I've retained the service of some highly skilled warriors. I'll need you to gather them for me," said Tazuro.

Stunned, Jinenji dropped to his knees, bowing like mad. "Thank you for sparing me."

Tazuro's pleased disposition turned to one of discomfort. "Stop that."

Mid-bow, Jinenji did as he was told.

"Samasa, remove those shackles and feed him. Be sure to provide him with everything he'll need as well."

The vermillion woman released Jinenji from his shackles. He rubbed his wrists and shook out his ankles.

"Follow me," said Samasa, walking toward the corridor.

As they passed, the plump yellow man sized the sorcerer up.

What are you looking at?

Samasa returned the scepter by slamming it into Jinenji's arms. "I don't know what he sees in you."

"Wait!" Tazuro's voice froze their exit.

A lump developed deep in Jinenji's throat. *Did he change his mind?*

Hesitant, he faced the emperor.

"Samasa, Daizo. Wait outside."

The plump yellow man and Samasa walked out; closing the door behind them.

"You too, Doctor."

Although displeased, the doctor exited the chamber through a door near the throne.

"Aren't you forgetting something?"

Jinenji began to sweat heavily. "I don't recall, Your Grandeur."

"I want to hear every—last—detail."

Jinenji told his story and a weight catapulted from his shoulders.

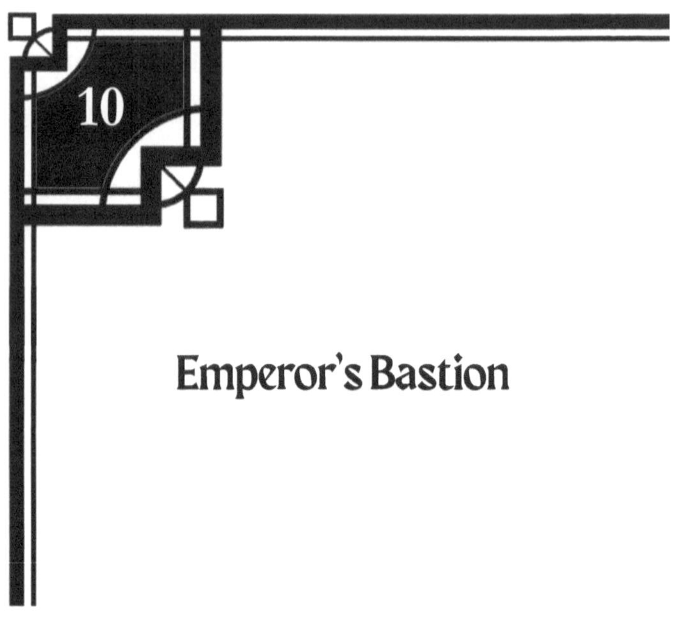

10

Emperor's Bastion

Jinenji's tapping foot rivaled the sound of bullets spilling from an automatic gun. With a stomach full of rodau chicken and potatoes, he was eager to continue his redemption.

Where is she?

The blue lights meandering around the foyer exasperated his uneasiness yet again.

I hope this isn't some sort of twisted trick.

As the thought passed him by, Samasa drove into the foyer with a different vehicle.

A Surface Cruiser? I guess that'll do.

After a heavy sigh and a sour expression, Samasa tossed Jinenji a rolled-up piece of parchment. "The locations are marked."

Jinenji unrolled the shabby parchment, allowing his eyes to fixate on a map. The marked locations stirred suspicion.

"Something wrong?" asked Samasa.

"When did it become wise to enter these regions unannounced?"

"It didn't," spat Samasa before tossing three more rolls of parchment at the sorcerer's feet. "Those are your targets."

To expel the building tension, Jinenji inhaled and then picked up the parchments.

"Tazuro expects to see all of you back here within the next two hours."

Samasa was halfway down the corridor before Jinenji could glance at a single parchment.

"Hey. What about the ignition code?"

Nothing but the echo of his own voice returned. He shook his head and hopped in the one-seater vehicle. Resting on the dash was a golden pendant; the same eye insignia from Tazuro's sword lay upon it. Jinenji fastened it to his shawl then searched for the code. He almost resorted to chasing after Samasa when he spotted it on the back side of the map.

I hate her. I really do.

The code awakened the engine, but years of worry and regret fell unconscious.

It's like I've been reborn.

Jinenji grabbed one of the rolls of parchment. Inside was a photo of an olive-toned man with a dirty blond mohawk. Earrings hung beside his neck, and tribal tattoos marked his temples and cheeks, not the sort to trifle with. All the necessary info peeked at Jinenji from the photos bottom right corner.

Name: Ventama.

Location: Pasanya Village.

Race: Centaur.

Looks like I'm headed for Pasanya Village. Jinenji pulled up beside a podium, identical to the exterior one in every way. *Wait. I need another code.*

He searched the map again and there it was, on the opposite corner from the vehicle code, written tiny as could be.

I'm going to kill that bitch.

The doors opened, and Jinenji slammed on the accelerator. Dark blue smoke shot from the exhaust as he left Omni Eye Fortress.

With all the enthusiasm one could muster, he ventured back into the wastelands. However, his enthusiasm didn't last long.

When does it end? he thought, passing another group of plump, yellow-skinned brutes. Each of which chased him on foot, giving up soon thereafter. *Good for nothing, ogres. Maybe I should go back and kill them all.*

Rocky, dust laden land transitioned into a desert full of great sand dunes. Limitations became clear in a hurry. Jinenji drove up the side of a big dune; it remained a looming mass of particles. Sand kept snagging his wheels, forcing them to spin in place. With a great deal of irritation, Jinenji got out and pushed. Not with his hands, but with a scarlet shield. The sun's sweltering heat gave him a relentless beating as he did so, cutting through every garment he wore to protect himself. Upon defeating the big dune, he celebrated, that is until he spotted another one. Its impossible proportions hindered his path even more. Using his last bit of strength, he carried on. As his body weakened, his resolve did too.

This is too much. I have to turn back. No, I can't. I won't be a failure. Not this time.

As his shield dissipated and his body collapsed, he nudged to the top. Beyond relieved, he looked below and saw Pasanya Village. Not far behind it towered a once great aerial warship. Its nose plunged into the sand and its tail cast a shadow over the village. He could hear every cry and creak of its rickety framework.

Thought that would've sunk by now.

The sorcerer flopped into the Surface Cruiser and pressed on the accelerator. Smaller dunes made for a bumpy descent, but they didn't prevent the vehicle from rushing straight at a building.

"No, no, no!" Jinenji hit the brakes, and the vehicle slowed to a stop, mere inches from collision. *That was way too close.*

Stumbling into the village under a daze, he searched for anything that could relieve him from the sun's abuse. At last, a gazebo where a horse laid in peace called out to him. He crashed to the ground beneath it and rolled onto his back, the persistent sun still visible through the gazebo.

"Leave me alone," he whined in a defeated whisper.

"How about you leave me alone."

Jinenji looked over to see a woman with delicate features and tribal tattoos across her forehead. As she stood, he realized that her bottom half was that of a horse.

"I'm sorry I thought you were—"

"Yeah, sure," she grumbled before trotting off into the sun.

Too tired to care, Jinenji lay back down. "Guess I should've checked first." A subtle giggle escaped him.

The sorcerer enjoyed a brief reprieve before scurrying about Pasanya Village. He went about it as fast his weary body would allow, going from one shaded area to the next. Whenever the sun touched his skin, he thought about shooting it out of the sky.

Evidence of a once affluent village was all around. Save for the doors, every building was built from sand hardened through some mysterious process. Incredible yet sad, it all looked on the verge of collapse. Upkeep fell by the wayside long ago. Graffiti defiled most surfaces, and potholes made the streets daunting to walk through.

All around were normal horses and other tribal tattooed centaurs dressed in tattered garb and damaged armor. A lone centaur elder sculpted a statue out of the same hardened sand used for the buildings.

Jinenji approached the sculptor, Ventama's picture in hand. "Have you seen this man?"

After taking a quick glance, the elder shrugged his shoulders and returned to work.

Jinenji moved on to a centaur couple he saw galloping by. "Excuse me. Do you know this man?"

They examined the picture and smiled. "I sure do. That's Ven," said the woman. "He lives in that house over there." She pointed to a home at the end of the lane.

"Wait, a minute," said the man. "He's a friend of ours. What's this about?"

"No need for alarm. He's been summoned."

The couple didn't budge.

"By who?" asked the woman.

"The emperor," said Jinenji, brandishing Tazuro's pendant.

In an instant, the couple's mistrustful demeanor cracked.

Scattered speech fell from the man's lips. "Oh. Um I, we—"

"It's fine. But I am in a bit of a rush."

Both centaurs stepped aside with haste. Jinenji reached the designated door and gave it a good knocking. Wood groaned as a small centaur girl cracked it open. Even she had tattoos on her face.

"Hello. Is there a man named Ventama living here?"

With major sass, the girl slammed the door. "Mom, there's a hagazo here asking about Dad."

The door swung back open and wobbled, the bottom most hinge being all that remained. It shocked Jinenji to see the woman he encountered under the gazebo. Her eyes lit with outrage.

"Baby, it's him! The perv I told you about!"

A fast hammering of hooves approached, seconds later, a six-foot centaur bolted into the entryway. "Who are you?" he bellowed, matching the photo from the parchment.

Jinenji jumped back, creating some much-needed distance. "Wait a minute!"

Ventama slowed his advance. "Hold on. You're that sorcerer, Ji-Ji—"

"Jinenji," replied the sorcerer with embarrassment.

"That's right. You know, killing you would net me a big reward."

"Not anymore. I've been exonerated."

Jinenji pointed to his eye insignia pendant; Ventama looked impressed.

"So, he sent you? He's finally ready for me?"

"Have you been waiting long?"

"You could say that."

Ventama closed his front door. It tried to fall, but he caught it in time. "Let's take a walk."

"Your wife didn't paint the best picture of me. I'm surprised you didn't take my head off."

A smirk creased Ventama's lips. "My wife is great and all, but she has a tendency to over-exaggerate."

Jinenji laughed, but Ventama's smirk vanished.

"She and my daughter are the only reason I'm even considering this. I'd thank her if I were you."

"Protecting our realm from the humans isn't high on your priority list?"

Ventama threw his defined arms up. "Fantastic. Is that what we're doing? Because that went so well before."

"Things will be different this time."

The centaur paced back and forth.

"You can better protect your family by keeping the humans out of this realm."

"The humans have never done anything to me. The way I see it, we're terrorizing them."

"You're wrong. They will come for us someday. Better to stop them now before they have the strength to do it."

His pacing grew faster and faster. "I don't know about this. It's been years since I met Tazuro. I expected him to send for me a long time ago. He said he would get me and my family out of this place."

"Our emperor is many things, but a liar—"

Jinenji received an irritable glare from Ventama.

"If he promised you riches, then that's what you'll get. One job. One! And your whole life changes."

"Fine. I'll do it. Let me tell my wife first."

"Can I count on you to make it to Omni Eye Fortress within the next few hours?"

"Yeah, I'll be there. Don't you worry, Mr. Sorcerer Man."

Jinenji continued his mission, leaving Pasanya Village in his rearview. Sand turned to dirt as he ate and drank from the rations he brought. Trees, bushes, grass and other forms of carmine foliage appeared along the road leading up to the mountains. The flowers alone possessed a multitude of colors. Taking a moment, Jinenji examined the second photo. A giant blue-skinned man with six arms and black void-like eyes stared back at him. Once again, pertinent info was written in the bottom right corner.

Name: Gonenga

Location: Oktau Mountains

Race: Juggernaut

I hope they're in a good mood.

As Jinenji neared the top of the mountain he killed the engine and continued on foot. The surrounding beauty escalated all the way to the summit.

Why was I living in caverns when I could've been living here?

He drifted between trees with odd shaped leaves and thick trunks. Footprints bigger than eight of his feet combined stained the ground. Rain water rippled within them as the ground rumbled. Through the hanging leaves came a male juggernaut with sapphire skin. His body was heavily muscled, and a patterned loincloth draped around his midsection.

Jinenji ducked behind a bush. *Damn. That's not him.*

Fidgeting with his loincloth, the juggernaut approached a tree. A yellow stream splashed the tree's base. Jinenji blocked his nose from the odor and made way for another bush further along. Rumbling re-ensued. Shivers ran wild across his shoulders as a presence closed in. He turned to find unsettling black eyes scrutinizing him from an inch away.

"Not every day I see one of you."

"Get away!" said Jinenji, jumping backwards.

The juggernaut stood up. "Hey, Orulle, when's the last time you saw a hagazo?"

Sounds of splashing liquid subsided, followed by more quake inducing footsteps.

"Been a while, buddy," said Orulle, peering at Jinenji.

"Stand back, both of you," said Jinenji, whose height only reached Orulle's waistline. "I'm on an important mission."

"Oh, lighten up, would you?" replied Orulle.

"Yeah. Relax. Save the tension for the ring," said the other juggernaut, his complexion like blueberries.

"Ring? What ring?"

"You're not here for the muzza matches?"

Jinenji gave the other juggernaut a blank stare.

"Oh buddy. You're missing out big time," said Orulle with a look of pity.

"Come along," said the other juggernaut, who lifted a flailing Jinenji onto his shoulders.

"Wait! I don't have time for this. I'm here to find someone."

"Really? Well, your best bet is the arena. Every juggernaut on the mountain will be there."

Despite his reservations, Jinenji trusted them. He clutched the juggernaut's wide neck as he went bounding through the forest, his loincloth swaying from side to side. The high vantage point allowed Jinenji to see a plethora of homes and buildings made of log. As they passed the quaint dwellings, a triangular ring came in to view as well.

Within it stood a teal toned female juggernaut, holding a brass megaphone that emitted dark blue smoke. She, too, wore a patterned loincloth around her midsection. A patterned cloth was also tied around her chest.

Hundreds of juggernauts, each a different shade of blue, sat in the stands around the ring. The women wore garments like the announcer's while the men matched with Orulle. Jinenji remained on the juggernauts shoulders as they reached the back row of the stands.

The juggernaut reached a hand up. "Names Barran, pleased to meet you."

"Likewise," said Jinenji, shaking Barran's hand.

Orulle reached a hand up, too, but Jinenji was quick to recoil. For a second, Orulle stared at his own hand before shrugging off the awkward exchange.

"We're not all angry brutes, you know," said Barran.

"Seems I—"

"Believed all the misconceptions?" finished Orulle.

Barran nodded. "We tend to stay to ourselves is all."

"We never refuse good company though," said Orulle with cheer.

The announcer's voice traveled throughout the arena. "First up, we have Darbol and Andro!"

Two male juggernauts, also wearing patterned loincloths, appeared. They vacated a log building in-between the stands and entered the ring. Another female juggernaut, dressed like the announcer, struck a gong located outside the ring. All in attendance flew into a frenzy. It sounded like furious thunder with each clap. Every whistle sounded like it could shatter glass. Jinenji had to cover his ears to prevent the drums within from bursting.

Darbol and Andro clashed head on. Jinenji found it difficult to keep track of their many hands, gripping and swiping at one another. After a brief struggle for dominance, Darbol locked Andro's limbs within his grasp. He outstretched Andro's arms then bashed him in the chest with his massive shoulder.

Andro moaned and stumbled back toward the edge of the ring. His feet slipped on it as he wobbled and tried to regain his balance. Darbol set upon him; he pushed his opponent out of the ring with each of his hands.

"And the winner is… Darbol!"

Most of the crowd re-commenced their rambunctious cheering. Disappointed Andro fans let a few faint boos loose.

"So, what did you think?" asked Orulle.

"It was actually pretty entertaining."

"I knew you'd like it," said Barran with the utmost of hype. "Get ready. The next match is about to start."

Jinenji became so wrapped in the festivities he let the time sensitive nature of his mission evade him. "It's been fun, gentleman, but I have to get going."

"Can't you search from up there?" asked Orulle.

The announcer's voice cut through the noisy crowd. "Next up, we have Derg vs Gonenga!"

Jinenji couldn't believe his ears. Male juggernauts approached the ring. One of them stood about four feet taller than the other and possessed bigger musculature. Despite this, the larger juggernaut seemed reluctant to enter the ring.

Nope. Not him.

The other moved into the ring like a ravenous shark on the hunt.

There he is.

"Derg? We're waiting," said the announcer.

As Derg dragged himself inside the ring the gong went off. More eardrum bursting applause followed.

"Gonenga, Gonenga, Gonenga!"

Every single member of the audience including Barran and Orulle chanted the name. Frustrated by this, Derg made a mad dash, grabbing Gonenga by the throat. Gonenga didn't so much as flinch. Instead, he stared a hole through Derg, who panicked. After prying Derg's hands loose, Gonenga headbutted him in the forehead. Derg became stunned and tried to maintain a standing position. Gonenga surveyed him for a moment then hoisted his body overhead. Derg rained elbows into Gonenga's face, but he did little more than wince. Every one of Gonenga's muscles flexed before he hurled Derg onto the ring's floor. He smacked face first and went still.

"One, two, three…"

Derg didn't move.

"Five, six, seven, eight…"

A couple of Derg's hands twitched.

"Nine and… ten! Gonenga wins!"

The announcer herself became elated and was not afraid to show it. Gonenga's brute force left Jinenji mesmerized; he could see why everybody loved him. Unwilling to supply any fanfare, the juggernaut walked back to the building between the stands. Without a word, Jinenji leapt from Barran's shoulders.

"Where you going, buddy?" asked Orulle.

"Thanks for all the fun guys."

"But there are more matches coming up," shouted Barran.

Jinenji pressed on, entering the log building between the stands. A dozen juggernauts awaited their turn. They gave Jinenji odd looks, but didn't bother addressing him. In a meditative position, Gonenga sat at the very back.

Jinenji tiptoed over to him. "Excuse me, Mr. Gonenga."

Refusing to acknowledge the sorcerer, Gonenga's eyes stayed shut.

"I hate to disturb you, but the emperor is ready for you."

Gonenga's eyes opened, but he still didn't speak.

"He expects you at Omni Eye Fortress within an hours' time."

The juggernaut glared at Jinenji who felt compelled to reveal his pendant. Gonenga climbed to his feet.

Is he going to attack me?

No attack came, but Gonenga did communicate via a simple head nod.

"So, uh… I can count on you to be there?"

Gonenga provided no further confirmation and walked out the back door.

I hope he shows up.

♦♦♦

Jinenji hiked to his Surface Cruiser and pulled out the third and final photo. Like the last two photos, information was provided in the bottom right corner.

Name: Orinsu

Location: Aglan Forest

Race: Vampire

I've been dreading this one. I hate dealing with vampires.

Orinsu's bloodthirsty expression seemed nothing short of pure evil. His braided hair, mauve skin, wings and long sharp teeth were disturbing to behold.

Hesitant, Jinenji searched the map for the best route forward and took it. Not long after, a forest abundant with trees the size of skyscrapers came into view.

He parked his vehicle in the open field ahead of the forest and crept in. The canopy was so dense the bright sun may as well have been a dim moon.

Every breath he took sounded amplified due to how quiet the forest was. Not a single bird chirping, deer prancing or frog croaking could be heard.

Is this place abandoned?

He retrieved his map and checked it again, ensuring he was in the proper place. *Maybe they moved on.*

Jinenji was not at all happy about the prospect of going to a fourth location. However, he knew facing Tazuro without completing his mission was suicide.

A faint rustle of leaves occurred. The sorcerer gazed up to find a few leaves falling with the soft breeze. Assuming it to be nothing of concern, Jinenji returned to the map. An entity of some kind swooshed overhead. This time there was no confusion, he was not alone. Gulping noises soon arose along with hiss like whispers.

"I can never get enough of these."

"Me either."

Whispers and gulps persisted.

"Their blood's so tasty, isn't it?"

"One of my favorites."

Right in front of Jinenji fell the corpses of saber-toothed wolves. They splattered hard on the leaf littered floor. The bloodstains on their pure white coats shimmered, even in the semi-dark.

Jinenji lit the top side of his scepter and held it like a torch. He moved in a circular motion, focusing on every inch of the canopy; he saw nothing but shadowy leaves. As he made his second pass around, what appeared made him jump. Horrible purple faces with blade like teeth hid amidst the leaves, eyes red, murderous, thirsty.

The faces burst forth along with lanky bodies and wings of substantial proportions.

Vampires!

With dizzying speed, they plunged. Jinenji couldn't react in time to stop one vampire from ramming him. His backside found the dirt with a loud crunch. He picked himself up halfway when the second vampire slashed at his throat with bloody claws. The sorcerer managed a haphazard block that resulted in his arm sustaining deep gashes. Like a pair of vultures, both vampires circled above.

"You're making a grave mistake," said Jinenji, gripping his wounds.

Both vampires sped straight down, criss crossing as they went. Scarlet sparks came forward in retaliation. Smells akin to rotten meat filled the air. Shrill screeches rang out as the vampires crash-landed. As fast as they fell, they stood. At last, Jinenji got a clear look at them.

They were terrifying to behold, their physiques gaunt, their behavior erratic and deadly. One was a female with grimy dreads; the other was a male so bald his head resembled a marble.

"Stop this! The emperor demands Orinsu report to the fortress," said Jinenji.

No amount of reason could pierce the volume of the vampires' hunger. They flew at Jinenji, one right behind the other. He couldn't see the furthest vampire very well, so he focused on the one closest, blocking her attack.

When she flew past, Jinenji expected the male to come next, but he was gone. A powerful kick found the sorcerers back. It almost pushed him onto his face. He resisted the fall then struck with his scepter. With an unsettling wail, the male vampire flew off again. The sensation of being stabbed three times at once brought Jinenji to his knees. Glancing over, he saw the female vampire release her claws from his thigh. Jinenji fired a bolt, but she dodged it.

"Dolsa. Gruck. Enough!"

A vampire decked in beautiful amber armor hovered beneath the canopy; he pointed at Jinenji. "Meet me in my quarters."

After further inspection, Jinenji realized he had found the third and final warrior. Orinsu touched down then pounded twice on the tree closest to him. An oval shaped sliver at the base of the trunk fell outward like a drawbridge.

"We've become more accommodating over the years," said Orinsu before flying up through the canopy.

Dolsa and Gruck went after him. From Jinenji's tunic came a jar containing ointment. Little dabs of the black goo stopped his wounds from bleeding. Extreme hesitance at his side, he stepped over to the hollowed-out trunk. He took a few peeks inside and jerked back each time as if he expected a ravenous beast to leap out. An elevator-like platform, a lever, and rope attachment waited inside. He glanced up, but it was far too dark for him to see where the trunk led. Imagining Tazuro's sword impaling him was all it took for Jinenji to take the risk.

The platform skyrocketed toward the canopy with a single crank of the lever. It stopped after ascending several hundred feet in a matter of seconds. Another oval sliver fell out from the top of the trunk. Arrays of elaborate suspension bridges and tree houses awaited. Sunlight still struggled to get through, even at the new altitude. Below was the canopy Jinenji thought marked the top of the forest. The forest kept many deceptions, trees of varying heights was one of them. A bridge lay before Jinenji. It harbored dozens of vampires, all perched on the railings, all a different shade of purple. They sniffed the air and licked their lips at the sight of him.

Don't try it, assholes.

"In here," said Orinsu as he went inside the largest tree house, its design unlike the others.

Jinenji passed between the other vampires, lamenting the fact his legs couldn't speed walk any faster. Each of the vampires breathed hard, letting their drool pitter patter his path.

Disgusting.

Jinenji entered the tree house to find Orinsu hanging upside down from a branch that jutted through the ceiling. Other than a few windows, there was nothing else.

"If your claims are true, my family and I will have to find another meal," said Orinsu.

"If I'm not mistaken, the emperor forbids the consumption of ginyai blood."

"The emperor forbids a lot of things. Don't get me wrong… I respect him, but sometimes you have to bend the rules a little."

A distressing heat crept through the sorcerer.

"So, are your claims true or not?"

"They're true. Don't worry."

"What proof do you have?"

As Jinenji felt around for his pendant, he discovered a tear where it used to be. "It must've fallen," he said, patting his chest.

"I'm not very fond of liars," said Orinsu, flipping down from his branch.

His face went close to Jinenji's; death and decay reeked from his breath. Jinenji prepared to stab Orinsu in the gut when a metal object hit the floor.

Jinenji glanced down, spotting his pendant which he retrieved fast. "See. I'm telling the truth."

"Hmm. Too bad. The hunt continues." Disappointment swept through Orinsu. "How does it feel to be part of the Emperor's Bastion?"

Confusion coiled Jinenji's face.

"It's the name Tazuro gave to his deadliest group of warriors. Somewhat corny if you ask me, but hey… I'm not in charge."

"There was never a name before," said Jinenji, taken aback.

"You've been gone for a very long time, Jinenji." Orinsu shrugged. "Things change."

"He expects you within the hour," said Jinenji, taking control of the conversation.

"I'll be there. After all, I still haven't tried human blood."

Accompanied by Jinenji, Orinsu stepped out of his tree house.

"He's free to go," said Orinsu to the now thirty or so vampires.

Each of them dispersed in fits of anger.

"See you there," Orinsu yielded a disturbing smile. "Tazuro must be in a good mood these days if he let you live."

Ignoring the remark, Jinenji took the elevator. Once at the bottom, he ran to his Surface Cruiser and sped off. His heart thumped like no other for most of the return trip. Before long, he arrived back at Omni Eye Fortress. Pulling up to the podium, he input the appropriate code. While waiting for the fortress doors to open, he almost experienced a heart attack. Gonenga plummeted out of the sky, wielding an enormous battle-axe with a matching helmet.

"Are you trying to kill me?" screamed Jinenji.

As the quaking ground stilled, Gonenga's mouth twitched into a half smile for a brief second. The doors opened, and they both entered. Jinenji parked next to Samasa's Surface Bolt and Gonenga stepped into the corridor. At that very moment, the Surface Cruiser sagged to the floor and its engine burst with sparks and dark blue smoke.

Shit. Well, at least it didn't break down sooner.

"I am genuinely impressed."

A familiar voice echoed around the foyer. Jinenji searched for the source of it and found the doctor. He stood at the entrance of a corridor opposite from the one Gonenga took.

"Part of me didn't expect you to still be here, Hallevi. Thought you would've started that institute you also talked about by now."

Hallevi's eyes flashed with reminiscence. "Unfortunately, plans don't always go accordingly."

"Can't argue with you there."

"I must implore you to consider collaborating once more. The things we could accomplish now."

Jinenji scoffed. "What? Haven't found a successor?"

"Of course not, attempting to replace the Chief Sorcerer would be futile."

Seventeen years ago:

Through a narrow lamp lit hallway. Down a steep stairwell that seemed to lead to misery itself. To the foot of an iron door emblazoned with the emblem of a grotesque creature.

Jinenji often traveled this path yet dreaded it each time. The sound of his knuckles against the iron reinforced his ill feelings. He knew he was in for an unpleasant couple of hours.

Dr. Hallevi opened the screeching door. "Ahh, Jinenji. Punctual per usual. Right this way."

Jinenji crossed over the threshold and as the door shut, the very air became stale, frigid and claustrophobic. He scrutinized the laboratory, and all it possessed. A plethora of machines and equipment lined the walls and floors. Many of which he did not know their purpose and hoped to never find out. Bone like pilasters lined the walls; the same design sprouted from the center of the ceiling like sun rays. All of it coated in faded blue paint. An iron table in the shape of a rhombus filled most of the space.

"So, how's it coming along?" asked Jinenji, approaching a series of vertical glass tanks.

A nude, human girl floated within one. Purple liquid enveloped her. Protruding from the back of her throat was a thick tube. Despite her circumstances, a blissful expression emanated from her sleeping face.

Hallevi sighed. "I've tried numerous methods, all failures to say the least."

Hallevi's eyes averted to another tank. It, too, held a human, but was absent of any liquid. The nude boy inside laid in a crumpled heap at the bottom, his body yellow and stiff. He'd been dead for hours. Next to that lay a pile of creatures—insects, mammals, amphibians, fowls and a few more humans, all deceased.

"Yours is all that's left, but I must admit… I have my doubts. If this proves unsuccessful, we'll have wasted yet another specimen," said Hallevi.

"I don't see why it wouldn't work. We're naturally stronger than humans. Infusing them with some of our soul energy should give them a boost."

"That makes sense, theoretically. But this has never been attempted."

"Isn't that what science is all about? Trial and error? Risk and reward?"

Hallevi adjusted his shirt collar and gave a side eye.

"Look. I've helped you with this experiment every step of the way. We're no closer to getting results than we were a year ago."

The doctor's side eye turned to one of shock, then defense.

"If this doesn't work, I'll bring you back five more specimens. How's that?"

"Fine. She's already been marinating in your energy for over a week anyhow."

Jinenji glanced at the scepter in his hands. "Great. Let's see if she's ready."

"If your hex succeeds, will it always take so long? I'm trying to build an army here. We need quick results. This is entirely too slow."

"Sorry. Don't know what to tell you. The human body is more complex than I thought."

"Well, can you at least perform more than one at a single given time?"

Jinenji resisted the urge to get angry. "Imagine running three or four complicated experiments at once. Imagine how taxing that would be. I have to monitor the hex frequently. Make sure it doesn't grow too fast or too slow. Something like that could potentially kill the host."

"You have no way of confirming that at this juncture."

"Actually, I think I do. The hex behaves like a symbiote. Overdo it and," Jinenji glided his thumb across his throat. "Plus, she's been fighting against the invading energy this whole time. I don't want to put too much strain on her."

Hallevi rubbed the space between his eyes, his glasses bouncing against his fingers.

"I suspect that my energy will eventually trump her resistance."

Scarlet energy emanated from Jinenji's scepter as he closed his eyes. A few seconds later, a look of surprise burst onto his face.

"It worked!"

"Come again?" asked the doctor, putting his glasses back in their proper place.

"My energy, it finished bonding with hers!"

"You're serious?"

"Stand back."

"What are you going to do?"

Hallevi went to stand at the other end of his table, opposite Jinenji and the tanks.

"I designed the hex to go dormant when complete. All that's left now is a little push."

Jinenji aimed his scepter at the floating girl, bathing her in a scarlet hue. Vomit spewed through her gritted teeth and her eyes bulged awake. Hair shed from her scalp and her skin turned pale as snow.

Hallevi winced. "How vile. What have you done?"

"I don't know why this is happening."

Both hagazo looked on in horror. Bones popped through the girl's fingers and toes while her teeth grew sharp. Her spine tore through her back and her breasts melted away, allowing her ribs to take their place. She convulsed for a bit then fell still.

"You killed her! I knew this wouldn't—"

The tank burst, sending purple liquid and glass shards everywhere. Jinenji brandished a scarlet shield while Hallevi ducked behind his table. Now a mutated creature, the girl pulled the tube from her throat. A slithering pink tongue unraveled to nudge the air like a hunting serpent.

Bloodshot eyes homed in on Jinenji as he backed into the edge of the table. With a pounce, the creature crashed through his scarlet shield and began slashing. Jinenji blocked every strike except the last which snuck through his defenses. Bony fingers cut him across the chest, sending him up and onto the table. Tumbling backwards allowed him to evade a stab attempt.

Hallevi opened a closet behind him and gave a frantic search through its contents. Like a wild hyena, the beast leapt onto the table. As a gunshot rang out, Jinenji fired a scarlet bolt. The bolt split the creature's stomach open as a bullet tore through its head. It fell off the table, landing lifeless on the cold floor. Glancing back, Jinenji saw Hallevi clutching a revolver.

"That was insane," said Jinenji, breathing heavy.

"That was..."

He braced for Hallevi's ridicule.

"Astonishing!"

"What?"

"Did you see how strong she became? She must've been using her soul energy instinctively. Like an animal. I've seen nothing like it."

"Yeah, but why did she change like that?"

"No matter, a manageable side effect."

"How? It was wild, completely *unmanageable*."

"How's your mind control these days?"

Jinenji reared his head back, almost flinging it off his shoulders. "We've been over this. I'm not ready for that."

"Not ready? You were trained by Rezvan himself."

"Did you forget he was banished? Didn't exactly get to finish my training."

Hallevi scoffed. "At any rate, I presumed you would've figured it out by now."

The sorcerer denied Hallevi a response.

"If we can control this creature, we can supply formidable soldiers, worthy additions to the army." Hallevi walked closer to Jinenji. "Think of all the glory we'll receive, all the praise."

Jinenji couldn't help but imagine what that would be like.

"All you have to do is perfect your mind control." A scheming smile appeared on Hallevi. "Had we offered anything else, we would've been laughed at, humiliated! But these, these… ghouls are a different story."

"It won't work. I'm not Rezvan."

"Don't be pathetic. I've attempted electroconvulsive therapy, alchemy, leucotomy, even hypnotism, each one a failure. But have I given up?"

"Even if I could do it right this very second, it wouldn't matter. We're too late to make the cut."

Hallevi offered a peculiar expression.

"I have to report to the emperor in an hour. He's planning to move ahead with the army as is."

"No! You must be mistaken."

"I heard it from Zathumor himself."

Trying to hide the pain in his eyes, Hallevi turned away.

"Looks like we'll have to wait until the next war to get our glory and praise."

"Well then," Hallevi forced his throat clear. "I'll prepare the battle tanks and the latest aerial warships. My apprentices are adding the final touches as we speak."

"Great, but that won't be necessary. The humans lack any real military prowess. They use more primitive methods of combat."

"All the more reason."

"That's what I said, but Tazuro wants to get up close and personal. Good old-fashioned sword play should do the trick."

Jinenji gave Hallevi a quick pat on the shoulder, he shuddered from the touch. Without another word, the sorcerer vacated the lab.

◆◆◆

Present day:

"I don't know, old friend. Where would I find the time?" said Jinenji.

Hallevi placed a hand over his heart. "The sting of rejection."

"Don't draw any conclusions yet. When this is over, I just might look you up."

Jinenji's sarcasm was unbridled.

"Pity, I've begun work on a submersible vehicle. There are some minor issues, but it's coming along nicely. The komera won't know what hit them. You might want to get in on that before it's too late."

"Too late? I'd say I got a few years to think it over."

Displeasure emitted from Hallevi as Jinenji proceeded down the corridor. Keeping his distance, Hallevi did the same. Daizo opened the door of Tazuro's chambers yet again. Gonenga, Ventama and Samasa were already waiting inside. Ventama now wore jade armor with an empty hexagonal chest plate. Faint signs of rust could be seen throughout the once immaculate garment. A long, collapsed fan dangled on Samasa's belt at the small of her back. Tazuro, the torture device, Celeste's remains and Orinsu were nowhere to be found.

The nerves within Jinenji went haywire. *Where is he?*

Sounds of the chamber door reopening made Jinenji's eyes shoot over. Orinsu flew in, now shrouded in a long, hooded cloak. A sigh of relief exhaled from the sorcerer.

Moments later, Tazuro entered through a doorway next to his throne. A black cape swooshed behind him like a shadowy ghost. He moved to the center of the chamber with an air of invincibility. At over seven feet tall, he stood above all but Gonenga.

A little, orange-skinned girl rolled in atop a metal ball, like a circus performer. Pointy ears poked through the hood of her shawl, and moonstone fastened to her chest. From the center of her nose to both earlobes was an ornamental nath. It jangled like a pair of maracas.

Everyone in attendance rushed to form a single file row before the emperor.

"Nobody told me I'd be working with a goblin," said Daizo with disgust.

Samasa spoke under her breath. "Shut up. Are you trying to get yourself killed?"

Daizo went silent then finished falling in with the others. Once the formation was complete, they all knelt down.

Tazuro went up and down the row, scrutinizing all of them along the way. "Each of you was chosen because of your unique skill sets. You are the best of the best from your respective races, the best of the best from the Ginyai Realm itself."

Everyone beamed with pride, none more so than Jinenji.

"I expect great things during our mission." The emperor stopped in front of Daizo. "Many of you don't know each other. Some of you belong to a race that despises another."

Cold sweats appeared all over Daizo's skin.

"This should go without saying, but it seems there are those of you who need a reminder."

Making eye contact with the emperor was more than Daizo could handle, he looked elsewhere fast.

"The days of killing each other for petty reasons are long gone. We're all ginyai and we'll remain united as one." The emperor resumed pacing up and down the row. "Your only concern right now should be conquering the humans. They, along with the stubborn komera, will regret their resistance."

While everyone else nodded in agreement, Daizo writhed with hatred.

"We've been given a second chance. We can't afford to waste it. First, we'll survey the current status of their realm and with Jinenji's years of experience draft up a strategy."

When it seemed Jinenji's prideful expression was at capacity, it spread even further.

"This time when we return home… we return home victorious." Tazuro halted near his iron throne. "Now stand Emperor's Bastion. We have work to do."

As if choreographed, everyone rose together.

"May Malubris reign supreme," shouted the emperor.

Everyone shouted back. "And may his supreme reign last for all eternity."

When seated, Tazuro pressed an indentation in the armrest of his throne. The bottom transformed into a square covering that extended out then up to the waistline. Matching iron legs burst from both sides. They raised the throne high off the ground. With zoganite smoke wisping from its backside, the throne walked away like an overgrown spider on the prowl.

Tazuro moved into the foyer; Jinenji followed along with the others. While they waited for the fortress doors to open, Samasa approached the emperor.

"Any room in there for me?" she asked in a seductive manner.

The doors opened and Tazuro proceeded without offering Samasa a passing glance. Downtrodden, she entered her Surface Bolt.

Daizo already sat in the passenger seat. "Can't say I didn't see that coming," he remarked.

"Oh, shut up," replied Samasa as Gonenga passed by.

Ventama couldn't help but watch the juggernaut. "How are you? Name's Ventama."

Gonenga grunted, then left in a hurry.

Disappointed, Ventama turned to Samasa and Daizo. "What's his deal? Is he always so pleasant?"

Samasa spoke in a nonchalant manner. "Well, when you grow up getting bullied for being the smallest of your race, you learn to be the meanest."

"The smallest? He's enormous!" exclaimed Ventama.

"Rumor has it he used to travel around challenging anyone and everyone. They say he's been in a thousand battles and only ever lost once," said Daizo.

"Well, shit. Glad he's on our side."

"You can say that again," said Samasa before driving outside.

Orinsu exited next, his wings almost reaching both sides of the foyer as he flew out. Giddy and energetic, the little goblin girl rolled out right behind him. Realizing he had no means of transportation, Jinenji ran in front of Ventama before he could gallop away.

"Can I…?" he asked, pointing at Ventama's back.

"Come on. I hate doing that."

"It'll be for a short while."

Ventama shook his head fast. "Can't you wave your little staff and fly or something?'

"All right, fine. I'll—"

"Get on," groaned Ventama.

"Really?"

"Hurry before I change my mind."

Thrilled, Jinenji hopped on and grabbed Ventama's waist.

"Shoulder!" screamed Ventama as if he'd just been electrocuted.

Surprised, Jinenji removed his hand.

"Grab… my shoulder."

As soon as Jinenji moved his hand, Ventama was on the move. Average ginyai as well as those clad in black armor cleared a path before bowing on bended knee.

Jinenji held his head high. *Peasants.*

A small girl resembling Tazuro and Samasa ran in front of the convoy. So did a boy of similar stature with bug-like features. They both swung sticks at one another in play. Tazuro paused, watching them with a stern eye. The rest of the convoy paused as well. Two women rushed onto the path.

"I'm so very sorry, Your Grandeur," said a bug-like woman as she wrangled the boy.

"Yes. So very sorry to get in your way," said a red-skinned woman while bowing.

Tazuro lowered the frontal compartment of his Spider Throne and stepped out. "Step aside, both of you."

The children froze and the women looked to one another in terror.

"Please don't, Your Grandeur," pleaded the red-skinned woman.

"Punish me instead," said the bug-like woman while bowing.

"Move," said Tazuro with more bass in his tone.

As Tazuro walked over to the children, the women cowered away. Both of the children quivered beneath him.

He took the stick from the apple-skinned little girl. "Preparing to be a noble kezai warrior, are you?"

While quaking in her tiny shoes, the girl nodded.

"And what about you, young man? Training to be a warrior, too?"

A shaky nod left the boy.

"There aren't many vulbortas in my army. I could use someone like you."

Much too mortified, the boy didn't speak.

Tazuro pointed to the goblin in his company. "See that girl over there? She isn't much older than the two of you, and yet she fights for me. She also collects a sizeable income, believe it or not." Snapping the stick in two, he handed half of it back to the little apple-skinned girl. "My men brought her to me about seven years ago, when she was but an infant. Her entire family succumbed during the unification. But not her, she survived. You don't find willpower like that very often." The emperor transitioned to a combat stance. "So, I took her in. And now she's one of the toughest warriors in all the realm." Crouching some, he aimed his stick at the children. "You want to stand like this and strike like that." With a sideways swing he smacked the kezai girl's stick. "You try."

Hesitant at first, the kezai girl imitated the move.

"Very good." Tazuro looked at the boy. "Your turn."

Following his friend's lead, the vulborta boy imitated the move as well.

"Yes. Good. That's what I like to see. Keep it up and you'll be fighting beside me in no time."

The fear enveloping both children disappeared.

"Now run along and practice."

Both of the frightened mothers received their children and smothered them with hugs and kisses. Tazuro re-entered his throne and proceeded forward with his convoy.

Up the broad, treacherous trail of the cylindrical cliff they went. Entering the mouth of the cave was different for Jinenji this time around. Instead of worry and uncertainty, he was confident and ready. Upon dismounting Ventama, Jinenji stayed beside the entrance with everyone else. Tazuro went before the Gateway. His mere presence forced it to awaken. Pink, kaleidoscope patterns appeared like they were afraid to keep him waiting. He went in and the others followed.

The Spider Throne turned into more of an octopus as it swam about. Orinsu had no trouble using his wings for propulsion. The little goblin girl held her ball and flutter kicked. Nobody dared so much as a smirk at Gonenga who swam awkwardly with his many appendages. Samasa and Daizo swam while pushing the Surface Bolt from the rear. Ventama struggled with his galloping, but things got easier once he added his arms into the equation. Jinenji swam with zero issues this time around.

As they all gathered in front of the Gateway, the wobbly image of Kinichi's Chamber arose, unencumbered by the translucent, white, energy barrier. Tazuro turned to the sorcerer, an elated expression across his face.

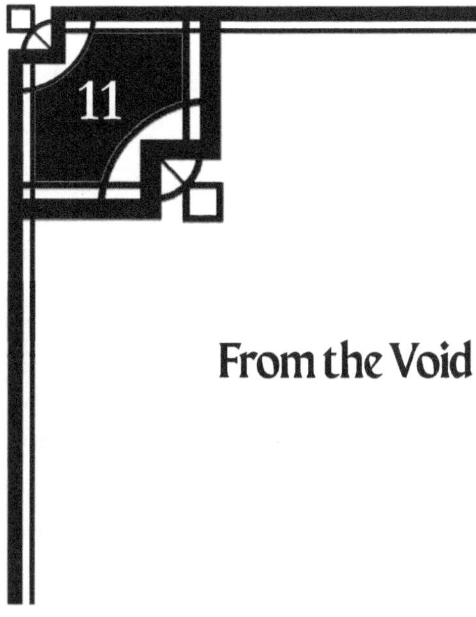

From the Void

As Obake lay within desolate blackness, heavy rain came down upon him. The relentless raindrops jerked him from his slumber. After a long, puzzled stare, he slammed his eyes shut, shook his head, then peeked again. The blackness remained.

What is this place?

He ascended and tried to brace onto something. It disturbed him to see the absence of a floor beneath his feet. Not even a pool of rain was present, the raindrops kept falling deeper.

Daring not to move another inch, he searched for a door, a window, anything that could lead to freedom.

"Anybody here?"

No one answered.

"Anybody here? Help!"

Only the storm replied.

Obake took a timid step forward and envisioned himself plummeting to wherever the rain was going. Yet, the invisible floor caught his footsteps again and again until the worry of plummeting took its leave.

He ran hard and fast, using the hope of discovering an exit as propulsion. Before long, he noticed that his stamina persisted; motivation to go faster. Determination accompanied every stride, but the void didn't care.

Sopping wet and miserable, he sank. *I guess this is it.* Defeat sank him even lower. *That thing is still out there. They have no idea.*

The thought made Obake perk back up. "I have to warn them somehow!"

"Warn who about what?"

From the rain came a familiar shape that transfigured into a young woman with silver hair.

"Meilana! How did you? How long have you—"

"Long enough to see you running around like a doofus."

Afraid Meilana might deform back into rain, Obake approached with care and caution. Bringing her close, he caressed her face. Meilana stared into Obake's eyes as he leaned in. He couldn't wait to kiss her thick, soft lips.

"Keep it in your pants, kid. Your grandmother's here for crying out loud."

Obake wheeled around to see his grandparents.

"Oh, let them be. We've done much worse," said Bao-Ang.

Joy swelled within Obake. "What! I'm so happy to see you guys."

Bao grinned. "I know I'm a little rough on the eyes these days, but I'm still a woman I'll have you know."

Obake laughed and embraced the two of them. "I'm sorry about what I said before. I overreacted."

"Nonsense. Don't worry your little head about it," assured Bao.

Yokai ruffled Obake's shoulders. "It's in the past now. We're just happy to see you. Could you maybe pick a beach next time, though?"

"I second that. All this doom and gloom can't be healthy." Yumo peered out from behind Yokai and Bao with a mischievous smile. "I was going to pop out and scare you, but it looks like you're stressing out enough as it is."

"You're here too!" said Obake, starting their elaborate handshake.

"Hey! How come we don't have a handshake?" asked Meilana in sarcasm.

With a chuckle, Obake pulled her close again.

"So, what's the deal, Green? Can't escape from a little void? I know I taught you better than that."

A shrug jumped from Obake's shoulders. "I tried, but it goes on and on. If only—"

"You knew where to look." Bao stepped aside to reveal a glowing white light in the distance. "We're counting on you."

"You can stop him, babe. I have faith in you."

"You know about him?"

"Of course she does. We all do," said Yokai.

Yumo nodded. "Your girl's right. You can stop him, but not from in here."

The light enticed Obake's gaze. "Are you… coming with me?"

"This one's up to you," said Meilana.

Bao caressed her grandson's green mane. "Being by yourself doesn't mean that you're alone."

"Now hurry! Before it disappears," said Yokai, reaching for another embrace.

Meilana joined in, followed by Bao and Yumo. Obake refused to let go; he wanted the moment to last forever. Even in a storm ridden void he was happy as long as his loved ones were by his side.

To his dismay, they all returned to the rain in one fell swoop. In sheer desperation, Obake grabbed at them, but all he got were fists full of liquid. His face twisted with sadness, but before the tears could well up, he remembered the light.

"No! Don't!" he screamed at the shrinking exit.

Charging forward, he dove headfirst at the now pebble sized light. As it overtook him, the light became blinding.

Jolting awake and gasping for air let the foul stench of death circumvent Obake's nose. The floor, the walls, the ceiling, and the Gateway were all familiar. He was back in Kinichi's Chamber, back with the dead, back to reality. His chest screamed with agony. A dark bruise glossed over most of it. A heavy item shattered in the next room, followed by thrashing and wailing.

It's you. Isn't it?

Before Obake could take a single step, the Gateway activated. As it came alive, he contemplated his options. Dropping back to the filthy floor was his best one. He slowed his breath and observed through his eyelashes.

Jinenji entered the chamber, followed by Ventama who couldn't take his stare from the floor. The little goblin girl rolled in, smelling the air as she went. Samasa and Daizo pushed the Surface Bolt inside, sweat gathering on both of their brows. Orinsu flew through with his head on a swivel.

Gonenga walked in right after, his nose flinching from the smell. Tazuro entered last, placing his Spider Throne to the far-left side of the Gateway. While descending the platforms, he marveled at Jinenji's handy work. Obake's heart slammed against his ribs like a prisoner ramming their cell bars.

"All this for me? You shouldn't have," said Tazuro, his smile so broad, so satisfied.

Jinenji's face lit with happiness. "I knew you'd be pleased, Your Grandeur."

"Everything's just how you described. Imagine the possibilities. Take notice, Emperor's Bastion. This is how you serve me properly."

Boiling with jealousy, Samasa rushed to bow at Tazuro's feet. "I'm ready for my first mission."

The emperor rubbed his beard, scrutinizing her. "So eager, I like it."

With her face near Tazuro's groin, Samasa bit her bottom lip and stared into his eyes.

A sensual expression flooded Tazuro's face. "Well then, let's get started." He moved closer, putting his groin against Samasa's cheek. "My sword…"

Samasa bit her lip harder.

"Get it for me," said Tazuro, his expression turning to stone.

Samasa bolted to her feet, her disappointment impossible to hide. "Of course, Your Grandeur. Where should I look?"

"One moment," said Jinenji as he went into the nearby office.

Moments later he returned with two maps and an inkbrush.

Inside of one map, he circled something then handed it to Tazuro. "They're very close by."

The emperor scanned the map while Jinenji circled something in the other map and threw it at Samasa's feet.

"The location you'll be headed to is marked."

Samasa nearly lunged at Jinenji, but she refrained in the end.

"Whoa. I'd be careful if I were you," said Jinenji, quite smug.

"Am I supposed to be scared?"

"Of me? Not at all. The humans, yes."

Confusion found its way to Samasa, Jinenji carried on.

"They created a golem to guard the sword. I was pretty disappointed when I couldn't beat it. I tried on several occasions too. Who knows, maybe you'll have better luck."

"Naturally. Let a real warrior show you how it's done," said Samasa, ascending the platforms to her vehicle.

Jinenji chuckled to himself.

"Daizo, go with her," commanded Tazuro.

The ogre perked up, his mouth full of dead flesh.

Ventama looked upon him with disgust. "Ever heard of a banana?"

Daizo walked past the centaur, making eye contact all the while. "If you die out there," He slurped down the sliver of flesh dangling from his tusks. "Just know that you'll live on inside my belly." With both hands, Daizo shook his round stomach.

Ventama sneered. "Can't believe I have to work with this guy."

"I'm pretty sure they've been dead for hours already," said Orinsu, picking up a corpse of his own. Upon sniffing it, he reared back and threw it down. "Ugh! How can you eat these?"

Daizo shrugged as he ascended the platforms and entered Samasa's vehicle. "More for me."

Tazuro locked eyes with Samasa. "Use your soul energy wisely. We don't want the humans to panic yet. And Daizo, stay close to her."

Daizo grunted then began turning away. Right before his head turned fully, a look of hate arose. The ogre placed a sausage fingered hand on Samasa's shoulder. She drove down the platforms then exited the chamber.

"Orinsu, I'll need you in tip-top shape. Go get something to drink, but don't let anybody see you."

"Will do, boss. Be back in no time."

Orinsu flew straight through the chamber's open window.

Tazuro stared at Obake. "Is that him? Is that Obake?"

Oh shit.

"Sure is. He managed to fight off the transformation. They all tried, but he actually pulled it off. Pretty amazing, to be honest," said Jinenji.

The allure of curiosity compelled Tazuro to approach.

No. Don't come over here.

Obake repeated the phrase in his head, but Tazuro walked over nonetheless. His heart thumped faster and faster as the emperor came to stand over him.

"He looks just like him," said Tazuro.

Jinenji joined his emperor. "He truly does. I wouldn't be surprised if they're secretly the same person. Only thing giving it away is the hair."

Thrashing and wailing from the other room recommenced.

"What was that?" said Tazuro, now concentrating on the room.

The goblin girl rolled over to the door. "I'll check it out."

In that moment, Obake rushed the window. Gonenga grunted while Jinenji's eyes popped out of his skull. Ventama's jaw dropped and the goblin girl snickered. Obake soared through the open window and hurdled toward the garden.

I'm sorry, Yumo. I'll come back for you. I promise.

He couldn't believe how far away the garden was. Nor could he believe how fast he was heading toward it.

I don't think a tuck and roll is going to cut it.

Sounds of a shattering window blared from overhead.

Something's coming!

The garden drew closer with each passing moment.

Should I use it? I have to.

With every muscle tensed, Obake released spurts of Shadow Cloud. As if struck by lightning, he seized with pain and aborted.

Shit. What do I do now?

A powerful force clamped onto the back collar of his keikogi. His trajectory reversed in an instant.

What the fuck?

From his peripheral he saw a black, snake-like creature with a horn and feathers.

In a full panic he wrestled, but the creature gripped tighter.

"Let me go!"

With its clawed hands, the creature lifted Obake onto its backside. Obake then held onto the creature for dear life.

What's happening?

After a moment, he gathered the courage to glance down. A gash presided over the creature's left eye and a bronze key dangled from around its neck.

Obake's eyes bulged. "Yumo?"

No More Chances

"Ventama, go after them. You too, Kalida. Kill the bastard, but bring the creature back to me alive if you can. If not, its corpse will be sufficient. Just make sure there's enough left for an autopsy." Tazuro pulled his gloves tighter. "If any humans see you, kill them."

Ventama and the little goblin girl left without hesitation.

Tazuro aligned his eyes with the juggernaut's. "Give us some space."

Gonenga took several steps back, crushing corpses as he went. Jinenji trembled as his emperor's gaze fell upon him next.

"Everything I've said about you today, I take it back."

"Your Grandeur, I can make this right. Give me another—"

"No more chances!" Tazuro ambled to his throne and released his sword.

Jinenji dropped to his knees, groveling. "Please! This is… I know I can… if you—"

A fuchsia wave of light, royal in caliber, gushed from Tazuro's sword to travel the perimeter. Every corpse in the chamber, bones and all, disintegrated.

"Defend yourself, sorcerer."

Debilitating trembles arrested Jinenji.

Tazuro closed in. "Maybe your tricks will save you again."

Jinenji took a risky glance at the window. *Can I make it?*

In his peripheral he saw a silver object carving toward him. Instinct kicked in, killing his trembles. He phased away as Tazuro's sword blasted a scar into the floor.

"You won't get away this time, coward," said the emperor.

Hoping to find an ally, Jinenji looked to Gonenga who scowled at him.

Tazuro smirked. "You have not a single friend, such a pity."

Before he could phase again, Tazuro used his shoulder to ram Jinenji high against the back wall. As

Jinenji slid to the floor, Tazuro dashed at him. The sorcerer stood fast and held up his scepter, a desperate attempt at defense. Although he blocked Tazuro's next sword strike, he could do nothing about its sheer force; it sent him crashing through the wall.

Between all the debris, Jinenji spotted the narrow cliff side below.

I'm going to die. I'm going to die!

With his fingertips, he snagged the bottom of the hole he just created. Disillusionment plunged into his emotional reservoir.

That bastard. I won't take it anymore.

Two hagazo knocking on death's door, a child's voice calling out to them, and Tazuro's amused expression banged around in his skull.

He ruined my life. Jinenji lunged himself up through the hole. "I'll kill you!"

Tazuro waited as Jinenji created a scarlet energy shield and fired it. Without even looking, Tazuro reached a hand out. The shield exploded against it, sending fragments of energy scattering. Not even a scratch appeared on the emperor's open palm.

Fury rumbled within Jinenji, he conjured another shield and fired it. As the shield spiraled at Tazuro, the sorcerer followed close behind it. Repeating his former maneuver, Tazuro shattered the shield.

Thought so.

Jinenji transformed his scepter into a scarlet whip. It slashed through the fog of energy fragments and wrapped around Tazuro's forearm.

The emperor twirled the whip around his forearm, drawing Jinenji closer. With impressive speed, Jinenji returned his scepter to its original form. Scarlet bolts then fired point blank into Tazuro's face.

Got him!

Screaming in pain, Tazuro clutched his face then… stopped. He parted his fingers and glared through them. A gasp escaped Jinenji's lips, the emperor laughed. Not a single sign of damage was present.

"Fuck you!" screamed Jinenji. "You don't deserve all that power, you demon!"

"If I'm a demon then what does that make you?" mocked Tazuro.

"Shut your filthy mouth, you murdering piece of shit."

"Well now, aren't you the epitome of the pot calling the kettle black?"

"You made me do all of this."

"Spare me. You enjoyed every bit of it. You could've stayed here and lived the rest of your days with the humans. Instead, you returned to *me*."

With clenched knuckles, Jinenji pounded away at his temples. "Stop it. Stop!"

Twenty-One years ago:

"Nenj! Nenj!"

A tiny hagazo boy sat cuddled up with his nose deep in the pages of a book.

"Nenj. You don't hear me calling you?" said a young hagazo woman, appearing in the boy's quaint dwelling.

A single lamp shed light on the boy's walls. They were covered with drawings of ginyai wearing robes and wielding staffs. Toys made from twigs stood atop a shelf overflowing with books.

"Sorry, Mom," squealed Nenj, prying his face from a book called: **Analyzing Animals**.

"That's all right. Enjoying your book?"

The woman's yellow eyes peeked from behind white bangs, fixating on the rail thin boy.

"Yup!" said Nenj.

"Well, you're going to have to save the rest for later."

This unusual statement did well to pique Nenj's curiosity.

The hagazo woman beamed. "We're going outside!"

Nenj's energy spiked through the roof. Without hesitation, he dove into his trunk and fetched some warm clothes. Once dressed, he vaulted through the front door. A cavern with a circular foyer accepted him.

"Wait for me," said the woman, putting on her coat.

There was no shortage of doors built into the cavern walls; all unique designs, painted with vibrant colors. Some doors were open, revealing other cozy little homes.

Bats in great number sailed through the air. Their periodic screeching sent echoes bouncing about. A stone bowl in the foyers center brewed a bonfire. Dozens of hagazo congregated around it.

"Come to join us by the fire, Azlin?" asked a hagazo man, warming his hands by the licking flames.

"No!" screamed Nenj before his mother could answer. "We're going outside!"

"Yikes, kid," said the man as he rubbed his ears in annoyance. "What are you, like, five years old?"

"I'm ten!"

"Okay. Okay. Don't have to yell."

The man's boar-like eyes went well with his wide nose, but conflicted with his narrow lips.

"You sure he's not a girl?" asked the man, stroking his blond hair.

Azlin shot him a dirty stare and middle finger combination, but both gestures lacked any genuine conviction.

The man couldn't help but giggle. "You know it's not safe out there. Don't believe the hype."

Azlin paused dead in her tracks, her hair bobbing right below her chin. "Be quiet. The emperor fixed everything. We don't have to hide anymore."

"He's been at it for what… a year? Takes a lot longer than that to create any real change, sweetheart."

"You don't know what you're talking about."

"Come on. You're not really convinced. If you were, your boy would be out there playing every day. Not once every few months."

Azlin squirmed from discomfort. "It takes some getting used to is all."

"All righty, then. Don't come crying to me when your boy gets gobbled up by one of them insect things. Or worse! Gets all his blood sucked out by a damn vamp."

"That's it," said Azlin, her pale gray skin running hot with anger. "I've had it. I'm telling my husband."

"Ooh. I'm shaking." The man laughed and looked around for approval, but none came.

Grabbing Nenj by the wrist, Azlin sped off through the series of caverns that lay before them. Each segment had doors built into the walls, a bonfire lighting the way and hagazo roaming about.

"Mom, I don't want to get gobbled up or have my blood sucked out."

"You won't. Don't listen to him. He's a stupid, stupid man."

A gate stood before them and the snow filled lands beyond. Azlin went through it with Nenj then locked it shut.

Snow drifted from the early evening sky. Wrenching free of his mother's grip, Nenj dashed for it.

"Slow down, Nenj."

Once outside, Nenj found he wasn't the only child present. A little hagazo girl was already busy playing by herself. Nenj stuck his tongue out, catching snowflakes, when a snowball smacked against his arm. Familiar laughter tickled his ears; he looked over to see an excited hagazo man. He had pointy, unassuming features with brown hair that brushed his shoulders.

"Watch out. Here comes another!" yelled the man, his dark gray skin contrasting against the snow.

Nenj bent down to acquire some snow as another frosty projectile nailed his leg.

"Two for two. I'm on a roll," said the man, cheering.

Nenj laughed, retaliating with his very own snowball. Copying Nenj, the little girl hurled snowballs at an older man who stood nearby.

"Stop that. I'm in no mood. You're lucky we're even out here," said the grumpy fellow. "Your mom should be the one out here, since she wants you to see the snow so bad."

Halting in place, Nenj stared at the man in curiosity. Rapid shuffles of snow brought his attention back to Azlin.

"Artem, he's doing it again," she said, stomping toward the brown-haired man.

Artem stopped mid-swing, a frown curving his lips. "Who's doing what now?"

"Davugo! He's harassing me."

"Honey, I told you to ignore him."

"You need to go teach him a lesson."

Dropping his snowball, Artem hugged Azlin. "It's beautiful out here. Can't we just enjoy the moment?"

Azlin's arms dangled at her sides.

"Don't let that guy upset you," said Artem, his hug tightening. "He's a nobody, miserable and alone. That's all. Don't give him any attention."

Halfheartedly, Azlin returned the embrace.

"Look at how much fun Jinenji's having."

Artem glanced at Nenj, but he averted his eyes.

"Hey. Want to play?" said a teeny voice.

Nenj glanced over to see the little girl holding a fat snowball. "Uh, sure."

A snowball fight commenced. The girl's brown pigtails swished as she ran about tossing and dodging. Nenj soon suffered a firm snowball to the nose.

"Hold on," he said, wiping the snow from his eyes.

Another snowball hit his forehead.

"Hey! I said—"

Then another hit his neck. He turned and ducked; receiving several more to the back.

"You kid's play nice!" shouted Azlin.

But the little girl continued vaulting snowballs.

Rage boiled within Nenj as he spotted a stick poking up through the snow. He retrieved it and aimed at the little girl. A single scarlet spark shot out, striking her thigh.

The shriek she released caused her father to come running. "What did you do, you little shit!"

Prickles coursed through Nenj's hand as the stick crumbled to bits.

"We're so sorry, sir. Is she all right?" said Artem as he and Azlin rushed over.

"Get away from us!" The man scooped up his crying daughter and marched back to the cavern. "See! This is why we don't go outside," he barked, brushing his daughter's hair from her face.

Davugo stood at the cavern entrance with a look of complete contempt. "Who would've thought a boy like that would be one of them soul violators."

"I need you to shut your fucking mouth!" said Artem.

"I guess I shouldn't be surprised though. There's almost as many of them as there are of us."

Artem snatched Jinenji by the wrist and pushed past Davugo. Azlin flipped him off once more, this time with conviction.

"Come on, guys. Why the hostility? I just think it would be nice to know when there's one around. You know, for everyone's sake."

Ignoring Davugo, Azlin and Artem rushed Nenj home. As soon as they were inside, they slammed the door and locked every available bolt it had.

Artem stared dead in Nenj's eyes. "Didn't we tell you not to do that in front of anyone else?"

Nenj froze, his mouth agape.

"Go to your room!" shouted Azlin.

"But Mom, I—"

"Go!"

With slumped shoulders, Nenj did just that. Once inside, he cracked his door in order to spy.

"You don't think it's true, do you?" asked Azlin, her voice quivering.

Artem sat on the couch. "How am I supposed to know?" His face buried beneath his hands.

Azlin kept fidgeting with various items she pulled from the fireplace. "It can't be true. Why would they want to take kids?"

"Why do you think?"

"We have to run. We can't stay here."

"Where would we go? We'll die out there in that snow. We don't even know who's loyal to him and who isn't."

"We have to do something," Tears gushed from Azlin's eyes. "I won't let them take my boy."

Artem held Azlin tight and stroked the back of her head. "Relax. They're not taking our son. We'll figure this out, but we can't do much tonight. Let's try and get some rest."

Azlin shook her head. "No! We have to leave now."

"It'll take a while for them to find out. We have time. We'll go first thing in the morning."

Refusing to look her husband in the eyes, Azlin pulled free and ran to a bedroom beside Nenj's room. All night long, Nenj listened to his mother weep and his father tap on the floor with his foot. Unable to get comfortable or turn his brain off, Nenj tossed and turned until day break.

Heavy knocks on the door chased the morning silence away. Nenj rushed into the living room and saw his father bolt up and his mother scurry out of the neighboring bedroom. Neither of them made a move, so Nenj tiptoed to the door.

"Get away from there," said Artem, yanking his son back.

A voice spoke through the door. "Open up. The emperor of the Ginyai Realm demands it."

Azlin shot Artem a look of pure resentment before melting to the floor. Artem crept over and gazed through the peephole.

"If you don't comply, we'll be forced to enter against your will," said the voice.

Azlin's tears returned to drench her cheeks and neck. Artem undid the locks and opened wide enough for those outside to see a sliver of what lay within. Out in the foyer, a kezai woman wearing black armor stood ready. She pushed the door in, hitting Artem in the forehead with it. Three more of her ilk entered as he staggered back. One of which was male. All of which were kezai.

"Bring them to me," said a baritone voice.

The soldiers dragged all three hagazo into the foyer. Tazuro sat atop a long legged, lizard-like creature with winding horns. He looked youthful like aging had yet to notice him. A thick mane covered his head along with a clean-shaven face and slender muscles. As if in defiance of gravity, his horns curved toward the ceiling.

Twenty hagazo were present. All but three watched with worry. The man from the snow and his daughter held cheeky grins. Davugo's glare held a sinister twinkle.

Climbing down from the lizard-like creature, Tazuro approached Nenj. He stood over six feet, making him the tallest ginyai there.

"Is it true what they say about you?"

Nenj looked to his parents who flanked him.

Tazuro placed a finger on Nenj's chin, guiding it back forward. "Don't look at them. They can't help you now."

"You're the so-called '*emperor*' we've all been hearing about? You're just a kid," said Artem in defiance.

"Watch your mouth!" said the male soldier.

With a wave of his hand, the emperor silenced the soldier.

Like a spotlight, Tazuro's gaze found Artem, shredding his confidence. "I don't know how the hagazo do things. But we kezai come of age at fourteen." Tazuro turned his attention back to the reason he came. "Well, is it?"

Nenj nodded slow.

"Let's see it then."

"But I need a stick."

"Stop! Don't show him," screamed Azlin.

Cautious, Nenj turned to his mother.

"Focus on me," said Tazuro with a soothing timbre.

Compiled on a rack below the bonfire were logs of unused fire wood. One of Tazuro's female soldiers fetched a piece. She returned with the thinnest log she could find and handed it to Nenj. After pausing for a moment, he shot a spark at the bonfire. For a split second, the bonfires' flames sizzled scarlet then the log splintered.

Tazuro grinned. "Take him to Rezvan."

"No way! Rezvan. Really?" said Nenj with glee.

Azlin rushed between her son and Tazuro, her tears still streaming. "No! I won't let you have him!"

"It's okay, Mom. I'll learn in the morning and come home in the afternoon. You know, like the institute."

"Not exactly," said Tazuro.

Nenj's glee faded faster than a shadow hit by the sun. Like a feral cat, Azlin lunged at Tazuro.

With ease, Tazuro shoved her to the ground. "Take her away."

A female soldier restrained the scrappy mother.

"Please let them go, sir," said Artem, timid and weak.

The emperor rolled his eyes. "Bring him, too. He can work in the galvantium mines with his wife."

Frightened screams reverberated throughout the caverns as the soldiers hauled the family away.

◆◆◆

Present day:

"You worked my parents to death. They didn't deserve that!"

"Oh, but they did. They resisted the emperor."

Tazuro propelled a beam straight into Jinenji's face, stunning him. He then sent his sword cleaving through the sorcerer's midsection. Viscera wiggled free as his torso detached from his legs. Both halves of Jinenji collapsed to the floor and copious amounts of blood spilled out. Erupting with joyous stamps and stomps, Gonenga rattled the academy.

Tazuro stared at him with a pompous grin. "Still want that rematch?"

Gonenga's intimidating posture staggered.

The emperor couldn't help but chuckle. "Guard the front entrance. I have business to attend to."

Jinenji gurgled, his own blood choking him. *I don't want to die.* He gazed at the nauseating sight. *My body. No, no, no. This isn't happening.*

Tazuro picked Jinenji up by his hair, blood draining from his severed waist.

He slapped the hagazo across the cheek, imitated his voice and moved his mouth like a dummy doll. "Look at me. A poor, insignificant creature who could never measure up." With Jinenji's legs in tow, Tazuro strolled to the back wall. "Well, it's been fun."

Like pieces of garbage, he tossed both parts of the sorcerer through the hole. Despite it all, Jinenji never let go of his scepter.

Battle Beneath the Rain

"Head to your town. My grandparents should still be there." Obake kept a tight grip on Yumo's horn. "Is your dad there right now? We'll need him too."

Yumo didn't so much as make a peep. Obake peeled his eyes from the view ahead and glanced down. His heart took a major plunge. Much like a baby fighting sleep, Yumo's eyelids fluttered.

"Hey! What's wrong?"

Beyond the Yokai Mountains, their altitude dropped a great deal.

Oh, shit!

They descended toward the patchy plane of grass like a loose flag in the wind. Coming inches from colliding with a tree was enough to bring them to a sloppy landing.

"You all right?" asked Obake, dismounting.

Yumo panted and stumbled about like a newborn giraffe.

"Shake it off. We have to keep going. They might be following us."

An array of tall bushes off the beaten path invited them in.

"Come on, hurry."

It took some wrangling, but Obake got Yumo inside where he laid down, his body sprawled out like an uncoiled rope.

"How did you end up like that? You look like the dragon from Zhai Foong."

Despite considerable effort, the excitement in Obake's voice broke through. Yumo threw him a cold glare then continued catching his breath.

I feel bad, but at the same time, he looks so awesome.

Dead katanas, decayed axes and other useless hand-held instruments of war were staked throughout the area.

With a light touch, Obake inspected them. *Just my luck.* Either the weapons were so rusted they resembled tree bark, or they simply crumbled on contact. *There's no way I could wield my soul energy with any of these.*

Growls emanated from Yumo.

Obake wheeled around to him. "Why're you doing that? This isn't the time."

Yumo opened his jaws to growl some more.

Worry flushed the young ninja. "Don't tell me you can't talk anymore."

Yumo tried speaking again, but another stream of raspy growls was all that escaped.

"Okay, okay. Think," muttered Obake, pacing about. "My grandparents will know what to do."

With one claw, Yumo scratched into a patch of dirt. His message read: "What if we lead the monsters to Dotam?"

"That's a good point." Taking a careful peek from behind the bushes, Obake watched for pursuers. *Nothing.*

He then looked toward his home. The now distant Yokai Mountains showed no signs of activity.

"Looks like the coast is clear. I think we can make it. My grandparents might know how to turn you back to normal too."

Yumo shook his head fast.

Obake scoffed. "They may not look like much, but they're tough."

Scratching recommenced, Obake pretended not to notice.

"We're going to need all the help we can get. We have to kill those things. I mean, did you see them?" Obake shuddered as Tazuro's image flashed in mind's eye.

"Especially the big guy with the horns, we're going to need a lot of help with him."

Yumo's new message read: "We can't beat them. Let's just warn everybody and run while we still can."

His words and depressing demeanor conjured dread into the atmosphere.

"No. You're acting like a coward. I bet my dad wouldn't run. He'd be the first to fight." Hope and pride carried Obake's words. "You want to run, that's fine, but I'm going back."

Yet again, Yumo scratched into the dirt, his final message read: "Good luck, then."

Obake scowled, but not for long. A terrifying thought came crashing in. *Wait. That damn gray monster knows where I live. I have to find my nana and papa before they go back home.*

The urge to sprint came over him as a trumpet-like noise rose from behind. He and Yumo turned to see a long, purple diamond floating in midair. It transformed into a large hexagon of purple energy; Ventama and the little goblin girl exited from it.

A mix of shock and awe burst from Obake as he withdrew several feet. *What the—!*

In a seated position, the little goblin girl bounced atop her metal ball. "Hi! I'm Kalida. Want to play?"

"Yumo, back up!"

Kalida stared at Yumo in an inquisitive manner as he followed Obake's instruction.

"Listen. O-Obake, is it?" said the centaur, extending a polite hand. "Name's Ventama." His hexagonal chest plate swirled with the same purple energy as the portal. "Let's make this easier on everybody. Just come along quietly."

Obake didn't reciprocate.

With a sigh, Ventama lowered his hand. "We need that lizard… that uh… bird thing."

Yumo flinched.

"I don't know what the boss has planned for him, but I do know this. He's not going to hurt him."

Kalida glared at Ventama. "Yes, he is. It's not nice to lie, mister."

Ventama gritted his teeth. "Don't listen to her. She has no idea what she's talking about."

"Yes, I do. Gosh." Kalida stuck out her tongue then stood up, bouncing higher and higher.

With a roll of the eyes, Ventama continued. "I want to get this over with so I can get back home. Mind helping me out?"

"Fuck off, horse boy," Obake spoke with the utmost of aggression. "He's not going anywhere with you."

Ventama's lips wound tight. "Just remember, I didn't want to do this."

The centaur's fury filled gallop left the friends with a single recourse.

"Run!" screamed Obake.

Yumo's stumbling subsided so Obake hopped onto him. Instead of taking to the sky, they hovered mere inches from the ground.

With Kalida in tow, Ventama jumped on their heels. Another diamond blasted from his chest plate. Spiraling forward, it hit the air behind Yumo and transformed into a portal. Ventama galloped into it and vanished.

Obake and Yumo screeched to a halt as another diamond formed into a portal in front of them. It unleashed a charging Ventama, forcing Yumo to spin around. He didn't get far before a hand seized his tail. Like a whip, the centaur snapped the friends to the ground.

"My turn. My turn." Hands outstretched, Kalida rolled in fast. "Ba boom!"

Two geysers of dirt lifted into the air. They then morphed into hands the size of boulders. Before Obake and Yumo could process what happened, they were already caught in Kalida's surreal ability.

"Got you!" Kalida stuck her tongue out again, this time flicking saliva from it.

The friends struggled, making the dirt hands squeeze tighter.

"Not bad. You're not as useless as I thought you'd be," said Ventama.

"You're useless!" Kalida stamped her foot. "I used to want a pony, but not anymore!"

Ventama let a chuckle slip.

"Uh, boss. Those don't look like bandits."

Five dumbstruck men in yellow armor stood within the array of tall bushes.

Dotam Guards. Yes! Obake waved at the men. "Help! They're here to kill us all!"

Yumo spoke too, but once again, nothing but roars and unintelligible sounds came out.

"Son of a bitch, just my luck," said Ventama, face palming hard.

"What are they?" asked a guard with bright red hair.

"I think they're… monsters," said a balding guard, gripping his dropped jaw.

A hairy guard pointed at Obake. "Why's that kid squirming like that?"

"Are we on drugs? I don't remember taking any drugs," said a skinny guard.

A bearded guard stepped forward. "This isn't drugs, boys. Whatever this is, it's much worse."

"Dammit guys. I have to kill you now. You know that, right?" said Ventama with agitation.

"It speaks!" gasped the hairy guard.

Kalida rolled around in circles, singing an ominous little tune. "He's going to kill you. He's going to kill you."

"You hear that, boys? Looks like it's do or die," bellowed the bearded guard.

Ventama locked eyes with Kalida and she skidded to a halt. "Whatever you do, don't let them escape. I'll take care of these idiots."

Galloping straight ahead, Ventama made way for his new foes. Each of the men brandished swords and charged with accompanying battle cries. Ventama plowed through the first four as if they were made of paper. The bearded guard stood his ground, striking as Ventama got close. Using no effort, the centaur guided the striking sword away. He then latched onto the bearded guard's throat and choke slammed him.

I have to help them.

As Ventama prepared to stomp on the bearded guard, the redhead grabbed his neck from the rear. Taking advantage of the distraction, the skinny guard snuck up to the side of Ventama's hind legs.

"Get off me," grunted Ventama.

The redhead aimed to stab Ventama through the back, but got yanked off and throttled to the ground instead.

"No!" shouted the skinny guard, proceeding to stab Ventama's hind legs again and again.

"Bastard!" growled Ventama.

Using the redhead's crushed body, Ventama swatted the skinny guard. On impact, the force snapped the skinny guard's spine. Next came the hairy guard, he dashed in with a sword thrust. To his surprise, a jade broadsword jutted from the portal on Ventama's chest plate. It split the hairy guards head wide open.

"Sorry, pal," said Ventama, his broadsword burrowing back inside his chest plate.

The bald guard charged like a feral boar. "Die!"

"No. Don't!" said the bearded guard, but his concern fell on deaf ears.

Ventama dodged the bald guard's unrefined attacks then delivered an elbow to the top of his head.

"I won't… give up," said the bald guard, trying to remain upright.

The centaur seized him. "You have heart. It'll be an honor to give you a warrior's death."

A diamond shot up to the sky to form another portal. As if the bald guard were a mere rock, Ventama threw him at the portal. Once the bald guard's head disappeared, the portal cinched shut. His body plummeted, staining the green grass a deep red. Blood rained on the bearded guard's shoulders. He gazed up to see the bald guard's head falling from a different portal. Utter horror appeared on his face.

Distraught, he tossed the head aside. "You call that honor? You disgusting bastard!"

With his sword in hand, the bearded guard beelined for his opponent. Ventama crafted a portal then kicked into it with his hind legs. Another portal appeared alongside the bearded guard, releasing Ventama's legs into the side of his head. The light in the bearded guard's eyes extinguished as he toppled to his death.

This is insane. Maybe we can't win.

With an unsatisfied look about him, Ventama trotted toward Obake and the others.

No, no. He's coming back. Obake fixated on Kalida. "Hey! Little girl. Let us go."

Kalida made a funny face. "No way, he's having all the fun. I want to play some more, too."

With outstretched arms, Kalida commanded the dirt hands. They obeyed, crashing down palms first; the fingers then spread out like the bars of a cage.

Obake executed a series of punches and kicks, but the hand remained strong. "Let me go, you little demon!"

He glanced over to see Yumo biting and tail thrashing; his efforts also failed.

Kalida's voice called out. "Ba boom!"

The dirt hands transformed into giant spiders with ten legs each.

Color drained from Obake's face; he panicked and looked to his dragon friend. "Help me!"

Yumo focused on dodging his spider's venom. Each successful dodge sent the venom spilling onto the grass. To Obake's surprise, not a single blade of grass sustained damage.

What? How's that possible?

The strange occurrence made his panic subside. As he scrutinized the grass, a blazing inferno spewed from Yumo's jaws. With a shriek, Yumo's spider disintegrated into wisps of nothingness.

"Yes!" screamed Obake.

Feeling confident, Obake looked back at his spider; the mere sight of it re-induced panic. He flailed, but Yumo's flames doused it as well. Although engulfed in fire, the spider leapt away to spin webs at them. One web hit Yumo square in the mouth, gluing it shut. Obake dodged the few webs that came his way then closed the gap between him and the spider. Once within reach, he jumped and pounded on the insect with both feet.

"Hey! No fair," squealed Kalida.

Obake continued stomping until the spider's head became nothing more than a puddle of blood.

"Disgusting," said Obake, cringing.

In an instant, Kalida threw a temper tantrum, jumping, punching and kicking at the air.

Obake raised an eyebrow. "You know this is a fight, right?"

"Go ahead and tag me in, kid," said Ventama who was standing a few feet away.

"No, hush. I have an idea. Ba boom!"

The dead spider twitched back to life. Its mangled head opened at the mouth, giving way for a distorted version of Obake's face.

"What the fuck!" screamed Obake.

On a tube-like neck, the face slithered forward and opened wide. Decomposing yellow fangs lashed out, sinking into Obake's shoulder. It lifted him through the sky, he punched like rapid fire, but that did little to faze the horrifying creature. Sounds of shredding webs soon arrived, followed by Yumo's flames. They slashed and burned until the creature vanquished. Upon dropping back to the ground, Obake gazed at his shoulder in astonishment. Like before, there wasn't a single sign of damage.

Another tantrum sprang from Kalida, which resulted in her tumbling from her ball. "No, no, no! You... ah, you ass wipes!"

Obake jumped onto Yumo's back and they lifted off.

"No, you don't!" Ventama swiped for Yumo's tail, but missed. "Dammit!"

The friends soared again until a portal appeared above to swallow them whole. They coiled like a screw through a tunnel of purple dimensional energy.

What's happening!

Grass, trees, and other familiar scents found Obake as he and Yumo dropped from the portal. He welcomed the hard ground against his weary body. The trumpet sound above faded, and the spinning subsided.

It didn't take long for Obake to recognize the new surroundings. "Taulon Falls? What are we doing way up here?"

Obake peered from the mountain to the area he just came from. The deceased Dotam Guards were all that remained. A rhythm of cascading water drew Obake's attention. Looming over a five-foot ridge was a beautiful waterfall.

◆◆◆

Two months ago:

Obake wrapped Meilana in his arms as they admired Taulon Falls and all its glory. Vibrant stars illuminated the night sky while the waterfall played a tranquil melody.

"I'll admit it. You were right. This is kind of nice," said Obake.

"See. I told you."

"When you said you wanted to have a picnic, I wanted to jump off a cliff, but I'm glad I didn't."

"Hey!" said Meilana, elbowing Obake in the ribs in playful fashion.

He feigned a wince then held Meilana tighter.

She snuggled her head into the curve of his neck. "I love the night. It's my favorite, so calm and relaxing. I can let all my problems go," Meilana looked into her boyfriend's eyes. "What about you?"

"What about me?"

"Your favorite time of day, dork. What is it?"

"I never thought about it. Anytime is fine with me."

Obake's nose hovered above Meilana's head. Freshly bloomed flowers sprang to mind as he harvested the scent of her hair.

"The daytime is so hectic, so much noise, so many people, everyone expecting you to do this and do that. It's nice being left alone for a while."

"Yeah, but without the day, how could you know to appreciate the night?"

"Hmm, you have a point. I'll give you that."

"Can't give me what I already have."

"And what's that?"

"Common sense," Obake laughed. "Something you need to get."

A gasp left Meilana's lips, she delivered another playful elbow.

"Ow, that one hurt."

"That's what you get."

Meilana reached across the furry blanket beneath them to a wicker basket. Inside, a pouch begged to be apprehended. She conceded to its desire. Within the pouch nestled green candies shaped like tear drops. She tossed three in her mouth and hummed with satisfaction.

"Again with the Sweet Drops? I'm going to laugh when all your teeth fall out."

Pure lust flooded Meilana's eyes. "No way, I need to stay sexy for my man." She offered Obake some Sweet

Drops. "They're your favorite color."

"Green is not my favorite color."

Like a seductress, Meilana placed a Sweet Drop through Obake's lips.

"If you have to know, my favorite color is pink."

"No way?" asked Meilana in doubt.

"What can I say? I like flamingos."

"You're full of surprises, aren't you?"

Present day:

A frustrated Ventama and Kalida came sprinting out of another purple portal.

"I advise you both to stop resisting," said Ventama, brushing the dirt and grass with his hoof.

"Yeah, this isn't fun anymore so stop!" said Kalida, her salamander-orange skin turning bright red around the cheeks.

Distant lightning came to cut the sky, thunder clapped, gray clouds huddled and cold rain soaked Taulon Falls.

Obake leapt onto Yumo. "Sorry, but no can do."

They flew off past the ridge and up a boulder laden trail. The rain turned the hard dirt into slick mud in no time flat. Ventama kept losing his footing and Kalida's metal ball got snagged more than once. A suitable gap developed between the opposing pairs. The waterfall drew ever closer, so did the rambunctious voices of several unknowns.

"How much do you think we could get for all this?"

"Quite a bit, I'd say."

"We'll be sitting pretty, boys. More money than any of us has ever had."

"I'm going to buy so many whores."

Sitting in the natural pool beneath the waterfall were eight dirty and disheveled bandits. Each of them wore thigh high bathing shorts. An assortment of jewelry, weapons, and clothing laid out on the pool's edge. One bandit spotted the boys then did a double take.

"What is that?" he shouted, jumping to his feet.

His companions displayed the same reaction upon seeing Yumo. They raced to their weapons, half of them retrieving pistols, the other half crossbows. A portal came into existence, releasing Ventama and Kalida. All of the bandits took turns screaming in fright.

"Isn't this fantastic?" grumbled Ventama with another face palm.

"They sent monsters after us this time!" said one of the bandits.

"I'm never robbing Dotam again," said another.

A trigger-happy bandit fired his pistol. Diamonds vacated Ventama's chest plate and collided with the bullets, nullifying them. Another bandit fired crossbow arrows at Kalida. She ducked behind her ball. Projectiles went for Obake and Yumo too. They ran for cover behind the biggest boulder they could find.

Ventama caught the next round of bullets and arrows with his chest plate portal. Another portal appeared behind two of the bandits, their own projectiles released into them and they died in a hurry.

Kalida kicked her metal ball. "Ugly, nasty, snot faces." It ricocheted between three of the bandits then bounced back to her. Each of the bandits dropped dead. "I'm so cool."

Rearing onto his hind legs, Ventama fired a diamond high into the sky. It halted, spun for a bit, then shattered into hundreds of shards that showered the remaining three bandits. Throats sliced open, heads got stabbed and bodies got shredded. The shards soon dissolved into fading energy particles.

Shards rained on Obake and Yumo as well, but flames from Yumo's jaws took care of them.

"I love it when you do that," said Obake, pumping his fist.

Yumo smiled bright with his new sharp teeth.

Obake threw an arm around his neck. "I think I like you better this way."

Like glass dropping on solid ground, Yumo's smile shattered. Obake couldn't resist a snicker.

"I know you and your lizard friend are over there. Come on out so we can finish this," said Ventama.

Clamming up, Yumo shrank into the mud like a worm.

Obake's eyes pierced into his friend's very soul. "You got this. You took care of that bear, remember? What's a horse and a little kid going to do?"

Possibilities turned behind Yumo's eyes like the cogs of a clock tower.

"Besides, you're a dragon now." continued Obake.

With a chest puff and a muscle flex, Yumo held his head high. After nodding to one another, the friends emerged on either side of the boulder.

Ventama mustered his breath. "I gave you two so many chances to surrender, now I'm pissed. No more Mr. Nice Guy."

"Oh, excuse me. I'm sorry for not wanting to get kidnapped by a pair of random monsters," said Obake.

Kalida sneered, as did Ventama.

The young ninja glanced over at his friend. "All right, you take the horse guy and I'll—"

Yumo shook his head.

"What? You're literally breathing fire," said Obake. Irritation found Yumo.

"Come on. I can't use my soul energy right now. I don't have a conduit," said Obake.

At last, Yumo conceded. With no time to waste, Ventama seized the moment. His chest plate became a vortex, pulling his opponents closer. Utilizing all four legs, Yumo anchored himself to the ground. Obake anchored as well, but the vortex pulled him along anyway. Yumo chomped down on Obake's back collar, but the force ripped the collar apart.

Flying through the air, Obake plunged headfirst into Ventama's chest plate, his body contorting like a wound-up towel. The familiar purple tunnel carried the ninja away. This time however, he averted most of the portal's discombobulating effects. Down range, he spotted the jade broadsword floating in place. Its minor patches of rust spoke of a seasoned weapon that had seen countless battles. As he passed by, he went for it, but couldn't reach. Before long he went tumbling back into his own dimension, but his body didn't reconvene with the grass. Four portals surrounded him, each one a vortex, all pulling together in unison. Agonizing pain flared throughout his entire being.

He's trying to tear me apart!

Acting fast, Yumo soared over to provide aid, but Kalida's metal ball almost decapitated him. In retaliation, Yumo locked onto her and spewed fireballs. Her tiny stature made dodging the fireballs a breeze. Like a boomerang, the metal ball curved, returning to Kalida. It smashed into Yumo, knocking him into the natural pool.

Obake struggled against the vortexes as Ventama burst from the left side portal. He punched the ninja across the cheek then entered the portal on the right. Obake then heard him re-emerge from the rear portal. A sharp punch then crammed into his back. Ventama galloped past Obake then vanished into the portal at the front.

Calming his senses, Obake waited for any sign of Ventama's impending return. *Where are you? Where are— there!*

As Ventama barreled back through the front portal, Obake kicked him in the face, dead center. Each vortex dispersed. Incessant vibrations raced about Obake's body, but he stood tall regardless.

"I don't believe it," said an awe-struck Ventama.

The jade broadsword's handle jutted from Ventama's chest plate. He grabbed hold and yanked it out into the open.

"What's with you monsters and pulling weapons on the weaponless?" said Obake, assuming his combat stance.

Ventama responded with attacks, he slashed from every angle imaginable. In spite of its size, the broadsword powered through the air with ease. It even cut the trees and boulders unlucky enough to be in the way when Obake dodged.

I'm so screwed if he hits me with that thing.

A few glances from Obake fell on the natural pool; he discovered Kalida rolling back and forth on the edge of it. She appeared to be looking for the dragon as well.

"A little help here!" screamed Obake after dodging another deadly strike.

His scream drew Kalida's attention.

Oh, great.

As if a bomb detonated, Yumo exploded from the pool, catching everyone by surprise. Kalida tried to react, but Yumo's teeth ravaged her. He slung her around by the arm then threw her into the bushes. Bolting ahead, he hurled three fireballs at Ventama who knocked them away with his broadsword. Two diamonds then blasted at the ever-approaching Yumo. After dodging the diamonds, Yumo released a stream of flames. Ventama split the scorching blaze down the middle with his broadsword. It raged on either side of his body, failing to make contact. As the flames dissipated, Yumo slid past the broadsword. With scissor grip jaws, he clamped onto Ventama's neck, wrapped his body around him and squeezed.

The jade weapon plummeted from the centaur's hand. Obake raced to retrieve it as Kalida rolled up, covered in blood.

She stomped and screamed the entire way. "Stupid bird-lizard. I'm going to squash you! Ba boom!"

Two nearby trees morphed into one eyed cobras that stood fifteen feet tall. One slithered up to gape wide over

Obake and the other did so over Yumo and Ventama. A surprised Yumo loosened his grip.

"It isn't real. Don't let go!" screamed Obake.

Yumo pondered for a second then reapplied pressure.

"Don't eat me! Don't— let me go!" shrieked Ventama, gazing wide at the cobra.

Despite his brain's incessant pleas to do otherwise, Obake ignored the serpent. Both cobras swallowed their prey whole, but no pain followed. Obake opened his eyes to see the serpents had turned into wisps of nothingness.

Kalida became so upset she jumped from her ball to cry in the fetal position. "No, no, no!"

The centaur came back to his senses. "What? I thought I was…"

Rage induced shouts boomed from the centaur as he expanded his arms. Getting a hand free, he seized the dragon and began prying him loose. Yumo sank his teeth deeper.

"Get off!" roared Ventama.

He hammered Yumo's head, rendering him unconscious. Like a sopping wet noodle, the dragon went limp. Ventama clutched his tail then started to spin.

Preparing to swing the broadsword at his foe's legs, Obake dashed ahead. "Leave him alone!"

Yumo's body unraveled, slicing through rain like the blades of a propeller. A clang of metal stung Obake's ears.

"Take this!" yelled Kalida.

He paused in time to catch Kalida's ball hurdling at him. Assisted by every ounce of his strength, Obake slashed the ball, returning it. Kalida's scream rivaled the thunder as the ball struck her off the mountaintop. Obake dashed again, but Ventama dealt Yumo the same fate as Kalida.

Dread clutched Obake as he watched. "No!"

Ventama pivoted then sped close to Obake, attempting to reacquire his broadsword. Obake pulled away and suffered a strike that sent him skidding across the muddy grass. Another diamond went airborne then shattered, sending shards to carpet bomb the summit. Using the broadsword like an umbrella, Obake shielded himself. While the shards repelled, he advanced.

Spurts of Shadow Cloud emerged from the ninja, but they declined to teleport him. *Why? I thought I had this under control.*

Off to Ventama's right, a portal formed, and he shoved a fist into it. The attack materialized from another portal in front of Obake. Broadsword still overhead, Obake twisted and cut Ventama's fist. As the centaur yanked his bleeding hand away, Obake jumped inside the portal. Ventama's eyes bulged as Obake burst from the portal.

With one succinct motion, Obake drove the broadsword into Ventama's abdomen. Blood gushed and the purple matter within the chest plate dispersed into particles.

All four of the centaur's horse legs buckled. "Dammit… kid."

Obake let go of the broadsword, causing Ventama to drop. When the hilt slammed into the grass, the blade cut all the way through, even past Ventama's spine. Like an overflow, blood spilled over Ventama's bottom lip, and his eyes glazed over.

Why do I feel so bad about this? I felt worse with the samurai, but still. I don't get it. Are warriors supposed to feel this way?

As rain splashed and lightning painted the sky, Obake vaulted down Taulon Falls to find his best friend.

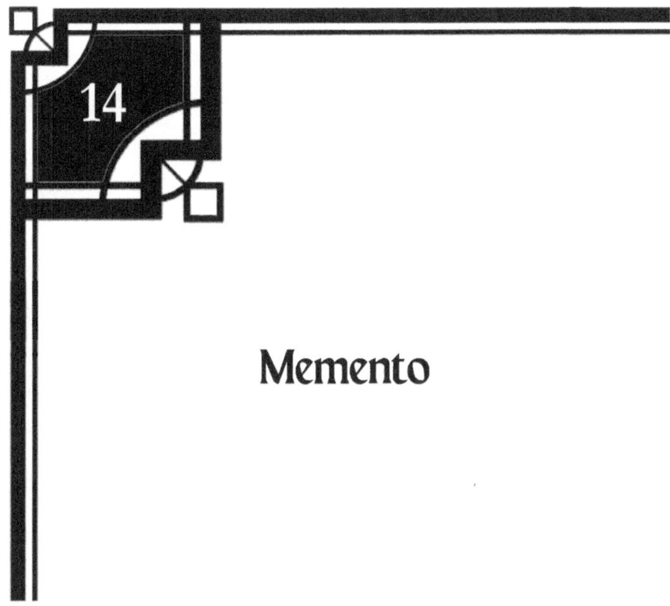

Memento

The rain showed no signs of letting up, instead it intensified with each passing moment.

Obake's agile movements departed, replaced with frantic slipping and tripping. "Yumo! Where are you?"

The mud oozing along the mountainside blanketed him whenever he fell. *Come on. Get up.*

Every few feet of his descent came with an examination of the vicinity.

His gut wrenched tighter each time he saw nothing. *You have to be around here somewhere.*

Soon enough, he felt thin metal smack against his zori sandal. Yumo's Stinger key went tumbling away.

He chased after it like it were a puppy leading him somewhere. After its brief display of acrobatics, the key became stuck in the mud accumulating at the base of the mountain. Obake fetched it then held it to the sky for a wash. Once devoid of mud, he put it around his neck and resumed.

"Ba boom!"

Kalida's voice soared between the splashing rain, whistling wind and clapping thunder. Tracing its source, Obake found the little goblin girl behind him on the mountainside.

She stood atop her now gashed up metal ball, huffing and puffing like an exhausted chimney. "Watch out, mud face."

Boulders wedged into the mountainside came barreling down.

Instinct took over. Obake made a run for it, but reconsidered before long. *It's not real. It's not real.*

He stood in complete defiance, waiting for the massive objects to pass. As expected, the boulders rolled right through him and vanished.

Obake smirked. "Your little tricks won't work anymore."

"I hate you!" screamed Kalida as she vaulted from the mountainside and rolled away.

The young ninja gave chase until he stumbled upon a trail of bloody feathers. He tracked them until his eyes fell upon Yumo who was laid out like a discarded strand of hair. Bruises and lacerations covered every inch of his body. Most of his feathers had fled and his tail was bent like a metal pipe. Several claws were missing and his tongue dangled from his gaping mouth.

Paralyzed by terror, Obake's eyes widened as far as they could go. His legs quivered, suddenly incapable of supporting his weight. Blood and rain water splashed as he collapsed next to his friend. Tears flowed so much they outpaced the rain.

Obake hesitated to check for a pulse, afraid to confirm what he feared most. "Get up. Get up. Stop playing around!" He applied pressure to the worst of Yumo's lacerations, but blood still seeped between his fingers. "Don't do this, please. Don't do this to me." Compressions came next, but when that failed, he pulled the dragon into his arms. *Please don't be…* He checked Yumo's neck for a pulse, no pulse arose. *I don't believe it. I can't.* Obake removed rainwater from Yumo's glassy stare. "Look. I got your Stinger key. I got it right here."

The key dangled in front of Yumo's face. Obake imagined him springing back to life then reverting to his original form. He imagined him grabbing the key then running off to find his motorcycle. Unfortunately, Obake's imagination proved too weak to defeat reality. The icy patron of death had his friend and wouldn't dream of letting go.

Obake laid his friend down. "I shouldn't have convinced you to fight. This is all my fault."

Tears didn't let up, even as he dug into the mud with his bare hands. His muscles burned, his fingers throbbed, but he didn't dare abate. Twenty minutes later, a shallow ditch big enough for a fire-breathing dragon was born. He picked up his friend and placed him inside. Pangs struck his stomach as if a butcher knife were gouging it open. After placing a sizable rock at the head of the grave, Obake inscribed: **Here lies Yumo, the greatest dragon of them all.** In that very moment, a piece of Obake died. Standing over the grave, sweaty, wet and dirty… he said his goodbyes.

"I'll miss you, Yumo. You'll always be like a brother to me."

Those responsible flashed in Obake's mind. Ventama's death no longer bothered him.

Overtaken by rage, he began a feverish search. *Where is she? I'll kill her too!*

Despite his efforts, Kalida was nowhere to be found, leaving Obake no choice but to abstain. Parting with Yumo proved to be the hardest of tasks. Obake kept glancing back until the grave became too distant to see. Setting his sights on the Yokai Mountains, he suppressed the anger attempting to gain dominance within him.

Thoughts of his grandparents helped to keep the anger at bay. *They have to be home by now. I have to tell them what's going on. I can't let this happen to anyone else.*

Without further contemplation, Obake raced home with Yumo's Stinger key swinging from his neck.

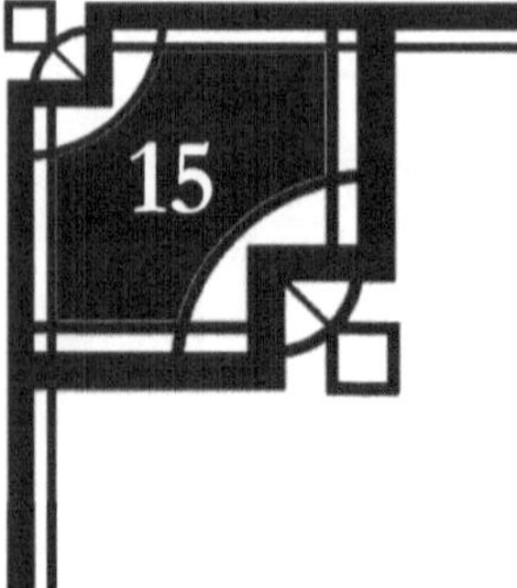

An Old Friend

Yokai resembled a pack mule while trekking up the slippery mountain, a wooden box strapped to his back.

Bao tapped at his heels with her hidden kodachi. "Faster, faster."

"If you don't stop that right now…" said Yokai.

"Relax, you grouch. I'm only kidding."

"How about you take it the rest of the way then, huh?"

"I would, but we're already here."

A sigh of relief left Yokai as he reached the top stairs of the trail. "I think I'm going to pass out."

He accelerated the rest of the way to his cottage and sank onto the porch. After peeling the straps of the wooden box off his shoulders, it crashed down.

"See, that's why I like to carry the box first. Hiking is usually hardest near the end," said Bao.

Yokai rolled his eyes then opened the wooden box, grumbling and muttering to himself.

Bao lit a cigarette then took a long drag. "Don't stress. We'll get by. We always do."

"You don't see the way those damn bank tellers look at me."

"Don't let it get to you."

"I don't understand. We used to find it hard to keep stocked, but now—"

Catching a whiff of tobacco. Yokai shot Bao an angry look.

She flicked the cigarette out into the slowing rain. "Fine, I'll do it when you're not around, like always."

With slouched shoulders, Yokai walked inside. "People used to love our medicine."

"Well, we didn't have to deal with Genopai before," said Bao, following him. "All those miles away and they're still able to keep up with Dotam's demand. We can't compete."

Yokai waved the statement off as if it were a pesky mosquito.

Bao aimed a finger to the sky. "I know. We could start selling puapo. It'll give us an edge, might even make us rich."

"Not a chance. That belongs to the Yokai Clan, no one else."

"Okay, then. How about this? Let's reconsider moving to Genopai. It'll be better for us, especially Obake. He needs the opportunities."

Yokai stopped in the middle of the living room, rubbing his forehead. "Not this again. This is our home, Bao-Ang."

"We live next to death and decay."

Yokai turned his back.

"Be reasonable, we could—"

"I won't leave my son!"

Bao slammed her fist against the wall. "Our son is gone! I loved him more than anything, but you have to accept that."

Despite the commotion, Yokai didn't turn around.

"We still have a chance to make things better for our grandson. If not for me, do it for him."

"I said no. Not another word."

Tears of frustration spilled onto Bao's cheeks as she rushed outside.

"Wait. Come back," said Yokai, now turning around.

Bao made an abrupt stop on the porch, frozen like an ice sculpture. *He's here!*

Her heart skittered about inside of her chest.

Escorted by shock and fear, Yokai arrived behind his wife. "It's him!"

Tazuro sat on a small boulder in the middle of the grassy field. His Spider Throne immobile beside him. He fixated on a sliver of rock, twirling it between his fingers.

Yokai pushed past his wife. "Get behind me."

With the utmost of caution, Yokai stepped down the stairs.

"It's a shame. A fine couple such as yourselves squabbling over trivialities." The emperor tossed up the sliver of rock and caught it. "How long has it been since we last spoke? Sixteen, seventeen years?"

"You made a big mistake coming here," spat Yokai.

Drawing her blade from its scabbard, Bao descended the stairs as well.

"Time really does fly," said Tazuro, tossing and catching the sliver of rock once more.

"You'll suffer for what you did to my boy," said Yokai, clenching his fists.

Tazuro feigned surprise. "I'm hurt. Is that anyway to greet an old friend?"

"I'll mount your disgusting head on a spike," said Bao through gritted teeth.

"Ah, Bao-Ang. I missed that fiery personality of yours."

Tazuro tossed the sliver again, but let it drop to the grass this time.

Rising to his feet, he cracked his knuckles. "You know, out of all the humans, I think I like you best."

Yokai opened a secret compartment in the wooden medicine box and fetched his claws.

The emperor approached his throne. "Can you believe there were times when I thought I'd be a failure for the rest of my life?"

"Your life won't last much longer," retorted Bao.

Unperturbed, Tazuro released his sword. "My dear sweet woman, you couldn't be more wrong."

Fueled by revenge, Bao and Yokai inched closer, striking distance was imminent.

"By the way," A smile crept its way onto Tazuro's lips. "Don't bother worrying about that grandson of yours. He's more than likely dead by now."

Fury gripped the elder ninjas. They launched an all-out assault. Yokai went for the gut, but his attack got deflected. Bao performed a high flip, slashing at the scalp. This too got deflected.

"Your son did it better." Tazuro laughed, his deflection sending Bao flipping over his head.

The claws returned, this time aiming for the neck. As Bao landed, she sent a kodachi slash at the ankles. Leaping high, Tazuro dodged both moves then stabbed the grassy field. Fuchsia waves of royal light burst forth in all directions. Both of the elder ninjas went tumbling about. Scrapping to a stop, Bao ended up on all fours. Yokai rolled a few times before springing back to his feet. Straight from Bao's voice came a potent scream. Tazuro became trapped within its sonic wave.

"Not bad," said Tazuro.

A purple bog bomb generated in Yokai's hand. A beam of light generated in Tazuro's. As Yokai's bomb grew, Tazuro fired. His projectile broke through Bao's sonic wave with little trouble.

Yokai looked to his wife. "Watch out!"

Without breaking her scream, Bao dodged the beam of light. *Oh no.*

The emperor's sword spiraled through the air, aiming for Bao as well. It stabbed the ground beside her feet, silencing the scream.

"Dammit!" barked Yokai, seething from anger, he hurled his bomb.

Dashing away from the threat, Tazuro made a sharp turn. Like a homing missile, the bog bomb tracked him to deliver a direct hit. Purple, blazing flames engulfed the emperor. Streams of smoke billowed from his body while he crashed onto his backside.

Bao's face lit with relief, then uncertainty. "Did we win? Is he—"

"No time. Go!" screamed Yokai.

Like a pair of lions who hadn't seen a meal in days, they pounced. As their blades were set to pierce Tazuro, he sprang up, kicking them both. Clutching their abdomens, the elder ninjas scrambled away.

"Aww, you two okay?" asked Tazuro with delight.

"Don't get cocky, asshole. You haven't won yet," yelled Bao, a slim stream of blood trickling down her chin.

"We're just getting started," grunted Yokai.

Tazuro's cape swooped and flapped as he strutted over to reclaim his sword. "I'm impressed, but you two couldn't beat me then. You think you can beat me now?" Drawing the blade loose from the ground, he held it out to be examined. "I can't wait to slice through your decrepit bodies."

One swift motion later and two speeding beams of light set aim for Yokai and Bao. They both dodged and returned fire. By avoiding a sonic scream and knocking aside a bog bomb, Tazuro came out unscathed.

"I wonder how you'll manage this," said Tazuro, releasing a fearsome blast that tore across the field.

"Hurry!" bellowed Bao in terror.

Yokai leapt onto his wife's back. The blast was primed to sweep them away, but Bao's intonation levitated them to safety. Their cottage however, was not so lucky. The blast demolished the entire living room.

"Our home!" yelled the elder ninjas in unison.

Seeing half her home in shambles elicited a whirlwind of emotion in Bao. *He's taken everything from us.*

"He has to die!" roared Yokai.

Bao soared over the emperor and Yokai dropped a hundred explosive bog pellets.

"Haven't dusted off those old bones in a while, I see," said Tazuro, proving much too fast for the payload.

Bao circled around, attempting to shred Tazuro with the same scream that kept her and her husband afloat. Sonic waves burrowed deep trenches as the elusive ginyai jumped to safety over and over. Making a sudden vertical loop, Bao caught the emperor off guard. He narrowly escaped the next set of pellets that erupted in his vicinity.

"Almost got me that time," gloated Tazuro, putting out a few embers on his forearm.

Clouds met Bao as she flew higher, giving Yokai time to craft his biggest bog bomb yet. It sloshed and warped until it matched a giant pumpkin in size.

Yokai heaved the bomb with expert accuracy. "Let's see you get out of this one!"

The bomb descended upon Tazuro with high speed. *It's going to hit.*

A devious grin came over Tazuro's mouth as he shot the bomb with a beam of light. It dispersed into dozens of smaller homing bog bombs. Flickers of concern replaced Tazuro's devious grin. His sword went to task, slashing the bombs to smithereens. Despite the emperor's defenses, several homing bombs slipped through. As they detonated, a billowing cloud of sizzling smoke consumed him. To survey the damage, Bao and Yokai made a landing.

Acting fast, Tazuro burst through the smoke. With his sword extended, he spun into a powerful overhead strike. Yokai's block saved not only his own life, but Bao's as well. He countered with a swift kick to Tazuro's chest, but before he could pull his foot away, Tazuro seized it.

No. He's got him!

Bao's kodachi flew in, it missed, but her follow up elbow scored a strike to Tazuro's head.

The emperor dropped his sword. "That's it," He seized Bao's arm. "That's how you're supposed to fight."

With minimal exertion he lifted then slammed Bao aside.

"Stop it!" said Yokai.

A fierce punt from Tazuro sent Yokai gliding through the pull-up bar and his bedroom wall. Photos hidden below the floorboards went airborne as Yokai broke through the floor. They fluttered and swooped around like baby birds having just learned flight. All the while, a broken portion of the pull-up bar rolled to a stop at Tazuro's feet.

Inhaling along the way, Bao staggered upright. Before a peep could escape her vocals, Tazuro snatched her by the neck. Caught in a frenzy, Bao scraped and clawed at Tazuro's hand.

Harsh and unsettling wheezes dripped from her mouth. "Help… me."

Tazuro squeezed her neck tighter then lifted her off the ground. Her feet kicked like a swimmer ascending from great depths.

Bao's vision went hazy and the surrounding sounds muted. "I… I love you, Yokai."

Scrambling like a mad man, Yokai emerged from the cottage. "Let her go!"

On bended knee, Tazuro attained the piece of broken pull-up bar. Like a javelin, he pitched it at Yokai.

16

Izaru's Speech

Meilana reclined on a leather chair in a room rich with elegant decorum. Placards and trophies of medical accomplishments exhibited from shelves and glass cases. Medical supplies, a cornucopia of them, occupied a nearby table.

A middle-aged, dark-skinned woman hovered over Meilana. "They still look good." Through a shiny monocle she examined Meilana's wrist. "All right now dear, you're all set, but continue to be careful. You don't want them ripping."

"I will, Madame Weila. Thank you," said Meilana, caressing the stitches on her wrist.

As Madame Weila made way for a nearby cupboard, her bushy hair bounced like a shaken bush. "Stop by again in a few days."

"Do I have to come in so often? Most people wait a while."

"Yes, but most people aren't royalty."

Meilana breathed deep from aggravation.

"Plus, your mother insists. The last thing I want to do is get on that woman's bad side."

"She insists on making my life miserable."

"I'll pretend I didn't hear that. Now run along. You don't want to miss her speech, do you?"

Meilana entered the hallway and heard the chatter of city folk out in the courtyard. She sneered at the pearl statues of her relatives then ascended the stairs. Upon reaching the third floor, voices belonging to Juroiza and Agalo came within range from below.

"It should be me standing by her side. She doesn't even love him anymore," said Juroiza.

Agalo cleared his throat. "It's just for show, boss."

They too ascended the stairs, forcing Meilana to duck behind the solid marble banister.

"I don't care. I'm sick of all the hiding, all the faking."

"Well, uh, maybe things will change someday."

Their footsteps drew closer.

"Maybe, I don't know. I think I'm ready to break it off with her."

"She might have you killed if you do that."

"You're probably right."

Over the banister, Meilana watched the pair exit onto the second floor. Scurrying to her room, she fetched a knapsack from the closet. At her bedside, she reached under and retrieved her tanto, a pouch full with money, a pair of climbing claws and a grappling hook. After stuffing the items in her knapsack, she tossed it over her shoulder. On her way out the door, a glass jug of water caught her eye.

Snagging it from the top of her dresser, she sped toward the window. "Don't worry. The handmaidens will take care of you from now on."

Through her half open curtains, Meilana could see her mother's balcony. A slow drizzle of rain trickled upon it.

Speech? Who cares what she has to say.

As she watered the plant, an armored Izaru walked onto the balcony, her war-hammer resting across her shoulder. The crowd erupted with rhapsodic cheers. Pai Liu, wearing another elegant shozoku, accompanied the Grandmagistra. Cheering amplified at the sight of him. They both reveled in the praise before raising their hands to quiet the crowd. It took a few minutes, but the celebration calmed. Juroiza, Agalo and many other samurai stood atop the ramparts below.

Izaru spoke into a standing microphone powered by zoganite. "My loyal subjects, we thank you for joining us here today."

Ugh. She's so fake.

"Indeed. We understand how valuable your time is," added Pai Liu in earnest.

"Cancelling the graduation ceremony brings us great displeasure, but this urgent matter could not be delayed," said Izaru.

Meilana scowled.

Izaru placed her war-hammer down on its head. "Late Wednesday night, many of our loyal and cherished samurai were murdered."

The vast sea of people gasped.

"Not to be alarmed. We're currently looking into the matter," said Pai Liu as fast as he could.

Izaru glanced at Pai Liu with vitriol before recomposing.

"My husband's correct. We're conducting an ongoing investigation." She glanced at Pai Liu again, this time with devious intent. "We have reason to believe that ninjas were responsible."

Anger festered amongst the people.

Pai Liu gazed at his feet. "We don't yet know for certain that ninjas played a part. The investigation is ongoing."

Izaru squeezed the handle of her war-hammer before speaking again. "That's correct, but if our findings prove what I fear most." Her voice filled with forced sorrow, followed by a well-played drop of the eyes. "We'll have no choice but to act."

It was enough to make the crowd want to detonate.

"If the ninjas have dared come into our home, they will regret it. If they have dared to cross us, we will get revenge," said Izaru with passion.

"She's really going through with it," muttered an awestruck Meilana.

"If we must, we'll finish what my father, Gazzo the Great, started. We'll finally bring the ninjas under our rule!"

Pai Liu opened his mouth then shut it without uttering a sound.

"So, I ask all of you now." Izaru raised her war-hammer to the sky. "When the time comes, will you stand and fight with your Grandmagistra?"

The people's anger blazed like a wildfire.

"Yes!" they roared.

"Will you uphold the honor of our clan?"

Everyone began thrusting their fists into the air. "Yes!"

"Will you defend our home?"

"Yes!" Their anger gave way to a series of chants. "Izaru, Izaru, Izaru!"

Unable to stomach anymore, Meilana raced to her mother's room. She crept inside unnoticed then tiptoed into the closet.

Her heart pounded. *Please tell me they didn't see me.*

She waited for her parents to come, but they didn't. Accompanied by a sigh of relief, she pulled the chain dangling from the ceiling. Dim light guided her to the back of the closet. The farther she went, the more it smelled of lavender.

Somebody's obsessed.

A glossy white cabinet stood between racks of clothing and other items.

There you are.

Yanking the knobs, she expected them to swing open but received resistance instead. *What? Since when is this locked?* Tanto in hand, she pried the cabinet doors open.

Another bout of anxiety washed over her. *Was that too loud? Did they hear that?*

The chanting outside was still in full swing.

Okay, okay. I'm good.

A silver key attached to a white ribbon hung on a hook; light glinted across the Gazzo Clan crest it bore. Meilana stuffed the key in her knapsack and headed for the closet door. As she pushed it open, the thump of footfalls halted her progression. Observing through the gap, she waited.

"I'm truly blessed to serve as your Grandmagistra," said Izaru as she and Pai Liu entered the room.

"I think it would be wise to alert the other clans of your intentions." Pai Liu sighed. "I'll arrange to have kotaos sent out to each of them."

"Who do you think you are? Undermining like this," said Izaru, closing the balcony doors.

"I was—"

"Shut your mouth! It seems you've forgotten your place. Need I remind you?"

Pai Liu smiled, pushing his glasses up the bridge of his nose. "That won't be necessary."

"Good. Now go find something useful to do."

Without another word, Pai Liu left. Izaru's eyes turned watery, and a single tear broke through. Shock hit Meilana like high voltage. She couldn't recall a time she'd seen her mother in a vulnerable state. Wiping away her defiant tear, the Grandmagistra left as well. Meilana waited a solid minute before feeling the bravery required to vacate. The castle was vacant, giving her ease of passage to the back entrance.

Behind the castle was another bridge that led across the moat. On the other side sat two buildings. Using the stolen key, Meilana opened the building closest to her. A plethora of weapons and armor awaited her. Three stone pedestals in the middle of the room lured her further inside. Each one possessed a name. **Izaru** engraved the one to the right. **Gazzo** engraved the one in the center. **Meilana** engraved the one to the left. The pedestal attributed to Izaru was the only empty one. Gazzo's pedestal held armor that saw more than its fair share of combat. On Meilana's pedestal lay two pauldrons, two gauntlets, two greaves, one fauld and a long katana handle, all of it coated in shimmering purple. Donning each item gave Meilana the feeling of invincibility.

She paused to admire herself in a body length mirror on the wall. "I look good."

Her hands glided across her hair which now flaunted two long braids. Soon thereafter, she checked for a clear coast then dashed into the adjacent building. An assortment of automobiles sat waiting to be driven. On the wall opposite the entrance hung every automobile key.

Something small should do the trick.

In no time at all, her heart set on a midsized automobile with small wheels and a smooth exterior. With the corresponding key in hand, she sat. The engine boomed as she cranked the ignition. Three sets of feet approached in a hurry. She rushed out, placed the key back and hid within a larger automobile.

Juroiza busted in. "Spread out. Search everywhere."

"Yes, sir," said two samurai.

Meilana slinked back to the automobile's cargo area and listened as the search commenced.

"There's zoganite coming from this one, but nobody's here," said one samurai.

"They couldn't have gone far. Keep looking," replied Juroiza.

A lump attacked Meilana's throat as they opened automobile door after automobile door.

"Clear!" they yelled upon completing an inspection.

The passenger door of Meilana's hiding spot swung open. From behind a few boxes, she watched a samurai search high and low. His eyes soon drifted to the cargo area. Suspicion came over him; he raced to the tailgate for a better look. Meilana moved to the front seat then ducked under it.

The samurai opened the rear doors. "Hmm, all clear."

"You think it could be one of them sneaky gaikaos?" asked the other samurai.

"Possibly. What I want to know is why we can't use these for patrols. All that walking hurts my feet. And those damn horses are a pain in my ass, literally."

"Would you shut up? We don't need automobiles to patrol the city. Horseback is plenty. Besides, zoganite isn't cheap. You know how frugal rich people can be," said Juroiza.

"Sorry sir, didn't mean to complain."

"Go search the perimeter."

"Yes, sir!"

In single file, the three of them marched outside.

That was too close. I need something quiet.

A few bicycles stood like beacons amongst the automobiles. Meilana took one and performed a delicate exit. Once outside, she glimpsed Juroiza and his subordinates heading toward the castle. Mounting the bicycle, she peddled to the unmanned back gate and unlocked it. Careful not to make another alarming noise, she opened the gate like it was made of fragile glass.

With the wind in her braids, she careened behind the ramparts and into the forest.

On her way to Illumino Lake, memories of Obake's fight with Juroiza appeared in her mind. *I want to see him so bad.*

The thought drove her to ride faster and faster. Giggles from two feminine voices grew louder the further she rode. Stopping behind the nearest tree, she waited for the women to reveal themselves. A brunette city woman sporting a bowl cut and a blonde samurai with a ponytail ran throughout the bushes.

The blonde gave chase until she caught up and embraced the brunette. Their faces lingered close before a band of leaves fell upon them. Startled, they gazed up. A lanky arm descended, clutching the blonde's ponytail. Her blood-curdling scream sent a shiver slithering up Meilana's spine. In a blink, the blonde disappeared within the canopy.

"Am I seeing things?" whispered Meilana.

Screams from the brunette discharged into the gloomy day. It provided Meilana with several additional shivers.

Orinsu dropped from the canopy. "Quiet, girl." His incapacitated victim draped lifeless over his arm. "Can't you see I'm trying to be discreet?"

Sheer horror consumed the brunette, she buckled to her knees. The last of the rain fell as the vampire plunged his fangs into the blonde's neck.

Meilana stalled as if glued to the ground. *I don't know… what to do… is this even real?*

Resolve mustered in the brunette, enough to compel her to crawl away. Caught in the moment, the vampire paid her feeble escape no mind; he instead snapped the blonde's neck as if it were a brittle twig.

He then guzzled the samurai's blood before tossing her onto the wet grass. "So sweet," he said, licking the excess from his fingers.

Compelled by absolute adrenaline, the brunette got up and ran for dear life. Meilana wanted to help, but couldn't convince her feet to join in. Orinsu's wings burst out, pushing his cloak behind like a cape. He tore through the air then sent a gust of wind to flatten his prey.

Picking the brunette up, Orinsu chuckled. "Did I knock you down? How inconsiderate of me."

She squirmed, slapped and screamed until Orinsu let her loose.

With maniacal laughter, he flew after her again. "Where are you going? Was it something I said?" A simple chop to the neck made the brunette's eyes go white with unconsciousness. "You'll make a fine dessert."

Upon seizing the brunette, Orinsu paused, sniffing the air like a bloodhound. His gaze then steadied on Meilana's current hiding spot.

Both of Meilana's hands clapped to her mouth. *He knows I'm here.*

A conversation approached Illumino Lake.

"Those dirty gaikaos, coming to our land. Killing our people," said a gruff male voice.

"I can't wait to get my hands on one," said a raspy female voice.

The soft voice of an adolescent boy arrived next. "They still have to investigate, remember? The ninjas might be innocent."

"Shut up!" said the other two voices in unison.

Staying low, Orinsu glided away, heading in the chasm's direction. The brunette hung from his arms like prey caught in the talons of an eagle.

Once out of sight, Meilana's feet functioned again. *I just stood here. I can't believe I just stood here. What's wrong with me?*

Ducking low, Meilana scurried over to the blonde. Her pale skin and bloody neck made Meilana's stomach coil. She returned to her bicycle, hopped on, then puked all over the tree.

Attempting to calm her nerves, she wiped her mouth then spoke aloud. "I have to help. I can't let that thing have her."

"Who's there?" asked the raspy female voice.

Meilana rode off and put a distant Orinsu in her line of sight. He flew up and over the Colossal Divide moments later. Even though her thighs burned, she peddled harder. As she approached the chasm, she leapt backwards off the bicycle, letting it fall in.

Racing to the Colossal Divide, she produced the climbing claws and began her ascent. "Come on, come on." Half way she threw her grappling hook, which failed to catch the first and second time. "Dammit, hook you piece of shit!"

The talon hooked on the third attempt. Sweat poured as she climbed fast.

At the top of the Colossal Divide, she scanned the Shinobi Empire. *There it is!*

With his wings tucked back under his cloak, Orinsu made way for the Yokai Mountains. Meilana rappelled twice as fast as she climbed. Half way down, she put away the grappling hook and slipped back into her claws. She then climbed down until she reached a safe dropping distance. Marred by hesitation, she stayed for a moment before letting go. On impact she rolled, sparing her legs any pain. In a full-blown sprint, she pursued the vampire as he went through a green torii gate at the start of the muddy trail. He failed to notice her due to the distance still between them.

"How am I going to get her away from it?" whispered Meilana, running through the torii gate.

A quarter of the way up the mountain, Meilana came to a junction. The trail on her left led to Obake's cottage, but the trail on her right was rife with clawed footprints.

She glanced between the two trails. "What if she dies before I reach him? Wait a minute. He should be at his academy right now."

Meilana followed the footprints all the way to the top where they vanished.

Kinichi's Academy loomed above her as she stepped off the trail. "Where is everyone?"

Approaching the academy's gate almost turned deadly. Gonenga sat on the ground, deep within the garden. His giant battle-axe lay flat across his lap.

Meilana's soul wanted to flee from her body at the sight of him. "Oh, no. Oh, no. I have to be dreaming."

A tiny bird stood chirping and bouncing in Gonenga's open hand. With his thumb and index finger, he gripped the bird's head.

No, don't!

The juggernaut smiled then began petting the tiny bird.

"What?" squealed Meilana.

Her squeal drew Gonenga's gaze. She dove behind the perimeter wall to avoid it. Heavy footsteps rumbled the ground. In a crouched position, Meilana ran along the perimeter wall toward the back of the academy. The wall traveled to the very edge of the cliff side. A few centimeters of land extended past the wall, enough space for Meilana's toes to stabilize. Hugging the wall, she shimmied along the edge with her claws as support. As Gonenga rounded the corner she slipped out of sight. Respite found her when she made it to a section where the land extended out further.

"This is too much," she mumbled through bated breath.

Rumbling footsteps started again, but this time they trailed away. Spatters of blood dripping down the cliff side stood out to Meilana. As she approached them, Gonenga's footsteps grew louder until they ceased altogether.

After a sigh of relief, she reconvened her investigation. "That's a lot of blood."

The spatters painted a good length of the cliff side before fading. More spatters stained the academy wall as well. They guided Meilana to the hole above. Using her grappling hook, she scaled up to it. She then entered after confirming the chamber to be empty. Foul odors of death permeated. Dark red and pale-yellow stains covered the floor along with many points of damage.

With her nose pinched, she kneeled and touched one of the floor's many scars. "What happened here? What if…"

Imagining her boyfriend lying dead was enough to make tears drop. As she struggled to control her emotions, she spotted the Gateway. Its transcendental aura made her want to run far away. The sound of metal stabbing dirt disrupted the eerie silence. Tazuro returned in his Spider Throne, a peek outside unveiled as much.

Not another one.

"Anything interesting happen while I was away?" asked Tazuro.

Gonenga shook his head.

Tazuro began scaling the academy's exterior. "As expected."

Meilana bolted all the way down the stairs to the first floor. Searching for another adequate hiding spot, she found a door labeled: **Basement, Faculty Only**. She crept in, shut it and found another flight of stairs. Dingy lighting from ceiling mounted lamps flickered. The muggy smell and cobwebs made the place unnerving.

On the dusty steps, Meilana could make out footprints matching Orinsu's. *It's down there.*
A tarnished steel door stood in her way. Against her better judgment, she opened the screeching barrier and ventured forth.

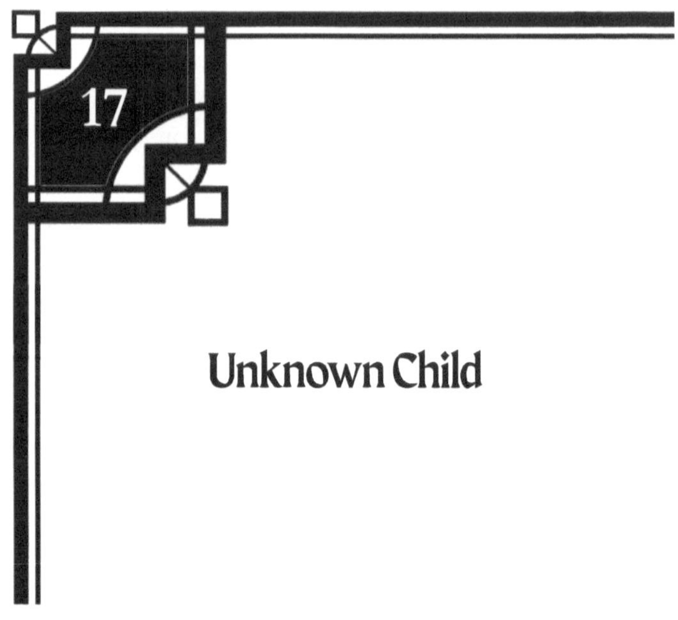

17

Unknown Child

Obake found sprinting too slow, he considered each moment that passed a moment wasted.

They better be okay!

At the foot of the Yokai Mountains, a green torii gate stood ready to receive him. He went straight through it then vaulted up the stone stairs. Although they were wet and muddy, he didn't slip or fall once. His agility and finesse had returned. A hike that would usually take forty-five minutes took half.

Wavy stretches of land were all that remained in Obake's way when the trail spit him out. Summoning even greater speed, he ran until disturbing imagery came into view. Destruction had befallen his home and it became more apparent the closer he got. He soared over the low standing bamboo fence to find the living room a sopping mess of debris on the mountainside.

"Papa! Nana!"

As he feared, no one answered. Part of the pull-up bar now stuck through the back wall of his grandparent's room. Blood eerily dripped from the end of it.

"Nana, can you hear me? Papa, answer me!"

Near the front, he peered through the hole in his grandparent's room. Blinds covered both windows, making it rather dark. Unable to make out more than a floating silhouette, Obake drew closer, but couldn't bring himself to enter. Fear of what horror may await kept him outside.

A wheezing voice drifted over to him. "O… ba… ke."

Turning around, he stared into the field where blades of grass waved in the wind. However, there was a spot that didn't wave, a spot in the middle, where somebody laid still.

Tears cascaded from Obake's eyes. "Nana!" The panic he felt upon leaving Taulon Falls returned. "No please, no."

Dread entered the equation as he raced over, kneeling beside her. In misery, Bao stared up at her grandson, breaking a part inside of him. Her eyes marred by pain, so full of desperation, her body defeated, so frail. Obake couldn't take it; he collapsed and grabbed Bao's shivering hand. Deep finger shaped ligature marks wrapped around her throat.

With her free hand, Bao placed it on her grandson's cheek. "I'm… sorry."

"Stop it. Save your strength." Obake rummaged inside Bao's sleeves and patted down her pockets. "Where's the puapo? That'll fix this. I need you to tell me where it is, Nana."

"It's too… late."

"Don't you say that, dammit!"

"I should've told you the whole—"

"No. Listen, I don't care about that anymore. I'm going to get you some help." Obake's arms wrapped around Bao and prepared to lift. "Here we go. You're going to be okay."

A whisper filled Obake's ears. "I'll always… love you… Froggy."

He pulled away to gaze at his grandmother. Sheer disbelief struck as he watched the light within her eyes flicker out.

He caressed her face. "Get up. I'm going to get you to a hospital." When that failed, he shook her back and forth. "Wake up! Please wake up!"

Realizing she would never wake up again, Obake held her closer than he ever had before. He sobbed so hard he couldn't catch his breath. The part inside of him that broke earlier died a most gruesome death. For the second time, he lost a piece of himself.

"Nana, where's Papa?" he asked before returning her body back the way he found it.

Deep down, he knew she wouldn't reply. Deep down, he already knew where his grandfather was. Upon returning to the hole, he worked up the courage to enter. As his tear-filled eyes adjusted to the darkness, he saw him. The pull-up bar pierced Yokai through the chest, hanging him on the wall like a painting. Copious amounts of blood seeped from his wound.

"Papa!" Obake scrambled forward, tripping into the shallow pit of photos on the floor. *This can't be real.*

Back on his feet, Obake tried applying pressure to Yokai's wound, but the pull-up bar made that impossible.

"I have to get you down."

In a panic, Obake tried pulling his grandfather off the pull-up bar, but the awful squishing sound his innards produced hindered the young ninja. Consciousness swelled into Yokai; he looked around in a dazed stupor.

Shock came over him when his sights landed on his grandson. "Promise me."

"Papa, stop talking."

His bloody hand reached out. "Promise me... you'll get somewhere safe."

"Take it easy. I can fix this."

Blood spilled through Yokai's barred teeth and his hand came to rest on Obake's collar. "Promise me you won't fight him." With a surprising amount of strength, he pulled his grandson close. "Promise me!"

Now face to face, Obake could see the urgency in his grandfather's expression.

Yokai's grip waned. "Say it! Say you won't—"

For the second time, Obake watched the light flicker from a loved one. For the third time, a part inside of him died, another piece lost.

Obake dropped to the floor, sobbing until the anger he repressed invaded. No longer did he desire to turn it away, no longer did he care to run from it. Now fully prepared, he embraced the anger with open arms.

Wiping away his tears, Obake ascended, sadness replaced with vengeance. With one swift motion, he took Yokai off the pull-up bar and laid him down. After retrieving Bao from the grassy field, he laid her beside Yokai.

He covered them both with blankets then said his goodbyes. "I should've been here to fight with you. I failed." Before leaving, Obake took pause. "I'm sorry, Papa, but I can't make that promise. I'll get revenge for the both of you, for Yumo. I'll kill every last one of them."

To the bathroom he proceeded, once inside, he ransacked it. Only when he opened the drawers under the sink, did he find what he searched for. Below the middle drawer's bottom sat a secret compartment. Two puapo canisters laid there. With them in hand, he ventured back to his grandparent's room.

Near their bed stood a wooden mannequin dressed in a green kimono and matching hakama. It also exhibited two gauntlets, two greaves and armored jika-tabi boots. Each armor piece shined black and gold. A hooded cloak draped over the mannequin's head, and a metal half-mask tied around the neck by way of rope. A sign nailed to the wall above it read: **In honor of our son Bakemono, the savior of the Human Realm.** All of his father's old belongings fueled Obake's vengeful mentality even further. Wearing those belongings provided the bit of familial comfort he now sorely lacked. In the mannequin's hand rested Bakemono's naginata, Mizuchi. Obake attained it, collapsed the handle then tucked it into his belt.

One shrapnel bomb, one kunai, and two shurikens lay at the base of the now naked mannequin. Every projectile went into Obake's possession, he then put Yumo's key behind his kimono for safe keeping.

Ready for battle, he walked over the shallow pit. Family photos in and around it garnered Obake's admiration. Most of the photos contained his grandparents and himself; he took his favorite and tucked it away. Some of the photos contained his mother and father. Obake seized one and stared at it for a while. He then tucked that photo away as well, but there was one photo that perplexed him. Next to the cathedral in Yokai City stood his father, mother and a small boy he knew nothing of. The child looked to be about seven or eight years old. Long, jet black hair grew from his head, and features similar to Obake's made up his face. Though the child wore a big smile, a sinister aura lingered upon him.

Obake stuffed the photo in with the rest. *Who is that?*

He racked his brain, trying to recall something, anything. His anger enhanced, realizing his grandparents had hidden yet another piece of information. Unwilling to aim his anger at them, he added to the hatred concocting in his soul for the ginyai.

Outside, he gripped Mizuchi and put on his mask and hood. "I'll be back to bury you both properly," he said, taking a final glance at the cottage.

Kinichi's Academy visualized in Obake's thoughts; he summoned his soul energy and teleported. Shadow Cloud discharged the young ninja into the garden. Gonenga still remained there. Half a dozen tiny birds bounced on him. He took time petting each one. A squirrel and a turtle vied for his affection as well. Obake's sudden appearance seemed not to bother Gonenga.

"Stand up," said Obake, removing Mizuchi from its scabbard.

All of the critters scattered as Gonenga rose to his feet. Even in the presence of Gonenga's immense size, Obake showed no fear.

Basement

Stale air circulating the basement reminded Meilana of rot. Some ceiling lamps were out, but many shed light, showing a basement that hadn't been disturbed in months, until now. Meilana drew her katana handle and pressed on its center. Blades jutted from both ends, turning the object into a double-bladed katana. With her weapon at the ready, she followed Orinsu's foot prints for several paces. They vanished near his cloak, which lay crumpled on the ground. She averted her eyes to the ceiling, some twenty feet above. Expecting to see her blood sucking nemesis, she braced herself. Much to her relief, he wasn't there.

Dozens of columns obscured her view. Each carved with an animal design like a totem pole. No other choice presented itself, so Meilana ventured further. She slashed while rounding each column until she spotted who she had come for. The brunette sat propped against a moldy wall on the opposite side of the basement.

"There she is," gasped Meilana, rushing to her.

She had yet to regain consciousness, her skin colder than the atmosphere itself.

"Hey," whispered Meilana.

No reaction.

"Hey, wake up," she whispered louder. "I'm here to help you." She tapped the brunette's face, still no reaction. *Please, don't tell me she's already dead.* Meilana opted to hiss. "Wake up now!"

That did the trick.

The brunette jolted awake, her eyes bulging with fear.

"Get away, monster!"

With no other choice available, Meilana restrained the brunette as she tried to bolt. "Relax. I'm not a monster."

Struggles and screams continued until Meilana slapped her across the cheek. "Snap out of it."

Stunned, the brunette stopped resisting.

Meilana let her go. "What's your name?"

"Grandheiress, it's you," said the brunette, staring with astonishment.

"What's your name?" repeated Meilana.

"It's… Umoi."

"Umoi, great, call me Meilana. I'm going to help you get out of here, okay?"

Umoi's jaw dropped. "No, you can't. There's this thing out there. It murdered my friend."

"Look, I know you're scared, but you have to stand up."

"I need to hide," said Umoi, shaking her head in opposition.

"Bad idea, trust me. We have to go. That thing you're talking about could come back any second."

"I never left," Orinsu's frigid voice crept from above. "You're the one from the lake. I remember your scent," he said, clutching the top of the nearest column, evidence of salivation on his tongue.

"Run!" screamed Meilana.

Finally heeding Meilana's advice, Umoi raced for the stairs.

"Get your own food," said Orinsu with a chuckle.

Flying low, he aimed straight for Umoi. As he was about to dig his amber glove into her spine, Meilana drop kicked him. Several feet away, his ribs slammed hard against a different column. Umoi stalled to survey the commotion.

"Go, go!" said Meilana, urging her forward.

Eager to resume the chase, Orinsu flew back up, his mischievous attitude eradicated. Nothing but hate and disdain filled his visage now. He administered his next attack, but Meilana ducked then countered. Her blade grazed Orinsu's stomach, releasing trickles of blood. The vampire retaliated with a swipe of his amber glove. Instead of flesh, his glove cut the strap of Meilana's knapsack, dropping it to the ground. Attempting to cut Orinsu again proved unsuccessful. By soaring up near the ceiling, he avoided the attack. With a glance, Meilana saw that Umoi had yet to make it out. Orinsu's attention went back to her as well.

Meilana scowled at the vampire. "You can't have her."

"Jealous? Don't be. Once I'm done with her, it'll be your turn."

In a flash, Orinsu went whipping in and around the columns.

"Weave! Weave!" screamed Meilana.

Umoi didn't listen and got tackled for it. Orinsu bared his yellow stained teeth. His breath was so hot and foul, it reeked from a distance. Screams of terror exploded, Umoi slapped and clawed the vampire which served to excite him. With impressive speed, Meilana ran over and slammed into Orinsu. He went skidding across the ground while Meilana took Umoi and hit the stairs.

As Meilana went to slam the steel door, Orinsu rammed it full force. Through the gap, he snarled and swiped, but a good push caused the door to latch; time enough to escape perhaps. Jumping up the stairs, Meilana hoped to catch Umoi who had already made it half way up. Seconds later, the steel door melted off its hinges. What looked to be yellow saliva had splashed all over it. The girls finished speeding to the top of the stairs.

"Leaving so soon?" said Orinsu while flying at them.

Meilana dove out onto the first floor with Umoi in her arms. Missing by a hair thin margin, Orinsu collided with the wall.

"Get behind me," said Meilana as she and Umoi got up.

Orinsu entered the first floor too, rage searing from his bloodthirsty pupils. "You're going to regret interfering with me."

Motion registered in Meilana's peripheral.

She turned to glimpse Umoi high-tailing it toward the front entrance. "No! Not that way!"

Once again, Umoi didn't listen.

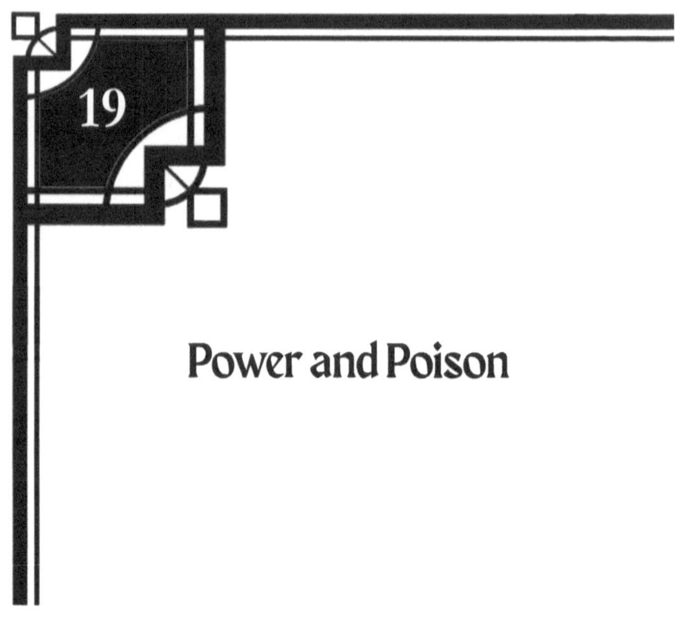

Power and Poison

In the here and now, fear found no home within Obake. Pure indignation seethed too heavy inside of him.

Like the glare on a window, light passed over all of Gonenga's skin. The ninja ignored what he saw, he instead extended Mizuchi's handle and darted forth. The academy's doors swung open, cutting Obake's advance short. He expected the emergence of another foe, but received Umoi. Upon spotting Gonenga, she screamed enough to rupture her vocal cords. Acting on impulse, the juggernaut jumped toward Umoi.

Obake teleported her out of harm's way. "Where did you come from?"

She squirmed and shoved until she broke free of Obake's protective embrace.

"What's your deal?" said Obake, taken aback. "I'm trying to help you."

Umoi sprinted for the perimeter wall, but never breached it. Gonenga long jumped over top of Obake and landed right on top of her. Like an old dog put to death via shotgun, Umoi yelped aloud. The crunch of her bones and the splatter of her blood reverberated around the garden.

No! Why did she have to do that?

Orinsu came through the academy's doors next. Unlike Umoi, he had company. Meilana gripped his leg as he flew overhead. Time slowed to a crawl for Obake as he followed their movements without blinking. Kicks rained on Meilana as she tried cutting the vampire down. Before long, a foot to the face dropped her into the garden.

"Meilana!" Obake raced to her as time returned to normal.

After shaking off the pain, Meilana spotted Umoi's dead body under Gonenga's feet. Her eyes welled at the sight of it. She clapped a hand to her mouth then glared at her boyfriend with suspicious eyes. This puzzled Obake until he remembered his mask and hood. He dropped the hood and pulled his mask off, letting the attached rope hang the mask like a necklace.

Meilana's face lit up. "Obake!"

Almost oblivious to the imminent threats, she jumped into his arms. She squeezed so tight, his breathing became impaired, but he didn't mind one bit. He enjoyed her flowery scent, her satin skin, her soothing embrace and her puckered lips moving in for a kiss. All of it culminated in a mixture that calmed the fire storm within him. As the rage simmered and his lips were inches from hers, the ground quaked and wings sliced the air.

"I think we have a few issues to deal with first," said Obake.

"I think you're right."

Diving into a barrel roll, Orinsu outstretched his amber claw. Like a sentient drill, he went straight at the couple, intent on gouging through them. Meilana charged then flipped forward, her katana clashing with his claw. The force knocked them apart. Icy blue coursed through Meilana's veins the moment she landed. Wisps of vapor dispersed from her body like a frigid breath in the winter. One katana stroke later and three pristine ice crystals went bustling off. By flapping both wings, Orinsu repelled them.

Meilana cut the first, dodged the second and caught the third. "Think fast," she said, sending the ice crystal stabbing into Orinsu's chest.

He skyrocketed, wailing in pain.

She's… amazing. I had no idea.

Fast-paced, heavy footsteps drew close. Obake re-applied his mask and hood. On the terrain below his feet, a puddle made of Shadow Cloud appeared. Gonenga's battle-axe came swinging, but the ninja submerged into the puddle, dropping below the terrain. Elsewhere on the terrains surface, another Shadow Cloud puddle appeared. Mizuchi shot from it, slicing the juggernaut's leg. A clang rang out.

What was that?

With unbridled speed, the blade retracted from whence it came. Unfazed, Gonenga thrust his battle-axe into the Shadow Cloud puddle. After a brief pause the puddle flared out to cover a larger radius. The juggernaut lifted with his middle set of arms, but the battle-axe plunged regardless. Confusion washed through Gonenga before he enlisted his bottom set of arms. In the end, their addition helped him to pry his battle-axe loose.

The Shadow Cloud puddle dissipated, but another formed at Gonenga's rear. Obake erupted from it, slashing up the length of his enemies back. Sounds of grazing metal accompanied the attack. Not even a wince of discomfort crossed the juggernaut's face.

Am I hearing things?

Swinging around, Gonenga sliced with his battle-axe. It failed to hit anything other than licks of Shadow

Cloud due to Obake teleporting. Gonenga stomped and roared as Obake materialized above. Mizuchi slithered from its handle to slash the ginyai in a multitude of ways. Each slash hit where intended, but once again, they were accompanied by clangs.

What is going on!

Baffled, Obake landed, examining his enemy. Baiting another attack, Gonenga puffed out his chest and pounded on it. Obake obliged. With a sideways motion, Mizuchi sliced Gonenga's bare throat. The same sound of metal striking metal blared.

No fucking way.

Bewilderment rained on Obake's parade, giving Gonenga time to grab and hurl him a good distance. Obake tumbled deep into the garden and a putrid stench located him. His limbs defied the commands of his mind. All he could do was peel his head from the ground. In doing so, he glimpsed Meilana evading a stream of poison from Orinsu's jaws. She ducked, jumped, dodged and everything in between. His poison sent various trees, bushes and flowers to an untimely demise. While everything perished, Meilana jumped into a small pond she found hiding amidst some bushes. Poison splashed against the surface of the pond, becoming nullified.

"Smart move, he can't get you in there," mumbled Obake, floundering to his feet.

"You'll have to come out, eventually," said Orinsu, ceasing fire.

Ice crystals shot from the pond like skyward arrows.

Orinsu scoffed and sent them away with a gust from his wings. "You'll need much more than that."

Much more arrived. A giant spike of crystal ice protruded to the sky. Like a surfer, Meilana hitched a ride upon it. Caught by surprise, Orinsu almost got impaled. With his back to the gloomy sky, he flew higher, sparing himself such a fate. The spike only reached but so high, forcing Meilana to abandon it. By utilizing an impressive vertical leap, she collided with Orinsu before he got too far. Her feet then thrust into his abdomen like a pair of battering rams. In addition, she gripped him by the throat with such viciousness, her fingers became like knives.

"Yes! Get him," cheered Obake.

Orinsu's amber claw tried slashing the features from Meilana's face, but she dodged too fast. Undeterred, Orinsu secreted poisonous yellow vapor from every pore. Stunned, Meilana embarked on a fifty-foot drop.

Obake hobbled toward Meilana. *No! I can't lose anyone else.*

His aching body wouldn't move fast enough and his Shadow Cloud refused to manifest. Wrapped in absolute desperation, Meilana rubbed her eyes nonstop. Coughing and gagging came next, but none of it lasted long. The ground below was primed to flatten her. By hurling an ice crystal at it, she saved herself from certain death. Her small crystal grew into another giant spike, allowing her to catch hold and slide down.

She's going to make it.

Rocky chunks of terrain smashed through the base of the ice spike. Before it could fully crumble, Meilana flipped away to safety. As if his battle-axe were now a shovel, Gonenga cleaved more sizable chunks of terrain at his enemies. Due to a lack of options, Obake forced his weary body to dodge.

Three of Meilana's ice crystals unleashed at Gonenga, but they shattered on contact. "What the fuck!"

"Be careful. His skin is stronger than steel," said Obake.

"Are you serious?"

One final chunk of terrain sped at the couple like a comet; Meilana slid under it and Obake sidestepped it.

"In that case..." Meilana sent what looked to be the same attack at Gonenga's axe hand.

Her deceitful little ice crystals struck their intended target. They went to work freezing the juggernaut's entire hand.

"Nice one!" said Obake, submerging into a new Shadow Cloud puddle. *All right, I have to ignore the pain.*

Gonenga's immense strength crippled the ice fast. Obake burst from a puddle below Gonenga and kicked him so hard, his helmet flew off. Enraged, the juggernaut slammed his battle-axe. Obake sank back into his Shadow Cloud puddle, causing the battle-axe to sink along with him. Refusing to let go, Gonenga's middle set of arms submerged. He pushed against the ground with his bottom set of arms, but it proved useless this time.

From beneath the puddle, Obake observed the realm above. A glob of yellow poison glided into view, heading straight for Meilana. In the nick of time, she evaded it. The poison splashed a bed of roses, killing them.

Meilana clenched. "Stop ruining the garden!"

I need to hurry.

Obake moved the Shadow Cloud puddle under Gonenga's feet, pulling his middle set of arms along for the ride. Gonenga looked to be assuming a sort of Yoga pose when panic set upon him.

"Give me my axe!" he roared, performing a double stomp.

The vibration caused the puddle to spit Obake out like a mouth regurgitating spoiled food. With the Shadow Cloud puddle gone, Gonenga's middle set of arms became trapped in the ground. Using his upper set of arms, he grabbed Obake from the air and tossed him.

Orinsu took notice. Five wing flaps later and he seized Obake in his grasp, taking him sky high.

"Let him go!" screeched Meilana while unleashing an ice crystal.

After evading the ice crystal, Orinsu spit into his hand and waited for another poison glob to generate.

Obake released his naginata, hoping to disrupt the attack, but the poison glob headed for Meilana anyway. On retraction, Mizuchi cut open Orinsu's cheek. This angered the vampire to no end.

Yet again, poisonous vapor secreted from Orinsu's pores. A great deal of it this time. It enveloped Obake, paralyzing him. "Safe travels," said Orinsu as he dropped his catch.

Head first, Obake plummeted. *I can't feel anything.*

Waiting to regain sensation, Obake used his bird's-eye view to search for a safe landing. Another large ice spike drew his gaze. It erected between Meilana and the poison glob Orinsu had launched. On contact with the poison, the ice spike melted.

Ripping his arms from the ground, Gonenga spun his battle-axe toward Meilana like a rogue carousel. All she could do to stay alive was fight from a distance. With another freeze crystal, she halted Gonenga's battle-axe in its tracks. One glance at the frozen battle-axe compelled Gonenga to rip a tree from its roots. By chucking the tree, Gonenga nearly crushed Meilana's legs. Like a rock through water, the tree crashed through the academy wall. Two more trees went spiraling at Meilana. She dodged the first by a landslide, but almost lost her head to the second. Gonenga's attention shifted above. Meilana's jaw dropped as she watched her helpless boyfriend draw closer to death.

Obake's willpower and determination weakened the paralysis. Fragments of ice splintered as Gonenga smashed his battle-axe against the perimeter wall. He then held the edge of his battle-axe underneath the ninja, waiting for it to split him in two. Obake came within inches of death when an ice crystal knocked the battle-axe off course. Regaining control, Obake flipped upright and cut the battle-axe's handle. Gonenga's eyes bulged at the falling axe-head. A flurry of punches followed, but Obake avoided them all.

Orinsu snuck up behind Meilana. "I'm sick and tired of you two!"

Keeping his distance, Orinsu threw another poison glob.

"Freeze it!" said Obake.

A crystal ventured out and froze the poison glob, but it didn't halt. Meilana jumped out of the way, the glob passed her and went toward Obake and Gonenga. While Gonenga prepared another punch, Obake teleported under the poison glob and issued a kick. The force of the kick propelled the poison too fast for Gonenga. It shattered against his body, drenching him. He screamed in agony as the poison ate his face, arms and torso.

"How does it feel!" said Obake, teleporting onto the juggernaut's shoulders.

Gonenga squeezed Obake with his upper set of arms, causing his body to start cracking. When he thought the pressure would make him pop, Gonenga's arms melted all the way to the bone.

"Die!" screamed Obake.

Mizuchi pierced the top of Gonenga's bald head, down through the bottom of his chin, his black eyes drooped low and went still.

"I didn't mean to, I... Tazuro will kill me," said Orinsu, falling into utter shock.

Meilana sliced Orinsu, snapping him out of it. Her follow up kick to the gut sent the vampire running. A chase ensued until Orinsu lifted off. Deploying yet another giant ice spike allowed Meilana's pursuit to continue. Like before, the ice spike grew only so tall. She jumped from its edge again, but failed to reach Orinsu this time. His flight speed increased tenfold.

Unable to land back on the ice spike, Meilana was due for another free fall, but Obake teleported before her. A foot boost helped her catch up until Orinsu reached another level of speed. Obake appeared again, hurling a shuriken into Orinsu's back. That slowed him down a great deal. Obake turned to Meilana and grabbed her by the wrist. She grabbed his too, and he threw her even higher. Soaring upward, Meilana caught Orinsu. Horrified, the vampire spun around to stop the impending attack. He could not. Meilana unleashed more than a dozen strikes, her katana slashed through his body each time.

On Meilana's return trip to the ground, Obake appeared for a third time. With his arms wrapped around her, he teleported back to the garden. Seconds later Orinsu hit the ground, but not all at once. Many pieces of him fell at different intervals. His arms and legs flopped about on impact and his wings drifted down like feathers. His torso and head bounced as if they were a pair of sports balls. While disturbing, it was also quite satisfying for Obake.

Extreme passion called the young couple to stare into each other's eyes. Without uttering a single word, they both rushed in for a long overdue kiss. It didn't take long for that kiss to turn into a full-blown make-out session. Vigorous caressing accompanied next. An image of Obake's deceased grandparents flashed through his mind. Yumo's lifeless body flashed soon after. Peeling his lips away, Obake wiggled free and stepped back.

Meilana's hurt expression beamed into his soul. "Did I do something wrong?"

"No, I uh—"

"I get it. This is weird. We just killed those things and I'm already all over you."

Obake staggered, his body heavy, lethargic.

Meilana looked beyond concerned. "What's going on?"

Obake sat with his arms draped over his knees. He took several deep breaths to find his bearings.

"You're scaring me," said Meilana.

"Sorry. I don't know what happened."

"You don't know what happened? I think you had some sort of panic attack."

"That's not it. I'm just tired."

"You know you can talk to me, right?"

"I know. Forget about it, okay?"

"If you're scared, I understand. Look at me. I'm terrified right now."

The ninja shook his head in annoyance, but Meilana continued.

"Like, what were those things anyway? Wait a minute. Are they the genai's or whatever?"

Dead classmates and dead senseis flashed behind Obake's eyes. "Stop it."

"That means your grandparents were telling you the truth the whole time," said Meilana, speaking like a detective who just cracked a tough case.

"Stop," said Obake with more aggression, but Meilana was too lost in thought to hear him.

"That means—"

"I said shut up!"

Meilana flinched then scowled. "What's your problem?"

"They're dead."

"What?"

"All of them."

"Wait, who's—"

"Everyone… my grandmother, my grandfather. My best friend, my classmates. My senseis, my parents. Everyone!"

Shaking with fury, Obake screamed at the academy's top floor.

The color drained from Meilana's face and tears fell over her cheeks. "I had no idea. I'm so sorry."

She sprang forward, embracing her boyfriend. Obake's arms dangled at his sides, unable to return the embrace.

"I have work to do," muttered Obake while gesturing to Yumo's Stinger.

Astonishingly, it still leaned against the tree, unscathed.

Obake removed the Stinger key from around his neck. "Take this and get somewhere safe."

"Don't tell me you plan to fight more of them? I saw a red one with these huge horns—"

Meilana glanced up, gasped then clapped both hands over her mouth. "There it is."

Without looking for himself, Obake made way for the academy's entrance.

"Please don't fight that thing. We barely survived just now."

Ignoring her words, Obake pressed on. Meilana grabbed at his wrist, but he jerked it away.

"I know you're capable of handling yourself, but I want you to get out of here. I'm not sure if I'll make it through this," said Obake.

"You don't have to do this alone. We can go get help," said Meilana, keeping pace with Obake.

"Who'd believe us? Plus, you're not even allowed to be here."

Meilana fell silent.

"What would they try to do to you? I won't let that happen."

Obake stopped then turned to his girlfriend. He could see the gears in her brain attempting to locate a valid counter argument.

"Take the Stinger and get back to your empire as fast as you can. This is something I have to do." Leaning in, he kissed Meilana on the forehead. "I want you to go and be happy."

After shoving the academy doors open, Obake crossed over the threshold.

"Wait! You're not breaking up with me that easily." Meilana sped forth. "I'm going with you whether you like it or not."

Prepared to protest, Obake opened wide, but Meilana pressed a finger to his lips. She then leaned in close. Their kiss was brief but special.

As Meilana pulled back to caress Obake's hair, he noticed bloody stitches peeking from behind her gauntlet. "How'd that happen?"

"Oh, that? Nothing but a weak moment," she said as if indifferent to the matter.

"It's bleeding. Here, take this."

Obake pulled out one of his puapo canisters and handed it over. "It's a very powerful elixir. My Nana—never mind."

Meilana opened it and took a hesitant whiff like she expected it to bite her nose off.

"What was that?" asked Obake.

"What? Medicine always smells funny."

Obake burst out laughing, Meilana did too. However, once they were all the way inside the academy, the magnitude of their predicament stole their laughs away. Meilana took a quick sip of puapo then tucked it away inside her kimono.

"You can have this back now," she said, holding out Yumo's Stinger key.

"Keep it, just in case."

Without argument, she placed the key back around her neck. As they went up the stairs to the dining hall, they couldn't help but peek around every corner and under every table.

"So how come you never told me you could do all that ice shit?" asked Obake.

"How come you never told me you could do all that shadow shit?"

Obake grinned. "I guess there's still a lot we don't know about each other, huh?"

"We'll have to fix that now won't we?"

"We will. How about starting with why you never told me who you really are? I thought you were an ordinary samurai from the Bushido Empire. Then I find out you're royalty!"

Such talk sowed dread into Meilana's expression. "To be honest, I wanted you to like me for me. Not my heritage. And I was afraid you'd treat me different if you knew what I could do."

"I can respect that." Obake adopted a look of satisfaction. "You never know who's going to judge you." A subtle hint of embarrassment ran through Obake's features. "I thought you might call me a defiler if I told you about the Shadow Cloud."

Meilana smiled in understanding.

"How did you learn to use the ice?" asked Obake.

"My mother. That's about the only good thing she's ever done for me."

The couple soon found themselves standing before the shut doors of Kinichi's Chamber.

Obake put his mask back in place. "Let's take this asshole down."

Weapons at the ready, they kicked the doors in.

No bodies. They're all gone. But how?

All that remained of his senseis and classmates were stains and damage. Tazuro sat on the uppermost platform, preoccupied with eating from a plate in his hand. Beside him sat a clear glass filled to the brim with yellow liquid. To the far left of him sat the Spider Throne.

"Where's that gray monster? Bring him to me, Kalida, too," said Obake.

Tazuro bit into a chicken leg. "I wasn't expecting guests. Had I known, I would've made you both a plate."

"Turn them over to me and I might go easy on you."

Without so much as a nervous twitch, Tazuro guzzled his drink. "Wow. This is absolutely delicious. What do you call this delightful beverage?"

"It's just, lemonade," said a dismayed Meilana.

"Interesting, we have that, too, doesn't taste nearly as good—"

"Nobody cares about your piss water, demon."

Mizuchi ejected, aiming straight for the ginyai emperor's face. At the last possible moment, Tazuro tilted his head out of the way. His focus remained on his plate, even when Obake retracted Mizuchi. After licking his fingers clean, Tazuro made eye contact with the couple. Meilana couldn't help but flinch. Obake however, remained unnerved.

"I hate that damn naginata." Tazuro set his plate aside and brushed his hands together. "You know, those were some good ginyai you killed out there. You had no right." A pensive crescendo swept upon the emperor then faded as fast as it arrived.

An analytical squint creased Obake's eyes. *He's upset. He's actually upset.*

"So, you were saying, Jinenji and Kalida. Well, Jinenji, how should I put this? He's gone to a better place. I made sure of that. Now Kalida's a different story. But what could you possibly want with her? She's just a child."

Obake gritted his teeth.

Tazuro approached his Spider Throne and claimed his sword. "Looks like you'll have to make do with me. But trust me when I say this. You'd have it no other way," Tazuro winked at Obake. "After all, I'm the reason everyone you love is dead."

The words hit like a boat crash. Racing in, Obake thrust his weapon at Tazuro's heart. With a twist of his torso, the emperor evaded it. He then dealt an elbow to the back of Obake's head, slamming him flat on his face.

"As for your grandparents, I killed them myself," said Tazuro.

Obake teleported behind Tazuro and unleashed a brutal kick. Tazuro snatched the ninja's ankle, tossing him back toward Meilana who stood petrified.

"Pathetic, you thought Jinenji was responsible?"

"You'll die slow for what you've done."

"I'm terrified," said Tazuro, imitating a shiver.

Obake went berserk, slashing in every way imaginable. With relative ease, the emperor dodged every slash. "You should've seen their faces."

"I'll slice your throat open."

"All those skills and they still begged for their lives. What cowards."

"Liar!"

A Shadow Cloud puddle formed beneath Obake's feet and he sank into it. In rapid succession, several additional puddles appeared around the chamber. Tazuro ignored all but the one below him. From the puddle's depths, Obake reached up, pulling Tazuro's leg. The emperor didn't budge an inch. Instead, he stood there laughing before plunging his sword into the puddle. Meilana shrieked with worry. Blood seeped from Obake's arm as he elevated from the Shadow Cloud puddle.

Seizing Obake by the throat, Tazuro brought him to eye level. "I'm the reason you don't have a mother."

As much as Obake wanted to, he couldn't hide his confusion and anguish.

"I'm the reason your father died at the Gateway like a fool," said the emperor, taking notice.

Confusion and anguish intensified within Obake.

"They never told you, did they?" asked Tazuro.

Obake said nothing, Tazuro's surprise turned to utter glee. A crystal of ice struck the emperor's hand, freezing it whole. Utilizing a push kick, Obake broke free and glided back to stand next to his girlfriend. Tazuro scrutinized his hand then dispersed the ice with a few shakes.

Words staggered from Meilana like a runner at the end of a strenuous race. "I'm sorry I—"

"Don't worry about it," said Obake while rubbing his neck.

"Together this time?" said Meilana, capturing a deep breath.

A warm gaze and assuring nod found Meilana, a gift of confidence from Obake.

"Don't you want to know what happened to them?" taunted Tazuro.

Ignoring the question, Obake closed the distance. Once within range, he vanished. The wisps of Shadow Cloud left behind obscured his opponent's vision. Six ice crystals came slicing through the wisps. Even with the Shadow Cloud obstruction, the ice crystals stood no chance.

Each missed their intended target. Obake emerged upside down, using the ceiling as a springboard. The emperor bolted away, leaving the floor as Obake's only victim. Meilana came in fast with a kick, but Tazuro blocked the attack. She then followed with a flurry of katana slashes.

Taken by desperation, Obake tried removing Mizuchi from the floor; it loosened ever so slow. As Tazuro blocked Meilana's last strike, she stumbled. Vicious kicks sent her smashing against the wall displaying spears. They cascaded on top of her and she fell unconscious.

At last, Obake heaved his weapon free. He sprinted at the emperor who dropped him with a gut punch. Encumbered by fear, Obake watched Tazuro walk away to pick up three fallen spears. He bent and twisted the spears as if they were common threads of rope. Two of the spears got tied around Meilana's wrists and one got tied around her neck. The tops and bottoms of each spear were then shoved through the wall. Meilana jolted awake to find herself stuck like a decoration.

"Relax for a while," said Tazuro with a smug tone.

Squirm as she may, the samurai's new shackles held strong. "Get these off of me!"

She kicked at Tazuro's calves, but that aroused his laughter.

"I find it astounding that they never told you the story," said Tazuro, waltzing back over to Obake.

Grabbing a fist full of green hair, Tazuro dragged Obake across the floor. He then tossed the ninja to lay below the bottom most platform.

Tazuro sat on the middle platform, placing a foot on Obake's chest. "Get comfortable. You're in for a real treat.

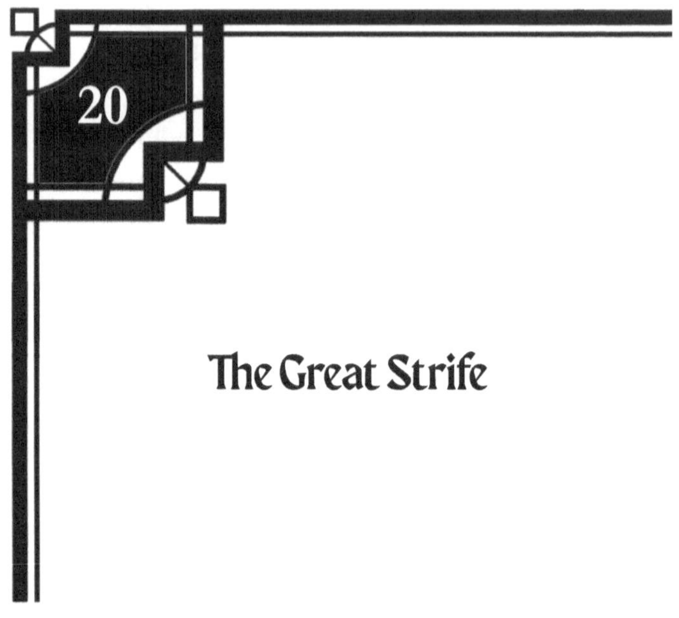

20

The Great Strife

Seventeen years ago:

To smell something other than sulfur was strange for Tazuro. *I thought every realm smelled like home.*

He inhaled the frigid air, letting it fill his lungs to capacity. A subconscious sense of enjoyment developed as the breeze brushed past. Grass massaged his six sharp toes as he exited the Gateway.

So soft.

It took a moment, but his eyes adjusted to the sun peeking from behind the horizon. His fresh shaven head attracted its light.

What a peaceful place, tranquil even. Jealousy swelled as he became conscious of his thoughts, and he made sure to suppress them. *Such blasphemy, if Malubris knew...*

Tazuro's itchy cheeks warranted frequent scratching. After all, they just started showing signs of a beard. Jinenji joined him, so thin and awkward; his blood red hair tickling the tops of his shoulders. A young man with bee-like eyes and wings to match came through the Gateway next. He didn't share the same issue as Jinenji. His black, stringy hair dangled well past his shoulders and three smaller eyes on his forehead glanced around. Next to exit was a female vampire that moved about like an ape. Another ginyai walked out behind her. Aside from metal armbands, he wore no armor and only minimal clothing. With his brown fur, cat-like ears and wolfish snout, he defined savage.

Jinenji was first to speak, breaking the silence. "As I reported, Your Grandeur, the city is about four hundred and fifty yards that way."

Jinenji pointed past the ridge overlooking the Serpentine Trail. As everyone focused their attention toward it, four hundred ginyai soldiers flooded the area. They spilled into every nook and cranny of the valley. The Gateway stood near the edge of the cliff, opposite the Serpentine Trail. It had no space to speak of once all was said and done. Many ginyai species stood in attendance. Kezai, goblins and hagazo made up the majority. A couple dozen centaurs, an equal number of vampires, a handful of ogres and some juggernauts had arrived too. Aside from the fellow with the bee eyes, one additional vulborta attended, and the savage man was the only wudaigo. Despite their enormous numbers, the ginyai snuck about like rabbits in the night.

Tazuro gazed at the ape like vampire. "Tozzmun."

She stopped sniffing everyone's feet and gave Tazuro her undivided attention.

"Tell me what you see."

Tozzmun's wings were draped around her like a cape. She unwrapped them and took to the sky. A leather pouch tied to her waist was the nicest part of her ensemble. Every other garment looked pillaged from corpses long dead. From her pouch came a set of binoculars, she used them to survey the land. As Tazuro awaited her return, an unsuspecting middle-aged couple came strolling through the Tree Corridor.

Dammit.

Their faces filled with terror upon seeing the horde of ginyai. Darts sank into their necks before they could part their lips.

Dropping back to the ground, Tozzmun returned a blow dart and binoculars to her pouch. "There are two look outs over there," she said, through a lisp.

The emperor stroked Tozzmun's head as if she were a pet. "We need to move quickly."

He turned to Jinenji, who gulped.

"Take them out."

Jinenji sent licks of scarlet energy through the tip of his tungsten scepter. His skin altered from gray to ebony. Black dreadlocks replaced his red hair. His hands shrank and his body gathered muscle. By the end of it all, his eyes had turned from piercing green to warm brown.

"Never ceases to amaze me," said Tazuro.

Before long, the army marched along the Serpentine Trail as quiet as could be. A rectangular sword, so golden it made the sun jealous, shimmered on Tazuro's back. The eye insignia upon it matched those found on banners held by some of the soldiers.

Once they'd gone high enough for Tazuro to peer over the ridge, he halted their advance. Yokai City rested right where Jinenji said it would be. Two lookout towers stood on either corner of the perimeter wall, each housing one ninja a piece. The wall doubled as protection from outside threats and a boundary to keep people from falling off the mountain. Nothing but the main entrance led to more land, cliffs surrounded the rest of the city in its entirety.

"I'll be listening. Don't mess this up," said Tazuro.

"You can hear from that far?" asked Jinenji.

Tazuro grinned then borrowed Tozzmun's binoculars. With anticipation, he watched through them while Jinenji continued onward.

"Baraiko? That you?" asked one of the lookout ninjas.

He wore a gray and green keikogi with a mask and hood covering most of his head. Tazuro could only see his eyes and the pale skin around them. Jinenji offered a kind smile and a wave.

"That's him," said the other lookout ninja who wore the same clothing, but was darker around the eyes.

"In the flesh," said Jinenji, showing off his wingspan.

"You're usually not up at this hour," said the darker ninja as he pulled on a lever next to him.

"I recently heard that the early bird gets the worm." Jinenji sighed. "The early bird gets no rest is more like it."

They all laughed together like a trio of good friends.

"Yeah, right, got yourself a little concubine, don't you? We won't tell anybody," said the pale ninja with a grin.

A forced laugh departed from Jinenji. Between the look-out towers, the wall separated in the middle. Double doors formed and opened to a cobblestone street. Aside from a few stray cats, it was empty, too young in the day for most. Vibrant and auspicious, the city looked marvelous. Not a single imperfection could be located. It resembled an untouched model of a city more than a place people truly lived.

The darker ninja leaned out of the tower. "What's that you got there? New weapon?"

"Ah… yes. Crafted it a fortnight ago. What do you think?"

"Weird, but I like it."

"What about your armor?" The pale ninja took a peek for himself. "That new, too?"

Jinenji glanced at his brown and silver armor which now fit too tight. "Something like that."

In rapid succession, Jinenji fired scarlet bolts at both lookouts. One died with a strike to the heart, the other with a strike to the neck.

Tazuro led his forces to the main entrance then halted them. "You four will come with me and Jinenji."

Two male kezai, one female hagazo and the man with the bee-like eyes perked up as Tazuro singled them out.

"Rinjado, I need you to grab a handful of soldiers and come along as well."

With his tail swinging in excitement, the savage ginyai made his selections.

"As for the rest of you, when you see a flaming arrow in the sky, lay waste to everyone and everything."

Each member of the army smiled. Having little time to waste, Tazuro went inside with all those appointed. Thanks to Jinenji's disguise, he made short work of any morning lovers unlucky enough to step outside.

"How much further?" asked the emperor.

"It's the house next to the cathedral, past the fountain," said Jinenji.

They entered a cul-de-sac and passed a decorative fountain. An immaculate house with platinum doors presented itself. Next-door, an illustrious cathedral made most neighboring buildings appear basic.

"Sorcerers are in that cathedral." Tazuro laid eyes on Rinjado. "None of them, not even one should survive."

Rinjado set off with his small platoon.

"Zathumor, I want you to remain here with Jinenji."

The man with the bee-like eyes nodded.

"If anyone comes outside, don't hesitate."

Baraiko's husk dripped from Jinenji, reverting him to his natural state.

With morbid amusement, Tazuro watched. "Disgusting, but I just might have to learn that someday."

Jinenji tried holding back a big grin. Zathumor tried hiding his envy.

Tazuro scooped up his other subordinates then jumped onto the roof of the platinum doored house. "Launch the signal."

One of the male kezai swiped an arrow against a flint. Bright flames arrived to overtake it. The kezai released the flaming arrow to the sky. Roars of combat rushed in, swallowing the faint sounds of the morning. The massive army went to work tearing through the sleepy streets. Through doors, walls, windows and rooftops they went. First order of business consisted of slaughtering all in sight. Those who escaped their homes got murdered in the streets. Women with small children, women with newborns and pregnant women alike were among the first to die. Straight away, ginyai slayed them in their desperation to flee. Husbands and teenagers accustomed to shoemaking, farm work and fishing wielded tools and whatever else they could find. Their makeshift weapons were useless against the might of ginyai weaponry. As their agony imbued screams sliced about, Tazuro plunged his fist into the roof. One swift jerk later and a hole large enough to fit a barrel appeared.

A young, caramel-skinned man slept on a couch in the living room below. Dark blond hair, tied in a ponytail, dangled over his shoulder. Black and gold armor along with a green outfit covered his anatomy. The sudden crash tore the blond man from his slumber. His left eye shined blue, his right green, both squinted with confusion.

"Go!" commanded Tazuro.

All three soldiers dropped into the room below, brandishing swords upon landing. A blue-haired woman, standing behind the couch, backed against the wall. She held a sleeping newborn tight against her bosom. Despite her horror filled screams, the baby remained asleep. Tufts of forest green hair sprouted from the baby's scalp like blades of grass.

Mizuchi rested on the floor beside the couch, and the blond man seized it. Mere seconds later, the female hagazo lunged at the blue-haired woman. With a dash and powerful swing, the blond man knocked the sword from the hagazo. He then slashed her from chin to ear.

A portion of her head parted from the rest. The kezai men were next in line.

One charged while the other kept his distance and shot an arrow. The blond man rolled toward the braver of the two. After the arrow whizzed overhead, the blond man untucked and sliced through the pair of legs coming at him. He then ejected Mizuchi. It swirled through the air, impaling the archer. Not taking any chances, the blond man stomped on the leg-less ginyai's head then pulled the archer toward him. As the archer sped closer, the blond man stepped aside. Momentum carried his foe through the wall. The archer dropped a small distance before blasting through the cathedral wall as well.

"Hurry, get out of here!" said the blond man to the blue-haired woman.

She stood there, doe eyed, fear draining her tanned skin to a blanched white.

"Vai, now!"

Vai snapped out of it. She then scrambled over the ginyai corpses with her baby still nestled.

A small boy with long, jet black hair came running into the living room. "What's going on?"

Vai took his hand then disappeared down the hallway.

Tazuro grinned. "You're every bit as skilled as Jinenji said you would be, *Bakemono*."

A confused expression returned to the blond man. "How do you know me?"

Tazuro placed a finger over his lips. "Shh, that's a secret."

Fuchsia energy left the emperor's hand then arrived at Bakemono's chest. Its power sent him hurtling backwards through the window. Glass carved up his body until he smashed onto the fountain out in the cul-de-sac. Tazuro watched with glee as Bakemono's consciousness fled.

Like a triumphant statue, he surveyed the overrun city, admiring the mayhem like a painter would a finished piece of art.

Rinjado crashed out of the cathedral doors. One after the other, his platoon members fell into the street along with him. Bloodied and broken, the platoon members each succumbed to their wounds. A tall man wearing a gold bracelet, a stumpy lady wearing a diadem and a young woman wearing pink diamond earrings followed. All three of them dressed in extravagant robes and exuded mocha colored skin.

After wiping blood from his mouth, Rinjado rushed at the trio on all fours. His movements outpaced lighting itself. A glass sphere, with a jewel like symbol inside, hovered above the stumpy lady's hand. Turquoise bolts fired from it, but they missed Rinjado by a long shot. The young woman turned her staff into a whip made of translucent white energy. She swung it at the wudaigo, but only succeeded in whipping the air.

As Rinjado passed her by, the tall man tossed five seals made of parchment. Each adorned with unusual markings. All of them missed except the last. It latched onto Rinjado's chest as he soared through the air. Thin wires made of bright green energy wrapped around him. He dropped hard and the wires squeezed.

With a flex of his muscles, Rinjado broke the wires off. He then bit into the tall man's ankle. Once upright, Rinjado slammed the tall man's face into the ground multiple times. Somewhere along the way, his neck broke.

A little girl with the same mocha complexion and the same extravagant robes emerged from the cathedral. A look of euphoria was stained onto her face.

"Get back inside," said the stumpy lady, full of tears.

The young woman glanced over. "Do what Mom says!"

Hiding her euphoria, the little girl ran back inside. Tears flowed from the young woman's eyes as well, but her tears were infused with rage.

Rinjado dropped his kill then licked the blood in between his teeth. "Say goodbye to daddy."

The brutality on display amused Tazuro. He couldn't peel his focus away from Rinjado until the pitter patter of footsteps caught his ears. Ten individuals wearing ghostly green masks and the same attire as the lookouts accosted him. A flurry of kunais, shurikens, and ninjatos rained upon the emperor. Not an ounce of worry came over him. It was less than child's play to evade, deflect and counter against all of the attacks. Most died there on the spot. Some went off the cliff side into the ocean. What remained died in the street beside Bakemono's house, all but one that is.

This ninja hung back, lobbing spit that turned into needles upon leaving her lips. Tazuro's golden sword deflected the needles back from where they came. One penetrated the ninja's throat. She collapsed—dead—and dropped her ninjato.

Soul energy can be so bizarre sometimes.

Painted with a smile of bliss, Tazuro began blasting at buildings and homes. More than a dozen erupted with bodies and debris, all of it going sky high along with shrieks of anguish. Yet, the ten ninjas from before would not be the last to arrive. In response to the mayhem, two hundred additional ninjas appeared. As they laid waste to the invading forces, the tide of battle began to shift.

How's this possible? Tazuro surveyed the unfolding events then found himself drawn back to Rinjado's exploits. *I made a wise choice bringing him aboard.*

The wudaigo was biting into an energy shield erected by the stumpy lady. Even as the young woman fired bolts at his back, he carried on.

"That stings!" said Rinjado, before shattering the shield with his bite.

He then used his teeth to tear into the stumpy lady's neck. As he ate, she placed her orb point blank and fired a bolt. Like Rinjado's teeth, the bolt ate until a gaping hole was left in the wudaigo's torso. In disbelief, the young woman fell to her knees.

Tazuro scoffed then jumped down next to Zathumor and Jinenji. *Seems I have to do everything myself.*

"Is this all they have to give?" said Zathumor, impaling a ninja with his daggers.

Jinenji blasted a ninja in the face then gazed at Zathumor. "You're still not using your soul energy? Are you sure you're not tainted?"

"Tainted? No! Don't try to lump me in with them." The vulborta glanced at his fists. "I just can't control it yet."

"You're no better than a common soldier without it."

Anger curved Zathumor's face, but it didn't have time to fully develop. Through all the sounds of war came a cheery yell from on high. A younger Kinichi straddled the back of a dead Tozzmun. Using his left hand as an extension of the mind, he maneuvered the vampire. With his right hand as a second extension, he pushed, lifted, tossed and slammed every ginyai he came across. Two rings, one on each hand, shimmered sapphire in accordance with his attacks.

Jinenji shot a scarlet bolt at Kinichi. "What the fuck?"

Kinichi dodged then pushed the sorcerer into a house using telekinesis. Tazuro released a beam at the unorthodox pilot. With his telekinesis, Kinichi stopped the beam in midair. A toothy grin spread Kinichi's lips. That same grin faded as he struggled to hold the beam at bay. It inched closer like a leashed dog trying to fetch a bone. Soon enough, it broke through, striking Kinichi's ribs. Staying on his feet, he surfed Tozzmun onto the ground. Zathumor flew at Kinichi, his wings buzzing as they carried him. A telekinetic lift seized the vulborta mid-flight. This prompted Tazuro to advance. Kinichi gave the emperor a telekinetic push with his other hand. It did little more than slow him down so Kinichi sent Zathumor hurtling at Tazuro.

With an annoyed snarl, Tazuro knocked Zathumor aside, then reconvened. "You're getting on my nerves."

The telekinetic push began losing its strength and distance closed between the warriors. Exhausted, Kinichi couldn't keep Tazuro at bay any longer. Using one hand, Tazuro reached for Kinichi then grabbed his head. As the sadistic kezai squeezed, Kinichi wailed in pain.

"The sound of a crushing skull is very loud. It'll be twice as loud for you," said the emperor.

An explosion distracted Tazuro. By the time he located its source, Kinichi was safe behind younger versions of Yokai and Bao-Ang.

Bao clenched a lit cigarette in her mouth. "You're one ugly son of a bitch, aren't you?"

"I'm not sure ugly is a strong enough word," said Yokai, bearing his claws.

Like a disappointed father, Tazuro looked upon Kinichi. "Let's hope you two are more entertaining than he was."

"If it's a good fight you're after, then I think you'll be pleased," said Bao, her kodachi at the ready.

Yokai stepped in front of his wife.

The emperor sighed. "If you have to protect her, then why bring—"

An ear-piercing shriek came, followed by a soaring Yokai. The power from Bao's intonation advanced Yokai at high speed. Tazuro's golden sword came around to collide with Yokai's claws. Yokai went airborne then let bog pellets rain.

He's pretty good.

Through the slimy explosions, Tazuro attacked once more. Yokai blocked, but went crashing through the second floor of a bakery anyway.

"You'll regret that," said Bao.

Her next scream projected chunks of cobblestone, so Tazuro's sword assumed the role of a shield. As the cobblestone chunks deflected every which way, Tazuro got close. His fist planted so far in Bao's abdomen she exposed her breakfast. Her cigarette floated in the digestion as Tazuro prepared to lop her head off.

"Over here!"

Soaring from the bakery, Yokai kicked his enemy in the cheek then flipped away.

Tazuro shrugged. "I'll admit. I'm having fun, but this can't go on forev—"

Bao and Yokai barreled forward, crisscrossing each other on the way.

"I wish you'd stop cutting me off," roared Tazuro.

The ninjas attempted to cut into the emperor, but he stabbed his sword into the ground and seized their wrists.

"You humans have more bite than I thought," he said, before skipping the ninjas across the ground like pebbles on a lake.

Not to be deterred, Yokai dropped an unavoidable bomb. Tazuro sustained the full brunt of its explosion. In retaliation, he fired another beam that curved skyward. The emperor met the beam in the air then spiked it with his sword. As a result of the beam's impact, Yokai and Bao went spiraling. Nearby cheers erupted. From his periphery, Tazuro glimpsed Jinenji and Zathumor observing in delight. Although bruised and bloodied, Yokai and Bao didn't stay down for long.

"You two don't know when to give up," said the emperor.

Bao cracked a smile. "Give up? Never heard of such a thing."

"This is all very interesting. It's rare when one's reputation holds true."

"I see you've done your homework," said Yokai.

A streetlamp flew Tazuro's way. He smashed it to smithereens then turned to its origin. Kinichi stood surrounded by hovering debris. Jinenji and Zathumor tried to intervene, but Tazuro stopped them.

The kezai and the telekinetic ninja locked eyes before the debris started to fly. Multiple sword slashes and a few dodge maneuvers kept Tazuro safe.

What the—?

Yokai surfed along on a plumbing pipe. Tazuro's golden sword swatted the pipe, but not before Yokai took a dive. Both sets of Yokai's claws impaled the emperor's torso.

"Hurts, doesn't it?" said Yokai with a backwards leap.

Bao came surfing next, a piece of the fountain as her transport. She jumped off the fountain piece, letting it clobber Tazuro. She then released a scream so powerful it brought Tazuro to his knees. In came Kinichi with a telekinetic press.

Two oversized bombs manifested in Yokai's hands. "Now's our chance."

He threw them forward with astonishing speed. Fuchsia energy burst from Tazuro as he roared like a pride of lions. The sonic scream and telekinetic press severed. Kinichi and Bao spun off in different directions. Tazuro sprinted forward to address Yokai's bombs head on. One after the other, they exploded against him, shredding his armor. Yet he didn't stop. Yokai filled with terror. He couldn't prevent the emperor from sending a fist into his face.

"Who's next?" said Tazuro, circling in place.

All the fighting subsided. With most of the humans dead, ninja and civilian alike, all eyes were on Tazuro.

"This is what happens when you fight alongside the most powerful warrior who ever lived."

Merry making from the ginyai army mimicked a crowd at a competitive event.

Sinister ideas crept behind Tazuro's eyes. "Burn it all."

All of the ginyai equipped with bows shot fire arrows at the surrounding buildings. In a matter of seconds, the entire city turned infernal. Yokai, Kinichi and Bao went paper pale. More arrows released, but a gale force tornado forged from nothing to vacuum them up. Arrows whipped round and round until the tornado became a fiery whirlwind.

Astounding, I've never seen anything like it.

The whirlwind sped at the army. Many ran for their lives and still got swallowed whole. Flashes of a man appeared within the spinning flames as they feasted. Most of the ginyai turned to ash, but the fiery whirlwind didn't stop. It doubled back, heading straight for the Ginyai Emperor.

Tazuro crouched low, preparing to combat the flames. "Come on."

A few feet away, the whirlwind dissipated, revealing Bakemono. Ginyai fortunate enough to still be alive, stood transfixed by the blond ninja.

Bakemono exhibited a severed goblin head. "It didn't take much to make him sing. You might want to invest in better soldiers."

How? He should be dead.

Bao stared at her son, happiness and concern in her eyes. Yokai and Kinichi held matching expressions of shock.

"What do you say? Want to give it another go?" asked Bakemono, throwing the goblin head at the emperor's feet.

Tazuro discarded what remained of his armor. "Perhaps I underestimated you, Grandmaster."

"You underestimated us all."

Members of the army stirred. Their desire for destruction unsatiated. Tazuro declined to indulge them.

"No one's ever seen what I'm truly capable of. You should consider yourself lucky."

Bakemono bounced then stretched neck and limb. "I already do."

What is this man doing? Is he out of his mind?

The young woman who fought Rinjado with her family came sprinting over.

Kinichi lit up. "Delorma, you're alive."

"Where have you been?" asked Bao.

"Helping your son, I think he can get us out of this." Delorma now wielded her mother's glass sphere. "Everybody ready?"

"Hold on." Bakemono came to a standstill. "Let me have a crack at this guy first."

Tazuro chuckled. "You humans are so stubborn. Look around you. We've already won."

"Not yet!" said a charging Bakemono.

A flurry of crescent winds left his naginata in a hurry. Tazuro knocked aside the first two, dodged the third and cut the last. A beam then burst from Tazuro's palm. It chomped the air in search of Bakemono. He spiraled over the beam then unraveled with a thrust.

As Mizuchi came within range, Tazuro stomped it loose then swung his sword. "You're finished."

Bakemono performed a back handspring, letting the golden sword crash against the ground.

He then used the sword as a launch point and drove his knee into Tazuro's nose. "You were saying?"

"Don't get cocky," said the emperor upon dropping his sword.

A bout of fisticuffs ensued, Tazuro landed devastating blow after devastating blow. Although powerful, Bakemono's jabs did little to hurt the seven-foot kezai. The emperor's next punch missed, but his follow up kick turned Bakemono to jelly. Kinichi, Delorma, Bao and Yokai gasped at their companion's waning defenses.

"You should've played dead," said Tazuro, throwing a roundhouse.

Bakemono dodged then countered with a three-kick combo. The emperor slapped the kicks away as if they were troublesome flies. Adopting the behavior of a stampeding bull, Tazuro skewered Bakemono under his shoulder. Blood spilled, but the ninja merely winced from the pain.

"Down you go," said Tazuro, slamming Bakemono.

Tazuro pulled his horn loose, fetched his sword then slashed it. A single body roll took Bakemono out of harm's way and over to where Mizuchi laid. With haste, he released a gale force squall at his enemy. It swept Tazuro up then dropped him several feet away.

"Yes!" yelled Bao, Yokai, Delorma and Kinichi in unison.

The ginyai army however, grunted with displeasure.

"What's the point?" Brushing dirt from his body, Tazuro got up. "Why fight this?"

"I could ask you the same," said Bakemono.

"Are you so foolhardy you can't see that you're doomed?"

"Leave now and I'll let you live."

"You're already exhausted and injured. Your city burns. I still have an army of ginyai, and your best warriors are no better off than you." Tazuro raised his sword then turned it so that the eye insignia was facing his enemy. "Eye can see this. Why can't you?"

Fear billowed from Bakemono. The emperor laughed, mocking him. That very same fear arrived in Yokai and the others. Ginyai army members laughed too, none more so than Zathumor. Jinenji, however, didn't even smirk; he had the same look of fear about him as the humans. Bakemono gazed at the ground. Bao dropped to her knees. Delorma became sullen. Kinichi and Yokai both slouched.

Yesterday the ginyai, today the humans, tomorrow the avirra.

"There's more than one way to win a war," whispered Bakemono.

Surrounding laughter increased to an obnoxious level.

Shifting an ear toward Bakemono, Tazuro listened. "What was that? I couldn't hear you, your failures too loud."

"I don't know why you're here. I don't know why you're doing this. To be honest, it doesn't matter. You attacked my family, destroyed my home and killed my people. I don't give a shit how strong you are. You'll die here today."

The emperor's laughter wavered. "So, you're the speech giving type."

A death stare radiated from Bakemono. "They'll tell stories about the day you failed to defeat the Yokai Ninjas."

"All right then, enough talk," said Tazuro, his blade engulfing with fuchsia energy.

Using the wind as propulsion, Bakemono flew at his foe, prompting him to strike the ground with his sword. Energy rippled forth, spitting and licking fragments of itself. Mizuchi's blade extended to split the energy clear down the middle. Tazuro's face became the target. He ducked fast, but Mizuchi extended faster. It sliced Tazuro from the front of his skull to the back. Blood stained the air and rivulets streamed over Tazuro's entire face. Ecstatic cheers erupted from the remaining humans. Tazuro crumbled to one knee, letting go of his precious sword. With both hands, he applied pressure to his head, but the blood poured on as if in defiance. Jinenji stumbled over the sprawling debris while Zathumor and the ginyai army growled.

Bakemono huffed and puffed from exhaustion. Enraged, Zathumor flew up then dove at the grandmaster. Yokai intercepted by tossing a bomb at Zathumor's face. Hoarse, choking screams sailed the battlefield. Everyone winced and cringed, human and ginyai alike. Zathumor hit the ground then grabbed at his burning face, neck and chest. Nothing could alleviate his agony. The blood streaming from Tazuro's head began to slow, Zathumor ran to him.

"Help me. Please!" he begged, through purple flames and smoke.

Revolted, Tazuro shoved him away. Zathumor fell beside the corpse of a ninja in a ghostly green mask.

Steady pools of blood spread from under the corpse. Taking two big scoops of blood, Zathumor splashed himself. The bomb's effects nullified, but agony still clung to every bit of his charred skin.

"Jinenji! Where are you?" Tazuro glanced around and caught the sorcerer sneaking away. "What are you doing?"

With a swipe of his scepter, Jinenji unleashed a dazzle of scarlet sparks. As they tattered about, flashing and confusing everyone, he climbed onto the perimeter wall. Ginyai cursed him as he fled along its spine.

"You coward!"

"Pathetic!"

"Go ahead and run. We don't need you!"

Some of the ginyai even attacked him. Firing arrows and throwing rocks amongst other things they found lying around. Jinenji spared himself any damage by keeping a scarlet shield up as he raced to safety.

Yokai approached his son. "We should go after him." Delorma, Bao and Kinichi approached as well.

"We will," said Bakemono, still catching his breath.

"We might be in for another round." Bao-Ang rummaged through her kimono and out came a puapo canister. "Here. Drink up."

In suspense, Tazuro watched as Bao poured the magenta liquid past her son's lips. She then drank some herself before passing it around.

Bakemono stretched his body once more. "I love that stuff."

"We have to make it count. That was the last of it for now," said Bao.

Tazuro stumbled over to reclaim his sword. "Not only are you all a sack of warring insects. You're cheaters as well." Once he possessed the sword, his energy flared and his arrogance returned front and center. "Let's get back to business."

Members of the ginyai army closed in on the humans.

Bakemono twisted into the air, carried by the power of the wind alone. "Get back!"

Delorma dispersed. Bao, Yokai and Kinichi followed suit. As the grandmaster came back down, he stabbed Mizuchi into the cobblestone. An enormous tornado whipped about and tore off toward the emperor.

Tazuro's sword flew from his grasp upon clashing with the tornado. He could do nothing to prevent the tornado from enveloping him. Zathumor got swept up by its fierce current as well. It spun them both into a dizzy before settling into a calm flowing orb.

Every ginyai became awestruck and stopped in their tracks. The dizzy spell over Tazuro subsided, he prodded the orb. Although made of wind, it was solid to the touch.

"All right everyone, follow my lead," said Bakemono, leading an onslaught aimed at the remaining ginyai.

With her sonic screams, Bao set many ginyai up to get captured by her son. Yokai's bombs assisted in much the same manner. Kinichi and Delorma's soul energy made for an effective contribution as well. Before long, every ginyai had become trapped. Groups of five, ten, even twenty at a time floated within a single wind prison. Some ginyai became too confused and dizzy to fathom what had befallen them. Others hurled obscenities and threats from their confines. Tazuro could do nothing but watch.

Bakemono jolted up, stabbing Mizuchi at the sky as he went. Every wind prison elevated higher than the tallest buildings. In a frenzy, Tazuro jabbed and punted at his wind prison. Zathumor laid in the fetal position, hands over his melted face. Other ginyai attacked their wind prisons as well, but to no avail.

"Release me!" screamed Tazuro.

"Not a chance," said Bakemono. "Kinichi, you thinking what I'm thinking?"

With an enthusiastic nod, Kinichi used telekinesis to toss Tazuro's wind prison at the nearest flame-ridden building. As it howled into an orb of fire, Tazuro's energy detonated. It gushed, surrounding him and Zathumor. Flames encroached, but couldn't breach Tazuro's energy.

Delorma's jaw hit the ground. "He can do that?"

The grandmaster looked to Kinichi then pointed at the gaggle of wind prisons. "Burn them too!"

Kinichi threw Tazuro's flaming wind prison at them. An inferno took over the sky. One by one, every wind prison went a blaze. An orchestra of wails and screams played throughout the sky. Ginyai devolved into ashes that sprinkled over the smoldering city like monstrous rain, but Tazuro remained unscathed. His energy continued to hold the fire at bay.

That's right, you pathetic maggots. Wait till I break out of—

Convulsions seized Tazuro, lurching and lashing him.

"Look, he does need a weapon," said Delorma.

Lacerations appeared on the orb of fire like knife wounds on skin.

Bakemono shook his head. "We can't beat him like this."

"Yes, we can," said Kinichi. "He'll burn any minute now."

"No. He's too strong. He'll break out if we wait any longer."

"Are you sure?"

"No doubt about it, and if he gets his sword back, it'll be game over."

"So, what do we do, son?" asked Yokai, panicked and uncertain.

"We have to get to the Meditation Stone. Well, they call it the Gateway."

Bao's eyes darted around in confusion. "What do you mean Gateway?"

"That's where they came from. The Meditation Stone is actually a portal," said Delorma.

Kinichi and Yokai looked skeptical and flabbergasted at the same time.

"All these years and it wasn't just some old statue?" Bao almost choked on her words.

More lacerations emerged on the orb of fire.

"We're almost out of time. Come on!" said Bakemono.

Forlorn, Tazuro watched as his enemies left the city and sprinted before the Gateway. He couldn't believe it when they started raising their soul energies.

Dammit. He really does know!

The stone obelisk took its time adopting its true form. Its shimmering pink kaleidoscope mesmerized everyone.

"It worked. It actually worked." Bakemono looked at Kinichi. "Get ready to catch."

With an upsurge, Bakemono soared over the Serpentine Trail and onto a high building in Yokai City. He raised Mizuchi and gave it a mighty swing. A fleet of wind summoned Tazuro's orb of fire. It zoomed into Kinichi's telekinetic orbit; he took hold of it then pushed it at the Gateway.

Despite extreme fatigue, Tazuro obliterated the orb of fire with another burst of energy. "I won't let you win!"

The convulsions plaguing him subsided. Kinichi's telekinetic push wavered. Bao assisted him by shrieking a sonic wave. Their efforts repelled Tazuro to the brink of the Gateway. Sheer determination allowed Tazuro to stomp forward like a rhinoceros. Zathumor, who still refused to let go of his face, slid into the Gateway and disappeared. Blood leaked from every orifice on the emperor's head. He stomped forward regardless. Yokai's legion of bombs and Delorma's bolts also did little to disrupt Tazuro's advancement.

"We can't hold him for much longer!" cried Delorma.

Floating into the fray, Bakemono blasted another gale force squall at the emperor. Everyone's combined attacks finally pushed Tazuro through the Gateway which reverted to a stone obelisk.

In misery, the emperor floated within the pink kaleidoscope, he contemplated giving up, but the sound of defeat was too much to bear. Like a giant bell smashing through a street, it banged away in his ears. Re-igniting the Gateway, Tazuro let it blossom to completion. A translucent, white energy barrier now guarded his path. Warped images of the humans came into view on the other side.

The emperor punched the translucent barrier until cracks streaked through it. "You think this is over!"

Delorma sprang to action, dumping more energy into the translucent barrier. At a snail's pace her energy reversed the damage. Tazuro worked faster. For every crack that faded, his punches added seven more. Racing to Delorma, Bakemono rested a hand on her shoulder. The others followed suit.

"Use our soul energy!" said Bao.

"No," Delorma shook her head. "If I take too much, you'll die."

"We'll be fine," said Yokai.

Uninhibited streams of Delorma's energy deployed into the Gateway. As she syphoned the soul energy of her comrades, the streams amplified.

Thundering punches from Tazuro became no more than muffled thuds. "Damn you all!"

Yokai ripped his hand away as if he got electrocuted and Bao knocked on death's door, but Yokai pulled her off. Kinichi grew light headed and fainted on the spot. Bakemono became the last one left to syphon from.

"Let go. Bakemono, let go! We'll find another way," said Delorma.

"Listen to her," pleaded Yokai while grabbing his son.

"There *is* no other way," said Bakemono.

Try as he might, Yokai couldn't pull his son away.

A gentle smile of acceptance came over Bakemono's face. "Dad, it's going to be okay."

Yokai froze as the realization of what was happening hit him.

Delorma wept. "We can run, all of us. Together."

Bakemono held on with tenacity. "Keep going, please. We can't let him win."

The emperor's punches started to shatter the translucent barrier all over again.

Bakemono gripped Delorma tighter. "Take it all, now!"

Through pouring sobs, Delorma syphoned what remained of Bakemono's soul energy. Tazuro noticed his punches losing effect, but he was too exhausted to punch any harder. As the translucent barrier gathered more nourishment, its density enhanced. Sounds coming from the Human Realm muffled once more. Before everything went completely silent, both Bakemono and Tazuro collapsed.

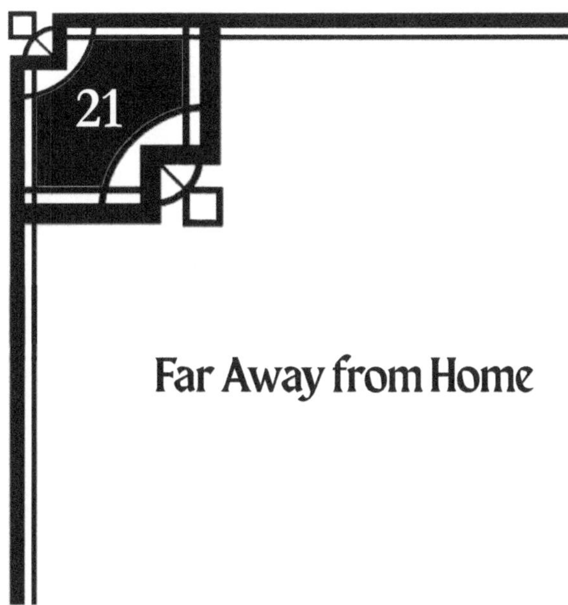

Far Away from Home

Present day:

Both of the young warriors went glacier cold. Tazuro glanced between them, engrossed in their every emotion. Obake's stomach tussled with itself. Meilana ran out of tears to shed, her eyes red and puffy. The emperor removed his foot, allowing Obake to scamper away like a rodent.

Clutching the stabbing pain in his chest, Obake winced. "I don't believe you."

"Denial will get you nowhere," said Tazuro.

"Why would I listen to a sick fuck like you?"

"Because the truth is always more satisfying than the lie."

Obake ransacked the caverns of mind. *This has to be a trick.* Clues he discovered over the years combined with Tazuro's story like puzzle pieces. *But it all makes sense.* Warmth soaked him to the bone. *They didn't die as cowards, they stood strong and they fought back!*

In the presence of Obake's radiance, Tazuro's gleeful disposition dissolved

"What? Did you expect me to cry, monster?" A smirk crossed Obake's lips. "My clan, my family, they won. They beat you, asshole."

Bolts of rage cracked in Tazuro's eyes.

"Even with an army and all your power, you still lost? What kind of conqueror are you?" said Obake in a taunting manner.

With a lunge, Tazuro seized the ninja then hurled him against the platforms, making the Spider Throne rattle.

Sluggish, Obake scaled the platforms, his eyes steady on the Spider Throne. *If I can just get in there, maybe I can—*

Fingers wrapped tight around Obake's ankle. Kinichi's Chamber turned upside down. Blood rushed to Obake's head like water down a sinkhole.

"You think you know loss? I'll show you loss," said the emperor, holding Obake up with a single arm.

Once more, Meilana pushed and pressed on her bindings. "Stop it, stop!"

Tazuro heaved his blade at Meilana, it pierced the wall centimeters above her head. Her next sentence imprisoned itself within her throat.

"You're going to feel exactly how your despicable father made me feel," said Tazuro.

Obake flopped to the floor then smacked against the platforms as Tazuro dragged him before the Gateway. After it sparkled to life, Tazuro chucked Obake inside.

An endless pink kaleidoscope captivated the ninja. *What is this place?* He tried moving, but his legs floundered beneath him. *It's like... the ocean.*

The emperor rushed in after him. "Not so cocky now, are you?" he said, acknowledging Obake's wide-eyed bewilderment.

"Fuck you." Obake attacked with all the strength he could generate. *What is this?* Instead of Mizuchi swinging with the usual cheetah-speed, it crawled like a turtle.

Again, Tazuro seized Obake, this time by the collar, his movements unimpaired. The pink kaleidoscope morphed into streaking lights as the warriors sped in further. Another Gateway came into view before long.

Obake's hands ran moist. His limbs fidgeted. He writhed, kicked, punched and everything in between. Nothing worked.

"Where are you taking me?"

"Imagine wanting to save your people, your loved ones. Keep them from a terrible fate." Tazuro's words reverberated throughout the vicinity. "Now, imagine you're trapped, unable to do anything about it. All you can do is wait for everything to come crashing down."

Coming to a stop, the emperor surveyed the other Gateway. "You pray to Malubris. Ask for mercy. But you worry he's no longer listening."

Who's Malubris?

The image of a cave swam in place of the Gateway's stone makeup.

"What am I saying? You won't have to imagine."

A strong punch crashed into Obake's cheek. He went soaring through the Gateway, bouncing on the jagged cave floor. Until his body met a stalagmite, it didn't stop. Through a steady blur, he investigated, the Gateway returned to solid stone.

No, no, no! His heart dissected itself. *This can't be happening. He has her. I have to get back there.*

Obake's lungs restricted. Infrequent sips of air could be stolen, but nothing more. The bones in his hand quivered and cracked on their way to obtain the Puapo Elixir. Clammy fingers reached inside the pocket of his kimono. Their slippery state let the canister slip. It made a getaway toward the cave's mouth like a prison escapee. Before long, it teetered on the edge of disappearance.

"No, please!"

On Obake's crawl to reclaim it, every fiber ached and wailed. He took the puapo canister from the edge with surgical precision. Magenta liquid went spilling down his throat, soothing it, refreshing it. A drink or two survived the ordeal, but not in vain. Obake's internals embarked on a revitalization mission. His tense muscles relaxed, knots softened, and stinging concluded. As the puapo continued to work, he dozed off to the land of dreams.

Behind the Mask

Obake drifted in and out of consciousness. By his fourth reawakening, a state of sheer alarm possessed him.

Where am I? How did I get here? His dulling pain acted as a potent reminder. *It wasn't a dream. Is this... the Ginyai Realm? No, can't be.*

Desperate yet hopeful, he returned to the Gateway. It continued its stone obelisk disguise.

How do I turn it on? Thoughts of Jinenji poured in. *Wait. I think I know.*

Mizuchi laid close by. A slew of fresh scrapes careened its galvantium build. *Shit. It's all scratched up.* He cradled it like an infant. *Sorry, dad.*

Ear splitting screeches blared from overhead.

"What are those things?" Obake's eyes traced the multi-eyed bats as they swarmed the cave ceiling. *I have to get out of here.*

Accompanied by his weapon, he re-approached his one path home. Short, pathetic spurts of Shadow Cloud entered into existence. The Gateway remained within its slumber.

"Come on. Don't do this to me."

Refusing to be denied, he tried many times over. His soul energy grew weaker with each attempt. Even the Gateway itself seemed disappointed. Not a flicker of pink kaleidoscope patterns arose for the ninja.

With his fist, he hammered on the Gateway. "Wake up, dammit. Wake up!"

The possibility of death in a foreign realm punched Obake's psyche. Pessimistic thoughts ravaged him like a pack of hyenas on a gazelle. Tazuro's hateful words arrived to stab deep. Obake's stomach soon growled, saving him from the various assaults.

With urgency, he sifted through the vials, books, and contraptions he found around the cave. Nothing of sustenance presented itself. He turned to the bats and the other creatures of the cave. They didn't look very appetizing, not even for a starving warrior. No choice remained but to venture out into the unknown.

As he made his way out of the cave's mouth, he heard a pair of footsteps shuffle away. The stench of rotten eggs tickled his nose hairs. While imagining a horrendous creature coming for him, he took cautionary steps outside. Black clouds on an ochre sky, serrated pillars and a humongous volcano came instead.

That better not erupt while I'm here.

Obake flipped open his mother's pocket watch. *2:54 p.m. It still works.*

Scanning the horizon, he put the pocket watch away. A city of black iron buildings persuaded his attention from afar. An overwhelming desire to stay away swelled from within. Stepping out further allowed him to take in the ocean. Its color matched the sky, and the way its waves moved evoked a raging fire.

It's kind of pretty to be honest. Fish! There has to be fish in there.

Obake descended the treacherous mountain, ran past spiked cannonballs wedged into the coastline, then arrived at the ocean. It sloshed and gushed as if lashing out at the sky. Murky water made it impossible to see if any fish were indeed present. Mizuchi shot its blade into the water twice. Both times no fish returned.

"This is going to suck."

After dropping down to his underwear, Obake dove in head first. The subzero temperature frosted his very core. Violent waves thrashed him like a piece of driftwood. He wanted to get out, but his stomach complained. Capturing a deep breath, he submerged well below the ten-foot waves to a much calmer depth.

Fish of all colors, shapes and sizes swam around him. *They look so weird. I've never seen fish like these.*

Their strange designs and features made it difficult for Obake to choose.

Mizuchi skewered a particular fish then brought it back to be examined. *This has got to be poisonous.*

Its fat lips and foggy eyes didn't elicit much trust in the ninja. Another fish that looked similar to a salmon became ensnared next.

Maybe this one's safe.

On Obake's ascent, a joyful kezai peeked out over the ocean's surface. The closer Obake got, the more the kezai resembled Tazuro. His hair, nose, eyes, mouth and horns were all different. Skin another shade of red. That didn't stop Obake from going berserk.

Another one!

The Tazuro look-alike reached over the water with a fishing rod. Obake blasted up through the waves, slashing both of his arms off. Each arm fell into the ocean where the waves swept them away.

Through wails of anguish, the kezai man fell onto his backside. Removing the skewered fish from Mizuchi, Obake stood over the kezai man. His teeth chattered and his lips quivered as he wiggled away from Obake like a worm. Prepared to finish the job, Obake gained on him. A gaggle of voices stopped the ninja in his tracks. He looked over to see more kezai—an adult woman and three adolescents, two girls, one boy. They watched in horror at the events unfolding.

Although shocked, the kezai boy darted between Obake and the armless man. "Stop. Don't hurt him!"

"Oh no," said the kezai woman, sobbing. "It's a human!"

Both of the kezai girls held each other while shaking.

Not knowing what to do or how to think, Obake stepped back. "I'm so sorry I..." Shame and disgust brewed within him like a bad cocktail. "Let me help," he said, stepping forward again.

Shrieks spewed from the girls.

"Get away from us!" said the woman, rushing over to drag the armless man away.

"I won't let you hurt my daddy anymore!" said the boy.

"Please let me—"

A bright orange glow shined, and the ground shook. Before Obake's very eyes, the family began disintegrating. First their hair and nails sizzled away, then their skin. Eyes drooped from their sockets like sauce leaking off a countertop. Each of their skeletons blackened, then ashed away with the wind. Obake's stomach coiled from the revolting sight. The man responsible soon appeared within the fading orange glow.

Black, stringy hair dangled in front of his ghostly mask; the same mask formerly worn by members of the Yokai Clan. His fist came loose from the ground, a large crack in its wake. From his body fluttered a dark brown duffle coat. He brushed himself off and faced Obake. Silver chest armor, gauntlets and matching greaves told the story of a seasoned warrior. Severe burn scars on his neck corroborated that story.

"Why the fuck did you do that?" screamed Obake.

"Put some clothes on and we'll talk."

"That mask. Where did you get it? Who are you?"

"I don't have all day. You want to get out of this realm or not?"

Hesitant, Obake pondered his next move, but the prospect of going home was far too appealing. The black-haired man walked to the edge of shore, staring at the vast sea.

In record time, Obake put his clothes back on, but left his mask around his neck. "So, what's your deal? You kill them then offer me a way home, you some kind of psycho?"

"If I recall correctly, you sliced that guy's arms off, no?"

"That was an accident," said Obake with a choke.

"Some accident."

"I thought he was after me. I thought…" Obake's stomach coiled some more. "Look, I screwed up. But they didn't have to die like that."

"See, that's where you're wrong. What do you think would happen if word got out there was a human in the Ginyai Realm?"

Oh no. I really am in the Ginyai Realm. Obake caressed his forehead. "I didn't think about that."

"Thought so, but you're right about one thing. That family more than likely didn't deserve that, doesn't mean they aren't afraid of us."

"Us?"

"Every ginyai, bad, nice, or otherwise, will be out for your head if they find out. Mine included."

"You're human?"

"Of course, you imbecile. I'm almost out of this shit hole too, so I can't have you drawing unnecessary attention."

Obake examined the man as if he were an artifact in a museum. *Could he be the kid from the picture?*

Sticking to the shoreline, the black-haired man dashed away. "Come on. I never stay out in the open this long."

Obake followed and they soon came to a beach made of jagged sand. Boulders the size of small houses appeared to be the man's destination. He entered a formation of them, dipped his hand under the sand then lifted a hatch. A dark tunnel descending to unknown depths awaited. The man entered, but Obake peered in, opting to stay outside. Impatience found the black-haired man. His mask couldn't hide it.

"I don't have time for this. Get out of here then. You're not getting me killed."

"Why do you have that mask?"

Reaching up, the man went to shut the hatch.

"Okay, fine."

Obake entered as the man lit a torch on the wall with his lighter. He then pulled the hatch shut and locked it tight. With the torch in hand, he carried on down the tunnel's staircase.

"Oh great, you're some kind of pedo aren't you?"

"Shut up. If I wanted to harm you, I would've done it while you were passing out in the cave."

"That was you! I knew I heard something."

"Don't flatter yourself. I go up there every day. Despite all my training, my soul energy still isn't strong enough to wake that damn Gateway."

"It won't turn on unless your soul energy is at a certain level?"

"You're a real scholar, aren't you?"

Obake peered at his bruises and scratches, all of them far along in the healing process. "Maybe I can do it when I'm not injured, or hungry."

"Overconfidence—that can get you killed. A select few can power that thing and you aren't one of them. It takes much more than you or I have to give."

A sneer found its way onto Obake's face.

The black-haired man pretended not to notice. "You could train for years and still not have what it takes. Trust me, I know."

"How long have you been stuck here?"

"Seventeen years and counting."

"Seventeen years!"

"Yes, sir. It's been a real treat."

"But how did you—"

"Let's get some food in you first, and I'll tell you all about it. I take it, you like fish?"

A compact room with walls made of rock waited at the bottom of the tunnel. Above an old cauldron hung a holder fit for a torch, the man placed his torch there. Obake took a seat on a chair beside a lopsided desk. Next to that were a bed and a long cabinet. The man removed a parchment wrapped item from the cabinet then lit a fire under the cauldron. Water within it boiled and bubbled. Two familiar fish slid from the parchment, splashing into the cauldron. Obake's mouth salivated. From the cabinet came a jug and two cups as well.

"You like salmon, right?" said the man, pouring himself and Obake a glass of water.

"They have that here too?"

"They have everything here that we have there. Don't ask me how. That's way above my pay grade."

Obake examined the room. "You built all this?"

"No. Found it."

Fish transferred from the cauldron onto two separate plates. One of the plates found its way into Obake's hands.

An inquisitive look swept over the black-haired man. "So, what do they call you?"

Obake collapsed Mizuchi's handle then sheathed it within the scabbard at his waist. "Is this done?" he asked, prodding the semi warm fish.

The masked man neglected to answer.

"Uh, my name's Obake. What do they call you?"

"Teiku, pleased to meet you and all that nonsense."

Obake bit into the fish, then spit it out.

"You've got to be kidding me," groaned Teiku.

"What? Not my fault it's nasty."

Annoyed, Teiku grabbed hold of Obake's plate. "What were you expecting, gourmet?"

"Sorry, I'll eat it," said Obake, yanking the plate back.

He couldn't afford to go any longer without food. No matter how revolting. Each bite went washing down with water, but even that possessed a bitter flavor. Obake's expression mirrored a child having eaten a handful of sour candies.

With an exaggerated sigh, Teiku sat on his bed. "As I was saying, I've been trying to get out of here for the better part of seventeen years. I used to be a mercenary, did a lot of odd jobs with the Yokai Clan. Assassinations, reconnaissance, theft, you name it."

Stunned, Obake dropped a piece of salmon onto his lap. *Did this guy know my parents?*

To allow for food, Teiku lifted the mouth of his mask.

A tingle scaled Obake's spine. *Oh shit.*

Teiku's neck scars didn't stop there. They crept up his chin and past his bottom lip, the extent of their reach obscured by the rest of the mask.

With his index finger, Teiku tapped on the mask. "That's how I got this."

"You must've been special. The Yokai Clan didn't give those out to just anyone," said Obake with a twinge of suspicion.

"Lucky is more like it. I was honored to work alongside them as long as I did. One day it all went to shit though."

Wait. Was he there?

"Tazuro came along with his army and destroyed everything. A lot of people I cared about died that day. As for me, I lived. But not without the scars to prove it."

He was!

"Anyway, by the time I showed up, the city was already a war zone. I attacked the first group of ginyai I saw. They were huddled around the Gateway. Nine, maybe ten, I didn't care. I wanted them dead."

Obake became more attentive, soaking in every word like a rag through a spill.

"Our little skirmish caused the Gateway to activate. Next thing I knew, I was floating inside this weird, pinkish… place. After killing those bastards, I realized I was trapped." Teiku's shoulders waved, it was obvious that a cold tingle had passed through them. "I panicked when the Gateway suddenly opened again. I had no idea how to move inside that place. By the time I figured it out, Tazuro and his lackey Zathumor came flying in. That's when I saw Bakemono and the others, they saw me too. There wasn't enough time for me to get out. They created some sort of barrier and that was that."

Obake took a sharp gulp of water. It traveled his esophagus like a pebble.

"Tazuro was furious. I've never seen such rage. I took the full brunt of it. He took me to his fortress and strapped me down. He and Zathumor interrogated me for days. That's when I made the biggest mistake of my life. I made light of the bug-eyed bastard's burns. He sure looked *terrible*. But in hindsight, I should've kept my mouth shut."

Obake braced for the horror his ears were in store for.

"He took a torch and… Let's just say I'm not as handsome as I used to be. I did manage to escape though… my one consolation."

An uncomfortable silence permeated the cramped room.

"Are you mad?"

Curiosity tilted Teiku's ohead.

Obake continued. "You know, at Bakemono and his friends."

"No point. In war there's always collateral damage."

He can help me. I bet he wants Tazuro dead just as much as I do.

"So what's your story, kid? How did you end up here?"

"That's my family."

Teiku shot up from his plate.

"The Yokai Clan, that's my clan."

"You don't say. How's Yokai? Bao-Ang? Doing well, I assume. I knew those two pretty well."

A storm of depression thrashed Obake's soul. He glanced around the room, fighting back tears.

Teiku gave a heavy sigh. "You're kidding. They were such good people. How did it happen?"

"Tazuro came back. They tried to beat him. I tried to beat him. He's too much."

With slouched shoulders, Teiku stared up at the ceiling.

"He took everything from me." Obake jumped to his feet. "He has my girl. I have to get home. You said you knew how!"

"I do."

"I don't have years to train. I need to get back there now."

"You don't need years. There's another way."

Teiku reached into his coat, pulled out a flask and handed it over. "Here. Have some. It'll take the edge off."

After taking one whiff, Obake handed it back. "No, thanks."

"Don't tell me I've got a square on my hands."

"Dulls the senses."

"Can't argue with that."

Obake gazed into the slits of Teiku's mask. "So?"

"All right, hear me out. There's a necklace out there imbued with great power. It formerly belonged to a sorcerer called Rezvan."

Obake mouthed the name to himself.

"Those who can weaponize their soul energy use powerful weapons and other such objects as conduits, right?"

Intrigued, the young ninja nodded along.

"Well, Rezvan took it a step further. He developed a hex that enabled him to store soul energy inside of conduits. They're called bamalgas."

"What's the point of that?"

"Whoever has one can amplify their strength."

"Seriously?"

"All we have to do is get that necklace and we'll have the boost we need to wake up the Gateway."

"That's it? Okay, I'm ready."

"You should know it'll be a daunting task. The necklace is on another continent."

"Another continent!"

"Simmer down, it'll just take a few hours by ship."

"Where are we supposed to get a ship?"

"I know a place."

Obake paced around the compact subterranean room. "Why can't we find another sorcerer and force them to make us one?"

"Rezvan's the only one who can do it. He made two in total, and he's long gone."

"Dead?"

"Banished, he was always against the Human Realm conquest. As you can predict, Tazuro didn't like that very much. He took the necklace and gave Rezvan the boot. I'm surprised he didn't outright kill him."

What food remained on Teiku's plate vanished. "Nobody knows what became of Rezvan after that."

"If it makes you stronger, then why doesn't Tazuro use it?"

"Apparently, he does. I have no proof, but they say he has the other one." Teiku placed a hand under his chin. "I haven't found anything that indicates what his bamalga is, but if I had to guess, I'd say it's his sword."

"I did hear him say something about a sword. He sent some of his grunts to get it."

A snap burst from Teiku's fingers. "It has to be the sword then. There's no other explanation. It's not like he's the sentimental type."

"If I were him, I'd use both and become unstoppable."

"It's not that easy. Your body can only withstand so much. Tazuro himself isn't even that strong. Weren't you taught about soul energy?"

"I was. But anything's possible with enough determination."

"Fat chance. Remember what I said about overconfidence?"

Suspicion found Obake once more. "How do you know all this?"

"Study and research. I've had a lot of time on my hands."

Obake scarfed down the last of his salmon. "What's our first move?"

Teiku headed for the stairs. "Follow me."

23

Across the Sea of Fire

Deep within the jaws of the serrated cluster of pillars, Obake and Teiku waited.

"When's this lady supposed to show up?" said Obake, growing impatient.

"Any minute now."

"Who is she anyway?"

"A wudaigo. She comes by once a week like clockwork to sell furs. She'll be hauling a large wagon and—"

"We're going to hitch a ride."

"You got it. Should be simple to pull off. She travels by taram, and speed isn't what they're known for."

"Taram? That some kind of—"

"Just wait, you'll see."

"Well, if it's slow then why use one? Sounds dumb if you ask me."

"I wouldn't be so sure. What it lacks in speed, it makes up for in other ways. It's a valuable asset for fending off would-be thieves and ogres."

"Which ones are those?"

"The fat yellow ones, I thought we'd have to kill a few ourselves, but I haven't seen any. They typically like to hang out around here."

Hooves clattered a brief distance away.

Teiku darted out of sight. "Here she comes."

Obake ran to the backside of a pillar, pressed his back to it then put his mask on. An almond-brown horse of a creature came trotting along, pulling a rickety wagon. Atop its head, three spiraling horns swept this way and that; a majestic sight to behold.

I need to get me one of those.

The fur dealer straddling the taram scrutinized the vicinity. Shimming along the pillar, Obake ensured he was out of view. His foot nudged a hard, round object along the way. Below, the severed head of an ogre gazed at him. Flies the size of grapes mobbed it like a discarded confection. A few arms, torsos and legs lay strewn about as well. Four dismembered, pudgy bodies desecrated the grounds, leaving a vile stench wafting about.

I think I'm going to be sick.

Obake pinched his nostrils then darted to an adjacent pillar. As the taram passed by, the volume of its hooves increased. Careful not to touch any more severed body parts, Obake circled behind the wagon. As the dealer rode onward, the mound of furs in the wagon jostled. Teiku peeked from underneath them and beckoned Obake who began tiptoeing over. The fur dealer's cat-like ears swiveled, and the wagon halted. She turned around, but before she could spot the ninja, he teleported. Obake's head ended up behind Teiku's rear.

"Ugh!" groaned Obake before shuffling over.

"So, you're telling me we didn't have to go through all that trouble. You could've... poofed us in here?"

"It doesn't work that way."

"What do you mean?"

"I have to be able to visualize where I'm going. Hard to do that in a realm you've never been to."

"You should've told me what you can do."

Seconds later, the wagon drove forward.

"Look. I don't know you and I don't trust you. For all I know, you could be setting me up. You don't need to know everything I can do."

"I hate to break it to you kid, but I'm your one chance of getting out of here. You're going to have to trust me, at least a little."

After fifteen minutes or so, Obake's ears absorbed a

rambunctious city. He raised the fur over top of himself by a mere inch and took in the sights. Iron architecture dazzled him.

This isn't so bad. Don't know why I was afraid.

The line of ginyai waiting to be served at **Argett's Fish House** aroused memories.

When this is over, I'm going straight to Dotam for some lamol soup. Mmm, I can't wait.

Children ran rampant in the streets, play dueling with sticks. A little ogress wearing a fancy nose ring detached a wet finger, letting it drift over two yards into the ear of a wudaigo boy. His thick-framed glasses wiggled when he whipped around in search of the culprit. Before the wudaigo could catch her, the ogress' finger returned to the hand it came from.

Obake laughed under his breath. *Classic.*

Contented families shuffled by, one after the other. In and out of stores, they shopped. To and from restaurants they ate. Imagination overtook Obake, forcing him to envision the families disintegrating. Every man, every woman and every child became a pile of ash. He gasped, blinked a multitude of times and then glanced again. Families carried on, unharmed.

I'm losing my mind over here.

Obake didn't have long to ponder the strange vision because once again, the wagon stalled.

"Get your furs, warm furs for sale. Don't be caught

in the cold without one," said a scraggly voice.

At the wagon's tail end, the fur dealer appeared. All manner of ginyai swarmed her.

With haste, Obake covered himself. "We're fucked. How were you planning to get us out of here?"

"Relax, she never sells them all. She'll sell a few then keep moving. Once she does, we'll jump out."

The weight of the furs lessened and lessened.

"Are you sure?"

"I'm positive."

Hubbub grew louder by the minute. Obake peeked from under the fur again. A rowdy throng of ginyai exchanged their money for fur, too busy transacting to see him. Citrine coins a bit larger than carnelians, amethyst coins smaller than sapphires, and onyx coins the same size as emeralds dithered within eager clutches. Searching beyond it all, Obake found a sufficient escape route. At the top of an embankment stood a single building and it seemed devoid of activity.

As the fur covering him lifted off, Obake grabbed Teiku and teleported to the building. "You almost got us killed."

"What do you want me to say?" Teiku shrugged. "I've done that a thousand times. She's never sold that many."

Teiku crawled to the edge of the embankment, opposite the fur dealer and her customers. Obake joined him, but not without a few groans of disapproval. On the other side, the ocean waved to them.

"Right on time," said Teiku, delight in his voice.

Despite the rough waters, a ship approached with ease. Eye insignias hailed from its many sails. Leathery wings extruded from both the left and right sides. Its figurehead, a monstrous viper, devoured the air and a wicked tail extended from its stern. The ship was more of a red and black sea monster than anything. A wooden dock reached out to it like a handshake.

Thumping footsteps emanated from behind. Two guards wearing jet black armor began strolling up the embankment.

"Aren't we the epitome of luck," said Teiku.

"What are those ones called?"

Groans of disapproval now spilled from Teiku.

"You act like I've been here before," said Obake, his brow furrowed.

"The red ones are called kezai. The orange, goblins."

"Was that so hard?"

"Shut up."

With the building blocking most of their view, the guards had yet to see the infiltrators.

"I can't remember when being married wasn't a living nightmare," said the goblin.

Teiku and Obake slid toward the ocean on their bellies.

"All she does is nag me. Kerter, do this. Kerter, do

that. Why's there piss on the toilet seat? It's enough to make you sick."

"I hear you. My old lady's the same way." The kezai appropriated a feminine tone. "Take out the trash, Gurt. Stop by the store, Gurt. Give me a foot rub, Gurt."

Both guards laughed as their helmets poked over the top of the embankment.

"Hurry," whispered Teiku, dipping headfirst into the raging water.

Obake snatched a breath from the sky, rolled in, then submerged. *I don't miss this. Not by a long shot.*

Like an expert, Teiku descended to a safe depth. He then swam over and grabbed a support beam at the end of the dock. Sea urchins living there screamed in protest. Yet, their screams sounded more like relaxing lullabies than cries of discomfort. One hand after the other, Teiku scaled the support beam all the way to the surface.

Reluctant, Obake copied his partner. *Sorry, guys.*

As soon as he resurfaced the waves throttled him. He clung to the support beam for dear life. The ocean wanted to sweep him off to who knows where.

"They don't call it the Sea of Fire for nothing," said Teiku, letting off a faint chuckle.

The sea monster of a ship finished docking. Multiple footsteps and rolling wheels spilled onto the dock.

Bright orange glows radiated from Teiku's gauntlets.

"Come on."

Energy identical to a set of fists blasted at the sea floor, rocketing Teiku up and onto the back of the ship. *Whoa! That was awesome.*

Mizuchi ejected, its chain wrapping around the viper tail. As the chain retracted, it pulled Obake up along with it.

Side by side, the partners scurried across the deck. As they made it to the bridge, a male vampire emerged from the hull. Enjoying a puff from his pipe, the vampire stood at the ship's edge. Teiku snuck up behind to snap his neck. Sprinting over, Obake dug his fist in the vampire's gut. The vampire hunched over, gasping for air. Teiku released the vampire as Obake knocked him out cold.

"What's wrong with you?" said Obake in a whisper-shout.

"What's the problem? We just need the captain."

"Oh, so we're going to murder everyone else then?"

"These bastards work for Tazuro," Teiku whisper-shouted as well. "The very same Tazuro who killed your family."

"They aren't part of his army. They're just trying to make a living."

"And you know this how?"

Obake wanted to look into the eyes of a man who could kill so easily, but the mask made that rather difficult.

"How do you know this guy wasn't there that day?

He could've slaughtered a few hundred humans then decided to make a career change."

"And what if he wasn't? I can't make the same mistake again. I won't have any more innocent deaths on my conscience."

Clattering hooves interrupted their argument. Teiku jumped to the bridge's roof as Obake dragged the vampire behind it. Obake peeked and spotted a female centaur wearing a captain's uniform. She walked onto the deck with an ogress on her trail.

"How many deliveries we got left?" asked the ogress.

"Three, think you can handle that my lady?" said the centaur, her timbre soft and kind.

The ogress nodded, then departed for the front of the ship while the captain headed toward Obake and his victim.

No. Not this way. Obake examined the bridge walls and found a door right beside him. *Why am I picking such bad hiding spots lately?*

He hoisted the vampire and backpedaled to the opposite side of the bridge in time to avoid detection. Through a monocular, the ogress surveyed the ocean, too preoccupied to hear Obake's faint scuttling.

A whisper fluttered from Teiku as he craned over the bridge's roof. "Get her. I'll get the ogress."

With a nod of agreement, Obake went for it.

Eyes bulged from the captain's skull the moment

Obake dashed in on her. "What in the—"

Seizing her in a choke hold, Obake put the captain to sleep. Back outside, Obake saw the ogress lying contorted like vines on the side of a house.

"I didn't kill her," said Teiku.

Obake rolled his eyes then walked toward the hull's entrance. As he and Teiku descended into the ship, two voices emerged. Both voices mixed in with the clang of metal and cascade of rocks. The source of the voices brought them to a closed door with a glass window. Inside, a male ogre and a female kezai shoveled dark blue stones into a giant fuel tank.

"That stuff kind of looks like zoganite," said Obake.

"That's because it is."

"I don't get it. This is a totally different realm. Why's everything so similar?"

"I told you already. The creator purposefully designed everything to be that way. At least that's what they say."

By tilting his head, Obake indicated he craved elaboration.

"It's all a bunch of religious mumbo jumbo. Honestly, it doesn't matter."

Sighing, Obake threw the engine room door open and the ginyai inside were dealt with.

"All right, let's tie them up and wake the captain," said Teiku.

A flushing toilet went off. Another male vampire

shuffled from a nearby bathroom, trying to fasten his pants. Upon spotting the infiltrators, gasps of terror left his jaws. He spread his wings and bolted for the stairs.

"Intruders!" He yelled, as his pants slid down to his ankles. "Intruders!"

Teiku jumped on his back, slamming him before he could fly outside.

With his feet holding the vampire in place, Teiku choked him to sleep. "Let's find some rope."

In the cargo hold was plenty of it, winding around package after package. The partners took what they needed, then went one by one, hog-tying and gagging the ginyai. Once they relocated everyone except the captain to the engine room, they returned to the bridge.

Teiku slapped the captain's cheek until she came to. "You're going to take us to the eastern continent."

"I will be doing no such thing. I request to be released, sir," said the captain.

Teiku yanked her upright then shoved her at the steering wheel. His voice turned deep, guttural. "Don't make me repeat myself."

Obake's hairs stood on end.

Upon inputting a code into the interface of the steering wheel, the captain set sail. "Sir, I must say. There is a storm set to brew near the eastern continent. It would be most unwise to venture there today."

"How long have you been a captain?"

"Fourteen years, five months and twenty-two days, sir."

"Then I'm sure you'll manage a little storm."

A storm struck forty minutes into the voyage; it was anything but little. Ten-foot waves turned to twenty, then forty. They threatened to capsize the ship. Pots, books, clothes, rations and anything else not nailed down slid across the floor, slammed against the walls and crashed into the ceiling. Obake wedged himself in a corner to keep from tumbling about. Teiku wedged in the opposite corner. The captain slipped through two forty-foot rogue waves, but smashed through a twenty-footer. Windows on the bridge shattered, dispersing shards to nick the three voyagers.

"Why did I listen to you!" said Obake, glaring at Teiku.

"Now's not the time!"

The ship elevated fast, caught on the tongue of a rogue wave that increased to over fifty feet. Thunder became so loud it upset everyone's eardrums. Shoving the throttle forward, the captain sped up the wave as it started to curve. Lighting splintered the sky, making it appear like a cracked glass mural. Teiku pressed deeper into his corner. Frigid-sharp water splashed into the bridge. Obake could do little more than squint as the water battered him. Miraculously, the ship reached the wave's lip. It then tipped onto the wave's backside and went shredding down the length of it. Obake's stomach churned the whole way. All three voyagers cheered as the wave dropped them outside of the storm's confines.

"You're amazing, captain!" said Obake.

"Akoh. I'm Captain Akoh," she replied with a proud tone of voice.

"Well done." Teiku put a hand on Akoh's shoulder. "Looks like we commandeered the right ship."

"Uh, thank you. I think."

A beach appeared on the horizon. It soon accommodated the ship by allowing it to dock.

"Even with your hands tied, you got us here. I sure hope Tazuro's paying you well," said Teiku, snatching Akoh by the arm and guiding her away.

A piercing scowl emerged on Obake. *He better not do anything stupid.*

"Please, sir. This isn't necessary."

After stuffing a gag in Akoh's mouth, Teiku took her to the engine room. He hogtied her four legs together, then left her among the other captive ginyai. They all squirmed and mumbled from discomfort.

"Pathetic," said Teiku, slamming the door then turning to face Obake. "Ready for our next task?"

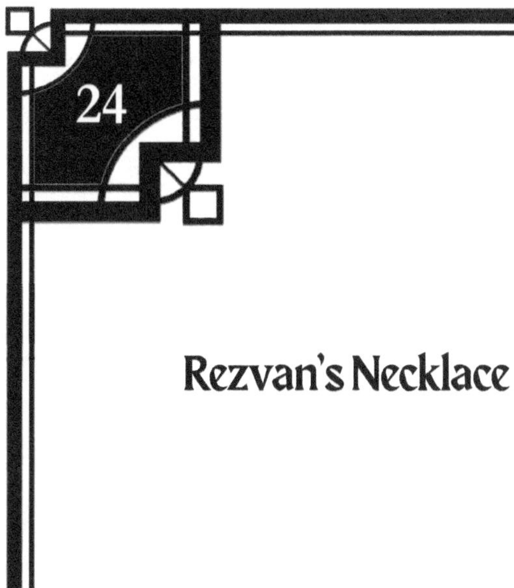

Rezvan's Necklace

Bones clattered and teeth chattered with every sopping wet step Obake took.

So, this is what misery feels like.

Shivers marched like a battalion through his core. He hugged himself, but the cold's hug overpowered his own. Unbothered by the circumstances, Teiku walked along. The fire fueling his determination seemed warmth enough. A meteor sized hole in the ground presented itself a quarter mile inland. Inside of it, one could see but so far. After the first ten feet, the hole became pitch black and spooky.

"Don't tell me we have to go in there," said Obake.

"I'm beginning to think," Teiku retrieved his lighter. "You don't want to go home that badly."

As Obake went to retort, Teiku ignited the lighter, then dropped feet first. His flame kept the blackness at bay for a while, but he soon disappeared within it.

"What did you do that for?" Obake waited for a response, but Teiku didn't provide one. "Hey! Are you all right?" He could hear nothing but pure silence. *He really is psychotic. Why would he...?* Nerves flared, making Obake pace back and forth. *What was he—?*

"You coming?" called Teiku from the depths.

"Oh shit! He's a ghost!"

"I'm no ghost! Hurry it up!"

"I don't know. That's probably what a ghost would say."

"I'm waiting."

"If you're a ghost, I promise I'll kill you again."

"Yeah, yeah."

I hate this guy.

A leap of faith later, Obake found darkness so thick he couldn't see his own feet. A tiny flickering flame came into view, enticing him like a moth. It illuminated Teiku who stood on a rocky platform.

Obake touched down next to him. "Very funny, it would've been nice to know we'd be jumping into a literal pit."

Another faint chuckle escaped the masked man. "Now where's the fun in that?"

"I didn't know you had a fun side."

Teiku held out his lighter, shining its flame on the surroundings. "This is one of the only known vulborta territories."

"Vel-what?"

Grumbles derived from the back of Teiku's throat. "They're another type of ginyai."

"How many different types are there?"

"Ten. Vulborta are especially dangerous. How should I put this? They're like... a cross between insects and humans, but they're not human at all."

A sweater made of fear knitted itself then slipped over Obake.

"You never know what you're going to get. The possibilities are endless," said Teiku.

He has to be joking.

"You could run into a grasshopper with a face like a human man. You might encounter a human looking woman with beetle legs. Even a human looking baby with antennae is possible. It can get pretty weird."

With his shoulders pinned to his ears, Obake scanned every which way.

"They live in these elaborate subterranean systems. I was lucky enough to find one of their deserted hideaways shortly after I got stranded here."

The caramel color of Obake's skin bled till it was whiter than salt.

"What's the matter?" asked Teiku. "I told you I'm not a ghost."

"You're serious?"

Teiku nodded.

"Insects? As in giant... bug things?"

"That's an interesting way of putting it, I guess. They do vary in size though. It all depends."

Obake shook like a wet dog trying to expel rain water. "I don't handle bugs very well."

"This day just keeps getting better and better," mumbled Teiku in disappointment.

"You got it from here, right?" said a reluctant Obake.

"Nonsense, let's move. We haven't reached the bottom yet."

Teiku jumped in further, forcing Obake to do the same. They encountered more platforms on the journey, but reached the bottom in no time.

"We're here," said Teiku. His lighter could find no more depths to descend to.

A tunnel large enough for a train loomed ahead. Glancing up, Obake saw that the meteor sized hole had become a watermelon sized hole. His mind frazzled at the thought of being underground with giant bugs.

"How many of them are there?" asked Obake.

"Nobody knows, could be thousands, could be millions." Teiku walked forward. "Hard to get a head count for a mostly subterranean species."

The ninja adopted a deep-set frown before shifting to a more optimistic expression. "Maybe this tunnel's abandoned, too."

"Tazuro would be a fool to leave this place unguarded. Two of the most feared vulborta around are said to be here."

Obake's frown snapped back in place.

"Many have tried to claim Rezvan's necklace, just as many have failed."

As if on cue, dozens of dead husks belonging to former ginyai treasure hunters surfaced.

"Case in point," said Teiku.

Their faces danced in the lighter's flame, forever frozen with pain and fear. Rays of ochre light presented themselves ahead. They poked through the ceiling to shine on an underground ravine full of columns and platforms. More of the dead were present. Some died recently, others many years ago. Teiku tucked his lighter away with one hand while covering the nose of his mask with the other.

Obake covered the nasal passages of his mask as well. "You smell it, too?"

Toxic smelling odor stained the air. Upon further inspection, the partners found the source. Brown gas billowed amidst the ravine's base. It drifted between every column and platform, hiding the ground. A sole rectangular slab extended to the ceiling. At the very top, embedded within the slab, was a shiny gold necklace adorned with red gemstones. It was on full display, inviting those bold enough to take it.

"There it is!" said Obake, pointing with Mizuchi.

Cautious, the partners moved out of the tunnel and onto the platform jutting from it. Their weight made the whole thing dip several inches.

Bells blared and a stampede echoed throughout the ravine. Loose bits of chipped wall fell as the stampede came to an abrupt halt.

An icy, shrill voice echoed. "Go on. Take it."

A horrifying woman peered down from behind a stalactite. Her eyes devoid of a soul, her hair like thorns on a bush.

"Yes, it's yours. Take it," said a second icy voice.

Another horrifying female face peered from behind a different stalactite. Long white hair flowed from her scalp and her eyes gave the same soulless stare, all four of them.

The first woman crawled around to the front of the stalactite, her lower half like that of a scorpion. Behind her, a long tail with a deadly stinger thrashed. Pincers took the place of hands. They snapped and clicked to no end.

The second woman revealed herself as well, her lower half like that of a spider. Each of her eight legs looked sharp to the touch. Four additional eyes and a fanged mouth extruded from her midriff.

"I don't… I don't think I can fight those things," said Obake, the hairs on his body standing at attention.

"Aww, poor little boy," said the spider woman.

"Get it together." Teiku grabbed Obake and shook him. "This is no time."

Perking up, the scorpion woman looked to her companion and smiled. "I'm Sukora and that's my sister Lugora," Malevolence swam in her vision. "As you can see, we've helped many a weary traveler."

On a thick thread of webbing, the spider woman rappelled to a platform across from Obake and Teiku. "Yes, perhaps we can be of some assistance."

"I don't give a shit what your names are," said Teiku, his fists glowing.

Lugora snarled. "Show some damn respect, you worthless vermin!"

"Come get your precious necklace," said Sukora, a look of contempt across her face.

Teiku fired his fist shaped energy at the ground and rose to meet Sukora. "Don't mind if I do."

She struck at him with her pincers, but he twisted away and countered with a well-placed punch. The impact sounded like a minor explosion.

Obake now stood alone with the menacing Lugora. Her eyes lit with excitement as he pointed Mizuchi at her and backpedaled. She jumped over to Obake's platform then weaved a thread of webbing. It bundled Obake up, except for his weapon bearing arm. Toxic gas wafted up at him as he wobbled on the edge of the platform.

Sukora fell from the stalactite onto a platform below. She shook her head in pain while Teiku landed in front of Lugora. Obake flailed his arm at Teiku, all the while tipping backwards into the ravine. He fell quite far before ejecting Mizuchi. It failed to reach the platform by a mere paper's width. As Mizuchi's chain shriveled, Teiku jumped across the ravine and grabbed it. He then landed on a long platform across from where Lugora stood. Obake retracted the chain and met the platform's edge where Teiku pulled him up.

"I won't save you again," The masked man ripped a hole in the webbing around Obake. "Get your head in the game."

With haste, Obake discarded all of the webbing.

"I don't get it. You fought Emperor Tazuro himself, but you're afraid of this?" said Teiku.

"It's not the same. Bugs, I—"

"Look, you don't have to fight them." Teiku pointed at the necklace. "That's your goal. Get that and we're golden."

Obake nodded as he imagined himself writhing in toxic agony. *What are you doing? Snap out of it already. You almost died, idiot. You're going to let these things take you out? After everything you've been through?*

Lugora jumped across the ravine, Sukora did the same.

"They're bugs, that's all, that's it," said Obake to himself.

The ninja could feel his resolve building, his soul energizing. Lugora landed first so Obake surrounded Mizuchi in Shadow Cloud. He then hurled the weapon at her. After leaving his hand, Mizuchi vanished then reappeared to spiral into Lugora's chest. Blood spurted from Lugora as Obake jumped at her. Grabbing hold of his weapon, Obake pushed Lugora with his feet. Toxic gas beckoned her as she dropped into the ravine.

Obake returned to the previous platform as Sukora tried squashing Teiku with a ground pound. He rolled from her path, but she spun around fast, her tail whipping Teiku into the wall. As he fell, his fists glowed. He clawed at the wall and scraped to a stop, but Sukora was already upon him. After sticking to the wall, she vice-gripped both of Teiku's arms in her pincers.

"Seems you're not the normal fodder we get around here. What are you?" asked Sukora, scrutinizing Teiku.

Obake made way for his partner. "Hold on!"

"No!" said Teiku, eyeing Rezvan's necklace.

Sukora licked her lips at Obake. "I'll be right with you."

Gazing back at Teiku, Sukora admired his bleeding arms. He yelled out in agony then kicked her in the nose with both feet. She reared back with a high-pitched screech. Teiku went to give her a second dose, but she released him. After falling a short distance, Teiku kicked off the wall. He then soared up to give Sukora a knee to the chin. Her legs lost their grip and like her sister, she dropped into the toxic gas.

Upon clinging to the ravine wall, Teiku glared at the ninja. "Would you go already!"

Obake acknowledged, then teleported onto the rock slab housing the necklace. Racing up it, he vanished every few feet, reappearing higher and closer. Multiple crashing steps went off below, pulling a glance from Obake. Lugora gained fast, a clear speed advantage at her disposal.

She's alive!

Near the top of the rock slab, Lugora's legs pinned Obake face down. The mouth at her midriff gaped wide then bit into his back. He didn't know which was worse, insect fangs ripping into his flesh, or the smell, hot and fetid like a sun-drenched garbage bin full of maggots. Fear mounted in Obake yet again, hindering his soul energy, preventing him from teleporting.

A crash went off, followed by glows of orange. The fetid fangs and heavy spider legs left Obake alone. Mizuchi drove into the rock slab to keep Obake from falling. Below, Teiku elevated with one energy fist. The other fist fired energy replicas of itself at Lugora.

Closing the distance, Lugora stabbed at Teiku with her razor-sharp legs. Teiku's gauntlet deflected her legs until one pierced his arm. Lifting Teiku overhead, Lugora aimed to slam him on top of Obake. Fast thinking led Teiku to twist and plant both feet on either side of the ninja.

"Go! I'll hold her off," said Teiku, Lugora's leg still embedded in his arm.

Obake climbed through Teiku's legs, fighting through the searing pain in his back. "Almost... there."

A shrill scream emanated from below, Obake followed it to Sukora. She launched from the toxic depths. On her approach to the ceiling, she turned upside down and stuck to it.

Her, too?

From the tip of her tail, Sukora sprayed toxic gas, the very same gas lurking in the ravine. It knocked Obake off the rock slab, but his hooded cloak and mask kept the toxic gas out of his system.

Teiku did well to keep Lugora at bay by blocking and blasting with his available hand. As Obake was set to plow into them, he vanished. He then re-materialized beside

Sukora and let Mizuchi slither out. Mizuchi moved fast, but Sukora moved faster. The naginata nicked Sukora's neck as she pinned Obake against the ceiling with her tail. He hugged her tail tight, refusing to let go, even as she slammed him not once, but twice. When her tail went for a third slam, Obake formed a Shadow Cloud puddle on the ceiling and submerged into it.

From within the puddle, Obake checked on Teiku. Lugora spewed an electrified web at him that shocked on contact.

Sukora watched the puddle, waiting to snip Obake to fleshy ribbons should he emerge. He did, flying from the shadowy puddle like a bat on a midnight hunt. As the webs electricity ran its course, Teiku convulsed and plummeted toward Lugora's midriff mouth. After passing Sukora, Obake fired Mizuchi into her shoulder. It plunged deep, giving Obake a sturdy anchor from which to swing. With his fingers outstretched, he caught Teiku's collar. They both swung over and under Lugora's swiping legs then up to Rezvan's necklace. Mizuchi retracted in time to gouge the rock slab.

"Grab the wall." Obake shook Teiku. "Grab the wall!"

Teiku was passed out cold and his weight numbed Obake's arm. With both hands occupied, the ninja searched for bright ideas. Before he could find one, Lugora barreled up the rock slab and rammed the partners. Obake's hold on Teiku was lost in an instant.

However, now that Obake had a free hand, he reached out, ripping the necklace from its home. He spiraled and tumbled, but got the necklace around his neck. A wave of power surged through his every fiber. His soul energy thundered with vigor, his muscles grew, his vision got sharper and his fear got decimated. Appearing on the platform below, he caught his falling partner with ample time to spare. The bamalga made Teiku feel much lighter in Obake's arms. He flipped Teiku onto his shoulder with minimal effort.

"Give it back!" screamed Sukora as she and her sister cascaded down the rock slab.

Obake jumped into the tunnel and sped through it, somewhat tripping over his own feet as he went. He wasn't used to his newfound speed.

Lugora came up right behind the partners. "You think you're fast? I'll show you fast."

She slashed at them with her available legs, but Obake sped up more, keeping her outside of reach. Teiku regained consciousness. As soon as his eyes caught sight of the sisters, he squirmed and jerked.

Obake held him in place. "Calm down!"

"No, you can't run. We need that bamalga!"

"We have it."

Within an instant, Teiku relaxed. They reached the first series of platforms as wisps of Sukora's toxic gas spindled by. Obake jumped onto the platforms and was amazed by how airy he moved. Even with Teiku on his shoulder, he jumped enough to clear a few platforms at a time before landing again. About halfway up, he teleported out of the hole then put Teiku down. Sukora and Lugora approached the top of the hole, Obake took off the necklace.

"Don't let them out!" he said, throwing the necklace to his partner.

Teiku caught it then slung it around his neck. A surge of energy washed through Teiku as well. He charged his fists, but they didn't glow this time, they shined. Two imperium level energy fists blasted at the side of the hole. A rocky avalanche ensued. Both of the sisters held on for dear life, but the falling rocks trampled them. The partners reveled in the sheer magnitude of the avalanche.

Obake smirked at Teiku. "We're even now."

For the first time since their meeting, Teiku let out a genuine laugh.

On That Day, So Long Ago

Tazuro emerged from the Gateway wearing an exultant demeanor.

"Where is he? What did you do to him?" screamed Meilana at the top of her lungs.

"Good to see you too."

Like a cornered coyote, Meilana struggled against her restraints.

A fit of laughter took the emperor. "You don't give up. Even when you know it's futile. I respect that."

"Let me go and we'll see how funny it is."

"You're an interesting one. I'm tempted to offer you a position in my army. Too bad the only good human is a dead one."

Meilana languished. "Why're you doing this?"

"Never fails," said Tazuro, an air of disappointment in his words.

"Tell me why!"

Tazuro took a load off on the middle platform. "First comes the anger. Then the reasoning and pleading. I've seen it so many times. Something all living things have in common I suspect."

"You don't have to do this. Please, just listen to me! You can stop. Right here, right now. There's no need for any of this."

A great deal of scorn leapt from Tazuro onto Meilana. "But there is."

"What could we've possibly done?"

"It's not what you've done. It's what you were created to do."

"What does that mean?"

"You humans are despicable. I'll take great pride in wiping you all from existence."

"We're despicable? Us? You come here and try to exterminate everybody, but we're the despicable ones?"

"I didn't want to at first. Believe me. I looked for every excuse imaginable. But then I sent my most trusted advisor to live amongst your kind."

Bewilderment surged through Meilana's eyes.

"He observed you, studied you… *became* you. The stories he'd tell whenever he returned solidified my stance. Murder, rape, kidnapping, pedophilia. War! The list goes on."

Meilana squirmed as if a grotesque entity had invaded her body.

"You're all so willing to kill each other for such trivial pursuits. Fortune, fame, land. Even meaningless objects like jewelry and vehicles."

"We're not all like that."

Tazuro's voice went a few octaves higher. "The ginyai however, we kill to survive. Shelter, food and water. Nothing more, nothing less. Are there rotten apples in the bunch? Sure. But they're the exception, not the rule. The same can't be said for you and yours."

Meilana pointed at the Spider Throne. "You got none of that by killing? None of it?"

"I fought to unite my people, to save them from each other. The money was fortuitous. More often than not, humans kill for the sake of it. Reprehensible."

"You're wrong. You're choosing to see the bad. We're more than what you say we are."

The emperor scoffed. "It was a matter of time before you found out about us. Before you aimed that insatiable appetite for destruction at my realm. I couldn't let it happen. I wouldn't. Especially not after everything I've been through."

◆◆◆

Seventeen years ago:

Tazuro waited within the confines of his chamber. A grandiose throne fashioned from the finest silver held him six feet high. Tapestries portraying glorious war-torn battlefields swooped and swayed from the ceiling. A puzzle of Mount Drakoba lay in his lap.

He tinkered about, looking for where to place the jigsaw piece between his fingers. *We'll move in while they're asleep. Kill them one by one. Would Malubris approve?*

Contemplating, scheming, strategizing—Tazuro's favorite past times.

A faint knock at the door stole the emperor's head from the clouds. "Enter."

As commanded, Samasa walked in.

She had yet to say a word, but her body spoke of a timid young woman. "He's here, Your Grandeur."

"Very good, you may go."

Jinenji crept inside. Samasa shot an ugly glare to his backside before shutting the door. At the foot of the throne, the sorcerer kneeled. He behaved like a child anticipating a scolding. Head hung low, eyes glancing up for milliseconds at a time, a pathetic sight.

"How are things going over there?" asked Tazuro.

"The humans don't suspect a thing, Your Grandeur. They still think I'm one of them."

"Who did you decide to impersonate again?"

"A man called Baraiko, a blacksmith. Even his wife and children have no idea."

"Hmm, you must be the greatest actor who ever lived."

"Not at all, my hex can do more than copy someone's physical appearance. I get their knowledge, memories, skills, voice, manner of speaking, I get it all. It's a fantastic thing to have. Disgusting to pull off, but fantastic nonetheless."

"You never fail to impress do you?"

Fear fled from Jinenji, giving him the confidence to look up. "You humble me, emperor."

"Odd, Rezvan never mentioned such an ability."

"He was never fond of the gruesome side of sorcery."

A good chuckle emitted from Tazuro and Jinenji.

"True indeed. So, this transformation ability of yours is self-taught?"

"It is, Your Grandeur."

Tazuro couldn't hide his fascination. "Keep it up and your future will only get brighter."

Jinenji gave a bow.

"Did you discover any more similarities while you were away?"

"As a matter of fact, I did."

Intrigue captivated the emperor.

"Remember when I discovered that they have cats, dogs and birds?"

"How could I forget?"

"Well, they also have rabbits, fish and foxes too. Again, they don't look all that different from ours. Take their foxes, for instance. They're missing more than a few tails, but there's no mistaking it."

"So strange."

"I overheard a woman call it a fox too."

"This coupled with the fact they speak our tongue is very perplexing to me."

"What could it mean?"

"I'll leave it to you and Hallevi to find out. Any luck in the lab?"

"Actually, yes. We've made significant progress today."

"Good. When will my soldiers be ready?"

"I'm very sorry, Your Grandeur. There are still some kinks to be ironed out."

Tazuro sighed. "You two have been at it for a while now. How much longer?"

Jinenji averted his gaze to the floor again. "Could be... years."

"Disappointing. Although, I've been considering the prospect of moving forward as is. I prefer to avoid ginyai casualties, but I can't afford to wait any longer."

As Tazuro descended the stairs of his throne, Jinenji gulped.

"Have Samasa summon Zathumor and Rinjado. We need to begin preparations."

A mixture of apprehension and excitement swelled in the sorcerer's facial features. "Yes. Of course."

After bowing even lower, Jinenji removed himself from the chamber. Two doors awaited on either side of the throne, both carving their own pathways deeper into Omni Eye Fortress. Tazuro chose the one to his right. At the end, a stairway ascended to a quiet room filled with vibrant oranges and exquisite browns. Patterned carpets slid along the floor and underneath two decorative dividing screens. Warm air partnered with the scent of pumpkin to make for a cozy atmosphere. Other fragrances attributed to autumn sailed through the room as well. The emperor went through the screens.

A small kezai woman laid on a bed thrice her size. Her white hair, deep wrinkles and withering horns acted as evidence of a long-lived life. Tubes injected into her forearm pumped white liquid from a rectangular, zoganite powered device. Dr. Hallevi sat in a chair at her bedside. His face wore the stress of a thousand bad days.

"How is she?" asked Tazuro.

"It pains me to say this, Your Grandeur, but her condition has not improved."

"I ask you to create powerful soldiers for my army and I get nothing. I ask you to create a new throne and I get nothing."

Hallevi tugged at his own collar.

"I ask you to find a way back into the Human Realm and I get nothing. I ask you to save my mother and again, I get nothing."

Copious amounts of sweat drained from Hallevi's pores. "Please, I must remind you. This isn't my area of expertise. The many medical professionals you hired couldn't ascertain the reason for her degrading health either."

"Explain to me why I employ you again, Doctor."

"Please, I'm not that sort of doctor. I want nothing more than to help your mother. She was so very sweet, always so kind to me. I hate seeing her this way."

"Wait outside."

"Emperor, I—"

"If I have to tell you again, you'll regret it."

Hallevi scurried from the room as fast as his scrawny legs could take him. Tazuro sat in the chair then took his mother's frail hand with his own. It was rough and cold, like handling sand paper left out in the snow.

"Mom, wake up. It's me."

The elderly woman lifted her eyelids as if they weighed a hundred pounds each. She stared at the ceiling like a baby seeing one for the first time.

"How did you sleep? Was the doctor nice to you?"

The base in Tazuro's voice quelled, it'd be hard to convince an eavesdropper it was actually him speaking. His mother peered over, gazing upon his face, confusion written on hers. Tazuro's heart took a dive. A dive that reversed the moment the woman smiled.

"My boy, come to visit your dear old mother, have you?"

So much happiness welled in Tazuro's heart. Tears of joy even found their way to the surface.

"Mom, I've missed you. I'm happy to see you."

The kezai mother reached up, wiping the tears from her son's cheeks. "If you're so happy then why're you crying, sweetheart?"

"These are happy tears. Don't you worry."

Terror apprehended the kezai mother. "Vampires, they're coming! Run and tell your father, hurry!"

She wiggled and writhed as much as her body could tolerate.

"Mom, stop. I've already taken care of them, remember."

Disbelief beamed from her. "You have?"

"They'll never hurt us again."

Comfort replaced the disbelief. "You mean it?"

"And get this. They work for me now."

She smiled bright, breaking into a joyous laugh that stopped when a cough seized her throat.

Tazuro snatched a glass of water from the bedside table. "I've even forced them to feed solely on animals," He then assisted his mother in drinking from it. "Kezai is officially off their menu."

"This is such wonderful news. You're astonishing, sweetheart. All that hard work, all your training, I always knew you'd set things right. Have you told your father? He'd be so proud."

Tazuro put the glass of water on the bedside table. A family portrait upon it lured his eyes. He found himself in the portrait first, then his mother, then a kezai man with horns as regal as his own. Tears came again, this time produced by loss. He couldn't bring himself to remind his mother that his father, her husband, had long since passed at the hands of a vampire. Enjoying the moment, however fleeting, was paramount.

"Not yet. I wanted you to be the first to hear it," said Tazuro.

The kezai mother continued to smile big and bright.

She rubbed her son's cheek and looked at him with pride. "Don't forget what Malubris has called upon you to do, my dear boy. The humans will come. And when they do it'll be just like the vampires all over again."

"I won't, Mom. I'll take care of everything. I want you to focus on getting better."

An expression of confusion found its way to the kezai mother again. "Son, is that you?"

A knife forged from pure anguish stabbed the emperor a dozen times over. "Yes. It's me. How're you feeling?"

"You look so handsome. It's so good to see—" Her smile continued, but the one exuding from her eyes departed.

A blank stare took over as her hand went limp and flopped onto the bed.

"Mom, Mom!"

Like an uninhabited shell, the kezai mother laid there.

Overcome with shock, Tazuro ran for the door, ripping it open. "Hallevi, get in here now!"

Seconds later, the doctor arrived at the bottom of the stairs. "What's happening?"

Tazuro fumbled over his words. "She's... I think she's..."

Present day:

"So, I'm supposed to feel bad for you? Is that it?" said Meilana.

"Pity isn't a currency I dabble in."

"Then why tell me your sob story."

"Sob story? Far from it, I wanted you to see how different we truly are." Tazuro got to his feet. "I see the way you humans look at us. You call us monsters, demons, but we actually care for one another."

"You're wrong. I have people I love too."

"Lies, humans only love those they stand to benefit from. There's no room for that in the utopia Malubris plans to create."

"Who's that? Your boss?"

"He's much more than that. He's the one, true, omnipotent being."

Meilana grimaced. "You're doing all this because some imaginary man in the sky told you to?"

A malicious grin came over the emperor as he approached his captive. "Imaginary? You pitiful creature."

"You're out of your mind," Meilana tried warding Tazuro off with wild kicks. "You're insane!"

"Quite the contrary. I'm saner than I've ever been."

Tazuro kneeled then swatted Meilana's kicks away. Before she could resume her coyote-struggle, he pinched her jaws.

"Let me go," she said in a muffle.

"You really want your freedom? Then earn it."

The samurai went still.

Tazuro flicked her head to the side. "I hope you like games."

Below the Thrashing Waves

The engine room's door squealed open like a symphony of frightened pigs. Muffled jeers from the captives wrestled Obake's ears into submission.

Teiku entered, looking about in a loathsome fashion. "Still pathetic as ever."

He untied Captain Akoh's bindings. Once free, her hind legs kicked at him. He dodged then arched back, slapping the spit from her mouth.

Oh shit!

"Come on. Get up," commanded Teiku.

Akoh found her footing and shimmied to him. A purple bruise blotted her cheek as if it had met with a paintbrush. He seized her arm and hauled her off. Obake went to shut the engine room door when the captives locked eyes with him.

Oh great. They're staring right at me. "Sorry," he said before finishing what he started.

Back inside the bridge, Teiku came nose to nose with Akoh. His guttural voice returned full swing to carry his words.

"For your sake, I hope you don't try anything stupid like that again."

What's up with this guy?

Akoh gave a vigorous show of submission then input a code into the ship's steering wheel. "What about the storm, good sir?"

Teiku headed for the deck. "Go the long way." As fast as his guttural voice came, it went. "Just make sure you take us back where you found us."

"Why would you tell her that? We don't have time to go the long way," said Obake, following him.

"Not like we have much of a choice, kid."

"There's got to be a faster way."

"We can cut through the storm and risk dying *again*, or we can go the long way and make it in one piece. Take your pick."

Obake ran a hand through his hair, an attempt to acquire more patience. "*Or* we could get stranded here. The windows are busted you know."

"Your point?"

"She might run for it."

"She won't. Trust me."

The engine purred and rumbled from the ship's bowels. A cocky head nod bobbed from Teiku, he then removed Rezvan's necklace.

Obake became perturbed at the sight of Teiku stuffing it inside his coat pocket. "What're you doing? You're going to lose it."

"Fat chance, I'd rather die first."

"Let me wear it. We went through too much trouble to risk it."

"When are you planning to pay me?"

"What?"

"Cash, coin, money. When should I expect payment?"

"Payment? For what?"

Obake searched his memory for a time when he ever agreed to pay anyone. Let alone a stranger.

"For being your damn tutor."

An immediate wave of discomfort struck the ninja.

"I'm teaching you about everything. I might as well get paid for my services."

Unable to do anything else with his embarrassment, Obake scowled.

"Listen. If you aren't strong enough, you can't wear something like this for long. It'll kill you."

As Akoh set sail, Teiku took a swig from his flask then re-entered the bridge.

Along with his shame, Obake accompanied him. *He's right. I don't know much about anything, do I?*

For a while, nobody uttered a single word. Teiku occupied the corner he had on the previous voyage. With his head against the wall and limbs relaxed, he napped.

Obake's corner welcomed him too however, he couldn't sleep a wink. Every time he closed his eyes, flashes of the dead stung like hostile wasps. Staring through the windows helped him ward off unwanted thoughts.

Comfort came as Obake watched the eastern continent get smaller on the horizon. *I hope I never see another vulborta as long as I live.*

Time came to a crawl, forcing Obake to keep checking his mother's pocket watch. 5:18 p.m., 5:26 p.m., 5:33 p.m.

Hold on, babe. I'm almost there.

Relieving the tension from battle, Obake dropped his mask, put Mizuchi away and outstretched his foot.

It nicked the lid of a wooden cargo box. *Hmm, I wonder.*

He retrieved it then brought forth a kunai. While he carved away at the lid, time sped up as if it were late for an appointment.

I think I'll make a—

Turbulence struck the ship despite the absence of a storm. As Teiku stirred, so did something else.

A sound like crackling glass trickled its way into Obake's attention. "Do you hear that?"

"Hear what, sir?" asked Akoh.

"That sound."

Tilting her ear to the ceiling, Akoh's brows pinched. "What is that? I've never heard anything like it."

The crackling persisted in conjunction with a black force field that crawled over the bridge. The ship jerked and stalled. Akoh's hands recoiled from the steering wheel as if it were ablaze. Obake dropped his half-completed sail boat carving.

Teiku jumped up, startled and confused. "What is this? Didn't I tell you not to try anything else?"

"Sir, you must believe me. I have nothing to do with this," said Akoh.

With the speed of a bullet, the entire ship submerged. The trio winced, expecting water to come thrashing inside, but the black force field kept the water at bay. Lower and lower the ship sank, Obake caught a fish like creature swimming past the window. It blitzed by too fast for him to get more than a glimpse. He did a double take as a grand city came into view at the bottom of the sea. Turquoise towers with decorative spires, pipe-like buildings with domed roof tops, spherical glass rooms and enclosed glass walkways arranged themselves throughout. Blazing white and yellow lights shot forth, illuminating Akoh's ship as it passed through its sprawling architecture. A building with a large opening in its wall awaited, covered by a bubble that appeared primed to burst at the slightest touch.

Akoh hugged the wheel, Obake and Teiku returned to their corners. Their efforts to brace proved unnecessary. The ship phased through the bubble with a subtle gyration. Several vessels, all designed to resemble various types of marine life sat parked. Chief among them were sting rays, dolphins and turtles. Akoh's ship came to rest in the very center of the waterless hangar. Not a soul emerged for minutes, minutes that felt more like hours.

A muscular man walked from behind the ship. With a humanoid physique and the head of a shark, he was peculiar to behold. Fins protruded from his forearms while the fin on his head played host to a marvelous crown. His long shark tail swam the air. Green scales took the place of skin. Reptilian teeth good for gnawing and gnashing lined his gums. He wore minimal armor, but what he had was ornate.

Teiku turned to Obake. "Komera, I've never dealt with them before."

"They're not particularly fond of Tazuro. I know that much," said Akoh.

Obake's mind ran wild with visions of the muscular komera devouring everyone alive. From a corridor marched a group of shark humanoids, two men and two women. One man was so frail he appeared related to the stem of a flower. The other man had more or less a normal build. One of the women possessed a neck so long, it looked like someone tried pulling her head off. The other woman had three appendages to speak of. Her left arm had been reduced to nothing more than a nub. Like the muscular komera, they also dressed in armor that appeared more ornamental than practical.

The muscular komera waved a hand, and the black force field destroyed itself. "Exit the ship nice and slow, hands where I can see them."

The trio did as they were told. Each soldier readied a spear. In a hurry, the normal sized soldier confiscated Mizuchi.

Obake resisted the urge to attack. *Fucking thieves.*

Even Teiku's gauntlets weren't safe. They got stripped away by the frail soldier. Akoh carried nothing for the one-armed soldier to take. A pat down commenced. Teiku's lighter and flask, gone. Obake's shuriken, kunai and shrapnel bomb, gone too. Once again, Akoh had nothing worth taking.

"Ah. What do we have here?" asked the frail soldier, swiping Rezvan's necklace from Teiku.

"No. You can't!"

"Shut it!"

Teiku lunged for the necklace and received cold steel at his neck. The one-armed soldier's spear yearned to make the plunge. All it needed was an excuse, Teiku didn't give it. He instead decided to keep his neck intact.

With a cheeky grin, the frail soldier searched Teiku's pockets a little more before yelling out. "Clear."

"Hands behind your backs," said the long-necked soldier.

She went from one member of the trio to the next, tying glimmering purple seaweed around their wrists.

Obake wrenched his arms apart. *What kind of seaweed is this?*

The further the seaweed stretched, the tighter it became.

With an inquisitive eye, the muscular komera observed Obake. "And what might you be?"

"Huh, me?" Obake let his wrists snap together. "I'm…" He looked to Teiku for guidance, but none came. "I'm human."

A drawn-out gasp jumped from the muscular komera. Chatter swelled amongst his subordinates.

"What kind of traitor are you?" Anger seethed from the muscular komera as he snatched Obake by the collar. "Working for Tazuro after everything he put your people through."

"Whoa, hold on a minute. I don't work for him. I'm on my way to kill him."

After the initial shock of hearing such a thing wore off, the soldiers burst out laughing. The muscular komera didn't partake.

He held onto Obake, stone faced. "Is every human this delusional?"

"He's telling the truth," said Teiku.

Upon releasing the ninja, the muscular komera bee lined for Teiku. "Why the mask? Something to hide?" His snout took a few whiffs. "Are you human, too?"

Nerves forced Teiku to clear his throat. "Yes. Look, you're interfering with something very important."

Ignoring Teiku, the muscular komera put Akoh in the hot seat next. "What do you have to say about all of this, centaur?"

Teiku tried slaying Akoh with his eyes, but she survived the ordeal.

"I'm afraid they're not being truthful, sir. They indeed work for Tazuro, as do I. May Malubris reign supreme."

"You lying bitch!" said Teiku, turning to attack Akoh.

All four soldiers restrained Teiku as an amused smirk curled Akoh's lips.

"That bastard has my wife," The muscular komera, now full of rage, drew close to Akoh. "You better pray you're a worthy trade."

Akoh's four legs quivered.

"Take them away," said the muscular komera.

The soldiers marched their prisoners through an enclosed glass walkway. Rainbows of fish and other sea life performed as they went. An oval shaped door with coral engravings met them at the end of the walkway.

Behind it was a chamber with more engravings. Kelp and clams embellished the walls. Sea grass and red algae embellished the ceiling and floor. Down the center of the chamber ran two thick parallel walls. Six openings were built into both.

"Get in," said the long-necked soldier.

One by one, the prisoners entered a respective opening. The frail soldier pushed a button on a podium near the entrance. Jet streams shot from the tops of the openings to form watery bars. Obake touched one with his nose, specks of water shot into his eyes. The bars were hard to the touch, but still held a liquid consistency.

"You can't break out, so don't waste your time," said the one-armed soldier.

The normal sized soldier glared at Obake then left with his comrades. Obake took a load off on his cell's uncomfortable floor. Teiku did as much in the cell beside him. Akoh stood in the cell straight across, a tight fit for her horse body.

"Well, it was fun while it lasted," said Teiku.

"You're giving up? Seriously?" asked Obake, scrambling to get a better look inside of Teiku's cell.

"Sometimes you have to know when to call it."

"I haven't known you long, but that doesn't sound like you."

In aggravation, Teiku's head rolled over his shoulders. "We're being held prisoner, thousands of feet below sea level, in an underwater city. I think it's safe to say we're officially done."

"If I can get my hands on a weapon or something sturdy, I can get us out of here."

"Oh, right. You're going to teleport us all the way back to the surface."

"We'll steal one of their ships."

"Did you see those things? By the time we figure out how to use one, they'll have killed us already. Or wait. Maybe we'll manage to make it out of the city only to crash and suffer a watery death."

Obake took a deep breath. Aggravation set upon him too.

"We were crazy to think we could actually pull this off."

"We're not quitting. I don't accept that."

"You don't have a choice."

Several minutes passed before Teiku spoke again.

"Hey, for what it's worth, I haven't had this much fun in years. We made a good team."

Did he just say something nice to me? This can't be good.

A warmth brewed inside of Obake. "Yeah, we did."

"Are you two falling in love?" said Akoh, an air of mischief about her.

Teiku grumbled, turning his back to her.

"What? No, that's disgusting," said Obake. "Cut it out before you make me sick."

"Captain," Teiku's guttural voice came back. "I don't care what it takes. I will make you pay for this."

Akoh moved deeper into her cell. Everything went quiet for a while until the soldiers returned.

The normal sized soldier stopped at Obake's cell. "You, you're coming with us."

Teiku stood up. "Where are you taking him?"

"Shut up," said the one-armed soldier.

While sneering at Teiku, the long-necked soldier pressed a button on the podium. The jet streams on Obake's cell slowed to a drip. The frail soldier pulled Obake out and back down the glass walkway they went.

Instead of returning to the hangar, they ended up in a cylindrical glass room. It traveled upward as far as the eye could see. Once the floor finished jiggling, it zoomed upward.

Maybe he's right. Maybe this is the end. What would Yumo do in this situation? Obake let a giggle run free. *He would've hauled ass a long time ago.*

"What's so funny?" asked the long-necked soldier.

In that moment, Obake didn't feel much like talking. He wanted nothing but to bask in the pleasant memory of his best friend.

At the top, the elevator opened to a magnificent hall. Walls within flaunted engravings of various royally dressed komera. They fit well with the glass ceiling and sea life swimming on the other side of it. A throne immolating coral reefs mounted a spiral pedestal. Sitting restless upon it was the muscular komera. At the throne's base, the normal sized soldier and the long-necked soldier stood sentinel.

"Your Kingship, the prisoner. As you requested," said the one-armed soldier, stepping aside.

Obake didn't budge and got pushed by the frail soldier because of it. The closer Obake got to the throne, the larger the komera king appeared.

"I need to know how to contact your emperor," said the komera king.

"He's not my—"

"Quiet!"

The komera king's raging voice made Obake wince.

"My scouts can find no evidence of his presence at Omni Eye Fortress. Where did he go?"

"He's in the Human Realm."

Both the komera king and the one-armed soldier glanced at one another, confirming they heard Obake's words correctly.

"Let us go. We have to get back there."

"To help your master? I don't think so."

"Would you just hear me out?" said Obake, taking a few steps forward.

The soldiers at the throne's base crossed their spears, blocking Obake's advance.

"All I want to hear is how to get a message to that bastard."

"We hijacked that ship and—"

The frail soldier attempted to cover Obake's mouth from behind.

"Stole the necklace so that—" Obake did his best to evade the frail soldiers' three fingered hand. "We could wake up the Gateway!"

As if frozen in time, the frail soldier stopped trying to silence the ninja.

"It's Rezvan's bamalga. We need it to take out Tazuro."

"Lies, two of the most vicious vulborta to ever walk this realm guard that," Pulling the necklace from his belt, the komera king let it glint in the light. "This can't be it."

"It's the real deal. Without it, we can't get home."

"You're telling me a couple of humans did what dozens of ginyai could not?"

"It wasn't easy."

"You're a gifted storyteller, I'll give you that."

"It's true. How about this? Check the engine room at the bottom of the ship."

Every soldier in the room scoffed.

"You'll find the whole crew down there. They'll tell you if we really work with them or not."

Curious skepticism enthralled the komera king. "The captain, she's setting you up out of revenge? Is that it?"

"Yes, exactly! I would never work with Tazuro. He's the reason my family, why everyone I love is…" Obake choked back the words. "He has my girlfriend. She's all I have left."

Obtaining a better look at the green-haired boy, the komera king sat higher in his seat. "Petta, Gudo. See if his claims are true."

Obake's face went bright with hope. "Thank you! Thank you!"

"But be very careful." The komera king glanced between Petta and Gudo. "They may have set traps."

"We didn't. Believe me," said Obake.

"Just go already," said the komera king.

Petta and Gudo slashed, poked and swiped at every nook and cranny. No corner was safe from their abrupt attacks. They examined the floors and walls with caution, all the while descending into the bowels of Akoh's ship. Gudo used her long neck to peer over every obstruction before progressing. Apt to avoid losing more limbs, Petta walked at a snail's pace.

Obake rolled his eyes at every one of their actions. "There aren't any traps down here. Can we get this over with?"

"Of course you'd say that," said Gudo.

A few paces later, the engine room made itself known.

"That's it. Right there," said Obake, pointing with his forehead.

With more precaution than before, Petta and Gudo ambled to the door, springing to either side of it. Petta peered through the window as if what she may see could blind her. She paused for a moment, long jawed.

Gudo began tapping her foot. "What? What's the matter?"

Oh great. Did they get loose?

Petta thrust the door wide. Inside, the five ginyai remained gagged and bound. Gudo went to work slicing off their bonds. Each of them climbed to their feet. The ogress, the kezai and the two vampires went wide-eyed with worry. However, the ogre ran toward Petta and Gudo.

"Back against the wall, now!" shouted Gudo.

Petta came in hot, almost stabbing the lot of them. "Do as she says!"

Fearful, the ginyai cooperated. Gudo snatched the gag from the ogre's mouth.

"Help us, please! The man with the mask and that green haired boy locked us in here. They're keeping us prisoner."

In synchronicity, Petta and Gudo's tense posture relaxed.

"That's him! That's one of them!" shouted the ogre upon seeing Obake. "Help us and the emperor will reward you handsomely."

"Idiot," grumbled the ogress.

"I see no vulborta here," said Gudo.

The ogre glanced at his shipmates in confusion.

"Their lack of knowledge can be excused." Gudo locked eyes with the ogre. "They in fact live under rocks."

"I don't under—"

"We despise Tazuro," said Petta, cutting in.

"No, wait! Maybe we can make a—"

Gudo reapplied the gag, shutting the ogre up.

Petta approached Obake. "Turn around."

Obake did so with reluctance. *I swear, I'll end this bitch if she tries anything.*

His wrists cheered with freedom as the seaweed around them unraveled. Turning back around, Obake found Petta's outstretched hand. He shook it without hesitation.

"Can never be too careful," said Petta. "Hope you understand."

"Fully."

"Mind giving us a hand with them?" said Gudo.

Together they marched the ginyai straight into the komera king's hall.

"He was telling the truth, Your Kingship," said Petta.

A warm smile seeped from the king. Petta and Gudo escorted the ginyai off to the prison ward. Obake couldn't help but wonder what would become of them.

The komera king looked to the base of his throne. "Azor, Beldur."

The normal sized soldier and the frail one stood at attention.

"Retrieve their belongings."

Moments later Teiku arrived, guided by Petta and Gudo.

"Considering you were honest about your lack of affiliation with Tazuro." The king tossed Rezvan's necklace to Teiku. "I think it's safe to say you're being honest about everything else."

Teiku looked the necklace over. "I'm glad we were able to clear this mess up."

"How long has Tazuro been in your realm?"

"He arrived this morning." Urgency stitched its way into Obake's tone. "He won't leave until he conquers it."

"Are there any warriors with him?"

"Yeah, there are. A lot of them are dead now though."

"Really? I don't believe it," said the king, his eyes enlarged.

"It wasn't easy. I barely survived."

"Are you telling me that you're responsible for their deaths?"

"I had help."

Leaning forward, the king placed his elbows on his knees. "The Emperor's Bastion are no run-of-the-mill warriors. Who did you say you were again?"

"I'm Obake."

The king's brows furrowed.

"My father was Bakemono," said Obake with pride.

"Well, that explains it. Strong bloodline, I see. Tazuro hated your father, ran his name through the mud endlessly. Jinenji was the only one he seemed to hate more."

Sadness swept through Obake's heart. "He's the one who let Tazuro back in. If it wasn't for him—"

Obake's tongue apprehended the tail end of his sentence.

"Did you happen to see a komera woman with them? She would've been a captive."

"No, there were only two females with him. One was a little goblin girl. The other was an adult, a kezai."

"Hmm, this could be our most opportune moment." The king drifted into contemplation. "Yes, might be our one chance."

Azor and Beldur returned with all of the confiscated items. Teiku wasted no time putting his gauntlets on. Obake caressed Mizuchi as if it were a pet.

"I've come to a decision."

Azor, Petta, Gudo and Beldur braced for their king's directive.

"Organize our forces. Today we show Omni Eye City what the Shuika City Dynasty can do. Today we bring Queen Celeste home."

The four soldiers cheered and thrust their spears into the air.

"Would you be so kind as to assist?" The king glanced back and forth between Obake and Teiku. "We could use powerful fighters such as yourselves."

Teiku gazed upon Obake, waiting for his response.

"I'm sorry. We can't. We have to get back as fast as possible," said Obake, as polite as could be.

"I understand. It was a selfish request. After all, you have someone special waiting for you too. I'll meet you in the hangar. Know the way?"

"Yup, thanks King."

"Call me Laozai."

♦♦♦

The warriors fell silent until they were alone in the enclosed glass walkway.

"How did you convince him we were telling the truth?" asked Teiku.

"Easy. I had our captive friends vouch for us."

Teiku ruffled Obake's shoulders. "Clever kid."

"Good thing we didn't kill them."

Obake's words held thick traces of ego.

Teiku's hands recoiled with insult. "That was a lucky call, and luck only goes so far. Keep it up and see how long you last."

Obake sneered all the way back to the hangar. As he and Teiku returned to it, a raucous bell blared throughout

Shuika City. For the next hour, they marveled at the influx of over seven hundred komera soldiers.

"That was fast," said Teiku.

Obake fell into a state of awe. "There's so many of them."

Laozai marched in last, and the legion sliced open a path for him. He opened the rear hatch of a large dolphin designed ship and a ramp slid out. He made it to the top then stopped to make an address. With a khopesh now in hand, he looked primed and ready for war.

"Tazuro is away. He's left his fortress vulnerable. All that's left to defend it are lowly guardsmen," Laozai held his khopesh high. "We will breach it and rescue the Queen. That bastard's arrogance will be his downfall."

All the komera began performing a ritualistic dance of sorts. While remaining in place they released heavy grunts, stomped their feet, thumped their fists against their thighs and swirled their heads. If they had ponytails, they would've swung like windmills.

"We may not be fond of violence, but that sad excuse for an emperor has left us little choice," Laozai began pacing the top of the ramp. "Kill anyone who gets in our way. My wife will be free today!"

The legion transitioned to a battle cry so bombastic, Obake wondered if those on the surface could hear it too. One after the other, soldiers boarded ships. Laozai beckoned Obake and Teiku; they both sprinted to join him. Seconds after they reached the bridge, the dolphin ship jettisoned, leaving streaks of zoganite in its wake. A komera with a multitude of scars maneuvered in the pilot's seat. Despite the wares of war tattooed throughout his body, he pushed on. Speed was at the dolphin ship's mercy. It cut through water like a spear in air and took no time getting within Omni Eye Fortress's vicinity.

"We're here," said Laozai.

Obake had time enough to apply his mask and prepare Mizuchi before the ship broke the ocean's surface. Fifty other ships surfaced around them in a triangular formation, Laozai's ship at the head. Omni Eye Fortress lay beyond the ridge overlooking the ocean.

"Raise it," said Laozai to his pilot.

The entire bridge lifted to the clouds, but it remained enclosed. Its glass build allowed Obake to see all there was to see. To look upon the Sea of Fire and the komera ships from on high was nothing short of breath-taking.

"Ready, aim, fire!" commanded Laozai.

Every soldier followed their king's command. Water missiles launched in unison from turrets equipped to each ship. Chunks of Omni Eye Fortress began to break off.

A cannon the size of a lighthouse emerged from the fortress's pointed roof top. Spiked cannonballs laid waste to komera ships, sinking them sometimes two or three at a time. Several ships returned below the ocean's surface while others stayed put, returning fire.

Komera that abandoned ship turned up on shore. Spears, swords and bows at the ready. They stormed the fortress and clashed head first with Tazuro's guardsman.

Laozai dipped low. "Open it!"

The scarred pilot input a code into the interface on the steering wheel. Glass walls around the bridge withdrew. The sounds of water missiles and spiked cannonballs increased in volume. Explosions went off all around, sending geysers up to shower everything below.

"Hold your breath," said Laozai.

With Teiku and Obake in his grasp, Laozai dove headfirst into the ocean. He lacerated through the water and onto the shore. Neither Obake nor Teiku could find words to fit their baffled reactions. A hail of arrows and cannonballs rained upon the trio. Laozai raised a hand and a black force field surrounded them. The arrows bounced off, but the cannonballs caused cracks to develop.

"On three, take cover under the dock," said Laozai.

Obake nodded, holding his hands out.

"One."

Teiku clanged the knuckles of his gauntlets together.

"Two."

All three of them took a swift breath.

"Three!"

Obake touched Teiku and Laozai then teleported under the dock. Water washed over their feet as it met with the sandy embankment.

Laozai shook his head, trying to shake off the dizziness. "Whoa."

"Sorry about that," said Obake.

"No, it's perfectly fine. Interesting ability."

Several arrows stabbed the top of the dock.

"Now do me a favor and save that girlfriend of yours," said Laozai, bracing for departure.

A spiked cannonball struck one of the dock's legs, destabilizing its infrastructure.

"I will. But I'll need a favor from you, too," said Obake.

"And what would that be?"

"Please don't hurt the civilians. They're innocent."

Laozai beamed. "You have my word."

The komera king dashed off. Even on land, he moved at immense speed. His force fields knocked arrows and spiked cannonballs off course as he went.

"You can't afford to hesitate anymore," said Teiku.

"Don't worry. My enemy's clear."

"Your enemies won't always be in matching uniforms."

Using the energy from his fists, Teiku jumped on top of the dock. Obake burst from a Shadow Cloud beside him. Dozens of guardsmen charged them, Teiku blasted away most, Obake sliced up the rest.

"Ba boom!"

A familiar voice navigated through the noise pollution and into Obake's ears. He glanced at Omni Eye Fortress to witness Kalida conjuring illusions. She transformed the cannon into a tongue covered with pus-filled boils.

Teiku watched in horror. "What *is* that?"

Fury overtook the ninja as he headed for the fortress. *There you are!*

"What are you doing?" said Teiku, rushing onto Obake's path.

"Get out of my way. That little bitch killed Yumo."

"Stop! You're going to ruin everything."

"Move before I *move* you."

Teiku flinched, but held steady. "What's her name?"

"What?"

"Your girlfriend. What's her name?"

Large breaths filtered into Obake's lungs. "Meilana."

"Meilana needs you right now. Not your revenge."

Obake's intense demeanor calmed. "I have to at least tell them it's an illusion."

"They'll figure it out, just like you did."

Komera soldiers fought the tongue and Laozai slayed opponents as the fortress's entry opened. Out came Dr. Hallevi, piloting a mechanized suit equipped with a flamethrower. Raging fire spewed at the komera as the doctor eyed them with focused hate.

"Who the?" said Obake, unable to peel away.

Teiku pulled Obake into a run. "That's Dr. Hallevi. He's a real scummy guy, does all sorts of heinous experiments on ginyai, willing or otherwise."

"Once we take care of Tazuro, we have to come back and help them."

"Okay, you have my word."

◆ ◆ ◆

The Gateway welcomed the pair as they arrived in its presence. It was somehow more inviting. Perhaps it could sense the bamalga's power.

As if he were holding a python, Teiku brought the necklace forth. "Whoever puts this on won't be taking it off until Tazuro's dead."

"You're going to help me?"

"Kid, getting home was half of my worries. The other half has obnoxious horns that I'd like to chop off."

"I was hoping you'd say that," said Obake, extending his knuckles.

With his own knuckles, Teiku bumped Obake's. "So, who's it going to be?"

"I'll let you do the honors."

Rezvan's necklace slid around Teiku's neck and like before, the euphoria of its power surged.

"Let's do this!" said Teiku, tucking the necklace behind his chest plate.

Both warriors powered up to the maximum. Obake's Shadow Cloud billowed and Teiku's fists shined so radiant, they bordered on blinding. The Gateway flickered from stone to pink, then back again, but the pair didn't dare give up. Nothing stopped them, not clenched teeth, not engorged veins, not throbbing muscles or pouring sweat. They persevered until the glassy pink kaleidoscope fully erased the stone. A momentous level of relief and a feeling of triumph engulfed the cave.

Like a starry night, the Gateway reflected in Obake's irises. "Let's go home."

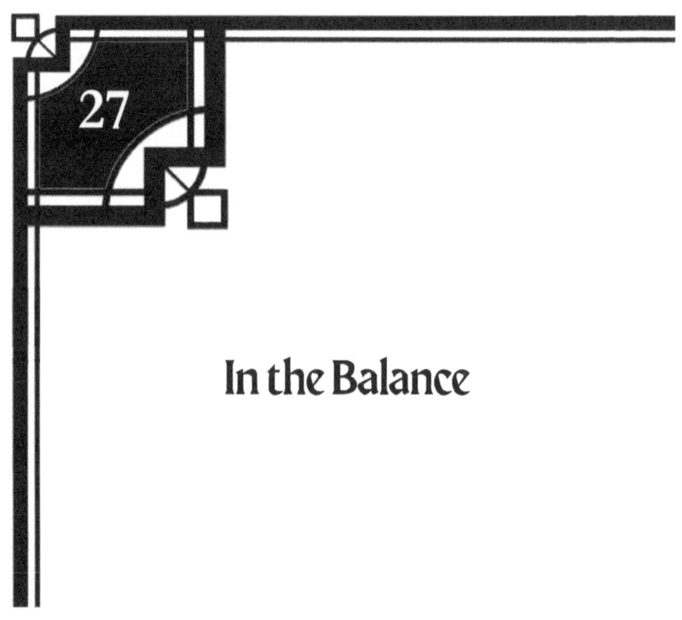

27

In the Balance

"Let's start with a simple one," said Tazuro, glaring at Meilana without blinking.

Her skin crawled like low tide heading up shore. "I don't even know what we're doing."

Tazuro rubbed his jawline. "Answer all three correctly and you can go home."

Sinister thoughts bubbled throughout his face.

He's getting off on this.

"What possesses one eye, but is blind to everything but its own twisted destruction?"

"Riddles? Seriously?"

Tazuro shot a hand to his sword, pulling it from the wall. "Wrong answer."

Meilana's palms flared in defense. "No, wait! Give me a minute."

The sword slacked into a counter clockwise twirl. "You have thirty seconds."

Meilana stared holes at the floor while pondering the riddle at hand. *What is it? Come on. Come on.*

"Give up?"

She pretended not to hear Tazuro as the answer trickled into her consciousness. "A Tornado!"

"Not bad," said Tazuro, approval curving his lips.

"My turn."

The emperor gave a soft chuckle. "I'm afraid this is more of a one-sided affair."

"But—"

"Ready? The next one's a bit more complicated."

"This isn't fair."

"Can you name a single thing that is?"

Trembles played through Meilana's body like a band of musicians.

"Two mothers enter a market accompanied by their daughters, but three women are present. How's this possible?"

Like a ghost in the shadows, the riddle blindsided Meilana. *Wait. I don't get it. Why don't I get it?*

Tazuro reveled in Meilana's rising struggle as it came to the forefront.

He whipped his cape behind him. "Have I backed you into a corner?" The cape fluttered as he began pacing before her. "I'm so very sorry about that."

Meilana's mind drove a mile a minute. "Can you… can you repeat it?"

Tazuro feigned a deep thought as he continued pacing. "Normally I'd refuse, but today I'm feeling generous."

In a mocking tone, Tazuro told the riddle again, albeit at a much slower pace. Under her breath and over and over again, Meilana repeated the riddle to herself.

"Tick, tock. Tick, tock. You can only say it in your head so many times before your brain goes numb," said the emperor.

Meilana envisioned her life bleeding out like a slit throat when it came to her. The answer, shining in gold plated letters.

"I got it. Because they're grandmother, mother and daughter."

Instead of irritation or aggravation, Meilana received praise from the emperor.

"The more we interact, the less I want to kill you." Tazuro covered his mouth as if he had let an unspeakable word slip. "I never thought I'd say such a thing. I must be going soft." His voice became like a stroke of thunder. "Last one!"

The sudden shout startled Meilana. She jumped, slamming her collar into the spear around her neck. She wanted so badly to sooth the throbbing with her hands. Tazuro's legs found themselves at a standstill. With his back to Meilana, he spoke the final riddle.

"You can escape the sword, you can escape disease, but none who live can escape from me. What am I?"

Unlike before, Meilana comprehended every word from the start, yet she didn't know the correct answer. No matter how much she searched through the information in her mind, she came up empty, every one of her neural pathways hindered by an impenetrable blockade.

Why am I drawing a blank? Why? This shouldn't be so difficult.

"I saved the best for last," said the emperor, smirking.

Meilana shut her eyes and fastened her brows. In between the flashing spots of white, an answer appeared. One she wasn't too confident of.

Please let this be it.

"Time's up."

"Uh… is it age?" said Meilana with a cringe, her heart thumping.

Tazuro smiled in pleasant surprise. "You are…"

An enormous sense of relief captivated the samurai. *I did it. I get to live.*

"Incorrect."

As Tazuro laughed, Obsidiana's life bled out in her imagination again. The miniscule amount of hope she had drained to nothing.

"Don't be upset. Many have wagered their lives against that riddle and come up short."

Tears welled in Meilana's eyes. "You're lying. I'm right."

"Are you now?"

"You can't accept that you've lost!"

"I'll admit that you were close."

Meilana's tears flowed like rivers. "You're a sore loser, a cheater!"

The emperor sighed. "From the moment each of us is born, our paths in life have already been predetermined. Some call it fate, others call it…?"

Like a mound of sand falling on top of her head, the answer arrived.

"Destiny," muttered Meilana, through shock and disappointment.

"Correct, destiny. The one thing that controls us all. I'm not so bad considering."

"You're wrong. I choose my own destiny, no one else."

Tazuro steadied his blade parallel with the ground. "Don't be so naive." He swiped, nicking Meilana's throat enough to draw subtle trickles of blood. "Yes, now that's what I like to see."

The blade returned to its former position, nicking Meilana a fraction deeper.

She sobbed, but didn't panic. "Fine, you win. Get it over with already."

"Perhaps your luck will improve in the next life."

As Tazuro prepared to chop off Meilana's head, the Gateway howled to life, luring Tazuro's gaze. A single shuriken spun into the chamber. Tazuro braced, but it whizzed by him, striking the spear around Meilana's right wrist. Sparks flipped as both the shuriken and spear shattered to the floor. Mizuchi slithered out next, heading straight for Tazuro. He dodged to safety as Obake spilled from the pink kaleidoscope. Worry and rage were the only words Tazuro's body language cared to speak. Meilana's spirits lifted on wings of power. With more leverage at her disposal, she reached a foot out and planted it on top of her katana.

The emperor stood mesmerized. His mouth opened to speak, but words struggled to assist him. Teiku entered the chamber next, his shining fists rebounding off the walls.

The spear around Meilana's neck froze to pieces in her icy grip. Teiku and Obake jumped from the platforms, readying for an offensive.

"What's wrong? I thought you'd be happy to see me," said Obake.

Genuine concern passed through Tazuro's eyes. "You've become quite the party crasher." His horned head darted between the two warriors. "And I see you've invited a guest. Rude if you ask me."

"Well, I didn't, so shut your fucking mouth."

Meilana used ice to suffocate the spear around her

left wrist as well. It elected to be more stubborn than the first two spears, but it crumbled in the end.

"That feeling," said Tazuro, putting an unusual amount of focus on Teiku.

All three warriors surrounded the emperor, their killing intent made the chamber pulsate like a heartbeat.

Obake's forehead wrinkled and throbbed. "You should've never come back here, monster."

28

Spider Throne

Like a pair of rockets, Teiku's fists hunted Tazuro. However, every punch missed the mark, leaving Teiku vulnerable to a knee in the gut. Teiku's armor did well to dampen the impact, but Tazuro's knee still left him on all fours.

Ice crystals, courtesy of Meilana found their way into the folds of Tazuro's cape. He was quick to slap the crystals aside with it. As the crystals crumbled at Obake's feet, he released Mizuchi for a chain link slash. Tazuro caught the chain then kicked Teiku at Meilana. His rolling body took Meilana's legs out from under her. With immense vigor, Tazuro swung the chain. Unwilling to let go of Mizuchi, Obake lifted off. Through the air he went, bludgeoning his partners. The trio scattered about like loose marbles.

"This is the most fun I've had in years," said the emperor.

Obake locked eyes with Teiku. "Let's take his sword. That way we'll have two bamalgas, one for each of us."

Teiku hammered a fist to the floor. "Son of a bitch!"

"What?"

"That's a different sword."

"You're joking?"

Teiku's guttural voice took center stage. "Forget it. We don't need it." He sprang up to expel not one, but two imperium level energy fists. "Dodge this!"

Although small at first, the fists enlarged the further they went. Pulsating with desperation, strength and malice, they filled the entire chamber.

Following Teiku's instruction, Tazuro leapt through the ceiling. The energy fists went on to bulldoze the back wall beside the Gateway.

"Fuck!" said Teiku, raring to meet Tazuro on the roof. "Teiku wait!" said Obake.

The masked warrior stared at Obake like somebody would a complete stranger.

"I know you're mad. I am too. But we have to work together."

"Better listen to him," Tazuro peeked through the

hole he made in the ceiling. "Strategy is key."

Ignoring Obake's advice, Teiku blasted off, smashing his own hole through the ceiling.

Meilana became perturbed. "What's with this guy? He's going to get us killed."

"I don't know. I think he's losing it."

"Should we—"

"I'll handle him."

Obake leapt onto the roof to find Teiku standing a few feet away, seething on the precipice of blind rage.

Tazuro admired the vast view from the roof's ledge. "Such a beautiful place and yet I hate it all the same. Probably as much as you hate me." Tazuro beamed in amusement at Teiku. "But why is that?"

Teiku caressed the burn scars knitting throughout his upper chest and neck.

"Go on. Spit it out. You know me, don't you? What vile thing did I do to you? Tell me so I can bask in it."

In reminiscence, Teiku's eyes swiveled about.

"Or don't. I'll figure it out, eventually. You're oddly familiar as is."

The sun began its retreat in order to welcome the night. Streaks of burning light frayed the arriving blue shroud, giving way to dusk's moody atmosphere.

Meilana came through the hole in the roof like a catapult. "Hey, let's use our heads here."

As if in a trance, Teiku fixated on Tazuro. Obake placed

a hand on Teiku's shoulder, only to get it thrown off.

Teiku's voice no longer shifted, his guttural timbre had taken over completely. "Stay out of my way."

Bounding across the rooftop, Teiku revved his fists, unleashing another onslaught. The emperor avoided Teiku's hatred induced strikes while his gauntlet-covered fists produced more power and speed by the minute. From above, Obake stabbed like a bolt of lightning. Tazuro's sword clashed against Mizuchi, reversing Obake's trajectory. His sword then rippled toward Teiku and cut through his chest armor. The emperor followed that by slamming his foot against the roof. A wave of energy gushed out to carry Teiku away.

Mizuchi shot into the roof then pulled Obake along. He barreled like a human cannonball, but his double kick failed to connect. Tazuro sidestepped the maneuver, then axe kicked Obake, much to the dismay of shattering roof top shingles.

Eager to turn the tide, Meilana delivered a series of vicious attacks with her katana. Tazuro foiled them all, even the ice spikes crawling up like reanimated corpses. Like an acrobat, Meilana vaulted and sliced at the emperor. Seizing her in midair, Tazuro slammed Meilana, inviting an ice spike to pierce her thigh. A splitting scream clawed through Meilana's voice. Obake stood up to help her, but Tazuro punted him away.

"I know I should end this now." Tazuro walked back

to the roof's ledge to absorb the sunset. "But I'm having way too much fun."

Despite the searing pain, Obake raced over to his girlfriend. "You're going to be okay."

He lifted Meilana off the spike then teleported to the other side of the roof. Teiku lay nearby, barely able to hoist himself to a seated position.

Obake placed his puapo canister to Meilana's lips. "Here, drink."

Through moans and whines, Meilana did just that. Her bleeding decreased upon consuming most of the puapo.

"On second thought, I'd better err on the side of caution," said Tazuro, watching.

Obake drank from the canister as well then threw it over to Teiku.

"Thanks," said Teiku after drinking every last drop.

"Mind if we work together now?" asked Obake, doing all he could to show his disappointment.

Teiku nodded, doing all he could to hide his embarrassment. "We still have to be quick. I don't know how much longer I can withstand this necklace."

"What necklace?" asked Meilana.

"I'll tell you about it later," said Obake.

Teiku braced. "I hate to interrupt, but—"

A millisecond later, Tazuro unleashed massive attacks upon them all. His sword defied all logic, spitting in the face of physics itself. The trio mounted a solid defense, but a sword slash got through. Like a shark's fin carving the ocean's surface, Tazuro's blade carved Obake's chest. Blood departed the ninja while Meilana slid in for a leg sweep. Tazuro jumped to evade it before stomping at her. If Meilana hadn't flipped into a back handspring, her bones would've been pulverized. Teiku flew in with a kick that collided against the emperors blocking forearm.

"Not quite!" said Tazuro, shoving Teiku away.

A thundering energy beam galloped from Tazuro's hand. It burst into tiny particles against Teiku's crossed arms. Obake scampered closer, bloody chest and all. He pitched Mizuchi then vanished, re-materializing behind his opponent. Dropping his weapon, Tazuro snagged Mizuchi as it tried imbedding in his face.

With his other hand, Tazuro blocked Obake's incoming kick. "Useless."

Obake vanished again, appearing in a handstand position atop Mizuchi. He activated its chain mechanism and the blade shot forth, slicing Tazuro's cheek open. Swinging down, Obake kicked off his opponent, taking the naginata with him. Near Tazuro's feet, Teiku punched the ground and blinding light discharged. Into the light, Meilana pounced. With no sword, Tazuro extended a hand in defense. Meilana's double-bladed katana pinned Tazuro's hand to his chest.

"You like that?" roared Meilana.

Frigid ice bloomed from her katana, spreading

across Tazuro's chest. Pained groans left him to circle the battle like a sparrow. Although Tazuro proceeded to flex every available muscle, the ice cracked very little. Teiku came forward once more, sending Tazuro flying upwards with a scathing uppercut. From a Shadow Cloud above, Obake stomped Tazuro onto the roof.

"Can't catch a break, eh antlers?" taunted Obake.

"So that's it," Blood streamed through Tazuro's grid locked teeth. "I knew I felt it." He climbed to his feet. "But it doesn't hurt anymore. As a matter of fact, I barely even feel it at all now."

The trio looked at each other in confusion.

"Such flawed logic. Bringing that to me," said Tazuro, blood sliding down his beard.

Obake smiled. "Damn. We really fucked you up, didn't we?"

Tazuro pointed at Teiku's neck. "You shouldn't be wearing that. A man of your caliber won't last much longer."

Teiku looked down to see Rezvan's necklace dangling loose. He stuffed it back behind his chest armor.

"Don't even think about it," said Obake.

"Let's kill him and get it over with!" said Teiku.

Meilana's brows pinched. "Why is that necklace so important?"

Tazuro, swaying like a drunk, retrieved his sword.

"Leaving the poor woman out of the loop? How cruel."

Enraged and offended, Obake choked his naginata.

"That's no ordinary necklace, young lady," Tazuro pressed the eye insignia on the hand guard of his sword. "It's a bamalga and I want it back."

Melodic clicks played from the sword like the notes of an instrument. A similar melody sauntered from below, chased by the sound of spinning gears and shuffling metal. An iron spider leg burst through the roof straight into Teiku. He went airborne then crashed onto one of the falcon statues.

More legs came up to knock Obake and Meilana into the air as well. Their weapons flew from their hands, whirling to a halt near the roof's edge. The ninja and samurai weren't fortunate like their weapons; they went off the roof and tumbled in search of a lifeline. From that height, the garden below looked like a miniature mock up.

Each of the joints in Meilana's fingers stretched to snag the roof's ledge. Obake fell behind her, hugging at her hips. His weight almost ripped her delicate grip loose. Like ribbons caught in a draft, they dangled.

"I'm going to slip!" cried Meilana.

"Hold on!" Obake climbed up to grab a bit of ledge for himself. "I got you."

He assisted Meilana back onto the roof, where they reunited with their weapons. Teiku and Tazuro's small holes combined into a big one as the Spider Throne entered the battle. Like a frog preparing to leap, the throne ducked low.

Tazuro jumped inside of it then fixed his sword into the headrest. "Now where were we?" he said, sitting with a cocky exuberance.

You've got to be kidding me. How many spiders do I have to fight? Obake sighed. *Well, at least this one's not real.*

The iron arachnid crawled over top of Teiku, who was still in the process of remembering where he was.

"That's right. My bamalga," said Tazuro.

Spider legs stabbed at Teiku who evaded by mere centimeters. There wasn't much room on the roof's spine to evade for long. After the second rolling dodge, Teiku fired an energy fist into the Spider Thrones underside. It staggered for a fraction of a second. When a spider leg went to stab at Teiku again, an ice crystal froze it in place.

Obake came along, shattering the leg to dust. "Get out of here!"

A backwards tuck and roll brought Teiku to his feet. By the grace of luck, he dodged another spider leg attack and launched himself skyward. As gravity compelled him to return, he revved a fist, intent on tearing through Tazuro and his iron arachnid. An unseen spider leg slipped in to thrash Teiku. He took the impact and then clutched the spider leg with all four of his limbs.

Meilana watched in horror. "What are you doing?

Get out of there!"

"No!" Teiku pummeled the spider leg with one fist. "He has to die by my hand!"

"If you don't get out of there, he never will! We have to re-group!" said Obake.

Teiku stalled, thinking for a moment before letting go. He landed and made a run for it, but the throne wasn't done with him. It stretched a leg out, knocking his feet out from under him. A new ice spike, big enough to make a tree self-conscious, jutted from the roof.

"Dammit!" screamed the samurai.

The ice spike only grazed the side of the Spider Thrones cockpit. Obake slipped in between the iron legs. Tazuro shifted gears to hold him off. With a dash and a dodge, the ninja made it to the cockpit's underside. Mizuchi was slow to pierce it, giving the throne ample time to ground pound. Obake teleported away as Meilana raced up her ice spike, jumping from the tip of it. Both blades of her katana coated themselves in a sharp layer of ice. Latching onto the cock pits brim, Meilana tried loping Tazuro's head off. Tazuro gave her attacks the slip then maneuvered his throne in search of Teiku. Meilana shifted her focus to the Spider Thrones interior control panel. She stabbed it, all the while releasing enough ice to elicit malfunction. The internal gears snapped and crackled, spitting zoganite smoke every which way.

Tazuro gave Meilana an angry right hook. "You, bitch!"

She fell to the roof as Teiku got up to run again. The Spider Throne tore across the roof after him. An iron leg knocked him flat as he neared the hole in the roof. He rolled onto his backside, shining fists blasted up. They did little to repel the Spider Throne. Another leg went forth, pinning the masked warrior. With Mizuchi's chain, Obake cinched two of the Spider Thrones rear legs together. Although her nose was a bloody mess, Meilana dashed in to slice the bound legs. They froze on contact, enabling Obake to collapse the legs into scrap metal. Balance compromised, the throne struggled to remain upright. The malfunctioning control panel worsened. Cold vapor seeped from every facet of the machinery, rendering the Spider Throne useless.

Tazuro jolted out of his seat then drew his sword. "Be sure and send greetings from the afterlife."

Like a missile, he took to the sky. He seemed to go on forever until he slowed down to launch a beam of extreme proportions.

Flushed full of fear, Obake turned to his girlfriend. "Come on, hurry!"

They rushed over to Teiku. He was still there, trapped under the Spider Throne's leg. Like a drunken bar fighter, his gauntlets issued lazy punches to the leg.

"Do your thing," said Obake.

Meilana froze the spider leg and Obake shattered it.

"Get out of here!" yelled Teiku as bits of frozen metal rained over him.

Brushing the words aside, Obake reached out.

Teiku slapped Obake's hand then stood up to shove him. "Don't touch me!"

"What's wrong with you? You said you were going to stop doing this."

"I have enough soul energy left to end this." Once again, Teiku's gauntlets charged to an imperium level, bursting with their brightest shine yet. "Die, fucker!"

Two enormous energy fists blasted at the sky. They collided with Tazuro's beam, wrestling it for domination. An explosion soon colored the night sky like fireworks.

"Did he, do it?" asked Meilana, watching the commotion play out.

"I can't tell. It's too bright."

As the blinding light faded, Teiku slumped to his knees with a crunch.

Meilana's shoulders curled to her ears. "He doesn't look too good."

Obake scoffed. "He looks like shit is more like it."

The couple reached for their masked companion.

"Let's hurry. That bastard might still be up there somewhere," said Obake.

Like a returning aircraft, Tazuro dropped in front of Teiku, confiscating the necklace.

Obake deployed a desperate attack. "No!"

Tazuro repelled the ninja with a beam. Meilana tried her hand next and failed in the same manner.

With a delicate touch, Tazuro brushed Teiku's hair back. "You actually thought you could handle such a power?"

Teiku couldn't keep his head from flopping side to side.

Between his fingers, Tazuro fiddled with the necklace. "I remember the way this would sap my soul energy. Even when it was all the way across the room, I could feel it, feeding on me."

Obake tried getting up, but a sensation like that of a thousand needle pricks hit him. "Don't let him take it."

"Teiku, run," said Meilana, getting up just to collapse seconds later.

Tazuro gazed at the necklace like a parent would a newborn baby. "How drained I'd be. I thought Rezvan poisoned it against me. But two bamalgas were too much for me back then. I wasn't strong enough." A flourishing smile emerged on the ginyai emperor. "I am now."

The bamalga dropped around Tazuro's neck, setting his soul energy ablaze. It spiked and swirled like a mighty storm of death.

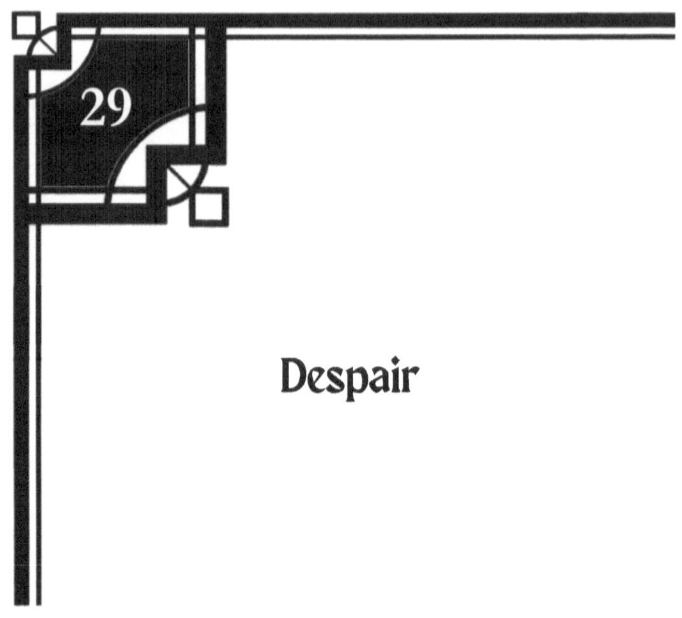

29

Despair

Night fully commenced. As if wind had chased clouds into hiding, the moon and stars glittered in unobscured glory. Yet there was no wind, at least not the kind created by nature. Only winds present were those generated by Tazuro's tumultuous energy. His energy swooshed aboard a vessel of tenacity and lashed aboard a vessel of furor.

Teiku dug into the roof with one hand and held his mask in place with the other.

"No, no my friend, I'd very much like to see who's under there," said Tazuro, reaching a hand toward Teiku.

Relinquishing his grasp, Teiku allowed the winds to shove him back through the hole in the roof.

Obake got to his feet, fighting through his pain to grab hold of Meilana. "Time to go."

A Shadow Cloud puddle formed beneath his feet. They plunged through the roof and into Kinichi's Chamber.

"Could you warn me next time?" said Meilana upon reuniting with the floor.

"Come on," said Obake, sprinting to retrieve Teiku who was lying on the floor.

"I'm not crazy, right?" Meilana sprinted alongside her boyfriend, fighting through her pain as well. "That necklace made him stronger, didn't it?"

Obake hoisted Teiku over his shoulder like a fresh cut log. "You're not crazy."

Meilana hugged herself. "What are we going to do? There's no way we can beat him now."

Tazuro dropped beside them, his wild energy now absent. "She's right, you know."

A Shadow Cloud puddle formed below Obake once more. "Get ready!"

He snatched Meilana by the waist and submerged into the dining hall, but he didn't stop there. Not until the first floor became their surroundings did he pause to gather his thoughts.

"I know what you're going to say, but we have to go get help," said Meilana, trembling.

"We'll be putting people in danger."

"Do you have a death wish? If we stay here—"

"I don't care what it takes. I'll find a way to stop him. Now go."

"Stop protecting me!"

"Meilana, I—"

"We've been through this."

"Let me go," slurred Teiku.

Obake shook him in anger. "Shut your ass up."

Meilana retrieved her puapo canister. "We're going to need this then."

"I was hoping we wouldn't have to use that so soon. But what choice do we have?"

Obake laid Teiku down and peeled up the bottom of his mask. As Meilana went to administer the elixir, a fuchsia beam battered her hand. She cried out in pain. The canister smacked against the floor, leaking its precious contents.

Tazuro stood on the threshold of the front entrance. "There you go again, trying to ruin all the fun with your special drink."

Meilana grimaced. "You're one to talk. Why don't you take off that necklace?"

"You're delaying the inevitable." The emperor held his sword out, ensuring that the eye insignia upon it was aiming at them. "Eye can see this. Why can't you?"

Like a stampede, Tazuro dashed at his enemies. He was set to cleave them to pieces, but Obake teleported away, along with his partners.

Outside, in the wrecked garden, Obake hid Teiku behind the tree chaperoning Yumo's Stinger.

"Don't leave me here," said Teiku through more slurred speech.

Obake wasted no time arguing. He instead raced to the center of the garden with Meilana.

A solemn mood infected Obake. "We'll beat him."

Uncertainty was all Meilana could muster for a response.

"How touching," Tazuro walked out into the garden. "Last words I presume?" He caressed Rezvan's necklace. "Where's your friend? I'd like to thank him for bringing this to me."

The emperor jumped all the way over to where Obake and Meilana stood. Through shock and fear, the young warriors attacked with everything they had left. Not a single one of their katana or naginata strikes connected. Punches and kicks fared no better, Tazuro tanked their blows. He grew bored and stabbed the ground with his sword. Fuchsia lights of royalty veined beneath the terrain until they burst like geysers. Dozens of light geysers sliced every which way, nothing was left unharmed. Not the remains of Gonenga, Orinsu and Umoi, not the trees or the bushes, not the plants or the rocks, not the perimeter wall or the academy. Nothing except for Meilana and Obake, that is. Thanks to quick feet and good timing, they remained intact.

The young warriors fled into the academy, taking cover behind the staircase. The light geysers soon dissipated.

"And to think, they haven't even returned with my old sword yet," Tazuro gloated. "Imagine what I'll be able to accomplish with two bamalgas."

We were right. But where's the other sword?

Meilana shot a concerned look at her boyfriend. "They? Who the fuck is *they?*"

"Ginyai, there are two more out there."

"And you were going to tell me this when?"

"I don't know. After we were done here, I guess."

Meilana harrumphed.

Obake took a risky peek. "I'd love to see you try. I'll be the first to cheer when the bamalgas rip you apart."

Tazuro flared a hand. "Don't confuse me with your caliber. If anyone can do it, I can." A perfect, round beam formed to the proportion of a small boulder.

As if sentient, the beam sped onward, disintegrating the staircase.

Oh, shit!

Wide eyed, Obake went left, ending up in Sensei Pelssa's classroom. A panic induced Meilana went right, straight into Sensei Gwell's classroom. Instead of dispersing, the beam hovered in place, thinking, contemplating. It opted to follow Obake. Desks, chairs, bookcases and anything else the beam touched ceased to exist.

What is that thing?

Utilizing a Shadow Cloud puddle, Obake phased through the ceiling. He expected the beam to continue its pursuit, it opposed his expectations. Meilana became much more alluring all of a sudden. Obake darted across the dining hall until he was above Sensei Gwell's classroom. He created another puddle then dropped his upper body through the floor. Meilana let ice crystals fly, but the beam progressed right through them.

Obake held Mizuchi out toward Meilana like a lifeline. "Hurry!"

She grabbed hold and Obake pulled her through the ceiling at the last minute.

"I didn't know power like this was possible," said Obake, ushering Meilana to the center of the dining hall.

Try as she may, Meilana couldn't shake her bewilderment. "This is insane."

All of the lunch tables rattled about, despite the lack of a land tremor.

"Here it comes!" screamed Meilana.

The beam shaved the floorboards as if they were mere hair follicles. Before the beam got close, Obake teleported away with Meilana in tow. Back on the first floor, they caught Tazuro waving his finger around like a musical conductor. The beam soon arrived to swirl around the couple. With each pass the beam made, it closed in like some sort of diabolical trap.

"I'm tired of being treated like a damn toy," said Meilana.

"Yeah?" Obake zeroed in on the emperor. "Me, too!"

Perfect timing at their disposal, the couple slipped past the beam and rushed ahead. Similar to a beckoning gesture, Tazuro curled his finger. Obeying its master, the beam tore off. It nipped at Meilana's heels as she ran behind her boyfriend. Obake placed a hand behind his back and opened it wide. A crystal of ice formed and Meilana gave it to Obake. His hand froze, but he neither winced nor shuddered, he just vanished into a Shadow Cloud. Meilana ventured into the cloud, slinging ice crystals as she went. She threw so many that Tazuro couldn't afford to trace Obake's movements. As the last ice crystal crashed against Tazuro's blade, Obake rose up to his waist from a Shadow Cloud puddle on the floor. He stabbed Tazuro's thigh with the ice crystal, freezing it in place. Stomach first, Meilana slid across the floor and wrapped around Obake. He descended, sucking her into the floor as well. Obake then shifted backwards and ascended to the first floor again, Meilana still hanging on. Full of joy, they popped out of the Shadow Cloud puddle and watched the beam slide right into the ginyai emperor.

The ensuing explosion shook the entire academy. Floors splintered, walls and ceilings charred black. Meilana stood beside her boyfriend as he shed the remaining ice fragments from his hand. What remained of the beam lingered on as harmless particles. Tazuro kneeled among them, agony as his companion. The bamalga called out, requesting to be commandeered. Obake obliged.

"Don't… touch it," said Tazuro, breathing hard.

"Looks like you're having a hard time." Obake spoke with a mocking inflection. "Allow me to help." He ripped the necklace from around his foe's neck and held it up to Meilana. "Interested?"

Meilana moved Obake's hand away as if it were contaminated. "I don't want anything to do with that thing."

"Guess it's my turn then."

Obake missed the immense power provided by the bamalga. He understood why the likes of Teiku and Tazuro coveted it so much. At the same time, he hated the fact that he needed or wanted it at all.

How do I get to this level on my own?

"You dirty little bastard," said Tazuro as the damaged floor beneath him gave way.

Meilana peered into the claustrophobic basement. "Do you think he's dead?"

"No way, but at least now we can finish this."

A few paces away lay the puapo canister.

Obake fired a finger at it. "The puapo!"

Meilana scooped it up and gave it a light jiggle. "Not much left." She offered it to Obake. "Here, you have some first."

Obake peeked inside of the canister. Less than half of its contents remained.

"I won't be needing it now." He handed it back to Meilana. "Can't say the same for Teiku though."

Obake dropped into the basement, Meilana followed. The ceiling mounted lamps that still worked blinked like fireflies. The totem style support columns exuded malevolence. Their animal designs seemed ready to come alive in the night.

Meilana eyed the debris at her feet and found it vacant of ginyai royalty. "He's gone."

"Looking for me?" said Tazuro, ramming his shoulder into Meilana.

She went skidding hard into the wall, her consciousness wrestled to stay active.

Obake started toward her. "Meilana!"

The hiss of steel through air made Obake pivot. He seized Tazuro's blade hand mid swing and squeezed. Tazuro's knuckles and joints cracked, and his ligaments screamed. The sword plummeted to the ground; Obake took his chance and kicked it away.

"Let me go!" said the emperor, wiggling and writhing.

Before long, Tazuro pried his hand free then staggered backwards.

Like an apex predator, Obake motioned in on him. "Where's all that arrogance now, asshole?" Dark memories of lost loved ones arrived on skeletal birds of misery. *I want to stomp him to a bloody pulp. I want to cave his fucking skull in.* Blade first, Obake stabbed Mizuchi to the ground then dropped his hood and mask. *I'm going to enjoy this.*

The young ninja assumed his combat stance. A great deal of hate exuded from the emperor before he bounded at Obake. With a soaring elbow he aimed to shatter every bone in the seventeen-year-olds face. However, the drill-like attack was not without its flaws, a defensive weakness exposed itself, one Obake exploited. After a swift evasion, Obake deployed an uppercut to Tazuro's ribs. They crunched like dead leaves in autumn. Subsequent attacks soon followed from Obake. Two jabs to the chest, a hook across the right cheek and a roundhouse across the opposite cheek. Each blow against Tazuro felt more satisfying than the last.

Blood leaked over Tazuro's bottom lip, so much so he spit gobs of it. Fuming, he discharged a harrowing series of melee strikes, none of which were a success.

"Impossible. I won't lose again!" screamed Tazuro.

Obake punted him into a panda themed column, wrecking it. Two chunks of the column became subject to Tazuro's whims. He threw one chunk then barreled forward. The chunk came so fast Obake nearly failed to dodge it. By the time he did, Tazuro was already smashing the other chunk over his head. Rivulets of blood weaved throughout Obake's green hair as the emperor bashed him through the column of lions. Pain journeyed across Obake's tailbone and then up through his back and neck. Like an indignant ram, Tazuro came charging.

By seizing both of Tazuro's horns, Obake kept his guts intact. A sharp knee to the stomach brought the emperor to his knees. Summoning great strength, Obake swung Tazuro at a column carved with falcons, destroying it.

Dust and debris fell from the ceiling; it even slouched some. The emperor rolled to a halt near his sword, upon noticing, he scrambled for it.

Not good.

Obake could do nothing but race to apprehend Mizuchi. As soon as his fingers made contact with the naginata, he teleported before Tazuro. Mizuchi erupted with Shadow Cloud. Tazuro slashed, triumph exuding from his pupils. Clashing against Mizuchi caused Tazuro's sword to burst into fragments. The force of the clash also drove Tazuro clear across the basement.

Obake hurled himself through the air, prepared to finish the job, but his body convulsed. *No! Not now.* He plummeted, hitting the ground. *I need more time.*

"Ah, there it is." Tazuro grinned. "Right on time."

"What's happening?" cried Meilana.

"You should be proud." The emperor ambled toward his enemy. "You held on far longer than I expected."

Meilana clawed at the wall in an effort to stand. "Hold on. I'm on my way," she said, yet her legs couldn't accommodate her desire.

"Did you really think you'd last long enough to kill me?" said Tazuro.

How's he still going? The ceiling slouched more, drawing Obake's gaze. *That's it. That's how I end this.*

Despite the unimaginable anguish, Obake wrestled his convulsions into a manageable state. Mizuchi erupted with Shadow Cloud once more, Tazuro paused in his tracks.

"Obake, I can't... I can't..." Tears streamed from Meilana's puffy eyes. She wanted to stand, to help. "I love you," she shouted in desperation.

"You better," said Obake with a euphoric smile.

A plume of Shadow Cloud blasted from Mizuchi. Meilana froze with fear and confusion as the plume swept into her. Within an instant, she disappeared.

"Quite the ladies' man," said Tazuro, snapping a hand forward.

Obake whipped around in time to snag the emperor's wrist with his free hand.

"Turn it over." Tazuro's fingers flared, reaching for the necklace. "It no longer serves you."

Dammit. I'm getting weaker by the second.

With rapid speed, Obake sheathed Mizuchi then retrieved his shrapnel bomb. As he pressed the button like protrusion upon it, the ginyai emperor snagged his wrist.

"What are you doing?" said Tazuro, his eyes bulging.

The ninja smirked and let the bomb drop. The clink of it hitting the floor thieved breath from Tazuro's lungs. Obake vaulted ten feet high, clearing the blast radius. The explosion sent shrapnel and smoke permeating the basement. As Obake flipped over Tazuro's head, he released Mizuchi once more. Like a dancing ribbon, it wound tight around Tazuro's body. Upon touching down, the ninja held his naginata steadfast like a bull wrangler. The smoke's thickness thinned fast, revealing an emperor peppered with fresh, blood-soaked wounds.

"I won't… I won't… lose!" said Tazuro, lurching and thrashing with surprising strength.

The kunai in Obake's possession went gliding through Tazuro's foot, anchoring it. "Stay put!"

A plume of Shadow Cloud left Obake's hand to hit a portion of the alligator column. It vanished, leaving the ceiling to wobble with instability.

Two left.

Convulsions returned with a vengeance, but Obake fought through them. He continued to vanish portions of the remaining columns, first the column of frogs and then the column of dolphins. By the time Obake finished, he had no weaponizable soul energy left. Like a dying banshee, the ceiling began an endless series of moans and groans.

Tazuro struggled against Mizuchi in a full-blown panic. "You'll die, too!"

"As long as I take you with me!" said Obake, holding firm like iron.

No matter how much he squirmed, Tazuro couldn't get free. As the ceiling caved in one piece at a time, Obake thought about his realm. He thought about all the people who would never experience suffering at the hands of Tazuro.

He thought about his grandparents, Yumo, his mother, his father. *I wonder if they'd be proud of me.*

Through the multitude of holes in the ceiling, Obake saw the entire academy falling in on itself. While Tazuro screamed, Obake closed his eyes and waited… peacefully.

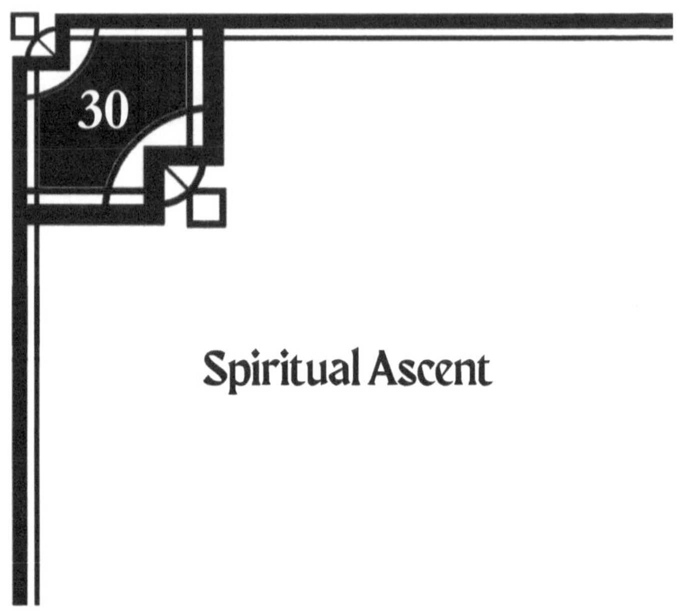

Spiritual Ascent

Obake thought venturing to the precipice of life and death would be a one-time occurrence.

Feels familiar. Oh, I remember now. Should've known I'd end up back here.

He imagined inky black desolation, a heavy storm and invisible ground. However, the pitter patter of rain was absent, distant thunder too, and his heart didn't swell with the hope of escape.

Peeling his eyes open let in a shock to the senses. A sprawling sandy beach, abundant with breezy palm trees, sleeping otters and a warm cheerful sun greeted him.

Wow. It's gorgeous here now.

He marveled at the horizon, where the different shades of blue kissed. Extra fluffy clouds waltzed on top of the horizon line, transforming it into a dance floor.

I wonder what it would feel like to lay on one of those clouds.

The smell of saltwater and seaweed, the flapping wings of seagulls and the tender ocean waves contributed to sending Obake's thoughts adrift.

"Hey! Are you in there?" Meilana stood off to the left, dressed in her glossy white bathing attire. "I like what you've done with the place," she said, imitating someone of extreme sophistication.

"How good of you to notice," replied Obake, going along with the act.

Upon standing up, Obake noticed he was wearing his black swim shorts.

Without giving it a second thought, Obake walked over and placed his hands on Meilana's hips. "Are you safe? Did you get away in time?"

"I'll need about a month of recovery, but I'll be fine."

Their embrace and subsequent kiss moved Obake's very soul.

"Now this is more like it!"

Obake turned inland to find Yumo walking toward them, glancing around as he did so. He was no longer a dragon, but a young man wearing fire red swimming shorts. Tears bubbled in Obake's eyes as Yumo reached out to begin their usual handshake.

Obake yanked Yumo in for a hug instead. "I can't believe you came to see me, especially after I let you down like that."

"Come on. Turning into a dragon was actually kind of cool. The whole not being able to talk thing, well that's a different story."

"That little girl, I couldn't stop her—"

"You did all you could. Now where's your papa? I bet he'd love it here."

"You're right about that," said Yokai as he sat on the edge of the tide, his blue swimming shorts extending well past his knees. "Bao-Ang. Look at this place would you."

Bao-Ang peeked from beside her husband, her toes splashing the salty water. "For a kid who's been to the beach only a handful of times," A modest, one-piece bathing suit hugged her body. "You sure do have a vivid memory of it."

Obake fumbled over himself to get to them. He dove on top of the elder couple like an excited puppy, his tears overflowing.

Yokai wrapped an arm around his grandson. "Dry those eyes, Green. I'm enjoying this beach. Don't ruin it for me."

Bao smiled from ear to ear. "We know what you're thinking Froggy—"

"I thought I could catch you in Dotam. I was so stupid. I should've gone straight home! If I was there I—"

"Would've died, too," Yokai interjected.

"We all have to go someday. It was our time," said Bao, placing an arm around her grandson as well.

"If it's any consolation," Yokai beamed with pride. "You did a stellar job at avenging us."

A strange, yet warm sensation washed over the young ninja.

"You're so much like your parents," said Bao.

"I am?" said Obake in awe.

Bao gestured toward the ocean. Obake glanced over to see Bakemono and Vai in the distance. From knee high water, they beamed bright smiles at their son.

Obake sprinted into the water then hesitated. "Is that really… them?"

He stared at his parents, transfixed.

"That peace you found just before you got here. Hold on to that," said Bao.

Looking back, Obake saw his grandparents, Meilana and Yumo all huddled together.

Yokai gave Obake a determined look. "It should be your most prized possession."

Meilana spoke with comfort in her voice. "Don't let anyone or anything take that away from you, babe."

"Yeah, you can't inspire peace without having some of your own first," said Yumo.

As Obake pondered their words, he shot a glance back to his parents. They nodded at him, then floated up toward the sun, the brightness overtaking them.

"Wait!"

From his periphery, Obake saw Meilana, Yumo, Yokai and Bao disappear into the sun as well.

"Don't go!"

Unencumbered sadness ran wild in Obake until he himself began to float. All around, below and above, the very fabric of the environment shattered like glass.

"What's going on?"

The slivers of the environment plummeted away one by one, revealing pure white nothingness that flared brighter than the sun it replaced. Obake pinched his eyes shut, an effort to shield them. The white radiance was still quite apparent.

Don't freak out. Peace. Hold onto peace.

With each passing moment, the stinging white nothingness outside of Obake's eyelids dimed. A hesitant peek turned into a full-blown survey of what lay below.

Like the clouds on the beach's horizon line, Obake waltzed above the remains of Kinichi's Academy. *How did I—? What am I doing way up here?*

The aftermath was remarkable. Kinichi's Academy was now nothing more than a pile of wreckage. Even the Gateway perished to mere rubble, its fractured top, sticking lopsided above the chaos. Obake searched closer and almost hyperventilated. Meilana and Teiku rested under the tree shading Yumo's Stinger, outside of the debris' reach.

They're safe. Obake took a deep inhale. "Hey, guys! Up here!" His voice didn't carry. "What's happening right now?" He gazed at his feet and saw that they were transparent. *Why do they look like that?* Examining the rest of himself, Obake realized he was entirely transparent and had no clothing to speak of. *I'm naked! Where are my clothes?*

Initial instinct urged Obake to cover up, but a more peculiar sight caught his attention. As if the wreckage were transparent as well, Obake saw clear through it. He braced himself for what he was sure to find in the basement. Wedged between all the damage and mayhem was his own mangled corpse. Despite its damaged state, an expression of peace persisted. To his astonishment, Mizuchi remained intact. Obake followed its chain to Tazuro, who was disfigured and contorted. Horns snapped, jaw slacked and limbs crushed.

"It's finally over."

Obake re-focused on Meilana and Teiku. The knowledge of how to fly flooded into his mind from out of nowhere.

While making his way over to them, his feet turned into golden specks and trickled away. *What's happening to me?*

His thighs, waist and hands did the same, followed by his abdomen and chest. The strange phenomenon didn't stop there; it took his shoulders and neck too.

I'm fading. I'm—

Obake stole one final look at Meilana before disappearing in a shimmer of gold.

Pronunciation Guide

To help with pronouncing unique and original words found

throughout the novel.

<u>Characters</u>

Obake
(oh, bah, k)

Meilana
(may, lah, nuh)

Juroiza
(joo, roy, zuh)

Agalo
(uh, gah, low)

Izaru
(e, zah, roo)

Pai Liu
(pie, loo)

Gazzo
(gah, zoh)

Bao Ang
("bao" is pronounced like *bow* and arrow, "ang" is
pronounced like gang)

Yokai
(yo, "kai" is pronounced like sigh.)

Mizuchi
(me, zoo, chee)

Yumo
(yew, moe)

Katshi
("kat" is pronounced like cot, she)

Naivu
("nai" is pronounced like sigh, voo)

Morrgo
(more, go)

Zhai Foong
("zhai" is pronounced like sigh, foong)

Jiaou
(gee, ow)

Eshra
(esh, ruh)

Jevoss
(jeh, "voss" is pronounced like dose)

Gwell
(pronounced like swell)

Tezza
(teh, zuh)

Pelssa
(pel, suh)

Batta
(bah, tuh)

Kinichi
(key, knee, chee)

Kauzo
("kau" is pronounced like cow, zoh)

Oldro
("ol" is pronounced like goal, dro)

Forru
(foe, roo)

Jinenji
(gee, nen, gee)

Argett
(arr, geht)

Samasa
(suh, mah, suh)

Daizo
(die, zoh)

Tazuro
(tah, zoo, row)

Hallevi
(hah, "levi" is pronounced like petty)

Ventama
(ven, tah, muh)

Gonenga
(go, nen, guh)

Barran
(bah, rahn)

Orulle
(o, rule)

Darbol
(dar, bowl)

Andro
(anne, dro)

X

Orinsu
(o, rin, sue)

Dolsa
(dull, suh)

Gruck
(pronounced like chuck)

Kalida
(ka, lee, duh)

Azlin
(azz, lin)

Artem
(arr, "tem" is pronounced like gem)

Davugo
(dah, voo, go)

Weila
(way, luh)

Umoi
(ooh, moy)

Tozzmun
("tozz" is pronounced like oz, "mun" is pronounced
like bun)

Zathumor
(zah, thoo, more)

Rinjado
(rin, jah, doh)

Bakemono
(bah, k, moe, no)

Vai
(pronounced like sigh)

Delorma
(deh, lore, muh)

Teiku
(tay, koo)

Kerter
(pronounced like murder)

Gurt
(pronounced like dirt)

Baraiko
(buh, rye, koh)

Akoh
(ah, koh)

Sukora
(sue, core, uh)

Lugora
(loo, gore, uh)

Petta
(peh, tuh)

Gudo
(goo, doe)

Laozai
("lao" is pronounced like cow, "zai" is pronounced like sigh.)

Azor
(a, "zor" is pronounced like door)

Beldur
(bell, "dur" is pronounced like purr)

Locations

Bushido Empire
(boo, she, doh)

Gazzo Castle/City
(gah, zoh)

Nuojo Grand Chasm
(new, oh, joe)

Shinobi Empire
(she, no, bee)

Yokai Mountains/City/Ruins
(yo, "kai" is pronounced like sigh)

Hoitunji Ocean
(hoy, ton, gee)

Taulon Falls
("tau" is pronounced like cow, lawn)

Dotam
(doh, tom)

Genopai
(geh, no, pie)

Ginyai Realm
("gin" is pronounced like tin, "yai" is pronounced like sigh)

Magyor
(mag, your)

Pasanya Village
(puh, sahn, yuh)

Oktau Mountains
(ahk, "tau" is pronounced like cow)

Aglan Forest
(ag, lawn)

Shuika Dynasty
(shoe, e, kuh)

<u>Unique Words</u>

Tabi
(tah, bee)

Kimono
(key, moe, no)

Shozoku
(show, zoh, koo)

Hakama
(hah, kah, muh)

Jian
(gee, ahn)

Naginata
(nah, gee, nah, tuh)

Tanto
(tahn, toe)

Katana
(kuh, tah, nuh)

Shuriken
(shoe, ree, ken)

Kunai
(koo, "nai" is pronounced like sigh)

Khopesh
(koh, peshh)

Keikogi
(k, koh, ghee)

Wangjin
("wang" is pronounced like wrong, jin is pronounced like pen)

Shamisen
(shah, me, "sen" is pronounced like ten)

Tatami
(tah, tah, me)

Original Words

Puapo
(poo, ah, poe)

Galvantium
(gal, van, tee, um)

Kantasian
(kahn, tah, "sian" is pronounced like the second vowel
in the word Asian)

Zoza Statue
(zoh, zuh)

Glissader
("gliss" is pronounced like kiss, "aider" is pronounced
like gator)

Ginyai
("gin" is pronounced like tin, "yai" is pronounced like sigh)

Zoganite
(zoh, gah, night)

Hagazo
(hah, gah, zoh)

Kezai
(keh, "zai" is pronounced like sigh)

Vulborta
("vul" is pronounced like dull, bore, tuh)

Wudaigo
(woo, die, go

Komera
(koh, mare, uh)

Muzza
(moo, zuh)

Bamalga
(buh, mal, guh)

Lamol Soup
(lah, mole)

Rodau Chicken
(row, "dau" is pronounced like cow)

Taram
(tah, rum)

XIX

Acknowledgements

Julianna, my wonderful girlfriend, you're the first person I want to thank. Not only did you believe in me, but you also provided feedback that helped make the relationship between a certain ninja and his grandparents all the more wholesome. I'd also like to commend your patience. As you know, when you read my early drafts, I got angry when you couldn't recall some of what you read. Like many creatives, I assumed that meant I sucked at my job. How easy it is to forget that we've all read something and missed a thing or two, we're only human after all. I can't thank you enough for continuing to support me, even at times when I didn't deserve it.

Duh Dude, my talented illustrator, your contribution was and continues to be tremendous. You took all of my rough sketches and breathed life into them. Had I not started working with you, I don't know where my vision would be. Even when your country, Ukraine, succumbed to the ills of war, you supplied a cover and other pieces of art I couldn't be happier with. You even put up with all my perfectionist qualities, any corrections I ask for, you complete. Thank you.

Belle Manuel, you gave my writing a proper polish and helped elevate it to the next level. You pointed out things I never could've caught, especially one that would've brought me shame had it not been corrected. Thank you for giving my manuscript such attention to detail.

Rob Donovan, you took my maps from rough sketches to works of art. I couldn't be happier with how well they turned out. Thank you.

Dad, you taught me the importance of being a hardworking man. Growing up, I often wondered why you put so much pressure on me, but now I see how important that was. Thank you for the life lessons you gave to me. I'm beyond sad that you're gone, but I'll always cherish the time we had together. You're my guardian angel now.

Brandon, honestly, I just might love you the most of all. You taught me how to respect and admire people from all walks of life. Your innocence and pure heart are aspirational. No matter what cruel people out there may think, your autism in no way makes you inferior. You're perfect just the way you are. Thank you for being my brother and simply… existing.

And last, but never least, thank you to each and every one of my readers. I can't thank you enough, because without you, I wouldn't be here. See you in the next one!

Also by Lee Obsidian

Book Two
Obake: Song of the Afterlife
(Coming Soon!)

About the Author

Born in St Louis, MO, Lee Obsidian moved to San Diego, CA at the age of two. As a child, he became fascinated with video games, comics, manga and anime; forms of entertainment that nurtured his unbridled imagination and granted him an escape. In his elementary school days, he developed a talent for creative writing. This resulted in him winning a district wide school contest, in which his unique picture book saw publication. Years later, he assisted his mentor with the creation of her very own children's book by producing the illustrations. Despite his achievements, as an adult, he put creative writing aside in favor of other pursuits. Yet and still, the wonders of the hero's journey compelled him to return to another story he originally crafted in his youth. After a few tweaks and a few updates, **Obake** was born! Lee Obsidian lives in San Diego, CA with his family.

Maps

HUMAN REALM
GAPALONA OCEAN
RINATORU OCEAN
HOITUNJI OCEAN
VUSHAMBU OCEAN
BUSHIDO EMPIRE
SHINOBI EMPIRE
INDRANA ISLAND
TOWER OF KNOWLEDGE
ASH FALL FOREST
YOKANA MOUNTAINS
IRON CAVALRY PENITENTIARY
KYILO ISLAND
GRAND COUNCIL CHAMBER
HONITO
MILLSTER
MONO FARM
ASURA RAVINE
NARA
FISHERMAN'S HAVEN
JADE ISLAND
NUUP GRAND CHASM
SAXISEN

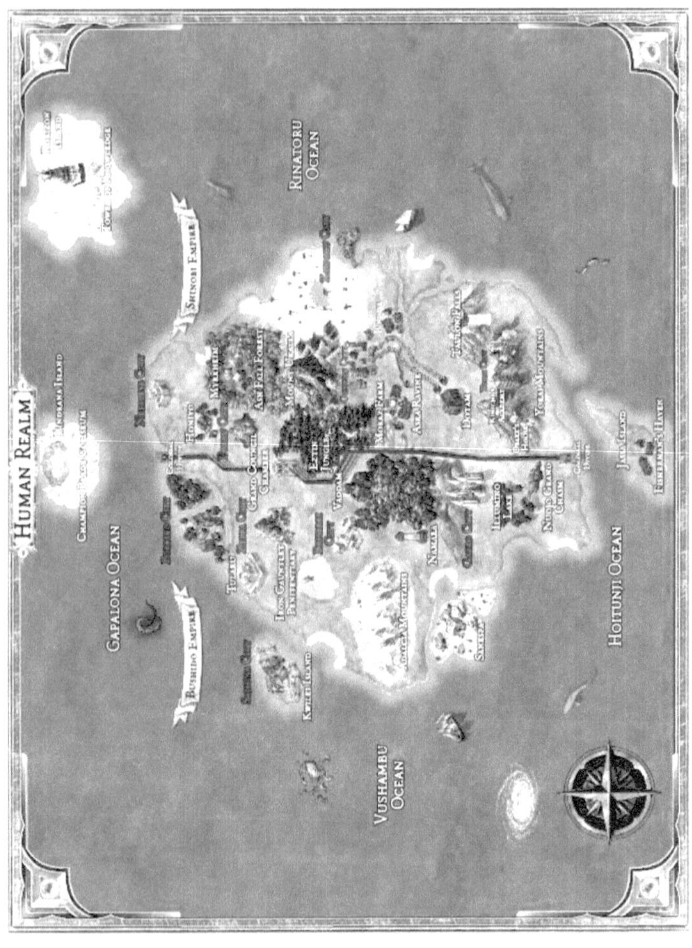

Ginyai Realm
Sea of Fire (North)
Zalaru Tundra
Mount Drakora
Gtralir Waterfall
Beyt River
Aglan Forest
Magyor Swamplands
Oxtau Mountains
Shuira City
Sukora & Lugora's Lair
Yetel Beach
Sea of Fire (West)
Vodex Caverns
Omni Eye City
Deptah Ravine
Sea of Fire (East)
Blacksmith's Manor
Pasanza Desert
Wastelands
Serrated Pillars
Lake Sarui
Gateway Mountain
Triku's Hideout
Valley of the Ozun
Three Tailed River
Sea of Fire (South)

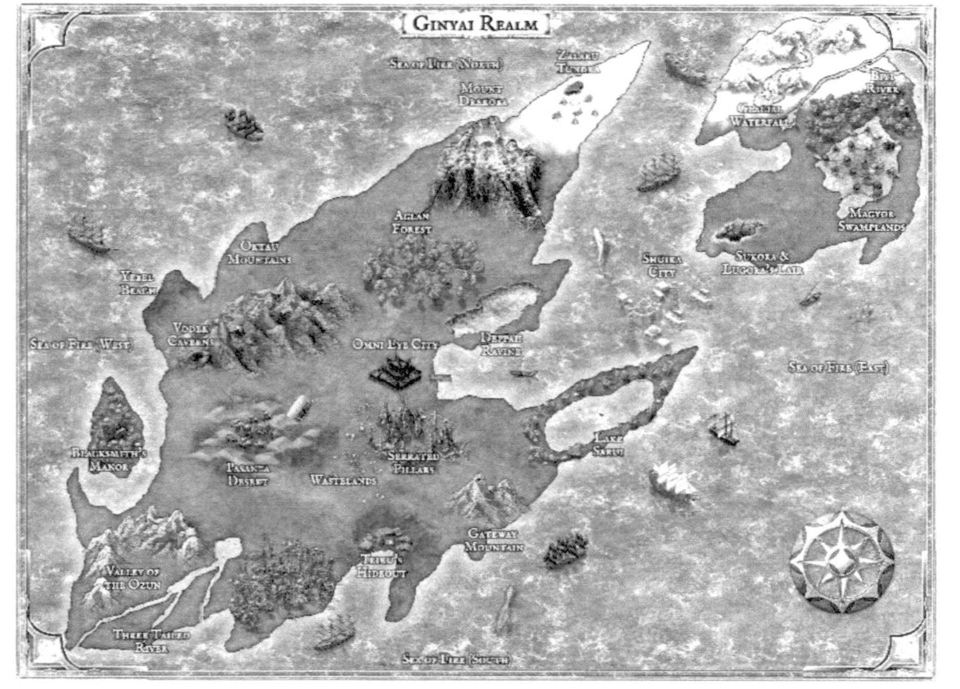

XXV